Grantville Gazette VI

BAEN BOOKS BY ERIC FLINT

RING OF FIRE SERIES:

1632 • *1633* (with David Weber)
1634: The Baltic War (with David Weber)
1634: The Galileo Affair (with Andrew Dennis)
1634: The Bavarian Crisis (with Virginia DeMarce)
1634: The Ram Rebellion (with Virginia DeMarce et al.)
1635: The Cannon Law (with Andrew Dennis)
1635: The Dreeson Incident (with Virginia DeMarce)
1635: The Eastern Front • *1636: The Saxon Uprising*
Grantville Gazette • *Grantville Gazette II* • *Grantville Gazette III*
Grantville Gazette IV • *Grantville Gazette V* • *Grantville Gazette VI*
Ring of Fire • *Ring of Fire II* • *Ring of Fire III*

Time Spike (with Marilyn Kosmatka)

JOE'S WORLD SERIES:

The Philosophical Strangler • *Forward the Mage* (with Richard Roach)

STANDALONE TITLES:

Mother of Demons • *Slow Train to Arcturus* (with Dave Freer)
"Diamonds Are Forever" (with Ryk E. Spoor in *Mountain Magic*)

WITH MERCEDES LACKEY & DAVE FREER:

The Shadow of the Lion • *This Rough Magic*
Much Fall of Blood • *Burdens of the Dead* (forthcoming)

WITH DAVE FREER:

Rats, Bats & Vats • *The Rats, The Bats & The Ugly*
Pyramid Scheme • *Pyramid Power*

WITH DAVID DRAKE:

The Tyrant

THE BELISARIUS SERIES WITH DAVID DRAKE:

An Oblique Approach • *In the Heart of Darkness* • *Destiny's Shield*
Fortune's Stroke • *The Tide of Victory* • *The Dance of Time*

WITH RYK E. SPOOR:

Boundary • *Threshold* • *Portal* (forthcoming)

WITH K.D. WENTWORTH:

The Course of Empire • *The Crucible of Empire*

WITH DAVID WEBER:

Crown of Slaves • *Torch of Freedom*

Grantville Gazette VI

Created by ERIC FLINT

Edited by Eric Flint & Paula Goodlett

GRANTVILLE GAZETTE VI

A Baen Books Original

Baen Publishing Enterprises
P.O. Box 1403
Riverdale, NY 10471
www.baen.com

ISBN: 978-1-4516-3768-7

Cover art by Tom Kidd

First printing, January 2012

Distributed by Simon & Schuster
1230 Avenue of the Americas
New York, NY 10020

Library of Congress Cataloging-in-Publication Data

Grantville gazette VI / edited by Eric Flint and Paula Goodlett.
p. cm. — (Ring of fire series)
ISBN 978-1-4516-3768-7 (hc : alk. paper)
1. Fantasy fiction, American. 2. Seventeenth century—Fiction. 3. Time travel—Fiction. 4. Alternative histories (Fiction), American. 5. Science fiction, American. I. Flint, Eric. II. Goodlett, Paula. III. Title: Grantville gazette 6.
PS648.F3G756 2012
813'.54—dc23

2011040769

10 9 8 7 6 5 4 3 2 1

Pages by Joy Freeman (www.pagesbyjoy.com)
Printed in the United States of America

To the memory of Cheryl Daetwyler, who died a year ago. And let us take this moment to express our respect for her husband Roger, who took care of Cheryl during the long years after she was incapacitated by a stroke. It's easy enough to say "in sickness and in health" when you're exchanging wedding vows. It's far, far harder to make good on the promise when and if the time comes.

Contents

Preface

Eric Flint

Every time I write a preface to an anthology, I remember the advice I got from Jim Baen a couple of years before he died:

"Whenever I open a book and see that it begins with a solemn, sober and serious introduction, I realize that reading this book would be an uplifting experience and do me a world of good. Hastily, I put it back on the shelves and go look for something fun to read."

With that in mind, I will keep this short and sweet.

The first four paper editions of the *Grantville Gazette* were simply print versions of the first four issues of the electronic magazine by the same name. Beginning with the fifth paper edition, however, we realized that we couldn't maintain the same system. Starting in May of 2007, the *Gazette* e-magazine started publishing on a regular bimonthly schedule, and it soon became obvious that Baen Books couldn't possibly keep up with the volume of stories being produced. So, beginning with *Grantville Gazette V* and continuing with this volume, these anthologies consist of the best stories selected from half a dozen issues of the magazine.

I need to add a caveat to the phrase "the best of." That's true... with the qualification that we always have to keep the length of the stories in mind. The *Gazette* is unusual in that, unlike most science fiction and fantasy magazines (these days, anyway; it wasn't always so), we publish quite a few long-running serialized stories. Many of these would easily qualify as among "the best of" the stories published in the *Gazette,* but for practical reasons we simply can't include them in these anthologies.

As with all the paper editions of the *Gazette*, I write a short story that doesn't appear in the electronic magazine. Following our long-standing custom, I write these stories after Tom Kidd, the artist for the 1632 series, has done the cover illustration—and I never know ahead of time exactly what that illustration will be.

It's admittedly a game, and probably a frivolous one. But I think that viewing cover illustrations as solemn, sober and serious endeavors runs the same risk that Jim warned about when it came to prefaces. Books of fiction may be more than simple entertainment—I try my best to make mine so, anyway—but they always begin there and you ignore that at your peril. The moment a reader finds that turning the page has ceased to be fun is the moment you lose that reader, unless your book is one of those which teachers and professors choose to inflict upon their helpless students. But books with cover illustrations like these almost never fall into that select category.

(More's the pity. Dammit, *I* was forced to read books I didn't want to when I was a callow stripling, so why shouldn't today's students suffer the same fate? Especially since this time around I might wind up making some money from the racket instead of spending it. Alas, 'tis not to be—proving once again that life ain't fair.)

If you enjoy these stories, I urge you to take a look at the electronic magazine from which they are selected. You can find the *Grantville Gazette* at www.grantvillegazette.com.

—Eric Flint
September 2011

The Masque

Eric Flint

— *1* —

Anne Jefferson studied herself in the mirror, then turned sideways and spent a few more seconds with the examination.

"The colors are pretty drab," she announced. "Comfortable, though, I'll give it that—way more so than modern-day Dutch women's apparel. At least it doesn't have a ruff. I hate those things."

She giggled. "I can't believe I just heard myself say 'modern-day' to refer to the year 1635."

Her husband Adam Olearius smiled at her reflection in the mirror. "I was born in this century so I can't say that I find the expression peculiar. Although people didn't use it much until you Americans came barging into the world. Changes came a lot more slowly before you arrived, so the distinction between past and present wasn't as great."

He studied her garments for a few seconds. "With the exception of fashion, of course. That's always changed rapidly."

Still looking at the outfit in the mirror, Anne shook her head. "I'll tell you what's odd to me, though. In the world I came from, women's fashions changed all the time. But men's clothing changed slowly, and it was even more drab than this dress I'm wearing. Suits, suits, suits. The colors were black, gray, navy blue and one or another shade of white. If you were really daring, you wore a light brown suit. Whereas here! Men's clothing changes every bit as fast as women's and it's even more flamboyant."

Olearius curled his lip theatrically. "One of the great drawbacks of your democratic system! In our sane seventeenth century, male fashion is determined by princes—who are not about to bury their effulgent glory under dismal colors and sober designs. In your world, on the other hand, male fashion was dictated by businessmen. Merchants, that is to say, a class of people whose adventurousness is entirely restricted to pecuniary endeavors."

Anne chuckled but didn't argue the point. Leaving aside her husband's analysis of the causes involved, she didn't disagree with him on the substance of the matter. She thought male costuming in the here-and-now was a marked improvement over that of the world she'd come from. Thankfully, the codpieces prevalent in the last century had fallen out of fashion. That would have been . . . a bit much to take, for someone who still had a lot of West Virginia attitudes.

She turned away from the mirror altogether. "Talk about princes! I still can't believe Ben Jonson is taking a personal hand in this masque."

"Do not get your hopes too high. I've heard he's declined a great deal from his glory days twenty years ago. That's the real reason he left England, I suspect, whatever he claims himself about the enmity of Inigo Jones and the earl of Cork."

Anne smiled. "It probably doesn't help that he's bound and determined to base the masque on that crate of stuff he got from Grantville. 'Memorabilia,' he calls it. 'Odds and ends,' is more like it."

"Or 'junk,'" added Olearius, perhaps uncharitably. He went to the door and opened it for her. "And now, my dear, we should go have an early dinner before making our appearance at the rehearsal. Even though"—his tone of voice was now definitely uncharitable—"I will be astonished if the esteemed poet has made much progress by the time we get there."

— 2 —

Ben Jonson studied the bizarre object in his right hand, his head propped up by the left. "Perhaps a token of esteem from the tritons . . ." he mused.

Standing behind him where the poet and dramatist couldn't see her, the young countess palatine Elizabeth rolled her eyes. It was obvious that Jonson was bound and determined to copy as much as he could of the masque he'd done thirty years earlier for King James, the famous *Masque of Blackness.* She thought the project was ill-conceived, herself. If for no other reason because the success of *The Masque of Blackness* had been due in no small part to the architectural genius of Jonson's partner Inigo Jones. His stage settings had been magnificent.

Jonson's *then* partner, alas. The rupture between the two men had been deep; it was now deep and bitter, since Jones had won the favor of Richard Boyle, the earl of Cork. So now Jonson was in self-imposed exile in Amsterdam and the Dutch architects and artisans at his disposal were not really up to the challenge of designing the monumental stage settings he insisted upon.

It would help, of course, if he'd actually finish the blasted thing instead of dithering. There was another rehearsal scheduled for that evening, for which both she and her brother Rupert had donned their costumes. It would probably wind up being a disjointed semi-disaster like the two previous rehearsals.

Rupert was leaning over Jonson's shoulder. He had his chin cupped in his hand in what he presumably hoped would be seen as a gesture of thoughtfulness—but Elizabeth was quite sure her brother just wanted to stroke his beard. Still shy of his sixteenth birthday, Rupert was inordinately proud of his whiskers.

In truth, he had some right to be. He was already six feet tall and was showing that extraordinary musculature that would make him a military legend in another universe. *Prince Rupert of the Rhine,* they'd called him. Rupert had vowed he would not pursue the soldier's career he'd followed in that up-time world. But Elizabeth had noted that her brother maintained a rigorous regimen when it came to his exercises in the *salle d'armes* run by his Dutch swordmaster. Such vows were easy to make; not so easy to keep.

"I think you should rather make it a token of esteem from

Oceanus," Rupert said. He pointed to the object in the poet's hand. "You could think of it as a symbol of the engirdling oceans in all their many hues."

Ben Jonson stroked his own beard. "Hm. Interesting idea, I agree."

In Elizabeth's opinion, the idea was idiotic—because *any* attempt to make the Rubik's Cube the center of a masque was idiotic. The ridiculous up-time contrivance was far too small to play that role. They'd do better to use the statue of the elf or even the club. What did Americans call the thing? A "baseball bat," if she remembered correctly.

The name was as idiotic as the Rubik's Cube. There'd been bats in two of the houses she'd lived in during her family's peripatetic existence following the expulsion of her father, the elector of the palatine Frederick V, from the throne he'd briefly held as King of Bohemia. The American club bore no resemblance to the creatures at all.

— 3 —

"George Monck's been executed," John Hampden announced, closing the door to the salon behind him. He came over to the big table in the center of the room around which a number of other men were seated and laid a radio message on the surface. "The news just came in. Thomas Fairfax, John Lambert and Thomas Horton were executed along with him. Horton was drawn and quartered first."

"*Bastards*," hissed Arthur Haselrig. "What about Denzil Holles? And Fairfax's son Ferdinando?"

Hampden pulled out a chair. "Still alive, I suppose. For how long remains to be seen." He sat down. "So far, the earl of Manchester is the only one who seems to have wormed his way into Cork's good graces."

"'Wormed' is the right word, too," said young Henry Ireton. "Unfair to worms, I suppose, but since 'swined' or 'toaded' aren't verbs it'll have to do."

There was real anger lurking under the humor. Still only twenty-four years old, Ireton was too young to have known any of the men executed by the earl of Cork. But like all of the men in the room, he'd studied the up-time accounts of the civil war that had begun in England—would have begun, rather, in another England in another universe—in the year 1642.

The history of that conflict weighed heavily on all of them, for all its insubstantial nature. Perhaps on none more than the man sitting at the head of the long table, Thomas Wentworth—who'd stopped calling himself the earl of Strafford because of it.

Wentworth studied young Ireton for a moment. In this world, the man was a lawyer—as he had been in that other. But so far he was only a lawyer, not the accomplished military officer he would become—would have become, had become, could have become—the grammar was maddening—in the up-timers' universe.

Wentworth suppressed a smile. And how must the youngster feel about having been Oliver Cromwell's son-in-law in that world? He'd never even met the Bridget Cromwell he would marry there. It would do him little good to do so in this one anyway, at least for the moment. The girl was still only...

Wentworth tried to remember the ages of Cromwell's children. Bridget was ten or eleven years old, he thought. Certainly no more than twelve.

If she was still alive at all. There'd been very little news of Cromwell since the escape from the Tower of London.

The men who'd recently been executed had played prominent roles in that civil war, as had the earl of Manchester. Would have played, it might be better to say. The reason Horton had been drawn and quartered was because, it that other universe, he'd been one of the commissioners of the High Court of Justice in 1649 and among those who'd signed the warrant for the execution of King Charles I of England.

In that universe, Horton had died of natural causes—disease, presumably; the American records were not specific—while serving in Ireland under Cromwell. In this universe, King Charles was still on the throne and his chief minister Richard Boyle, the earl of Cork, had seen fit to cut the matter short—along with the man himself.

In the universe the Americans came from, Horton's heirs had been deprived of their estate during the Restoration in the 1660s. Wentworth didn't doubt for a moment that they'd already been stripped of the estate in this one. Among his other charming characteristics, Richard Boyle was ravenously greedy. By all accounts, the king was mired in melancholia and paid no attention to the affairs of his realm. The earl of Cork had become for all practical purposes the military dictator of England and he saw to it that all property seized from "traitors" wound up either in his own hands or those of his close associates and followers.

"Why execute Monck at all?" asked Henry Vane plaintively. "Or Fairfax, for that matter? Both of them helped the Restoration in the end."

Wentworth exchanged glances with the man sitting at the other end of the table. That was Robert Devereux, the earl of Essex. He and Thomas Wentworth were more-or-less the two recognized leaders of the group. "More or less," because as yet the group itself was only more or less a group. It was still an association of like-minded individuals rather than the formally constituted revolutionary organization that both Wentworth and Devereux were striving to establish.

Robert understood the meaning of that glance. There was a great deal of personal friction between Thomas and Henry Vane, which stemmed from the fact that Vane had discovered in the course of perusing the American history texts that in that other universe he had disliked Wentworth for reasons having to do with the complex politics of the time. The cretin had chosen to adopt the same hostile stance in *this* universe—and never mind that none of the events which produced the hostility had happened in this world or ever would.

But it would be best to leave those embers unstirred. So Robert took it upon himself to answer Vane's question—and did so a lot more diplomatically than Thomas would have himself. It was a cretin's question, after all.

"Boyle's got his own ambitions, Henry, that's why. He doesn't want anyone at the court who could make a claim to the king's confidence, besides himself. Given the king's nature—even on his best days, which these aren't—that's not unlikely. Charles is petulant. Sooner or later, the earl of Cork is bound to annoy him. When that time comes, Boyle doesn't want anyone like Monck or Fairfax around whom the king might decide would make a suitable replacement for him."

Thomas Harrison grunted sarcastically. "Not all that likely, Robert! You're presuming that His Royal Idiocy has actually studied the up-time histories." He gave Wentworth a look that was not entirely friendly. "What actually happened is that he learned of the basic fact that concerned him—'they cut my head off!'—and then left it to Strafford here to learn the details and act accordingly."

Wentworth's jaws tightened, but he made no protest. It would be hard to do so, of course, since Harrison's account was fairly accurate. As for the harshness of the man's attitude...

Again, the weight of history. In this world, Harrison had had the good sense to flee England as soon as he heard of Pym's arrest. At the time, he hadn't read any of the up-time texts himself, but he'd sensed what was coming.

There was no guesswork involved any longer. In that other universe—and by now Harrison *had* read the texts—he'd been executed at the Restoration.

"There's no point in digging all that up," Devereux said mildly. "Thomas did as the king bade him do, which is the task of any minister. But he didn't go any farther than that, and he certainly didn't oversee the sort of wholesale slaughter that Boyle's been responsible for."

After a moment, Harrison nodded stiffly. "True enough. If I've caused any offense, Thomas, my apologies."

"None needed." Wentworth smiled ruefully. "It's not as if anything you said isn't true."

John Bradshaw had been silent, up till now. "I want to change the subject," he said. "What are we going to do about this *other* unpleasant news?"

Silence came over the room as the men sitting around the table exchanged glances with each other.

The *other unpleasant news* were the tidings that had arrived just this morning. Karl Ludwig, the oldest surviving son of the elector palatine, had assumed his father's title when Frederick V died less than three years earlier. Along with his mother Elizabeth, who was the daughter of King James and the current English king's older sister, he'd been residing in Brussels for years in what amounted to Spanish captivity. Very pleasant and genteel captivity, to be sure, but captivity nonetheless.

And now, it seemed, the eighteen-year-old Karl Ludwig had converted to Catholicism—taking with that conversion the best option the English exiles had to replace King Charles. No matter how unpopular Charles and his chief minister Richard Boyle might have become, there was no way the English populace would accept a Catholic monarch.

Harrison grunted again. Not sarcastically this time, though. The sound had an almost pleased quality to it.

"I never thought much of Karl Ludwig anyway," he said. "With him sworn over to the damn papists, that puts Rupert next in line—and I'll be the first to say I'd far rather have Rupert on the throne of England."

Wentworth sighed, and ran fingers through his hair. "So would I, Thomas, so would I. But Rupert will refuse if we raise the idea with him."

"Are you certain of that?"

"I'm afraid so. As most of you know, I've become rather close to the boy over the past months. I've never raised the possibility directly, of course—that would have been most inappropriate, with his older brother still in possible line of succession—but I know him well enough to know that he wouldn't accept. He's bound and determined to avoid the same career he had in the other world. He says he intends to become an inventor instead. Or possibly an artist. Or both."

"An inventor!" exclaimed Henry Vane. "That's absurd!"

Wentworth felt obliged to come to Rupert's defense. "Actually, later in his life—after the Restoration, I mean—Rupert became quite an accomplished inventor. And artist as well."

"It's still absurd," insisted Vane. "And he wasn't king in that world, anyway, so I fail to see the problem."

You wouldn't, thought Thomas. But he left it unsaid. Whatever else had or might change, the dictates of diplomacy had not, did not and would not.

Devereux pulled out a timepiece. "We need to go, gentlemen. It's almost five o'clock."

Wentworth rose from the table along with him. So did Hampden.

"Where are you off to now?" asked Bradshaw.

The earl of Essex made a face. "It's another of Jonson's masque rehearsals." His eyes widened. "But it occurs to me that since we'll be wearing masks anyway—incredibly elaborate ones, to boot—that you could go in my place."

Bradshaw shook his head, smiling. "What? So I could stand around being bored while that decrepit old poet tries to remember what he's about? No, thank you." He waved an airy hand at Devereux, Hampden and Wentworth. "You three splendid—no, resplendent!—fellows are more than enough to attend to the needs of protocol."

"Have fun," said Harrison, chuckling.

Henry Vane looked envious. Certain proof, if any were needed, that the man was a cretin.

— 4 —

"Wentworth, Essex and Hampden," said Robert Clifford. He spoke softly, with his head canted slightly forward to bring his mouth closer to the three men listening to him. "Remember. Those are the key targets."

"And if we succeed with all three and have time to spare?" asked Matthew Bromley.

The corner of Clifford's lips twisted in the manner he had when thinking. After a moment he said: "It doesn't really matter that much. Laud, of course. But the reason I didn't place him with the first three is because he never attends these affairs."

While he'd been speaking, Bryan Neville had been keeping an eye on the windows of the large house in whose shrubbery they'd hidden, although nothing beyond shadows could be seen through the curtains. Now, he chuckled slightly. "God forbid the once-and-still-imagines-he-is archbishop of Canterbury should participate in such frivolous pastimes."

Bromley frowned. He was quite devout and disapproved of using the Lord's name in vain. But he made no open protest. The other three men present were not devout at all—their leader Clifford fell just short of being an outright freethinker—and they were quick to ridicule.

"How soon do we move?" asked the fourth man. That was George Wilchon, who'd once been a bookbinder's apprentice in Norwich before his uneven temperament had caused him to be dismissed. A week later he'd stabbed his former master to death in an alley by way of revenge and discovered his current trade.

Clifford glanced at the sky and then at the windows. At Amsterdam's latitude, twilight was a protracted affair. They'd crept into the bushes after sunset but had had to wait a considerable time before it was dark enough for their business. By now, though, night had fallen and since they were just three days past a new moon there wasn't much light in the streets.

All of their targets had arrived and judging from what Clifford could tell the rehearsal had finally gotten underway. He'd wanted to wait for that to begin just as much as he'd wanted to wait for full darkness. The demands of the rehearsal would keep everyone preoccupied while he and his men made their entry into the house.

"No reason to wait any longer," he said. He eased his way out of the shrubbery, heading for the narrow pathway that led around to the back. The house wasn't quite big enough to qualify for the term "mansion" but it came very close. Happily for their project, the kitchen was in an isolated extension of the house and there was a rear service entrance. They should be able to get inside without much in the way of noise or fuss, and they'd only counted two cooks.

The cooks were both men, and would of course be very familiar with knives. But Clifford foresaw no great difficulty. Skill at cutting meat was by no means the same thing as skill at cutting men.

— 5 —

"No, no, no!" exclaimed Ben Jonson. The old playwright limped toward the center of the room. "You!" he said, pointing at Rupert. Despite the mask he was wearing, the young prince's height made him quite recognizable. "You're supposed to be still, not capering about! Go sit down until you think you've mastered that meager skill."

Rupert restrained his temper easily enough. He wanted to sit down anyway. Jonson couldn't seem to make up his mind about what he wanted and Rupert's feet were getting sore.

He strode over to the wall where his sister was sitting and flung himself into the chair next to her.

"I was not 'capering about,'" he hissed. "Just..."

"Moving a lot," said Elizabeth. Rupert couldn't see her face because, like him, she was wearing a full mask. But he was darkly certain she was smiling.

His sister was smiling, in fact. It was not an expression of derision, though, but one of sympathy. Elizabeth had had quite enough of Ben Jonson. The famous poet and playwright was irascible, bad-tempered—and worst of all, she didn't think he had all his wits about him any longer. He would yell at someone for not doing something Jonson had forgotten to tell them to do; and then yell at someone else for doing something he *had* told them to do but had since forgotten he'd done so.

She called it "senile" or "being in his dotage." Her instructor Anne Jefferson insisted that such terms were imprecise and unscientific and that Jonson suffered instead from one or another form of dementia brought on by his advanced years. Most likely something called "Alzheimer's disease."

Americans could be a bit tiresome. Had there ever existed a people more prone to making pointless distinctions?

Naturally, they had expressions for that too. *Splitting hairs. Crossing the t's and dotting the i's. Fussing over the fine points.*

"No, no, no!" Jonson yelled again, this time at a woman. Elizabeth wasn't sure because of the mask, but she thought that was Mrs. Hampden. She extended her unspoken sympathies still further with another smile.

— 6 —

As Clifford had foreseen, the cooks proved to be no problem. But there was a servant boy they hadn't expected, nine or ten years old and quick on his feet. Luckily, his shrill peal of alarm was drowned out by a shouting voice coming from the salon and Bromley caught him before he could call out again or flee the kitchen.

His little corpse joined those of the two cooks in the root cellar.

"Quietly now," Clifford said. He entered the dim hallway leading into the rear quarters of the house.

— 7 —

As one of the servants guided Anne and Olearius through the house, Anne could hear Jonson's hollering while they were still twenty feet from the door leading to the main salon. That was a solid, heavy door, too.

She sighed with exasperation. "I am really getting sick of that man."

Her husband smiled and drew back one side of his coat. Anne could now see a pistol tucked into his belt. "Have no fear, dearest. Should the old reprobate misbehave again, I shall—what's that charming American phrase?—plug him full of holes. Well. One hole, anyway. It's just a single-shot flintlock."

Anne's eyes widened with alarm. Well. Some alarm. Her husband wasn't a hot-tempered man. "Oh, please! That old lecher? I assure you that I can handle him quite easily myself—as I did when he made his advances, remember? You really didn't need to bring that on his account."

They'd reached the door to the salon and the servant began to draw it open. Adam's smile widened. "I was only joking. I didn't bring the pistol because of Jonson. I just don't trust Amsterdam's streets at night."

They came into the salon. Jonson turned and glared at them. "You're late! And why aren't you wearing your masks?"

— *8* —

"*Now,*" said Clifford. Neville, the biggest of them, kicked in the door to the salon leading from the back chambers. Clifford piled through, followed by Wilchon and Bromley.

The salon was packed with people. And most of them were wearing masks!

Clifford hadn't expected that. He and Wilchon had learned from casual questioning of one of the servants in a nearby tavern that their targets were among a crowd of people rehearsing a masque. But neither Clifford nor any of his companions had ever observed a masque in person, those being generally entertainments of the upper classes. Without thinking much about it, he'd simply assumed they weren't much different from the plays he'd seen performed.

One man sitting nearby was not wearing a mask and Clifford

recognized him from woodcuts he'd been shown. That was the earl of Essex, Robert Devereux, one of their main targets. He aimed his pistol and fired. The bullet struck the earl in the chest. He threw back his arms, the chair tipped over, and he fell to the floor.

There'd be no time to reload and Clifford didn't want to use up his other pistol for such a target. Essex might already be dying anyway. Springing forward, he reached the earl, seized him by the hair and drew him up to a half-sitting position. Cutting his throat took but an instant.

Behind him, he heard his companions firing their pistols. He could only hope they hadn't wasted the shots by firing at random.

Masks!

Adam Olearius was a diplomat, not a soldier. He didn't lack courage but he did lack an experienced combatant's trained reflexes. So he was paralyzed for a couple of seconds before he thought to sweep his wife behind him with his left hand while he drew his pistol with the right.

That delay probably saved his life. The assassins *were* trained and experienced in these matters, so they ignored him. He seemed to pose no threat and they didn't recognize him as one of the men they sought.

Two of the assassins fired at the same man, a tall fellow wearing a rather flamboyant multicolored cloak. He slumped instantly to the floor. The third fired at a man standing perhaps eight feet away. From the long, dark and curly hair spilling out from behind his mask, Adam thought that was probably John Hampden.

The shot missed. Partly missed, rather. The man with the long curly hair cried out and clutched his left shoulder. Blood oozed from between his fingers.

His assailant threw down the pistol, drew another, and took aim again. It was all very quick—but by the time he could fire, a woman had arrived and was trying to pull the wounded man to the ground. The shot struck her instead, right in the middle of her back. She coughed. Blood burst from her mouth and splattered over the mask of the man she'd tried to protect.

That *was* Hampden. Adam recognized the costume of the woman who'd been shot while trying to save him as that of his wife.

Finally, he drew out his pistol. And, in his excitement and nervousness, dropped it onto the floor. But the man who'd shot

Mrs. Hampden had ducked when he saw the pistol coming out, stumbled over someone who'd thrown themselves down in fear, and now stumbled onto his knees himself.

Both assassins who'd fired at the cloaked man had drawn new pistols and were advancing on Hampden. There was another assassin rising up behind them, too.

Rupert had no experience at all with this sort of bloody, brutal melee, and he was still only fifteen years old.

On the other hand, he'd been training with weapons for years and he was already immensely strong.

So he rose, turned, seized his chair and hurled it across the room. A great, solid oaken brute of a chair, as you'd expect to find in the salon of such a fine house.

The chair sailed across the room and struck the first of the two men about to shoot Hampden. He was knocked right off his feet and into the arms of his companion—who couldn't stop himself from pulling the trigger of his own pistol.

The bullet cut through the fleshy hip of his dazed partner, was deflected, and flew across the room to strike Rupert's sister Elizabeth in the head.

A glancing shot, luckily, and much of the bullet's force had already been spent. Still, it was a bloody horrible sight. She clutched her head, blood spurted through her fingers, and she fell out of her chair.

Rupert roared with fury, seized Elizabeth's chair—which had not quite tipped over when the girl spilled out of it—and sent that one hurtling after the other.

This second chair struck the two assassins, who were still tangled together with one of them holding up his partner. Both of them were knocked flat.

There was a third chair nearby. Rupert seized it and smashed it against the wall. A heavy oaken wall, as you'd expect in such a house. The force of the impact was enough to shatter the chair. The prince came away from the wall with a chair leg in each hand.

Dear God, that bastard's strong! Clifford aimed at the tall figure striding toward him and squeezed the—

Damnation! Some old fool stumbled in the way and the bullet took the top of his head off.

No time to reload. Clifford hurled the pistol at his opponent and drew his dirk.

Thomas Wentworth hadn't come armed to the rehearsal. But the man who'd murdered poor Elizabeth Hampden had fallen to the floor and was now trying to rise not more than six feet away. Wentworth balled his fist, strode over, and struck the man behind the ear. Once, again, again, and yet again.

Wentworth was a large man, quite well-built, and he was in a fury. The blows knocked the killer senseless.

Rupert's training finally took over. He recognized the stance and knife-grip of the man facing him as that of an experienced bladesman. There was a straightforward way to handle such an opponent, when you had a sword—which the prince didn't, but a stout chair leg would substitute quite nicely.

Especially because he had two of them. He hurled the one in his right hand at the assassin's head.

The man ducked, and when he came up with the knife leading the way as it should, Rupert smashed his hand with the oak table-leg. The assassin cried out and clutched the shattered hand with his other. Rupert now smashed both hands.

The training left him. Rupert's opponent was helpless, the prince was very young, and the swine had foully murdered his sister. He drew back the club and brought it down with all the power of an arm that had just turned two oak chairs into splinters.

"Rupert, no!"

That was Wentworth. But he barely heard the voice. The club crushed the assassin's skull like an egg. About the only difference was that a ruptured brain came out instead of a ruptured yolk.

Adam Olearius finally brought up his pistol, ready to fire. But it was all over.

One man was obviously dead, another had been beaten unconscious by Wentworth, and the two whom Rupert had knocked off their feet with the chairs he'd thrown were now being…

Olearius winced. Beaten to a pulp, it seemed, by just about every man in the room and a fair number of the women.

His wife Anne raced over, trying with the instincts of a nurse to halt the carnage.

Being honest, Adam couldn't wish her much luck in the project. It was all he could do not to race over himself and shoot one of the bastards.

Instead, he turned to help Elizabeth Stuart. Anne had glanced at her young protégé before running over to the mob in the center of the salon. With her experienced eye she'd immediately seen that while the girl's head wound was gory it wasn't really dangerous.

Once he reached her, Adam discovered that Elizabeth had come that realization herself. "Just get me a cloth of some sort," she said, continuing to press her hand onto the wound. Her lips were tight but she seemed otherwise quite composed. "Preferably sterile, although I don't know where you'll find a sterile cloth in this chaos and confusion. Is my brother all right?"

"Well—"

There came a now-familiar roar from the center of the room. The tall figure of Rupert rose up from the mob assailing the two killers. He held one of the men above his head.

Another roar, and the man was sent flying across the room to smash into the wall and slide to the floor, bringing a large portrait of a prosperous burgher down with him.

The boy's strength was really quite astonishing.

"Well. Yes. I'd say he's in good health." After a moment he added: "I'm afraid Ben Jonson was killed, though."

The princess nodded, a bit gingerly. "I'm sorry to hear it."

"Perhaps it's just as well. His reputation won't be ruined now, the way it seemed it might be."

"Yes. And I didn't like him. But I'm still sorry."

For someone born of such royal lineage, Elizabeth Stuart was really quite a nice young woman. So Adam's wife had told him and he saw no reason to disagree.

There came another roar. Adam looked over. Rupert was rising up again, with the other assassin in his hands.

Another wall shook, and another portrait came down.

So was her brother, for that matter. Allowing for the occasional—quite justified, Adam thought—insensate fury.

Give him a few more years, and the prince would be a frightful enemy for those who drew down his ire.

— 9 —

"But Hampden himself is all right, yes? That's what matters."

Wentworth tightened his jaws, restraining his temper. Henry Vane could be trying.

To put it mildly. The term "ass" came to mind also. For that matter, so did "asshole."

The look that Thomas Harrison was giving Vane made it obvious that he was entertaining similar thoughts.

"I would strongly urge you not to say that in front of Hampden himself," Harrison said. "John's likely to take his rage out on you. He was close to his wife, you know."

Vane looked vaguely alarmed. But then, Vane often looked vaguely alarmed about many things.

Ireton leaned back in his chair. "It's too bad we couldn't get any useful information from the surviving assassins." He slapped the table with exasperation. "You'd think among the three of them that at least one would know *something.*"

"Two of them, it'd be more accurate to say," grunted Bradshaw. "One of the swine the prince used to decorate the wall came out of the experience with his mentis pretty much compost."

Wentworth shrugged. "He probably didn't know any more than his fellows. It's clear enough that the one Rupert killed was the leader of the gang. These are just criminals, when all is said and done. Cut-purses and murderers-for-hire. Boyle hired them, obviously, but he would have worked through intermediaries. I doubt if even the ringleader knew who his ultimate employer was."

"Too bad." Ireton slapped the table again. "If we could just prove..."

Wentworth finally managed a smile. The first one, he thought, since those horrid events three days before. "I don't think it matters. The only person whose opinion is truly critical is the prince, and he's sure and certain—as only a teenage boy can be—that the earl of Cork was behind it all. Not to mention—"

Wentworth cleared his throat. This was perhaps a bit embarrassing. "Rupert, ah, also believes that he and his sister were among the assassins' targets. And he is purely furious about the assault on Elizabeth. Which he considers dastardly, unchivalrous, wicked, beyond all forgiveness—his terms, mind you—and for which he holds his uncle ultimately responsible."

Everyone at the table stared at him. Bradshaw cleared his throat. "I think it's almost certain that the assassins had no intention of harming the Stuart children. Probably didn't even know they'd be there."

"Supposition, supposition," stated Wentworth. "Who's to say?"

Ireton grinned at him. "And you're not about to suggest to the prince that his suspicions are unwarranted."

"No, I'm not. I believe Prince Rupert's thoughts are now running down an excellent channel and I see no reason to risk diverting that flow."

There was silence for perhaps a minute. Then Ireton grinned again. "It occurs to me that there never was a King Rupert of England in that up-time universe. Proving once again that predestination is as slippery as an eel."

Henry Vane frowned. He was clearly of the suspicion that theological error lurked somewhere in that statement by Ireton. Thankfully, he was not smart enough to figure out how or why.

— *10* —

"It's too bad about Wentworth and Hampden," commiserated Paul Pindar. "Would have been nice to get Laud too."

The earl of Cork shook his head. "The truth is, the scheme worked better than I thought it would. Essex alone is worth the cost."

The man who was England's ruler in fact if not in name rose and went to the window. From his vantage point in the royal palace at Whitehall he had a good view of Westminster as well as the City of London. He clasped his hands behind his back and spent a couple of minutes surveying his domain. The expression on his face was one of satisfaction.

"These sort of assassinations are always a toss of the dice," he said finally. "But even if they only partially succeed—or fail altogether, for that matter—there's no harm in trying."

The Monster

Gorg Huff & Paula Goodlett

The Eagle Flies

Magdalena van de Passe stood outside the building and stared. She paid not the slightest attention to what was going on around her; she had eyes only for the plane that was flying overhead. She had seen airplanes on TV, but she had seen dragons and giant apes on TV, too. A civilized person and old Grantville hand knew that just because they had it on TV didn't mean that they could do it in the here and now. It didn't even mean that it was real up-time.

She couldn't hear the engine, or maybe she heard it just a little; it might be her imagination. It didn't matter. The plane was real. Man had learned to fly and could do it in the here and now. And she was going to. She didn't know how, she didn't know when. But she was going to fly. Whatever the cost. She felt almost like she was flying now. After the plane had gone over and while people were running off to wherever they were running off to, Magdalena went back inside. She needed to be alone and to think. Her life had just taken a sharp turn and was running off in a new direction. She needed to catch up with herself.

Back in the building, she looked at the books that had accumulated over the last months. She had come to Grantville at the combined request of her father and her patron. An engraver from a family of engravers, Magdalena was here to learn about opportunities in that field and opportunities in general. To facilitate that, she was studying up-timer business practices. She had found it interesting; now she found it positively engrossing. Right there on her desk was a paper on the costs of mule trains and how they compared to barge traffic, the new rail lines, and trucks on the improved roads. What about airplanes? How much would they cost? How much could they carry? What were their hidden costs?

Suddenly, Magdalena's life was making another turn or perhaps she was catching up with the last one. The outline of a plan was forming. There were a lot of pieces missing, but she could fill those in; she was sure of it. Meanwhile she had some letters to write.

Dearest Father,

I pray that you will put aside your reasonable skepticism and gift me with a continuation of that trust you gave me when you sent me to this place of wonders. For what I have to tell you next may make you wish you had sent my brother instead.

Magdalena had been sent instead of her brother because she was probably the least trusting member of the family. Her brother was a talented artisan but "he'd buy the Brooklyn Bridge without even arguing the price," as she had heard Cora Beth say.

I would not believe the report I must now make lest I had seen it with my own eyes. Not ten minutes ago, I stood outside this very building and watched a flying machine overhead. With my own eyes, Papa. I would not accept such a claim on lesser evidence. Nor can I truly expect you to. What I do ask is that you begin to let yourself consider believing that it is possible.

I make this request because one thing came very clear to me as I watched the manmade bird sail overhead. There are no toll collectors in the sky.

Your Services No Longer Required

"Sorry, Georg. But with Jesse Wood running the Air Force..." Vanessa Holcomb actually seemed sorry, though they hadn't gotten along. Kitt Aviation was letting all the down-timers go, because Jesse Wood had beaten them into the sky and would be deciding who got the government contracts. They said they were going to have to cut back. The rest sort of flowed over him as he dealt with the fact that the sky was no longer his to claim.

Two days later Georg Markgraf paced back and forth outside the Gardens. This was a crazy idea. He wasn't any good with people; he knew that. Maybe he should try to join the Air Force...but the line was long for pilot training. Besides, he wanted to build planes more than he wanted to fly them. And the up-timers had that part pretty much sewn up, so far as the Air Force was concerned. He had tried the Kellys; they weren't hiring either. That left starting his own company.

Georg finally ran down and most of his guests left, but Farrell Smith stayed. "Kid, you are not good at public speaking. Your presentation skills are pitiful. You're not well organized and you get distracted. In fact, you pretty much suck at it."

Georg slumped and buried his head in his hands. "I know. I know. But I can build a plane." He thumped his chest. "In here, I know it. I have seen the designs at Kitt. Seen the designs at Kelly. I understand aerodynamics; the numbers and concepts make sense to me. I can do as well. Better. Because they are not considering what we can do now. They all concentrate on what can be salvaged, not what can be built anew."

"How do you mean?"

"Craftsmanship!" Georg held up his hands. "I don't mean fancy doodads. I mean the ability of a good craftsman to judge wood, its strengths and weaknesses, by feel. To shape it using the structure of the wood itself. I mean the skills of a good leather worker to make a saddle or a wine sack and pick the right leather for the right job. Those skills can be combined with your up-time tools and knowledge to craft airplanes."

Farrell kept him talking late into the night. Because the kid had a point. Just before Farrell left, Georg asked, "Do you think any of them will invest?"

"Not a chance, son. I'd be running too, if I didn't know you a bit and Dad hadn't said some good things about you." Farrell shook his head. "Those folks came here half sold after Jesse Wood's flight. You managed to convince them that investing in flight was crazy."

"What do I do now?"

"You wait. Just hang on and let me see what I can do." Farrell assured Georg that he'd contact him in a couple of days. The boy had good ideas. After listening to him talk about the monocoque design he had in mind, Farrell was convinced of several things. Georg Markgraf was as qualified as anyone in Grantville, outside of Farrell's father, Hal, to design aircraft. Georg wasn't, however, qualified to run a company whether it designed aircraft or made thumb tacks. And, finally, Georg had to be prevented from making presentations in front of potential investors at all costs.

Farrell paused, then turned back. "Georg, where are you staying?" With the kids moving out, the house was a bit empty. He'd have to clear it with Mary but perhaps the kid could stay with them. Farrell wasn't really qualified to run a business, either. He could put together a presentation, even if it would end up sounding like a lecture.

"I was sharing a room with a friend. It's paid for the rest of the month."

Farrell wasn't all that much of a salesman himself, but after years of teaching shop at least he could sound like he knew what he was talking about and keep on point. He made the presentations. The fact that his father was the one and only aeronautical engineer who had been brought with the Ring of Fire didn't hurt and the timing was good. After Jesse Wood flew and, especially, after Hans Richter soloed, people were ready to throw money at flight projects. It had been proven that it could be done down-time and the down-timers—even more than the up-timers—saw the potential benefit.

There were more than rational reasons for this. The simple fact was that the New US, and much of the CPE, was caught up in the romance of flight.

We Need a Bigger Plane

June 25, 1633
Dear Sirs:

TransEuropean Airlines is seeking bidders to produce one or more aircraft to open passenger and cargo service to various cities within and without the USE. The planes must be capable of carrying at least ten passengers or one ton of cargo for a distance of at least three hundred miles non-stop.

We will provide partial funding on approved designs. Further, we will provide aid in acquiring or constructing engines, within reason. We will provide final payment after successful test flights are completed.

On successful completion of testing of the first aircraft, we will guarantee to buy up to ten more, if the manufacturer can provide them to us within a reasonable period of time.

Contact M. van de Passe
Address: 2613 Makem Rd
Phone: 448-5767

Magdalena looked at the letter and smiled. The letter would go out to Kelly, to Kitt and to anyone else who might be doing anything serious in terms of aviation. It would also go out to potential investors to let them know that TEA was serious. Of course, TEA didn't actually have the money to pay for the aircraft yet. But, as the Bible didn't say, "Act as if you have financial backing and financial backing will be given unto you."

"I'm not sure I believe this." Georg Markgraf sat at the desk, staring at the computer screen.

Farrell glanced over. "What'ya got?" The computer was running an Excel spreadsheet, full of formulas, drag coefficients, lift calculations, wing stresses . . . all he had to do was plug in a few variables and out came a pretty good estimate of the flight speed, stall speed, ceiling, empty weight, loaded weight. In general, the results were the probable flight envelope of the projected aircraft.

"That letter we got from TransEuropean Airlines. It got me to thinking. So I started plugging in numbers to see what I got."

"Umm hum?" The spreadsheet had started with something Farrell's father, Hal, and Vanessa Holcomb had put together. Excel was such a powerful program that the various designers, including Georg, had started adding bits. More formula based on up-time books, then more based on experimentation to fill in the gaps. It was a pretty good tool by now, one that let you try things and get a rough idea how they would work.

"Well, I plugged in a hundred-and-twenty-foot wingspan and got a stall speed of like twenty miles per hour."

"Never work. With the materials . . ." Farrell stopped speaking because Georg was glaring at him. He had forgotten Georg's wing stress kludge.

"I know that." Georg's irritation was as evident in his voice as it had been in his look. Then he visibly shook it off. "We couldn't support even an eighty-foot wingspan. Not in a monoplane."

"A biplane? They're a lot less efficient. You only get about eighty percent as much lift for the wing area."

"Sure. But the upper and lower wings support each other, so they don't have to be nearly as strong. And if the lower wing is shorter than the upper, we only lose lift where both wings are involved. It lets us extend the upper wing farther out. With a seventy-foot lower wing, we could have a hundred-foot upper wingspan."

"What about drag?"

"A lot, but drag is a function of speed and this would be slow." Georg laughed. "To think I would ever call sixty miles per hour slow. I'm more concerned about the strutting disrupting laminar flow."

Farrell scooted his chair over to the computer and started to examine Georg's numbers for real. The four Jeep engines would only put out a grand total of maybe six hundred horsepower. But that was all this thing would need if the numbers were right. "A biplane with those? And have the darn thing *fly*?"

Georg waved his hand at the computer. "The spreadsheet says we can." He drew pictures in the air. "The upper wing would have a hundred feet of span, the lower seventy. The lower wing is as much to support and strengthen the upper as to give added lift." He sat back down at the desk. "I've got to check these figures. Go away."

Farrell did. There wasn't much point in trying to talk to Georg when he was calculating.

☆ ☆ ☆

Slowly, as he went through checking the formulas to be sure he hadn't dropped a decimal someplace, Georg began to believe it. It would be, he was convinced, unlike any plane that had ever flown. It would be more like a powered glider than an ordinary airplane.

Georg loved the DC3. He had ever since he had seen one in the movies; more so after he had read up on them. A lot of flight enthusiasts loved that plane, he'd discovered. The DC3 Dakota was perhaps the most-loved plane in up-time history. It was also totally out of the technical reach of anyone down-time. It had two radial engines, each putting out over a thousand horsepower. It was all metal construction and that much aluminum simply wasn't available. But it—or as close to it as they could get—was what TEA wanted.

The biplane that was staring back at him from the numbers on his computer screen would have over one and a half times the wing area of the DC3. It would need it, because it would have barely a third of the horsepower. It would need the extra lift just to get off the ground, as underpowered as it was. Its cruising speed would be less than half that of the Dakota's, but then its landing speed would be a lot less, too. With a full cargo load, it would have about five hours flight time. Right at three hundred miles.

It would carry a ton and a half of cargo, perhaps a bit more. The body would be a semi-monocoque construction—part of the structural support coming from internal bracing, part from the shape of the structure—made of a composite of fiberglass and viscose that they had been testing, making for a light, strong airframe. It would be a lot like the Dakota, except it would be made of fiberglass rather than aluminum. It would be well-streamlined, even the supports between the wings. But in power and speed it would be closer to something out of World War One or earlier.

"We really can do it." Georg pulled out a paper and pen and started to draw.

Hal Smith snorted. "I can see what the kid's gone and done, Farrell. He didn't know it, but he's reinvented the wheel. If he'd ever seen a picture of the *Ilya Muromets* built by Igor Sikorsky near the dawn of aviation, he'd have recognized it right off. This is as close a cousin to it as I ever saw."

"So it will fly?" Farrell asked. "I thought it would, but couldn't be sure."

His dad gave him the look that said "I always was disappointed in you." Then he nodded. "It'll fly... assuming you can build it."

"Hand me the scraper." Georg didn't look up. He had heard a sound and assumed it was someone who belonged there. An instrument was put in his hand. He glanced at it. "Not that one. The corrugated one." He stuck his head out from under the section of fuselage enough to see a pair of legs in the split skirts that all the ladies seemed to be wearing these days. He didn't recognize the legs. "The wiggly one."

Having received the right scraper, he went back to his work. "Sorry. I have to get this done before the viscose dries. It's like cardboard, you see. The strength comes from the shape and where the bits connect." Having gotten the fabric pressed into the grooves, Georg climbed out from under the section he was working on and looked at his unknown helper.

He saw a woman of medium height and quite a nice figure, but it was her eyes that really caught his attention. Intelligent eyes that were examining what he had been doing. "Ah... Are you looking for work? We don't have anything right now, but check back in a couple of weeks. We're expecting a big contract."

"I've seen cardboard. This doesn't look like it. Isn't cardboard supposed to have flat sheets on either side of the curvy bits? And aren't the curvy bits straight?"

Georg grinned. He couldn't help it. "I'm constantly trying to figure a way of putting it that makes sense myself. Corrugated cardboard's inside sheet is given a curvy fold in one direction because it's easier to do it that way in a cardboard making machine and because cardboard is mostly used for making boxes. The corrugations add strength, but primarily in one direction. We need the added strength to go in different directions at different places in the structure. So we adjusted the corrugations to curve around the structure to give added strength where we need it in the direction we need it."

Georg waved his hand at Joseph Kepler. "Joseph is the carver. I just told him where the stresses were going to be. We'll add a smooth top coat later for added strength and streamlining."

Farrell finally got off the phone and headed for the shop. He had to get Georg out of there before he blew the deal. When he entered the shop he found Georg and the crew talking with a young woman about engraving, and how it was sort of like the way they made the forms. "I hate to break this up, but Herr de Passe is on the way from TEA and we need to get Georg out of here before he opens mouth and inserts foot." Farrell looked around the shop. "And get this place cleaned up. Let's try to look like a real company that might actually be able to build the airplanes they want."

"Too late," Magdalena said.

"You're not ready for this thing yet, Georg," Magdalena said after they had shown her the designs for what Georg called the *Jupiter*. "I've seen what you're trying and like most of it, but you don't even have a single-engine plane in the air yet. Do you have any idea how much the fiberglass costs? It's too much to invest on a first plane. Finish the *Mercury*. You have a buyer for that one. Learn from it and refine your designs."

It clearly wasn't what Georg or Farrell wanted to hear. Well, it wasn't what Magdalena wanted to say. But facts were facts. After they had built a smaller plane that would fly, she would talk to them again. Besides, she didn't have the money to pay TEA's part of the cost yet.

Vrijheer Abros Thys Van Bradt found it necessary to leave Amsterdam due to the sudden arrival of unwelcome guests, an army of Spaniards under Cardinal-Infante Don Fernando. He was forced to leave behind most of his wealth, taking only his wife and immediate servants. He stayed with a cousin for a short period, but he couldn't spend his life there; he had business that needed attending. So in a matter of a few weeks he started making his way to the Ring of Fire. From what he understood, it was an excellent location to do business. He almost went to Venice, but he remembered a letter and a small investment he already had in Grantville.

As the primary patron of the de Passe family, he had been allowed to read the letter Magdalena had written to her father and he had believed it. More than the word of the flight, he was impressed with the cost analysis of other forms of transport that she had sent along. It was nothing he didn't already know, but it had taken him years of experience to get the feel for it.

He arrived in Grantville on August fifteenth, with very little cash on hand and much of his wealth locked behind a siege hundreds of miles away. He still had connections and, surprisingly, the Amsterdam guilders were worth more than expected.

"So, girl. Tell me about airplanes and this airline you've started."

Magdalena told him. She told him about the other investors she had lined up, about the costs she had calculated and what they would need. They discussed where they would get fuel, oil, pilots, aircraft and a host of other things.

He provided introductions to other investors and helped to persuade them to invest. The strategic reserve of fuel had been used, which had driven the price of fuel through the roof, but that was a temporary problem.

"Yes, but," Fredrich Kline, one of the investors, said yet again. "There is still the problem of shipping the fuel. That doubles the price right there, more than doubles it, I'd say."

"No, it doesn't," Magdalena said, "the fuel is a mix of fifteen percent gasoline and eighty-five percent ethanol. Ethanol is really just alcohol—twice distilled spirits. So even when you do need to ship the gasoline to the airport, you only need to ship fifteen gallons for every hundred gallons of fuel."

Vrijeer Van Bradt nodded. "It will take organization to set up airports and find the most economic way to get this gasoline to them. But Magdalena makes a good point. Spirits are available almost anywhere and—since they are not for drinking—the cheapest, poorest quality can be used."

It took some wheedling, something any artist learned to do early, and Magdalena expected that. Still, it hadn't taken all that much. For every lord who controlled a pass, there were a dozen merchants and lords who resented having to pay the tolls. It was only partly economics; a big part was anger and the desire to get some of their own back. They liked the idea of their cargoes sailing over the toll stations of "Baron-I'll-take-mine-off-the-top." That was where most of her investors had come from, people who had been hit with tolls or robbed by bandits.

Yes, it was a potentially profitable venture but the way their faces lit up at the thought of flying over all the tolls and risks of land travel... Magdalena honestly thought that some of them wouldn't care if they lost money on every flight as long as

"Baron-Off-the-Top" didn't get it. Of course, each of the investors had their own unreasonable "baron" that they had to deal with, whether it was a Lutheran school or a group of merchants that collected the tolls. In fact, more than a few of the investors collected tolls of their own. That didn't change the fact that they resented it when they had to pay them.

They finished the *Mercury* and sold it to Cristoforo Racciato. They did learn from it. The *Mercury* was a bit of a mishmash of concepts and Cristoforo was quite good about telling them where he was having problems with it as well as what he liked. Cristoforo was introduced to Magdalena and took her flying. Georg wasn't sure how he felt about that. He wanted very much for TEA to buy his *Jupiter* four-engine biplane. But Cristoforo was charming and Georg wasn't. So he found himself glad that Magdalena was flying in his airplane but wishing that Cristoforo was rather less charming.

Cristoforo munched contentedly on a sandwich. He loved eating in the air. In fact, he loved doing just about anything in the air. He checked the gauges on the *Mercury*, then glanced at the horizon. A storm front was building, but he figured he could beat it to Leipzig. Or at least find a field closer to Leipzig to set down in. A little later, looking back, he saw lightning and began to look for a good place to set down.

Five minutes later, he was still looking and the storm was getting close. He pushed the stick a little forward as the world turned into gray mist. Slowly losing altitude, he tried to get below the clouds where he could see to land. He was going to be late and Gus had said that the parts were needed in a hurry. He'd offered Cristoforo enough money for a dozen tanks of gas. While Cristoforo was trying to figure out how to explain to Gus that it wasn't his fault, the engine died. He tried to restart. He was losing altitude too fast, so he pulled back just a little on the stick and tried the engine again.

Between the added weight of the rain and the added drag of flying through raindrops, the plane was handling a bit differently than Cristoforo was used to. It went into a stall and he wasn't ready for it. The delay in his response cost vital seconds and Cristoforo's lack of experience cost more. Still, he almost made it.

He had managed to pull out of the stall, induced spin and had the plane level again but he had used up all his altitude doing it. He was going to land—like it or not—and he was coming in hot, fast and heavy. The field had been plowed and was in the process of being turned into mud by the rain. The *Mercury* bounced once on the top of a furrow but then a wheel hit *in* a furrow. The wheel stopped, but the plane didn't. It nosed into the mud, bounced again and landed upside down. The cockpit roof collapsed and his skull was crushed by the impact.

Heinrich Bauer heard the noise and went out in the rain to check it out. What he found was what was left of a plane in his field. Well, partly in his field, partly in Johan's. He wasn't the only one. Several of the villagers had come out to determine what the noise had been. After checking on the pilot and confirming that he was in fact dead, they retreated back indoors to try to figure out what to do.

The next day they sent a rider to Leipzig and started cleaning up the mess. They were later told that they should have left everything just where it was till the investigators got there, but by then it was much too late. They did collect up the bits of wrecked plane and scattered cargo and put it in a barn in case it might be worth something, but they had work to do.

It wasn't that they weren't sorry about the boy. He had never done anything to them but crash in their fields, and it was clear enough that it hadn't been on purpose. But he was already dead. There wasn't anything they could do for him. And they had no reason to believe that anyone could tell anything from the crash site that they hadn't been able to tell.

"Damned shame." Georg shook his head and continued to pick through the rubble of the *Mercury*. It had been sent to them by the Racciato family in the hopes they could determine what had gone wrong.

Cristoforo had been a good kid.

"It seems to me that he waited a little long before he tried to set her down," Farrell said. "Or maybe it was just bad luck. The clouds were pretty low that day from the reports."

Georg nodded. But he was busy going over the report. "Look at this. The villagers didn't hear anything until the crash. The engine must have died. Water in the carburetor, you think?"

"Hard to tell. We'll know more after we go over the engine." Farrell pointed to a piece of the wreckage. "It could be that the weight of the rain on top of the weight of the cargo pulled some screws loose."

On the strength of Cristoforo's praise they had gotten two new orders for Mercury-style aircraft. With his death, those orders had been canceled. Georg was convinced that they would have kept them, at least kept one of them, if the designer had been an up-timer. And they still didn't have a contract with TEA.

The Contract
November 1633

Whap!

Georg jumped. Magdalena could be fairly temperamental, but she didn't usually try to beat the table to pieces as she was doing now. "Ah, Magdalena? What is the matter?"

Whap! The file folders hit the table again while Magdalena worked out her frustrations. "They won't sell. 'We're going to build them, and fly them,' they said. So TEA can't buy their plane."

Georg cast a glance at Farrell, who hid a grin of relief. "We have the plans for the *Jupiter* ready, Magdalena. Well, almost ready."

Georg and Farrell had both been worried that one of the other aviation companies would beat them to the punch. Now, with the refusal to sell to TEA, they still had a chance. Georg, for more than one reason, wanted the sale to TEA. Not only did he want his own plane in the air, he was very interested in Magdalena, who appeared to return that interest.

Magdalena glared around the room. "I have a sneaking suspicion that you're not quite as sympathetic to TEA's plight as you pretend to be." Then just a touch of grin showed through the storm. "Never mind. Show me the progress reports. Where are you with the *Jupiter*?"

Magdalena was learning to be a pilot and had seen sea planes on TV since coming to Grantville but she wasn't an aircraft designer. An airport, while not that difficult to build, was needed for a large aircraft. At least she assumed it was. She didn't want a repeat of what happened to Cristoforo. Not with a plane full of passengers.

She asked Georg to replace the wheels with pontoons or make the fuselage into a hull.

Georg promised to look into it. It was only a couple of days later that he delivered the bad news.

"It won't work. Pontoons don't sit *on* the water, they sit *in* the water. They displace as much water as the weight of the plane on top of them, all the cargo and fuel it's carrying, plus the weight of the pontoons themselves. When the plane tries to take off they push that much water out of the way. All the way from the start of the taxi to lift off, and drag more water with them."

"But there are sea planes all over the movies from up-time."

"Yes." Georg snorted. "And thousand-horsepower engines to pull them out of the water." Georg's face was a picture of desperation. "The long wings that let us take off at thirty miles per hour are just that much more weight when you put the plane on pontoons. I talked to Herr Smith about it. The flying boats of the thirties used ten percent of their fuel loads on takeoff and landing. They ran those thousand-horsepower monsters full out—they had to just to get into the air—then they cut the power way down for level flight. I'm sorry, Magdalena, but with the engines we have, it would never get into the air."

"I'll hire Maria," Magdalena said. Maria was a friend from before she had come here. She had a knack for finding things in the National Library.

"Won't do any good." Georg glared at her. He was not, she knew, that fond of Maria. "I've already studied everything they have on aircraft."

Nor did he lack for ego. Sometimes Magdalena wondered what she saw in him. A lot of the time, actually. Yes, he was the smartest person she had ever met, but sometimes he was a real jerk. Of course, sometimes he was anything but.

"TEA needs a certain amount of flexibility if we can possibly get it." She gave Georg one of her best looks. "It's worth a try."

"*Eureka,*" Maria whispered. What she really wanted to do was shout. MSP Aeronautics was her first major client. They had hired her after their investors had insisted that the plane must be capable of water landing and takeoff. But who would have thought that she would find it in a *Time* magazine article? She read the first part of the article again.

> *Aug. 25, 1967*
> *Everything seemed normal when Test Pilot David W. Howe eased the LA4 "Lake" amphibian toward Niagara Falls International Airport earlier this month. He radioed a highly abnormal report to the tower: "Bag down and inflated." Seconds later he landed—without wheels—on a cushion of air.*

The article went on to describe—with a maddening lack of technical detail—the principles and basic structure of ACLG, Air Cushion Landing Gear, conceived by Bell's T. Desmond Earl and Wilfred J. Eggington. It was simple enough in principle—put an airplane on top of a hovercraft. At least that's the way the article made it seem. Maria spent the rest of the day getting a start on learning about hovercraft to try to fill in some of the technical details that the *Time* article left out.

"This doesn't make sense," Georg complained. "If this is so good why didn't they use it up-time? This article says it happened over thirty years before the Ring of Fire."

"I have no idea." Maria smiled. "I do know that a lot of stuff they had, they didn't use. Mostly it was because they had something better, but not always. Sometimes—" She shrugged. "—they just didn't."

"I think I might know," Farrell said. "Look at the date. By sixty-seven, little private airports were all over the place. I used to love to look at the planes as we went by one on the highway. Most planes had no need for amphibious takeoff and landing. So ninety percent of the potential market is gone before they start. As for the planes that did need to be amphibious, well, pontoons were a known tech. The FAA already had all the guidelines in place. The manufacturers knew how to build them, the FAA knew how to test them, the pilot knew how to check them before flight. By the time the air cushion came along in the sixties, it was competing with established, tested products.

"It probably would have cost Bell millions to jump through all the hoops the FAA would have wanted. For what? Maybe a thousand sales a year and liability down the line if someone blew the maintenance requirements and got themselves killed." Farrell shook his head. "I'd lay five to two that the bean-counters got hold of it and said, 'Don't bother.' Once that happened, well, they never took off because if you owned a plane you could buy pontoons but you couldn't buy this ACLG stuff."

"That's not the real question," Magdalena interrupted. "The real question is 'can we do it?' "

Maria pulled another file from her case. This one consisted of a report she had made after interviewing Neil O'Connor, who had turned out to be something of a creep. Neil was the proud owner of a home-built hovercraft that he had built after the Ring of Fire. After his discharge from the Army—a discharge he and his family didn't discuss—he used it to provide rapid transport down the Saale River. Because it was a hovercraft, it didn't care how shallow the water in the Saale was. It went right over sandbars without even noticing them. He could get you from Grantville to Halle in half a day. And right now the railroads were looking like they were going to put him out of business in the next year or so.

Neil was probably going to be needing a job anytime now, and building air cushion landing gear might well be his out. That hadn't kept him from hitting on Maria from the moment they had met. He was one of those up-timer guys that figured any down-timer girl would just naturally be thrilled to be his latest conquest. However, if Maria had it right, they were going to need Neil even more than he needed them. While simple in principle, air cushions weren't all that simple in practice. They weren't just skirts but a sort of a cross between skirts and leaky balloons. The design had to push the air inward.

Neil's air cushion was a series of tubes pointing at the ground, placed in a circle around the outer edge of his craft. There were two layers of plywood above that, with a gap between them. The fan was set into the top layer of plywood. When the fan was turned on the air was spread between the two layers of plywood and escaped from there into the tubes which inflated. The tubes formed an inward curving ring around the craft and as the air was forced through them much of it escaped into the area surrounded by the ring.

The way Neil explained it, there were three levels of pressure. The lowest pressure was the air outside the hovercraft. The highest was the air in the tubes and between the two layers of plywood. The middle pressure was in the area below the plywood bottom and surrounded by the inflated tubes. It was the way the air had to flow that kept the skirt of the hovercraft from blowing up like Marilyn Monroe's skirt in *The Seven Year Itch*. Neil had leered at her when he said that part.

The tubes were made of oiled leather, with removable thicker bits at the bottom where the worst wear was. Neil generally had to change out one or more of the extensions every trip, which was one of the reasons why his service was so expensive.

Maria hesitated but she was a professional. "There is another option."

Farrell looked at her and smiled encouragement, so she continued. "Hydrofoils. Herr Bell, inventor of the telephone, was working on hydrofoil landing gear from the beginning of the twentieth century. While it's clear that he got hydrofoils to work, I have not been able to see any case of a plane actually taking off using them. I have no idea why but I think they didn't work." After some discussion—and over Georg's objections—they decided to go with the air cushion landing gear. The *Time* article was proof that it did actually work.

The problem with air cushion landing gear became apparent as soon as they started to seriously look at it in terms of something designed to leave the ground. Once the ground was taken away the air escaped almost instantly, the skirt deflated and stayed deflated till the plane landed. Not till it was *going* to land, until it was *on* the ground. They worried over that a lot. It was the *Time* article that finally came to the rescue. "Bag down and inflated," the pilot had said. The air cushion on the plane up-time wasn't a skirt, not even a fancy skirt. It was a bag.

Building the Monster
January 1634

The ACLG required several changes in the design of the aircraft. The lower wings were shortened and their width increased. They became short stubby things, barely forty feet wide. The upper wings were increased in length. The *Monster* began to look less like the *Ilya Muromets*. While all this was going on, Georg was working out the thousands of details that go into making an aircraft. Where the control runs would go, how to save weight and drag while increasing lift.

Georg really wanted to use monocoque construction and mostly he did, but not all of it could be built that way. The materials he had to work with would actually increase the weight if he tried to make a pure monocoque plane. There were places where internal supports would be needed to save weight. But he spent weeks balancing the numbers to determine just where the internal supports had to go, where he could use the shape of the plane to provide the support. The good news turned out to be the engines. Though water-cooled, they were lighter than expected, if weaker than he wanted. He refined his estimates, did drawings, changed things around, did more drawings, refined his estimates again.

He got in knock-down, drag-out fights with Magdalena over weight versus cost, which didn't help his love life any. Lost some, won others, redesigned again. After that he got in knock-down, drag-out fights with Farrell, Hans, Karl and the guys in the shop over how to build each and every component. How to make the forms, how to angle the fabric, how much of which glue and resin to use, in what mixture.

Testing and Turnover

"Bag motor on." The putt-putt of the small lawn tractor engine that powered the two fans and inflated the ACLG was loud in the cabin. Farrell looked over at Magdalena and grinned.

He put the engine in gear. "Bag inflating." Farrell looked out the window and saw the large leather bag balloon out below the plane. He waited till the plane lifted on the air cushion, and he started the left inboard engine. The plane started to spin. They hadn't realized just how little drag there would be. He managed to kill the engine but not before the plane had made a full half circle and not before he had scared the heck out of himself and Magdalena. He felt a thump as Georg apparently leapt onto the plane. The door opened. "Magdalena, are you all right?"

Neil was sitting off to the side laughing his ass off. It rapidly became apparent that after checking to make sure she was all right, Georg's next intended destination was to murder Neil. Farrell almost let him. Air cushion landing gear apparently didn't include brakes. And air, it turns out, is more slippery than any grease.

"We'll have to work out some sort of procedure to handle it," Magdalena said. "Start the engines with the props feathered."

"It will take more than that, I'm betting," Farrell countered. "Each engine will be a little different. They'll idle at different speeds. What we're looking at is having to fly the plane from the moment the engines come on."

"Kickstands." Georg snapped his fingers. "Kickstands, like on the bicycles in town. One about twenty feet out on either wing. And maybe one near the tail. They'll have to be retractable. And they won't work on the water or even on muddy ground, but even if you land on water you should be able to taxi onto solid ground."

"But what about water and muddy ground?" Farrell pointed at the four levers that were the thrust controls for the four main engines. "We need something that will let us adjust the thrust on each engine to match the thrust on all the other engines. We'll need it in the water as well as on a runway."

They tried several things before settling on what amounted to an anchor. Near the tail, a retractable tail skid provided drag. Since the drag point was well back from the engines, uneven thrust twisted the plane less. It wasn't a perfect solution but it was workable.

Another day, another test, and this time the *Monster* only slewed a bit back and forth as Farrell brought up the engines. When Magdalena retracted the tail skid, off they went. The surprising thing was how fast it picked up speed till the air drag matched the engine thrust. They started to bounce a bit when the air speed indicator read twenty-five mph, which was before they were supposed to. Farrell gave it a bit more power and at thirty-two indicated air speed, they were off the ground. And drifting left. Farrell adjusted the flaps and the engines again.

It handled like a barge. Slow and steady. You turned the wheel and it took a while for the plane to turn. Banks weren't just slow, they were physically difficult. The *Monster* had a lot of wing and a lot of flaps and no power steering. In fact, it took both of them to bank it to any great degree. They made a slow circuit around the field and landed.

After that came the water landings. Any stretch of water a hundred feet wide was a landing field. Well, two hundred feet wide. Or a body of water that didn't have trees or too steep a bank.

Fields were landing fields, too, and they didn't have to worry about rocks unless the rocks were three feet tall.

Each flight brought them closer to the final turnover of the plane to TransEuropean Airlines. Each flight used more of the gasoline-ethanol mix that they had adjusted the engines to take.

Testing completed, TEA paid the final delivery payment. It was a great deal of money. Markgraf and Smith Aviation was in the passenger plane business.

TransEuropean Airlines
The Wietze Oil Field

Since its creation last year, TEA had been an airline without any airplanes. All outgo, no income. Arrangements had been made, deals agreed to, money spent—all on the basis of Magdalena's promises and the investors' hopes. Now they had a plane. They needed fuel. Well, gasoline. They had the alcohol stations. But they had been unable to contract for much gasoline, in the middle of a war, until they could show a working aircraft.

On a sunny Thursday afternoon, the oil men at Wietze looked up into a clear blue sky and saw a plane. It wasn't the first they had seen, but it was the biggest.

Quentin Underwood came out to see. As did Duke George of Calenburg, who owned the oil fields. Quentin was impressed, Magdalena could tell, but not nearly as impressed as the duke.

"There they are." Magdalena climbed down from the plane and helped an older gentleman down after her. The older gentleman was Vrijeer Van Bradt. And Vrijeer Van Bradt was here to buy gasoline. Lots of gasoline. He wanted it shipped to various places in and out of the USE and he wanted to make arrangements for some to be carried by the Jupiter itself.

If it wasn't carrying much of anything else the *Monster* could carry close to three hundred gallons of gasoline. When mixed eighty-five gallons of methanol to fifteen gallons of gasoline, that came out to seventeen hundred gallons of aviation fuel. Enough for fourteen three-hundred-mile trips.

Van Bradt looked at the approaching men, then looked at all the people who had stopped working to watch. He rubbed his hands together. "Time to, how do they say? Oh, yes. Let's make a deal."

The first trip to Venice was just the three of them: Magdalena, the copilot, Johan, and Vrijeer Van Bradt, along with a bunch of extra gasoline. As luck would have it, they arrived three days after Cardinal Mazzare. They hadn't had any intent to upstage the new cardinal of the United States of Europe, since they hadn't known that he was going to be there. Or that he'd been made cardinal for that matter. The neat thing was that he came out and looked at the *Monster* and blessed it. Then spent a couple of hours looking at the engines. The official name of the plane was the *Jupiter*. But its real name had come about when Colonel Jesse Wood had come by for a visit, taken one look at it and said "What a monster." From then on, no matter what Georg said, it was the *Monster*.

They spent three weeks in Venice that first trip and a week in Bolzano with Claudia de Medici. Now that a real live plane was part of the deal, they could work out the details of the agreements they'd previously made. Magdalena came away convinced that Claudia was one smart cookie. The deal they had worked out had real advantages for TEA and Claudia.

Among other things, it just about guaranteed them full cargo loads because Claudia got half-price for standby cargo transport. If they didn't have a full load, they stopped at Bolzano and carried what she wanted, carried it at about the cost of the flight. In exchange for which Claudia provided docking facilities and didn't charge tariff on what they carried. At the end of the year if they hadn't carried at least the required amount of her stuff, or offered to, they paid her a fee.

Having completed their business—and Cardinal Mazzare having done the same—they gave him and a few of his aides a ride back to Grantville.

A month later

Magdalena glanced back at her passengers who were crowding the portholes on the right side of the plane and over at her copilot. Their navigation had been just a touch off this trip. It looked like they would pass about a mile to the east of Munich, closer than the five to ten miles on most trips. They were also a bit light this time. Their passengers were two Venetian merchants who had business in Grantville, and Claudia de Medici, who was taking one of her free flights.

Magdalena grinned. This was still a very new thing and it was a first flight for all of their passengers. While their ceiling was higher, they were flying at about three thousand feet to facilitate sightseeing. One of the merchants pointed out a feature of Munich that he recognized. The other apparently missed it.

Claudia de Medici spoke up. "Signorina de Passe, might we go around again to get a better look?"

Magdalena looked over at Johan and shrugged. He shrugged back. They knew relations with Duke Maximilian were in the dumps, but heck. They weren't doing anything, just flying over. She started a slow right turn that would take them around Munich and if they lost a bit of altitude in the turn, that was all to the good. It made for better sightseeing.

On the ground, a captain of the duke's guard cursed. They were rubbing it in. The duke had been livid every time they flew near Munich. Now it seemed they wanted to rub salt into the wound, and there wasn't a damned thing he could do about it. At least, at first he thought there wasn't, but as they circled they got closer and lower.

The captain started shouting, "Load with canister! All cannons! And double the charge!" That got him a questioning look from the sergeant but they did it right enough. It took a couple of minutes for the plane to make the circuit around Munich and by the time they did, it had dropped to eighteen hundred feet and was less than half a mile from the wall. By that time, His Grace had arrived and the captain had the guns aimed at a point in space he thought the plane would fly through.

☆ ☆ ☆

"What are they doing there on the wall?" Claudia de Medici asked, just as the puffs of white smoke appeared.

It wasn't a golden bb, not even a silver one. The cannons missed entirely; no single bit of shot from those guns came within a hundred yards of the plane. They were much lower and closer to the cannons than they should have been, and the *Monster* was a big, slow-moving plane. Still, it wasn't close enough or slow-moving enough or, most especially, low enough to be hit by cannon fire. They weren't, however, far enough away to avoid being frightened by it.

What it actually was, was a loose copper fuel line, combined with suddenly ramming the throttles to their stops. The fuel line on the right inboard engine came loose and sprayed the hot engine with fuel. Johan had already kicked the rudder over and started to reverse his bank by the time the fuel line came loose. The engine didn't catch fire; there was fuel and oxygen in plenty but in spite of the heat of the engine, there wasn't a spark.

As the engine died, the torque of the left side engines was no longer balanced by the right side engines. The plane started a right roll and right yaw, bringing it closer to Munich and lower. Magdalena and Johan struggled with the controls. Neither of them were what an up-timer would call qualified. They had more time in the *Monster* than anyone else, but it was still only a few hundred hours. They had very little experience flying with one engine dead and none at all with it happening suddenly out of the blue.

"The right inboard engine is out," Magdalena shouted, while Johan tried to remember what he was supposed to do. Some of it was obvious; they were rolling right, so stick left. They were also yawing right, so left rudder.

Johan noticed that all the engines were at their max. Magdalena must have done it. Then what Magdalena had shouted penetrated and he cut the fuel to the right inboard engine. While Magdalena was holding the stick left, he throttled back on the left engines.

"Take the stick, Johan. I've got to adjust the trim."

It took a few minutes and almost five hundred feet to get everything as well balanced as they could. Magdalena pulled out a pencil and started doing sums. The *Monster* could fly with three engines. At least, with its tanks half empty. But three engines delivered unbalanced thrust, so the right outboard engine was being run full out.

They couldn't do that with the left side engines or they would end up going around in circles. As it was, they had the left inboard engine at about fifty-five percent power and the left outboard at eighty-five percent. The rudder was almost all the way over and they were in a slight left-hand bank to keep from slipping right. All of which meant that they were using about twenty percent more fuel than they should be using at this point in their trip.

They weren't in any danger of crashing, not as long as the right outboard motor held. They would just run out of fuel before they got to Nurnberg. As long as the left outboard motor held. They were stressing the heck out of it. The engine wasn't designed to handle that sort of RPM on a constant basis.

They had time before the fuel shortage became critical, but they needed that engine fixed. Normally, they would put down in a field or on a lake or river to fix an engine. It had happened a couple of times before and was generally no real problem. But to do it where people pulled up cannons and shot at you just for flying over seemed unwise. This was not a place where you wanted to land even for a few minutes and they didn't know how long the repair would take.

Johan was not as familiar as Magdalena was with engines. Generally, when they stopped to fix something, he held the tools. They discussed the matter in whispers, in an attempt to avoid alarming the passengers.

"I could go out on the wing and have a look." Johan didn't look happy about it but he didn't hesitate either.

"Don't be silly, Johan. You've never met an engine that you couldn't make worse by looking at it." Magdalena looked down at the rudder pedals; the left one was almost to the floor. "Besides, you weigh one eighty, I weigh one twenty. Which of us is going to do a better job of holding the rudder hard over?" Even with the trim set all the way it was still taking muscle to keep the plane straight and level.

He nodded. "What do we tell the passengers?"

At that point it became apparent that their whispered consultation had not had the desired effect. "You might try the truth." Claudia de Medici arched an eyebrow. "Just how bad is our situation?"

"Well," Magdalena hesitated. "It would be just inconvenient if the duke wasn't a crazy man. We'd just land, fix the engine, then be on our way."

Claudia nodded. "How far away were we when they fired at us?"

"Around eighteen hundred feet up and a bit less than half a mile off. Why?" Johan asked.

Claudia shook her head. "Crazy people, indeed. To have had any chance of hitting us, even to reach us at that range, he would have had to double charge his cannon. He was willing to endanger his men in order to have a very slight chance of hitting a target that was no danger to him. Just out of spite. I agree. I don't want to land in his territory. What options does that leave us? We seem to be flying well enough on the three engines remaining."

"There are two problems facing us. One is fuel. Flying this way takes more," Magdalena said. "The other is that we are overstressing the remaining right side engine. It will last for a while, but we don't know how long. The longer we wait before fixing the inboard engine, the worse it will be."

"How long will it take to fix the damaged engine?"

"We don't know yet. The only way to find out is to go out and look. Normally we'd land and look but in this case . . ." Magdalena pointed back toward Munich. "What I am going to do is go out on the wing and look at the engine to see what's wrong with it."

One of the merchants swallowed. "Go out on the wing?"

"It's not that bad." Magdalena smiled at the man. "I've seen it done and our air speed is low." She didn't mention that the only time she had seen it done was in the movies in Grantville.

The *Monster* had one real disadvantage when it came to wing-walking. Its streamlining. Handholds were hard to come by. Magdalena wing-crawled to the right inboard engine with one hand on the leading edge of the bottom wing. To keep the engine away from the water when making water landings, it was hung from the upper wing rather than sitting on the lower. There was a support that went from the bottom wing to the streamlined box it was in. But the bottom of the engine casement was four feet from the bottom wing and she was only five feet six.

After she reached the support, Magdalena carefully tied herself to it and looked around. She was terrified and at the same time exhilarated. Standing in the open with just three and a half feet of wing below her, twenty feet from the body of the plane. With a forty-five-mile-an-hour wind blowing in her face. She wanted to shout for joy. She wanted to get back inside the plane where it was safe. Her hands were shaking and that wasn't all. She wanted to jump Georg and would have if he weren't over a hundred miles away.

Instead, she took a few minutes getting herself under control. She forced the cowling open against the wind and examined the damage. By now she wasn't sure whether she wanted to jump Georg or kill him. The cowling worked fine on the ground. But in the air, with a gale blowing in your face, and that gale trying to slam the cowling on your hand, it sucked.

She found the problem easily and it was an easy fix. She decided that she could fix the engine right there, and there would be no need to land. She reached for the line and bumped the strut holding the cowling opened against the wind. It slipped and the forty-five mile per hour wind slammed the cowling against her back and head.

There wasn't time for it to build up much momentum or she would have died at that moment. As it was she was knocked senseless, and left dangling from the strap she had used to tie herself to the support.

Inside the plane Johan, Claudia de Medici and the two merchants watched helplessly as Magdalena dangled from the strap. Johan started looking for a place to put the plane down. Duke Maximilian be damned, and all his solders with him.

They had come just twenty miles since they had left Munich. No rivers of any size were within another twenty miles but there in the distance was an open field. There was going to be an unhappy farmer.

Johan cut back on the power to the remaining engines and started the bag engine. That was what they had come to call the small motor that ran the fans for the air cushion landing gear.

The farmer watched as the plane floated down onto his field, across his carp pond and out the other side. It stopped, still sitting on the big brown bag. He saw a woman—he thought it was a woman, it was hard to tell at this distance—dangling from one wing. Then he saw the large man come out of the plane and run along the wing to the woman. He thought of going to give aid, he thought of calling the local lord, but on due consideration, he decided that he didn't want to get involved.

He knew that the duke didn't like the people from the future. Had even been told that they weren't from the future, also that they weren't people but demons. He didn't know what he believed about them except that he didn't want either the duke or the people who flew mad at him.

Johan reached the still woozy girl only seconds after touchdown. He used some ammonia as smelling salts and that seemed to mostly do the trick. Magdalena had been semiconscious as the *Monster* landed and the spray from crossing the carp pond had helped. "Let me up, damn it. Where are we?"

"What? About twenty miles north of Munich."

"Well, if we were going to land anyway, what the hell was I doing out on that wing?"

Johan paused for a minute. "Got me. I'm not crazy enough to do it, that's for sure."

That was when Claudia stepped out on the wing. "I hate to interrupt, but since I doubt that they have any airplane fuel here and since Maximilian has never impressed me with his forbearance, perhaps we should see about fixing the engine and being on our way?"

Magdalena looked at Claudia, who was standing calmly on the lower wing of the *Monster*, shaded by the upper wing, and suddenly realized what "unflappable" meant. Claudia was unflappable. Magdalena got up. It hurt, but she did it.

Looking at the engine without the wind in her face, she saw a problem. The nut had been over-tightened and the threads had slipped. "Johan, get me the five-eighths-inch wrench, would you? And the vise grips!"

She had to bang the connection a bit to make it fit again. And she gooped it up to keep the stripped threads from leaking too much. She used the vise grips to lock it in place and taped that. All in all, it took almost fifteen minutes.

Fifteen increasingly nervous minutes. Johan had climbed up on the upper wing, which put him almost twenty feet off the ground and gave him a good view of the surrounding territory. About twelve minutes into the repairs he shouted down, "Riders!"

"How far?"

"A couple of miles, perhaps a bit more."

"I'm almost finished."

"Well, finish later. We need to leave. We'll make a short hop, ten miles or so then you can finish."

"Can't. If we lose the vise grips, we'll be even worse off. Just another minute. Go ahead and start getting ready for takeoff."

"Right! Ma'am, gentlemen... if you'll kindly take your seats, and fasten your seat belts for takeoff."

Claudia might have been unflappable, but Matteo dal Pozzo, one of the merchants, certainly wasn't. In a nervous voice, he asked, "How often does something like this happen? I don't mean being shot at, but having to land in the middle of nowhere."

"Not that often," Johan said. "Certainly a lot less often than it did in the early days of flight up-time. Our engines are better and better maintained. It does happen sometimes, though."

"So our cargoes aren't really safer than if this were a mule train?"

"Of course they are. A mule train spends the whole trip subject to being found by bandits. It can be tracked by them. We can't. For your cargo to be taken by bandits, they would have to be right where we happened to land. And be there right when we landed."

Claudia laughed. "Matteo, we have regular flights from Venice to the USE. That is worth millions. Granted, it's much more expensive than a mule train or even a coach. Still, it is faster and much safer."

While Magdalena was tying down the vise grips, she felt the plane shift under her as the bag inflated and took the plane's weight from the stands. She closed the cowling, and ran.

"The wind's from the south," Johan told her as she was strapping in. "And so are the troops coming our way."

There was really very little choice. They had to get into the air as quickly as they could. They took off into the wind and into the faces of the approaching riders. There were no puffs of smoke from the riders as they passed overhead at only a couple of hundred feet. But Magdalena could see them trying to get their flintlocks ready. And one guy waving a sword at them.

Magdalena couldn't resist. She stuck her thumbs in her ears, then waggled her fingers at him. She leaned back into her seat. "Let's try to keep this a unique experience, Johan. At least on this airline."

☆ ☆ ☆

Technical Notes:

The *Ilya Muromets* is, or was, a real airplane built by Igor Sikorsky in Russia in 1913. It had flight characteristics quite similar to those described for the *Monster*. It was Russia's large bomber during World War One, but was initially designed as a luxury passenger plane with seating for sixteen passengers.

Likewise, the air cushion landing gear is real as is the *Time* article on it. There is also a small hybrid hover/flair craft that is sold as a sports vehicle. The technology is proven but does have several drawbacks. The primary one is weight, after that comes the lack of friction. It's like taking off and landing on a slip and slide. Everyone seems to assume significant issues in terms of drag while in flight, but from the reports the drag issue is minor to nonexistent. Besides, parasitic drag is more of an issue for high-speed aircraft than for the sort of low-speed aircraft envisioned here.

The composite materials are a bit more iffy. There are several possible routes that might be taken to achieve the desired ends. The fabric could be the fiberglass we used, or silk, or even linen. The bonding agent might be glues or viscose, the material that is extruded into both cellophane and rayon. Viscose was originally developed to act as a coating for fabric tablecloths. It failed in that use because it made the tablecloths stiff. It apparently didn't occur to the inventor that there were circumstances under which that stiffness might be a good thing. If it had, we might well have had the composite materials revolution a century early in OTL. We can point to no instance of viscose and fiberglass being used together and the specific properties of that composite aren't known to us. It's a WAG.

What isn't a guess is that the down-timers, being made aware of the concept of composite materials that are light and strong, will experiment with the concept using the glues and resins they have. They will, we're sure, combine those glues and resins with up-timer knowledge of chemistry to make new ones. There is, for instance, a better than even chance that they can make carbon fibers within a very few years of the Ring of Fire. Carbon fibers are produced by baking polyacrylonitrile (PAN), however, lower-quality fiber can be manufactured using pitch or rayon as the precursor instead of PAN. Further heat treating can improve the quality. Our point, however, is that while what the particular composite is may be somewhat unpredictable, that some fairly decent ones will be developed is predictable.

Semi-monocoque is not quite the same thing as monocoque. What semi-monocoque means is that there are internal supports but fewer of them are needed because some of the stresses are supported by the shape of the structure. The use of corrugations, as in the skin of the Ford Trimotor, is a semi-monocoque; the corrugations in the aluminum add structural strength. Since then, quite a bit more has been learned about ways of effectively adding strength to materials through structure. And most modern aircraft, and car bodies, are of semi-monocoque or monocoque construction.

Birdwatching

Garrett W. Vance

Prelude

The flash was so bright it pierced her closed eyelids, waking her from her nap. A thunderclap followed, Pam Miller felt the deep vibration even in bed. *Spring storm, maybe I'll get up and watch the show.* After a few minutes with no further drama offered by the April skies she went back to sleep.

Awakening hours later in post-twilight gloom she felt disoriented. It took her a moment to remember it was Sunday and she was home in bed. A "mental vacation" she had called her lengthy afternoon nap, although she didn't feel particularly rested. She reached over to switch on her bedside reading light. After several clicks with no response Pam noticed the digital alarm clock was also dead. *Great, the power's out.* She fumbled around in the bedstand's drawer, groping for the flashlight she kept there; finding it, she got out of bed with a groan to make her way to the kitchen.

She had left the kitchen door propped open; a chill breeze blew through the screen door, smelling strongly of pine. Her nose wrinkled at the unusually powerful scent. Pam peered out into the darkness of her garden, her flashlight playing across the six-foot-tall tower of the bird feeder, then the row of large rhododendron bushes that made the border between her yard and the copse of box elders and maples stretching up the hill beyond. There were a few pine trees up there, she thought, but couldn't recall them ever putting off such a noticeable smell before. She shivered; the breeze was unseasonably cold, so she hastily closed the door. After a dreary dinner of cold pizza, which the candlelight failed to lend any romance to, Pam sighed and decided to call it a night. *So, this is the exciting life of the divorcee.* At least her ex-husband had helped warm the bed sheets.

The next morning she woke up before dawn feeling refreshed, finding the unusually cool air pleasantly invigorating. *It must have blown here all the way from Canada!* The power was still out so she made a fire in the wood stove that helped save on electricity in the winter. Soon she had a nice cup of rich "Italian Roast" coffee, milk, no sugar, warming her up, and sat down to enjoy the morning show at the little table she had placed beside the picture window looking out on the garden. Breakfast time at the bird feeder! A group of black capped chickadees were already enjoying some sunflower seeds in the pre-dawn grayness. Soon they were joined by a pair of rufous sided towhees, an attractive bird with a black head and rust colored sides. She sipped her coffee, enjoying the company.

Pam had always loved birds; it was fostered in her at a young age by her grandmother in Fairmont who delighted in the nature walks they took together through the friendly West Virginia wooded hills. She had learned their names and over the years had observed their habits. She never really thought of herself as a "birdwatcher," but her interest had only increased as the years went by. A well-worn copy of Peterson's *Eastern Birds* field guide lay beside a small but useful pair of field glasses on the table before her—nothing fancy, just a hobby. The birds had become regular company once she had put up the bird feeder. It was company she welcomed a little more than she liked to admit. After the divorce she had rented this little one bedroom house on the outskirts of town, a truly tiny place but featuring a spacious garden for her to putter about in. It was good to keep busy; between the garden and the birds she didn't feel all that lonely... most of the time. Morning with the feeder had become a daily ritual.

What in blue blazes happened to the power? Pam got up to pour herself another cup of coffee from the old copper kettle on the wood stove. Returning to the table she hoped that her favorite birds would make an appearance today; it would be nice to see them. A few minutes later her hopes were rewarded. A flash of flaming scarlet winged over the rhodies to alight on the bird feeder in red splendor. The cardinal had come. The brilliantly plumaged male dipped his crest at her in what she liked to think was greeting and proceeded to help himself to the sunflower seeds. Even in the lingering shadow of night he glowed. Soon he was joined by his olive hued mate who wore just a blush of rose on her head and wings—nowhere near as striking as the male, of course, but still a very elegant and beautiful bird.

She watched them closely as they ate and was mesmerized for a time, deeply enjoying their bright movement in the stillness of the dawn. *No wonder they were chosen as our state bird—we weren't the only state that had chosen cardinals, either!* The cardinals sometimes seemed to her as if they didn't even belong in a place as normal as West Virginia; they had the look of a fanciful jungle bird from some exotic clime, such was the glamor of their crest and hue. They brought a sense of wonder to her garden and she was awfully glad to have that... it was important. Everything else seemed so drab these days.

Her eyes were taken away from her cardinals by the fluttering of a new arrival at the feeder. A bird about the same shape and size as the towhee was now testing the sunflowers with an inquisitive peck. It had a brown back, a creamy light orange border on the lower breast curved up around an eye catching bright blue bib flashing from breast to beak. It was a lovely thing and she realized with some surprise that she had no idea what it was! A new bird for her list and one definitely not common to the area! She grabbed her field guide in excitement and began flipping through its pages in search of the new, her attention torn between studying the strange bird and trying to locate it in the pages. As she searched it was joined by two more, another sporting the blue patch and then a drabber brown bird that shared the same creamy breast and belly—the female, obviously!

"This is ridiculous." Making herself go slowly and concentrating on each page she made her way through the entirety of *Eastern Birds*. There was nothing that matched the strangers at her feeder. Eyes narrowed stubbornly, she went over to the small bookshelf by the bedroom door. She found the little *Golden*

Guide to American Birds she'd had since she was a kid. On a whim she also grabbed the rarely opened *Birds of the World* her ex had given her as a birthday present. It was a typical gift from him, an attempt to show that he knew what her interests were but a failure to know them in any depth. He didn't understand her birdwatching, or for that matter *her*, at all. In Trent's mind it was a pastime for doting little old English spinsters. *Which is what you are becoming, isn't it?* Shaking the bitter thoughts from her mind she hurried back to the table. Amazingly the new birds now outnumbered the ubiquitous chickadees; nearly a dozen of them feasted in her garden!

"All right then, so they've wandered in from the western states." she mumbled to herself. The *Golden Guide* was quaint and full of pleasant childhood memories but it was an overview of all of North America and really wasn't any use. She would have to order Peterson's *Western Birds*; strays were rare but they did happen. She picked up her coffee then nearly dropped it in surprise. The cardinals had flown away and a new bird had taken their place at the feeder. It was as large as the cardinals, its body was a powdery orange combined with patches of light gray and it sported a bright blue bar on its wing. In place of a crown it had light and dark stripes running back from its sharp beak. It called out in a harsh rasping call causing the chickadees to scatter away into the safety of the rhododendron. She had never seen this bird before but she knew its voice: it was a jay, and it sure wasn't blue!

"What the hell!?" She grabbed *Birds of the World*, flipping directly to the corvids, the family that included jays and crows in its genealogy. There it was in a color plate photograph. The Eurasian Jay. Definitely a European bird and here it was helping itself to her feeder.

Maybe one stray in a day but not two, not two in a whole season! The odds are too much against, especially across the damn Atlantic! She watched in amazement as the big bird made itself right at home in her garden, devouring the sunflower seeds with messy relish in the morning sunlight . . . the morning sunlight. . . . Pam stood up at the table, the wonder of the stranger birds forgotten.

Pam ran out the kitchen door into cold air, rife with the scent of too many pine trees. She stopped near the feeder, the birds scattering into the bushes at her intrusion. Pam watched the morning sun climb higher above the hill into a somehow too blue sky, no haze, no drift of pollution. The sun was beautiful, the sun was warm. The sun was in the wrong place.

"That's not possible." A lot of people go through their lives not caring or noticing where the sun rises and sets throughout the seasons and she was not one of them. Pam paid attention to things like that, to the world around her, and this was *wrong*. She stood very still in her garden as the shrill cries of a bird that shouldn't be there rang out in a morning that shouldn't be happening.

She was afraid to move for a very long time.

One Year Later

There was no coffee left. Pam sat at her table with a cup of hot water that she'd poured some fresh cream and a single drop of artificial vanilla into—a poor substitute but it made the morning a little warmer. She watched what she now called the "bluebibs" at the bird feeder picking at a meager assortment of flax and some wild grasses she had gathered. She couldn't give them very much since she was saving the sunflower seeds for next year's garden.

Pam frowned at herself. If she had been smarter last year she would have planted the entire yard in sunflowers! She, like everyone else in Grantville, had been too busy just trying to survive. Her cranky landlord's precious grass had been turned up to put in vegetables in the rush to grow enough food for a seventeenth-century German winter. Pam had grimly enjoyed that; the mean old coot hadn't even allowed her to plant a few trees along the road; such was his obsession with that damn grass. At least she'd had sense enough to plant one row of sunflowers in the midst of the chaos; twelve dried sunflower stalks from last year tied in a bundle leaned against the wall beside her garden window, their round heads full of seeds. There had been times when she had looked at those seed pods hungrily but had not allowed herself. If she could get enough of them growing this coming year she would have enough for the birds and not feel guilty. *No one starved, I'm right to hoard the seeds.*

A few black capped chickadees that had come with them through the Ring of Fire mixed with the native German birds at the feeder. They were tough little buggers; they had made it through the first winter and just may have a chance here. *I'm glad to see them, I just wish...* She knew she should just forget about it but she had never given up hope.... *I just wish the cardinals were still here.* She knew the chances of a breeding population were entirely too slim. Pam swirled her faux coffee around in the cup. She had been through it in her mind a thousand times. *First of all I can only guess at the number that came through with us. Anywhere between the six I actually saw at one time at the feeder and maybe ten... twenty... or more? Wishful thinking!*

By autumn of that first year there were none to be seen. She had spent every morning watching for them but now only the chickadees and the native birds came to her feeder. She sometimes tried to make herself feel better by considering that there were still lots of cardinals... across the Atlantic. It never really helped much and usually just made her feel more lost. Even so, she couldn't help thinking about her lost cardinals. *Were they eaten by some new unaccustomed predator?* Various stoats and weasels from the Thuringian forests had found their way to Grantville and the formerly spoiled up-time house cats turned hungry feral predators were probably the biggest danger. *Maybe they flew away too far to find each other again.* That was also pretty likely. The chances of a successful breeding population remaining here in Thuringia were extremely low. And even if they did, she wondered if it would really be a good thing.

Whenever nature's balance was changed something inevitably paid. Transplanted species had often become pests back up-time. The English sparrows and starlings brought to America to make it feel more like home had bred in such numbers that they often threatened native species. The starlings that had begun with only one hundred introduced to New York's Central Park in the 1890s eventually spread throughout the entire North American continent. It wasn't natural. *But then again, neither are we.* There was some small hope for cardinals in Europe, if they stuck together and could breed fast enough for their population to grow. *They are out there somewhere, out there in this time's Germany. I need to believe it.*

Pam found herself becoming more and more devoted to her birdwatching. It was a hobby that didn't require technology or resources that could be better spent on Grantville's survival. She began taking long walks around Grantville, sometimes even stepping over what she personally called "The Rim" to venture into Thuringia proper. This edge was becoming less and less apparent as West Virginian and German plant species mixed and mingled along the ring's edges. Grasses and runners had already covered most of the raw exposed earth created by the mismatched elevations. Nature at least was going to absorb the presence of this misplaced chunk of the world quietly. "Not so its people!" She laughed aloud thinking of the political turmoil their American presence had created across this century's Europe. *We are a weed that isn't going to die off too easily.*

On a fair June afternoon Pam was watching a flock of native birds playing in the pine trees at the forest's edge from a vantage point atop a crumbling Grantville embankment in the process of sliding into a Thuringian meadow at the rim. The birds were about thirty yards away across the meadow. She sat comfortably in the tall grass with her legs dangling over the rim *half in, half out*, enjoying the birds' antics with her field glasses. They were true beauties, bright lemon yellow with black wings and tail. She was quite sure they were orioles and had dubbed them such in her notebook. She put down the glasses to look at the pencil sketch she had made. It was in black and white; she was hoarding the lone box of colored pencils she possessed back at the house until she became a better artist. Around the simple but fairly accurate drawing she had described the colors in detail in her notes. At the bottom of the page she had whimsically written "Lemon Oriole."

"And why shouldn't I give you a name?" she asked the distant flock. *It's not like anyone else cares.* She had made nonchalant inquiries after European bird books at the school library and every private book collection in Grantville. *Oh, just thought it might be interesting to know what's in my garden these days.* Even a guide from Great Britain would have been useful as she knew it shared many species with the mainland. There wasn't a single one. *What the hell do coal miners care about European birds anyway?* This made her frown; she felt self conscious at her hobby. She had publicly kept her interest quiet, she really didn't want the other townsfolk to know how much it had come to mean to her.

Pam dreaded the day when someone would inevitably refer to her as "The Birdwatcher"—yeah, that would stick. "Then they'll be *sure* you're a nut." She thought of her ex-husband Trent down at the mine chuckling along with them. "*Yeah, I always thought she was a birdbrain!*" Pam blew a blast of air at a loose strand of hair that had fallen across her face. She knew she wasn't being fair; Trent wasn't mean-spirited like that. He would keep quiet and just shake his head knowingly. *Come on, let's not do this today. Just watch the damn birds, Pam.* She put the field glasses back up to her eyes. There were men there. A trio of rugged-looking men had come out of the woods and now walked along the tree line. One had what must be a crossbow strapped to his back and they all wore sizable knives hung from their belts. *Down-timers.* Most of the dangerous sorts had been scared off over the last year, but you really couldn't be too sure. She was far from any road and at least a mile from anyone's house. They may be just regular folks about their business . . . *or not.* Forcing herself to move slowly despite her racing heartbeat Pam pulled her legs up to her chest then slid on her butt backwards into the tall grass, keeping low. Any eye, animal or human, was attracted to quick motion. She watched the men continue on their path, snippets of their deep voices conversing in German came to her ears. She carefully turned over to crawl away from the bank's edge on her belly, not looking back. *They didn't see me.* She crawled through the grass until she reached the path through the maples she had taken to get there. She ran as far as she could until the stitch in her side grew too painful, then continued walking quickly home.

Later that night Pam sat at her table looking glumly through her notebooks. She had calmed down with the aid of some *kirshwasser.* Here was something she definitely liked about Germany. *Yay for booze.* She looked glumly at her notes. Her drawing of the oriole looked crude and amateurish to her now.

"This birdwatching thing is going to get me killed." Pam closed the notebook and stared at the darkness beyond the garden window. *I need to be more careful.* That was a fact. These were exceptionally dangerous times she now lived in. But she couldn't just stay in her garden anymore, it would drive her crazy. She had to get out.

Maybe I need to hire a bodyguard. She smiled and lifted the shot glass in a jaunty toasting motion. "Not a bad idea."

What the hell was I thinking? The next day Pam stood before a small crowd gathered near town hall. This corner had become an unofficial mustering point for Germans looking for work; as news of Grantville's opportunities had spread the population of the corner had increased. At the moment there were twelve men and four women, ages ranging from thirteen to sixty, in various degrees of health and what she considered shabbiness.

Pam tried to look nonchalant as she attempted to covertly eyeball them. Knowing they were on display, many of the would-be workers smiled broadly and bowed as if she were a visiting princess, which only made her more uncomfortable. *Oh, just do it, Pam!* Squaring her shoulders she approached a fairly tall fellow who looked to be in his early twenties. He was thin and obviously in need of several good meals but seemed strong enough; although there wasn't much of the warrior about him.

"Uhh, do you speak English?"

"*Ja!*"

"Good! What's your name?"

The fellow hesitated slightly, a worried look on his face. "*Ja?*" he replied hopefully.

This isn't working.

"Okay, thanks." Pam moved away from the young man, trying not to see his disappointment. She felt sorry for everyone here; desperation was heavy in the air. *I need someone with at least a little English; my German is just not good enough yet. Actually, I can hardly speak it at all. That's got to change.*

A determined-looking red-cheeked woman trundled up to her. She appeared to be in her late fifties but was probably only around forty. The hardships of this century could age people so quickly. Her round face was stern but had an honest look to it.

"I can English," she announced in a low, confident tone.

Pam smiled meekly. "I'm sorry, but I need a man, a *herr*... someone strong."

"Strong man." The woman nodded at her. "I know." With a businesslike bow the woman motioned for Pam to follow her. Pam did so, not really having a better plan. The woman led her over to a brick wall where a man was leaning. A wide-brimmed hat the color of dirty white socks that may have once had some kind of shape was pulled down over his eyes.

"Gerbald." She pointed at the man. "Gerbald!" she announced loudly to get his attention.

The man slowly looked up, peering out from beneath the uneven felt brim, looking first at the German woman then at Pam. His eyes were a beautiful cobalt blue within a woven nest of deep wrinkles. He stood slowly up from the wall and gave a nod to the approaching women.

"Hello. I am Gerbald." The pitch of his voice had a pleasant depth; there was weariness there, but Pam heard confidence as well.

"Gerbald *strong*!" the woman proclaimed with a proud smile.

Gerbald chuckled. "My wife, Dore." He leaned his head toward the determined woman. "Dore is also strong." His eyes creased further with amusement, the remarkable blue shining out. Dore stood taller and moved proudly to his side.

I like them. Pam smiled back at the pair. "I'm Pam. It's good to meet you."

Gerbald was around five foot eight inches tall with wide shoulders and a solid-looking build. He wore a battered sage green long wool coat crossed by a wide brown leather belt, mustard breeches and knee high brown leather boots; an ensemble which made Pam think *Robin Hood!* What looked to be a saber hung at his side; there was little doubt that he had been a military man of some sort. Pam thought he might be around fifty-five but knew he was likely older. In any case, he seemed to be hale and in good health and the sort of man that other men don't trifle with lightly. Her smile broadened.

"Were you a soldier?"

"Yes, a long time. Not now. Good soldier, not bad man." He looked a bit worried that his former profession might not go over well with this female potential employer.

"Soldier my job before, but I am tired. I don't like fight anymore, too sad. Peace." He looked at Pam hoping she would understand him.

Pam's instincts seemed sure that he was sincere and very likely legitimate in his claims. There were a lot of men like this in these times, men who would have been farmers or carpenters if not swept up by the omnipresence of war. Gerbald cocked his head at her, one eyebrow lifting the brim of his monstrously ridiculous hat slightly upward.

"You . . . you need *soldier*?"

"Yes. Well, not exactly. I need a guard. Someone to go with me outside of Grantville, into the forests and fields. I am looking for . . . *things*, in the countryside. You would guard me. Stop bad men from hurting me."

Gerbald nodded. "Yes, guard. I can do."

"Great!" She looked at the couple and realized there were a lot more things to discuss—how much would she pay Gerbald? Where did the two of them live? *I'll figure it out. I've done well today.* Pam was exceptionally pleased at succeeding in her mission; she was sure she had done better than she could have hoped. "Well, Gerbald, Dore, let me buy you a beer and we'll talk some more about the job." And so they headed for the Thuringen Gardens, a trio of contentment.

Over several rounds of the Gardens' fine beer, Pam learned a little more about Gerbald and Dore. He, like so many men of the age and region, had been a soldier for hire, and Dore his camp follower mate. He had left his last employer because his captain had ordered him to do something that Gerbald did *not* want to do, something he wouldn't go into any detail about. The name Magdeburg came to mind, but Pam did not press the issue. She knew he was being purposefully vague regarding many details of his soldiering career; it was perhaps better she didn't know. Dore sat stone-faced and silent during this part of the conversation. She was plainly deeply devoted to the man. Pam didn't hold their secrets against them; how could someone like her really understand the horrors that these people had faced in this war-crazed world they were born to? Her gut told her she could trust them and so she would.

Pam had asked around at the Research Institute about the going rate for German laborers in Grantville. She had told her co-workers that she wanted some odd jobs done around her house and yard; she was still intent on keeping her birdwatching habit very quiet. *Why do I do that? Just because Trent didn't get me doesn't mean they won't.* She pushed the thought out of her head, there would be time to indulge in "Pam analyzes Pam" later. Pam made a tidy wage in the current economy, her up-time lab work experience and scientific knowledge had significantly increased in value here under these extreme circumstances. She was useful and in high demand. *Now that's a new concept.*

She offered Gerbald a little more than the current going rate, much to Dore's obvious delight. She only needed him part time and wanted to keep him around—the hiring process was not a performance she wanted to repeat anytime soon! The deal was made and settled with a handshake. It turned out that the pair had lodging in a group shelter not too far from her place, which would be convenient. This news came as a relief to Pam. Her house was so cramped even for one that she had not been asked to take in refugees the last winter and besides, she very much valued her privacy. Gerbald and Dore walked her home so they could see where she lived and Pam went to bed, excited about the next day's birdwatching.

Pam got to the institute early the next morning. She worked like a whirlwind. She felt infused with boundless energy; now she was going to be able to go out past the rim and be as sure as anyone could be of her safety. There was no doubt that Gerbald could handle anything short of an army of bandits. She didn't take a lunch break and left around one, claiming she needed to go supervise the workers at her place. The days were getting long now and they would have plenty of time to hike out to her intended region of exploration and back before dusk. Pam's house was on the outskirts of Grantville at the northwest edge of town. *The new northwest, that is.* She and Gerbald would walk some gravel back roads and paths that didn't see much traffic these days.

When she arrived home, flushed from excitement and the extra speed she had put into her gait, she found Gerbald and Dore standing at attention on the road beside her front yard's edge.

"Hello, come on, come in!" She bustled up the incline of the long walk to her front door with them in tow. She had a big yard and a small house, just the way she liked it. She had kept her smaller back garden a private paradise of flowers and shrubs for her birds while the spacious front yard was now filled with row after row of rapidly growing sunflowers *(Her up-time landlord would* hate *that!)* watched over by an empty aluminum laundry tree. Except for a few rows of useful vegetables it had all gone to sunflowers this year. Her former landlord had mercifully been left up-time in Fairmont—the place was going to really be *hers* now and she could do with it as she pleased. She wondered sometimes if the bossy old coot had ever tried to drive out to Grantville on a mission to crab at her about keeping the lawn mowed precisely to his picky specifications only to find a chunk of this time's Thuringia in place of his property—that *would* be a surprise! *Now available in Marion County: Real German farm, quaint outbuildings, wooded setting.* Pam figured they would never know.

"Sorry about the mess. I live alone and I've just been too busy to clean much lately." Dore and Gerbald nodded politely, standing just inside the door as Pam bustled about the small living room's clutter, gathering her notebook and field glasses. She pushed a sweater for the cool evening walk home into her rucksack, threw it over her shoulder and headed for the door. Dore looked a polite question at her.

"Oh yeah, Dore... well, you can wait here for us if you like, just make yourself at home." She motioned to the overstuffed loveseat that was still partially visible under a week's worth of laundry in waiting. "Have a seat and take it easy!" Dore smiled sweetly, nodding her understanding. "See you later!" With an indelible grin etched on her face, Pam marched down the walk, Gerbald in practiced step behind.

They walked northwest passing Highpoint on their right. Pam was eager to visit a new lake she had heard had formed where the watercourse of a lazy Thuringian stream had found a big West Virginian hill in its path. She thought there might be some marsh birds there and it sounded like some interesting "rim" terrain that she hadn't seen yet. Even after a year there was something about that border between her original everyday world and this strange *(new? old?)* century they now inhabited that drew her to it. Seeing it, *being* at the edge helped make it real to her, something that watching cars be replaced by horses in the streets of Grantville and the loss of such everyday items as toothpaste and deodorants still failed to do.

The retired soldier wasn't a small talker, which suited Pam perfectly. They reached their destination at the top of a rolling hill ending abruptly in a razor straight plummet. Pam stayed well back from the edge which was now crumbling and unsafe—it would be a long fall. Below them a lake had formed, the top halves of dying German pine trees stood forlornly in murky water, the upturned roots of a West Virginia red maple that had lost its purchase were now a bleached tangle at the steep shore. She decided to make their way down the left side of the hill to a narrow flat spot along the rim where the water had flowed into a West Virginia hollow creating a narrow shady marsh.

"Gerbald, I'm going to be looking for birds. I'd like you to just stay quiet and keep your eyes open for any people." Gerbald nodded his understanding and backed off to stand under a nearby sycamore, calmly scanning the jumbled landscape. Pam pulled her field glasses out to begin looking for activity. A lone duck bobbed along at the far end of the new lake but it was too distant to make out in detail. A Eurasian jay gave a shrill cry from farther down the shore but remained out of view.

Around thirty minutes went by. Pam decided that there wasn't really much to see after all, so she wandered over to where Gerbald stood under the sycamore to collect him for the walk home. She noticed some of the "bluebibs" that so often visited her garden flitting about in the tree's higher branches. Even though these had become a regular backyard visitor she put the field glasses to her eye out of habit to watch their antics for a few moments while Gerbald quietly observed her. Shortly she joined him under the tree.

"Well, not much to see here. Let's start walking back, I guess." Gerbald, who instinctively understood her general preference for quiet, took this as a cue that it would be all right for him to speak.

"You are . . . seeing birds?"

"Yes, I am. I watch them." Gerbald nodded but made no further comment. Pam decided that she had to talk about her . . . *obsession?*—with someone and her new bodyguard was the only logical choice. If he were going to be following her around daily, he might as well understand what she was doing.

"I like birds. A lot. They are beautiful. I like to watch what they do, see where they live." Gerbald nodded understanding politely.

"These up here—" she pointed into the branches above them. "I call them 'bluebibs.' They are from here, Germany."

"Blaukehlchen."

"Pardon?"

"Blaukehlchen." He motioned upwards with his misshapen hat's brim. "Bird is named." Pam's eyes went wide.

"You know the name of that bird? In German?" Gerbald shrugged and nodded.

"Do you know the names of a lot of birds?" She felt an excitement growing.

"Some. They pretty. My father . . . he like bird. He tell name, I listen."

"Blau-kehl-chen." Pam carefully tried to pronounce the German name. "Blue . . . Chin?" She asked, pointing to her own chin. Gerbald smiled in what she took as assent.

"You know German a little."

"Not very much. That was just a guess! Well, I wasn't far off when I called them 'bluebibs' it seems." She grinned. Pam quickly dragged her notebook and pencil out of the rucksack. Beneath her drawing of the little blue-throated bird she now wrote *"blaukehlchen"* followed by "blue chin" in English. "So, now you have a name after all."

Somehow knowing the local name for the first German bird she had met on that shocking morning made Pam feel better. There was order here; wild things had been given names long before *her* coming and it made this century somehow less alien. *It wasn't like we ended up on Mars.* That rather chilling thought made the oddly patched together landscape before them look positively homey. *Mars would have been a short stay.* Pam pushed thoughts of a Grantville frozen and lifeless in the shadow of Olympus Mons firmly out of her head. She looked back at her notebook—an idea was forming.

Pam flipped to the "lemon oriole" she had drawn the other day.

"Gerbald, this bird is yellow and black." Gerbald looked at the drawing carefully.

"Pirol."

"Pi-rol?"

"Yes, I think. Yellow bird and here and here . . ." He pointed at the wings and tail. ". . . is black."

"Yes! I wonder if there is a direct translation for *pirol* in English. Well, it's a prettier sounding name than 'lemon oriole' anyway! . . . *Pirol.*" Pam realized that she was about to begin studying German in earnest.

"Gerbald, from now on when we see a bird, please tell me if you know its name in your language." An idea was forming in Pam's mind, she put it on her mental back burner to simmer—in time, in time.

"Yes, I do for you," he said with a note of enthusiasm. It was going to be a pleasant job helping this nice American lady watch birds.

On their way back Pam suddenly came to a complete halt. Gerbald had already learned to anticipate this and also stopped, quietly—there must be a bird in their vicinity.

"Over there Gerbald—look!" She slowly raised her hands to point at a nearby thicket. Gerbald, whose former profession had sharply honed his powers of observation in the field, saw a bird with a black head and rust colored sides hopping about the twiggy growth.

"I am sorry. I not know that one." He apologized in a hoarse whisper. Pam's face shone with joy.

"I *know*!" she was obviously struggling not to jump up and down. "Gerbald, that is an *American* bird! I didn't think there were anything but chickadees left! It's a *towhee*, from here, from Grantville! It's an up-timer bird!" Pam allowed herself the thought: *Maybe the cardinals made it through the year, too.* They watched the towhee for a very long time. If it hadn't eventually flown away into the darkening shadows beneath the trees it seemed likely they would have stood there until dark.

Back at the house Pam practically skipped up the walk in the gathering dusk, past the aluminum clothes tree festooned with her bed sheets and weeks' worth of laundry. It took a moment for the change in her yard's scenery to register—then she saw several of her bras and felt her cheeks redden.

"Let's get inside." She hastened Gerbald through the door into her immaculately clean living room. Pam's eyes widened. She had left behind a disaster area of clutter.

"Dore?" she called out questioningly.

"*Ja*, I am here!" Her voice came from the kitchen.

Pam entered followed by Gerbald who stood in the doorway so as not to crowd them in the narrow space. Dore was happily humming as she fussed over a big pot of what Pam had come to know as *spetzel* boiling away on the wood stove.

"Dinner!" she announced proudly.

"Dore! You didn't have to do that! I didn't expect you to work, I told you to just take it easy!" Dore, whose English was not as good as Gerbald's, looked to her husband with a worried question. He spoke to her in German briefly. Dore looked embarrassed.

"You . . . you not like I do?" Her tone was very meek.

Pam now felt bad for embarrassing the woman. "No, I don't mean that. You did great! Really, really good, I like it and God knows I have let the place go. I just didn't expect it." Pam pulled her pocketbook out of her rucksack. "Here, let me pay you for what you did today." She begin to pull some money out but Dore looked alarmed.

"*Nein!* No, good lady, I not do for money. I do—" Her English faltered and she began to speak quickly to Gerbald who nodded. He turned to Pam with a slight smile.

"Dore say she like to do for you. Money, she no need. You give me good job, Dore very happy! She do—" He swept his arm around to indicate the various housekeeping Dore had performed. "She do to say thank you." Dore watched Pam with a concerned look, afraid to have displeased her husband's new employer.

Pam rushed over to her and took both her hands in hers. "Thank *you*, Dore. You are very kind. I am happy to know you and Gerbald." Her face felt hot and flushed. Pam was not given to displays of affection and knew this about herself. Her ex-husband knew it all too well and she had admitted that she should have been more affectionate with her son Walt. She loved Walt very much, and had loved Trent once, too, but she just wasn't good with people.

Pam realized that she had been alone for a very long time now and there was something about the simple goodness of these two people she had barely met which was filling her with unexpected emotion. Pam held Dore's hands tightly and smiled at her, her lips trembling and eyes moist. The older German woman could see the pain there, and the hope; understanding without words. Dore squeezed firmly back and gave Pam a long look with her sensible hazel eyes, a look that said *"You are going to be all right."*

"You good lady. Good luck we meet you." Dore released her hands from Pam's grip with a last heartfelt squeeze, then led her to the door, shooing Gerbald outward. "You go, sit. We eat!"

Another Year Later

Pam, Gerbald and Dore established a routine that suited them all nicely. Five days a week, Pam and Gerbald went on birdwatching expeditions. On the fourth day, she would give Gerbald money for Dore to go shopping with for the next evening's dinner. On the fifth day, Dore came to the house with Gerbald and the groceries, did the laundry and general housecleaning and then made the wonderful dinner they would all share.

With the help of her new friends, Pam's German studies made rapid progress. Gerbald could read and helped her with her lessons on days when the weather was just too nasty to go traipsing about the countryside. The focus of her studies was of course the translation of German bird names into English, but she was learning to speak as well. She soon learned she had been mistaken in her assumption that the "*kehlchen*" in *blaukehlchen* meant "chin" in English. Even though it sounded like "chin" to her untrained ears, it meant really "throat." This turned out to be a common pitfall when learning a language that is a close cousin to one's own; the occasional appearance of "false friends," words that sound like they should mean the same things in both languages but really don't. The "bluechins," formerly "bluebibs" were now properly "bluethroats."

On the weekends Pam devoted herself to painting birds. She had perused a few artist's how-to books at the library, tried some of their suggestions and then decided that the best way for her to learn was to just sit down and *do* it. She had liked to doodle as a girl and recalled that she had always received A's in art, but never really believed she had any talent. It was possible she actually didn't have any talent, but she did have determination. Her paintings were not intended to be hung in a gallery after all. They were scientific works; their sole purpose was to catalog accurately the birds of Thuringia she encountered. She started by copying the illustrations in her own small collection of field guides. After she felt she had learned some of their basic techniques, she tried applying them to something closer to a live model, starting with a photo of a mallard duck. Her first attempt was definitely more "Daffy" than "Audubon" but she kept at it.

After this Pam began to paint in the field. She would quickly pencil sketch in the birds she saw, then try to capture their colors with her brushes. If they held still long enough, she would focus in with more detail. Gerbald offered quiet encouragement with approving nods as he kept his eyes open for intruders. Gerbald's steady and watchful presence made Pam feel safe, which allowed her to better concentrate on her work.

They had taken to ranging several miles past the rim on some days, seeking nesting grounds amongst the fields and forests of Thuringia. Although the situation had become fairly quiet in the region, there were still plenty of opportunities for brigands to sneak about. She and Gerbald had made it an unspoken rule to avoid strangers by staying hidden when they drew near. She had always considered herself fairly adept at moving surreptitiously in the field, but Gerbald proved to be a master of the art and a good teacher. They often made their way past other people under cover, off the road or path without those they observed ever having a clue they were in the vicinity. This pleased Pam who still preferred not to be seen wandering the area in the company of *a man* by fellow Grantville residents.

One Sunday afternoon in April, Pam walked into town to do a little shopping. Another year was beginning here in her new world and she felt amazingly optimistic about it. She realized that in many ways she liked her current life better than the one she had lived before the Ring of Fire. Why not? She hadn't felt this happy and focused in years. With a tinge of regret she wondered what her ex-husband Trent would think of her now. He had remarried of course. *Ah well, I'm glad he's found what he was looking for. Maybe I have, too.* Near the Freedom Arches, she saw a peddler's wagon parked at the curb. A cheerful-looking chubby fellow with a beard sat in a chair on the sidewalk. He reminded Pam of Burl Ives. Pam wandered over to the wagon.

"Hello good lady, welcome, welcome! I am a seller of beautiful things, please, maybe you like." He greeted her in accented but clear English. Pam was always impressed by the knack for languages Europeans possessed. She felt a surge of pride at her growing German abilities; there were a lot of up-timers who simply weren't bothering to learn the language that surrounded them.

Pam smiled at the fellow, stepping closer to look over the multitude of gewgaws perched on shelves in the wagon's open side or hung by hooks from the propped up panel that formed a protective awning. Tin whistles, whimsically carved and painted wooden toys, mounted deer antlers, etchings of famous buildings of Europe. She wasn't much of a collector of such fancies, but she was impressed by the quality of workmanship. It was apparent that the peddler had a fairly wide range, certainly not all of his goods were locally made. She looked at the jovial peddler as an idea came to her.

"Sir, you travel a lot, don't you?" The peddler stood politely when she addressed him.

"Why yes, of course! Well, as much as is safe in these troubled times, but my business takes me all about the Germanies and even down to northern Italy on occasion. I am always seeking new fineries for my selection. Do you like what you see?"

"Yes, very nice." Pam hesitated. *Oh why the hell not?* "I would like to ask you something. In your travels have you ever seen a bright red bird? It would be a new creature; it came to Germany with us."

"A red bird?" The peddler was somewhat surprised at such a question. "Why, I see many birds and animals in my travels, out on the open road as I am."

"This one I think you would notice. It's a beautiful bright red and has a black mask around its bill. On the top of its head is a pointy crest, like a hat." Pam's description was accompanied by a sort of pantomime of the cardinal's features.

The peddler nodded, a look of comprehension came to his eyes. "A red bird, face is black! Yes, yes, I have seen such a bird! I was down in Bavaria . . . here, I show you!" Pam's eyes went wide. The peddler ducked his head under the wood awning and proceeded to shift some of the items on his top shelf around. "Yes, here it is!" He pointed. Against her will, Pam followed the course of his finger to the shadowy upper shelves.

It was a bird. A red bird. A cardinal.

Stuffed.

Pam stood frozen in horror. The cardinal was posed with its wings outspread as if about to leap into flight from the gnarled branch it was mounted to. Glass orbs replaced living eyes, the beak open as if frozen in mid-song.

"Pretty nice, yes? A trapper sold it to me. He snared it in the woods last month. What a pretty bird, a nice display for your home!"

Pam started to cry.

Hours later, Pam sat at her window side table, a bottle of what was passing for whiskey these days half-empty before her. She poured herself another shot. Her bird guides, notebooks and precious painting supplies lay scattered about the floor behind her.

"God damn *people*!" The anger welled up again and she felt her face grow hot. She was on an emotional boat ride through fiercely stormy seas, rising on crests of towering wrath, sliding down into depressions of black despair. She hadn't eaten and the whiskey was only making her head hurt, the fiery liquid in her belly failing to warm the icy sense of helpless loss.

At five o'clock Gerbald arrived to begin the evening's work. Drunkenly Pam ordered him to go home. "No birds tonight," she said, her voice thick with pain and anger. Her head slumped onto the table with an audible thump, mind reeling with images of dead cardinals mounted in dead trees, forgetting Gerbald was even there.

The unflappable German's face creased up in worry, an emotion rarely seen there.

"I get Dore," he told her, exiting quickly.

Dore came through the door huffing and puffing. She was a bit on the heavy side and had run as fast as she could all the way to Pam's little house. Gerbald followed, barely having broken a sweat but face gray with concern for Pam. They found her still at the table, mumbling incoherently. One on either side, Gerbald and Dore gently lifted her, moving her over to the overstuffed loveseat. Pam began to weep softly, Dore held her close like a child, murmuring comforting words as she stroked Pam's hair. After carefully picking up the items Pam had cast on the floor in her despair, Gerbald paced about the room, his strong arms crossed in helplessness.

After a time, Pam became coherent enough to haltingly detail what had happened. Her friends listened closely with heartfelt sympathy. Dore made some thin chicken broth for her, gently feeding it to her as one would a small child. Pam had calmed down now and become sleepy, Dore helped her into bed, giving her a fond kiss on the forehead before turning out the light. Pam softly thanked her, the forgetfulness of sleep coming soon after, a welcome darkness.

Pam safe in bed and sleeping off her day's tragedy, Dore sat down on the loveseat. Gerbald sat in Pam's usual chair at the window side table, his brow furrowed in deep thought. Dore steepled her fingers contemplatively in her lap. They shared a long look of painful concern for Pam, whom they had begun to think of as a well-loved younger sister more than an employer. Pam didn't know how protected she truly was by these two strong-hearted Germans.

At last Dore spoke softly so as not to wake Pam in the bedroom behind her. "This bird. Show me."

Gerbald nodded. Opening *Eastern Birds*, he found the cardinal, Pam had shown it to him and he well knew it was her favorite. He walked the book over to Dore. "This one, the red one. It is special to her."

Dore studied the small painting carefully. "I can see that! It is an American bird from *up-time,* yes?" She used the English term for the concept.

"Yes. Some few of them came here with Grantville. She searches, but we haven't found one yet. Now she finds a dead one, it is too sad for her."

Dore nodded slowly. "Tomorrow we start," she announced confidently as she began the process of extricating her bulky form from the lumpy old loveseat. Gerbald brightened, giving her a hand up. She patted his arm affectionately.

"Yes. We will." He grinned.

"It is a red bird with a pointy hat," Dore told the women she worked with at the laundry.

"It has a black mask around its beak," Gerbald told the men he did construction work with during the day.

"If you see one, you must remember to tell me," Dore told the vegetable farmers who had brought their produce to market from the outlying farms.

"If you see one, do not kill it!" Gerbald told his companions at the tavern over a lunchtime pint of *dunkel* beer.

"It is an *American* bird," Dore told the mail riders at the post office.

"Tell your friends. Tell your neighbors."

"Tell everyone! The red bird must be found!"

Pam recovered from her upset more quickly than she might have expected. It was dawning on her that she had changed since the Ring of Fire. Her depressions had grown shorter and she hadn't the time for the long sessions of self pity she had once indulged in. The stuffed cardinal had been awful, a terrible waste but it was also evidence that at least one of her cherished birds had survived two German winters! There could be more. In retrospect, the incident lifted her hopes more than dashed them.

Her list of American birds had grown by a large number this spring; more and more species were emerging from the woodwork: tufted titmice, redhead ducks, turkey vultures, killdeer, ruby-throated hummingbirds, scarlet tanagers—it was incredible! She had even witnessed a confrontation at her feeder between a gray and orange Eurasian jay and an eastern blue jay! The

American blue jay had triumphed, boasting loudly in harsh jay tones as the native jay presumably fled back to the safety of the Thuringenwald—but for how long? It had some new competition!

It was strange how in that first year the American species had vanished from sight. Pam supposed it wasn't really unusual for animals to go to ground for extended periods when threatened. Perhaps the Ring of Fire had affected birds more powerfully and in different ways than it did mammals, which had continued their daily existence seemingly physically unaffected by the event. Birds had different senses, particularly migratory birds with their feel for Earth's magnetic fields. Who could know what havoc something like a journey through time and space would play on avians? Pam continued her project with a very welcome new wrinkle: Translating the names of the transplanted American birds into German!

Gerbald came up the road at a flat out run, his sage green coat tails flapping behind him. Pam, sitting on a lawn chair by the front door enjoying a pleasingly balmy May afternoon, watched in amazement as he leapt from the road over the short decorative fence at the corner of the yard to cut across the rows of sunflowers instead of ambling up the walk as he always did. Pam couldn't help but chuckle seeing his goofy misshapen hat bouncing just above the cheery yellow discs of their blossoms as he zigged and zagged his way up the yard. She stood up quickly, now worried that something bad might be happening to provoke steady Gerbald into such flight!

"Gerbald! What's going on!"

"Pam!" He paused for breath. He must have run a long way, as Gerbald rarely showed any strain when exercising. "Get your field glasses. We must hurry!" Pam only hesitated a moment before rushing into the living room after her gear. Gerbald waited for her by the road, obviously in a great state of excitement. Equipped, Pam ran down the walk to him.

"Can you run?"

"Yes, let's go!" Gerbald took off at a steady trot, Pam running behind. They headed down the road into town. As they neared the end of that odd mile, it occurred to Pam that she was in pretty good shape these days. *My God, this would have killed me two years ago!* A brief thrill of pride shot through her but was quickly brought down by a sudden dark thought—*People are going to* see *us!* Gerbald looked back to check on her progress. Pam raised her hand in a brief wave, *I'm all right, keep going.* Whatever it was it must be important. Gerbald well knew her feelings on the matter of exposing their activities. *This better be good, mein Herr!*

Rounding a corner onto the main street, Gerbald led her to the city park where a small group of down-timer women were talking in hushed tones.

"Dore!" Pam exclaimed as one broke from the group to approach her and Gerbald as they came to a halt at the grasses' edge.

"Pam! Oh, it is good. Look, look!" Dore's chubby finger, flushed red from the hot water of the laundry, pointed up into a tulip tree near the town's bandstand. Pam's eyes followed, a look of stunned disbelief now on her face.

"It is the one, *ja?* The red bird? The *American* bird?" Dore's voice was filled with hope that she was right. Dore reached for her, beckoning her to come closer.

Pam slowly advanced to take Dore's offered hand, her eyes unblinking as she continued to stare into the tulip tree's branches. It was there. It was really there. A red bird. An American bird.

The male cardinal tipped its head at her as if in greeting, just as it used to do at her feeder every morning. His mate, rosy blush on peach in the spring sun, hopped down a branch to join him. A third cardinal appeared above them. He looked to be a yearling. The young bird threw back his scarlet crested head. He opened his beak with a thrilling song, the loveliest music Pam had ever heard, a symphony in the park, a serenade, the bright music of her heart's desire. Tears came, soft warm streams of relief and hopes satisfied. She felt Gerbald's comforting presence at her side as Dore squeezed her hand—the woman was grinning like a kid on Christmas morning.

"How? How did you know?" Pam asked. Dore chuckled.

"Know? We know much! Pretty smart!" Dore tapped her temple with her free hand. She started to laugh happily aloud, but quickly realized the need for quiet and clapped the hand over her mouth so as not to startle the nearby cardinals, hazel eyes sparkling with delight.

Gerbald spoke softly in his deep tones. "I show her picture. We tell everybody we meet, look for that red bird."

"*Der Amerikanische rotvogel*!" Dore interrupted proudly. "My friends, washerwomen same like me, say today they see here in park. I send Gerbald!" If Dore grinned any wider Pam swore her head would split in two.

"I must thank them. And you." Pam hugged first Dore and then Gerbald who froze stock still in discomfiture. Shyly, he gave Pam's back a gentle pat with his large hand.

"You are happy now, Pam. We are happy, too," he told her. To his relief, Pam released him in order to take another long look at her wonderful cardinals. A number of Grantville children and their German schoolmates had approached, drawn closer by the scarlet birds in the tree.

"Hi, Ms. Miller!" one of the Grantville youths greeted her. "Those are cardinal birds up there, aren't they? Like back in America times?"

Pam looked at the earnest young face, a face full of curiosity and wonder. *I have another job ahead of me now.* Her decision was made so quickly and so decisively she didn't have time to be surprised by it. *Who are you and what have you done with Pam Miller!?*

"They sure are, honey! They came through with us. But see that smaller one up there? It was born here, in Thuringia. They live here now, same as we do. They even have a name in German: *Amerikanische Rotvogel!*" *The name* cardinal *might be a touch problematic given the religious tensions of these times. Back up-time I heard some folks calling it "redbird," I recall. "American Redbird," yes. That has a nice ring. Why not a new name in a new place?*

The girl smiled at Pam. "I saw a whole bunch of them over by my uncle's orchard. Ten or so! They sure are pretty." Pam's heart left her body to fly around the sun a couple times. *Joy, oh joy, oh joy!*

"Hey, who is your schoolteacher?"

"Mrs. Clinter."

"Okay. I'm going to come see her pretty soon. Do you think your class would like to learn more about birds?"

"Yeah, I sure would!" The other children who had gathered around all chimed in their agreement.

"That's good, kids. That's really good."

A week later Pam sat at her window in the dawn hour. She had grown to appreciate the sun's new path; it had given her garden more light in the morning. The cardinals—*rotvogels!*—had rediscovered their source for sunflower seeds and now joined the tufted titmice, *blaukehlchen* and chickadees for breakfast nearly daily. She had counted as many as twelve of her treasured birds at once so far. Reports were coming in from Dore and Gerbald's word-of-mouth network that they had been seen on the road to Magdeburg! The species had adapted and was now spreading.

Pam leaned back contentedly in her chair. She had prepared her notebooks and paintings for the show and tell sessions she was going to do at the school today—Mrs. Mason had been so taken with the idea that Pam had been asked to visit every class! Birdwatching field trips were being planned as well as a special summer nature program series that Pam would help implement. Pam learned that many of the town's educators shared her hopes to avoid some of the ecological misdeeds of the up-time past by engendering a love and knowledge of nature in the school kids. What a good place to start! She looked down at the two documents on her table.

The first was titled "Birds of the USE. A Field Guide to Native and Transplanted Species." She had made her lists and written up a plan for organization by bird type. What she was going to do about the scientific names of the European species she still had no idea—she would figure out something. "Is Linnaeus around these days?" The question was only half in jest—she had better find out!

The second was a proposal she was drafting. It could certainly use a lot of polish but she felt she had made a good start.

> *Citizens of the United States of Europe and their official representatives,*
>
> *The following is a formal proposal submitted by myself, Pam Miller of Grantville, based on my personal observations and field studies. The proposal contains two separate yet related issues.*
>
> *In Brief:*
>
> 1. *All transplanted American bird species (A list of sightings will be provided) be given protected status in the USE until we can determine what, if any, positive or negative effects they will have on the local ecology. I believe these animals have as much right to a new life here as we do and that we should allow them the chance to adapt as we have.*

2. *I would like to move that the cardinal, also known as the American red-bird and* Amerikanischer rotvogel, *be considered for status as the national bird of the USE. We are a new nation. We need a new symbol. I give you a bird that was once hailed as the state bird of West Virginia, a bird that is quickly gaining recognition amongst the down-timer population who admire its unusual beauty.*

A bird from the Ring of Fire. A bird that has survived the journey. A bird that is thriving here and spreading its range.

A bird like us.

Suite for Four Hands

David Carrico

Grantville
Late July, 1633

As he turned from closing the door of the Bledsoe and Riebeck workshop, Franz Sylwester found several pairs of eyes focused on him. "Well?" his friend Friedrich Braun asked expectantly. "What did the nurse say?"

Franz struggled to keep his expression solemn as he took his jacket off. He heaved a sigh and turned to hang it on a peg by the door. As he faced the others again, Marla moved closer and placed a hand on his arm.

"Franz," she started softly, obviously ready to comfort. He couldn't hold it in any longer, and broke out in a smile, then laughed.

"Frau Musgrove declares that my hand is good, is healed." He held his left hand up and flexed his fingers. The thumb, index and middle fingers moved easily. The ring and little fingers were still frozen in the same curved shape they had healed in after the knuckles were crushed in Heydrich's assault, but even those fingertips flexed a little. "So, I now have enough of a hand to hold things."

"Franz!" Marla squealed. She grabbed him and swung him around. "That's great news!" Friedrich, Anna and Thomas crowded around to slap him on his back in congratulations.

Ingram Bledsoe came in from a door at the back of the workshop.

"What's the occasion?" Marla bounced over to him and gave him a swift hug, leaving him looking a little surprised but smiling nonetheless.

The others stepped back from Franz, who lifted up his hand again and flexed the fingers, smiling. "Nurse Musgrove says I am not to come back, that I am healed."

"Congratulations!" Ingram stepped forward to shake hands. "That's great news!"

Franz held up his good hand for quiet, reached into his pocket and dug out a three-inch rubber ball. "Marla," tossing the ball to her, "please give this instrument of torture back to your niece. Tell her I thank her with all my heart for the loan of it, and that I never want to see it again!" Everyone laughed with him again, but they were all aware of how hard he had worked the last few months with that ball to rehabilitate his hand . . . squeezing it over and over and over again in every unoccupied moment . . . squeezing it until his arm ached to the elbow with the effort. They knew what drove him—the determination that he would not be a cripple, that in some way he would again be able to support himself.

Marla moved up and took his arm in both her hands.

"Franz," she said, "to celebrate this occasion, we've got a gift for you." He looked at her quizzically. "Anna, the first part's yours." Franz looked at his friend, wondering what was going on, while everyone else shifted around like young children trying to stifle exclamations. Anna walked over to a chest against the far wall, a chest that had come with them from Mainz, opened it up and took out a bundle wrapped in burgundy velvet. She handed it to Thomas, who passed it to Friedrich, who unwrapped the cloth to display a violin. As he held it out toward Franz, Marla felt him stiffen.

"That . . . that is . . . my violin," he stuttered.

"Yes," from Friedrich.

"How . . . how . . ." he stopped, swallowed, and forced himself to composure. "How is this possible? I smashed it . . . did I not?"

"No," Anna stepped up, smiling, "no, you did not. You did smash your bow that night, and you endeavored to likewise destroy your violin. You did indeed throw it at the wall that night, in your fever and your anger, but you ran out the door before you could see that although the scroll hit the wall above the bench, the body hit a cushion instead."

"The scroll was scraped," Friedrich added, angling the instrument to show the traces of the mar, "but I was able to smooth it down and apply new finish to it. And so," he said, pressing the violin into his friend's hands, "it returns to you. Both are somewhat older, both are somewhat stressed by your experiences, but you still suit one another very well. We kept it safe until you were ready to hold it again." He stepped back, leaving Franz to clasp the instrument he thought he had destroyed—to hold it gently and pass one hand in a caress over its top.

Still staring at the violin—*his* violin—Franz said, "Never has a man had friends such as you. When I regained my senses, in my wanderings after I left Mainz, I grieved over this, grieved most sorely. The thought that I had wantonly destroyed my violin, made solely for the creation of beauty in a world that has not enough of it, did try my soul indeed." He looked up, blinking, eyes bright with unshed tears. "And today you have restored it to me. I have not words to thank you as you deserve." He looked back down at it as the tears spilled over, caressed it again, then embraced it for a long moment, his cheek leaning against the scroll.

The room was quiet, everyone respecting Franz's emotions. He finally looked up again, smiled a little, and said, "Thank you. I thank God for you, my friends, who have saved me, and now have saved my violin as well. Now I am free of that guilt, and I am free to find someone who will take it from my hands to love it as I do and to play it as I no longer can."

Marla took his arm again and turned him to face her. "Now for my gift. Franz, you don't have to give it up. You can play."

Franz was shocked that she would say such a thing, and a flash of anger and sorrow went through him. "Do not mock me, Marla." Holding up his left hand, he said, "Even with the healing that has been done, I cannot finger the neck. I cannot play."

"Maybe you can't finger the neck with that hand, but I'll bet you can hold a bow with it now! Switch hands! Learn to play with switched hands!" Marla was grinning with delight and bouncing slightly in her excitement. Franz felt stunned. Was it possible? Could he do it? He felt dazed, as if he had been hit in the head. He saw Marla put her hand over her mouth to keep from giggling, so he was sure he looked as amazed as he felt.

"It's true," Ingram said, grinning himself. "I knew a mountain fiddler once who had an accident that left his left hand like yours. He just taught himself how to finger the neck with the right and learned to bow with his left. Last time I saw him, he was just as good that way as he was t'other."

Franz shuddered, and his jaw snapped shut. He felt an excitement building in him, and his eyebrows climbed to meet his hairline, causing Marla to giggle. He looked at her, and asked, "Do you think I can do this?"

"I know you can."

Taking a deep breath, Franz turned to Friedrich and said, "My friend, how long until you can make me a bow to grace the violin you have restored to me?"

"As it happens," Ingram interrupted, "that's *my* gift to you." He brought his hand out from behind his back, and presented a bow to Franz. "I always seem to end up with odds and ends of musical stuff. I've had this bow for ten years, never had a fiddle to go with it, never could bring myself to get rid of it. Now I know why. I was savin' it for you. It's made in the up-time style, not like the ones you're used to, but I believe you'll actually find it easier to hold with your hand the way it is."

"So," Marla spoke again, "you have your violin, you have your bow, you have your hand, and you have your friends. What more do you need?"

Franz looked around at the smiling faces, and smiled back. "Nothing."

"Then get started."

"As you wish, Mistress Marla," he said and danced away from the jab she aimed at his ribs.

— *Bouree* —

Grantville
August 1633

As he was giving the tuning knob a final twist, Franz heard the door open.

"So, have you decided yet?"

Franz looked up from his violin to see his friend Isaac Fremdling entering the choir room. "Have I decided what?"

"How you will string your violin, of course? Will you string it in the usual manner, or will you reverse the order of the strings?" Isaac pulled one of the chairs around and sat down.

"What do you think I should do?"

Isaac fingered his moustache, and after a moment of contemplation said, "'Twould perhaps be best to keep the usual order of the strings. In that manner you and another could play each other's instruments with no difficulty."

"An advantage, to be sure," Franz replied. "Yet think of this, if you will: it will likely be easier to learn to play again if each right finger will move in the same manner and in the same relationship to the strings as the left does—if to play an 'F' the related finger makes the same motion, only mirror reversed, if you will."

"A point," nodded Isaac.

"And then consider the bow. Would it not be easier to train myself to reproduce the position of the bow as in a mirror, rather than in a totally different angle and position?"

"Aye," Isaac nodded again.

"Well, then, Isaac, you have answered the question, have you not?"

"It seems that I have, at that," his friend laughed. "So you have decided, then?"

Franz chuckled, and held up his violin. "Friedrich has moved the sound post inside and made a new bridge. I just now finished the stringing and tuning. Behold, a mirror violin." He handed the instrument to Isaac, who examined it closely, tested the tuning, then attempted to place it under his chin.

"Pfaugh! It feels most unnatural to try to hold it under the right chin. But if anyone can do this, Franz," he handed the violin back, "'tis you."

"My thanks. I've no choice, you see, for now that I see a glimmering of light in the night, I will pursue it with all my heart."

Isaac looked at his friend, his expression sobered, and he said quietly, "I grieved for you when I heard of the attack."

Franz looked down, uncomfortable as always when offered sympathy. "I thank you, but as you are so fond of saying, 'The Lord giveth and the Lord taketh away. Blessed be the name of the Lord.' My pride needed curbing, I freely admit. I could wish that the manner of that curbing had not been so severe, and that I had been calmer and wiser and more considerate of my friends afterward. But it took long months of being alone before

I began to slowly grow wise, and it was not until I found my way here to Grantville that I could begin to understand how and why you would say that. The Lord gave, the Lord took away, the Lord gave again, and I have learned to bless Him no matter my circumstance."

"Then you are indeed wise, my friend, for there are few enough even of gray-hairs who possess wisdom that equals what you have just shared." Isaac paused for a moment, then chuckled.

Franz raised an eyebrow.

"My initial reaction to your misfortune was grief indeed," Isaac said, "but hard on its heels came indignation in harness with rage. I must admit that the thought of applying the consequences of the Golden Rule to Heydrich did cross my mind more than once or twice."

"Surely you did not..."

"No, I could not bring myself to do it in cold blood. But there were others of like mind, and I doubt not that their conversations did find their ways to Rupert's itching ears, there to alarm rather than soothe. In truth, he began to company with various fellows, brutes from low taverns, in fear of what had been rumored. And he found no ease in that none of the rest of us would be alone with him thereafter. All of us found it to be most humorous."

Franz smiled. "Well, I am not saintly enough to not find some small pleasure in hearing of his discomfort."

"Oh, aye, before we left Mainz he had become almost two men, one moment the loudest of braggarts, the next like a nervous hind when the hounds bell out. I have seen the man's head almost swivel completely in a circle as he tried to watch his own back."

"The wicked fleeth when no man pursueth," Franz chuckled. "It is perhaps the best vengeance. He will torment himself more than I could or would, and my hands and heart are clean."

"Indeed." There was another moment of quiet before Isaac continued, "As I said, I grieved when I heard. Of all my friends and fellow musicians, your love of the art is most like my own, and I knew well how I felt when someone attempted to take it from me."

Franz raised an eyebrow again.

Isaac made a hand motion as if brushing off a table top. "You know that I am out of the Jews, but I say nothing of my life before Mainz. I knew, however, what you would feel. I was born Isaac

Levin. My father is—I trust he still lives—a rabbi in Aschenhausen, where our forebears settled when the elector expelled the Jews from Saxony. Early in my years I showed promise of music, and he desired me to become a cantor. But other music enticed me, that which I heard from the taverns, through the windows of the merchants' houses and the doorways of the salons. I hungered for more than the Psalms, for more than the music of our traditions. The wealth that was to be heard away from the synagogue filled my heart. I could not see how beauty such as that could not exist in God's presence, but my father rejected it. He forbade me, he lectured me; as I grew older he reasoned with me. He even took a rod to me more than once.

"Finally, in my sixteenth year, he caught me once again slipping away from the door of a salon, and dragged me in front of the elders of our congregation. Right soundly he berated me, and demanded of me a solemn oath by the name of God that I would abandon foolishness and obey him in this. He ended by saying to me that if I would not, then I would no longer be his son. I would be dead to him."

Franz whistled.

"Aye. I was stunned indeed, as were the elders. They argued with him that he was being too harsh, that he should not emulate Saul who drove away David, but to no avail. And all the while I tried to think of life without the music that was so much a part of me. He withstood them all, seeming to grow ever more rigid, and when they were finally silenced he turned to me and demanded my answer.

"I grappled my wits together, and gave the only answer I could give. I still remember every word. 'Papa, I have tried to do as you say, but you were the one who instructed me that the Holy One, blessed be He, created music, that His very spirit guided David when he invented the lyre. Do not now blame me if that music calls me. Some men are called to trading; some men are called to farming; some men are called to the working of metal; some men are called to the study of Torah; and men such as I are called to music. If I do not swear, I am dead to you; yet if I do, I will be dead inside. You force me to judge between two evils, to cause a death either way. But in truth, it seems to me that the greater evil would be to forswear what the Holy One above has placed in me. Papa, it will be as you will it, but I cannot swear.'"

"A grievous choice, indeed, for a youth to have to make." Franz placed a hand on his friend's shoulder.

"But the tale is not finished. I saw at that moment that my father had never truly understood me, for all his wisdom in Torah and Talmud. I saw that he had fully believed that I would swear, for the shock of my choice well-nigh shattered him. A proud, upright man he was, but he turned away from me gray and old. It was as if a tall and vital oak in the full bloom of summer in an eye-blink turned to a dead and hollow husk. The light in his eyes died, for he had made his command in public in front of the elders of the congregation, and his own pride and authority would not let him recant. His face turned to stone, his very voice turned to gravel as he said, 'Thou art dead to me; Thou art dead to me; Thou art dead to me.' He turned away, and trudged out of the court and into the house. The elders followed him, silently, except that for a moment old Joachim Arst, a man I had never before cared for, came to me. As tears coursed my cheeks, he placed a purse in my hands, saying, 'I believe that I have lost some coins in the streets today.' Then he took my face between his hands, and said, 'Always remember, young Isaac who is now a stranger, the Lord giveth and the Lord taketh away. Blessed be the name of the Lord.' And so I am now Isaac Fremdling, Isaac the stranger."

Isaac brushed a hand across his eyes, looked at Franz and said gently, "And so I know somewhat of how you felt after Heydrich mauled you, for I know how I felt when I thought I would not have the music, and I know how high a price I paid to have it."

"Indeed," Franz said, aching in his heart for his friend, knowing the kind of desolation that had been dealt him. "How is it I never heard this, from you or one of the others?"

"Because I have not shared it these last five years; before now there was none who would understand, none who could know what I felt then."

Two young men—of different heritage, yet brothers in their love of music and the prices they had paid to have it—sat together in silence, contemplating things lost and things gained, and likewise contemplating the ancient wisdom of a man named Job.

— *Allemande* —

Grantville
Moments later

The door to the choir room crashed open, startling Franz and Isaac both. They had been wrapped so deeply in their thoughts they had not heard anyone approach. As the door panel bounced off the doorstop, a group of young men of an age with themselves broke into the room, arguing at the top of their lungs. They threw their books down on the tables at the head of the room and carried on with their heated discussion. Two of them in particular stood almost toe-to-toe, arms waving frantically. German epithets were bouncing from the walls and ceiling, the mildest of which were "Fool!" and "Imbecile!" The others quickly turned to egging their champions on, and if the volume did not decrease, at least the mass confusion did. Franz began to chuckle. They were such a sight: faces red, veins bulging on their foreheads, hair dancing wildly. He leaned over to Isaac, who was grinning broadly, and near-shouted in his ear, "I wonder how long Thomas and Hermann have been at it this time?" Isaac shrugged, but didn't try to shout over the din.

For a moment there was quiet, as both men ran out of breath at the same time. Chests heaving, sweat running down their faces, they stood glaring at each other. Nothing was settled, though—this wasn't even a truce. It was more in the way of a pause for breath in a long-fought duel between two very evenly matched opponents. That last thought caused Franz to laugh out loud, for although the two champions might have been evenly matched with their chosen weapons of words, little else about them was.

Thomas Schwarzberg, one of Franz's closest friends, was a very tall man. Even among the giants of Grantville he stood out; among the native down-timers he was more than the Biblical head and shoulders taller. On the other hand, Hermann Katzberg was short, even for a down-timer. Franz doubted if he was five feet tall, especially if he took off his boots with the built-up heels. He was stocky, though not misshapen, and reasonably handsome with dark hair. In Franz's mind, Hermann was more than a bit pugnacious, as he had just been demonstrating—possibly an in-born temperament, but just as likely an attitude adopted to keep the taller world in which he dwelt from overlooking him. It obviously irked Hermann just now that as much as he wanted to be nose-to-nose with Thomas, he was actually more like nose-to-navel.

The two were both excellent musicians, adept at several instruments, although each had one in which he was clearly superior. Hermann was perhaps the best harpsichordist that Franz had ever heard—better even than Thomas, which was praise indeed. Thomas, on the other hand, was far and away the finest flautist it had been his pleasure to hear, although Hermann, in his turn, was more than competent with a flute. Neither man had met the other before they came to Grantville, Thomas at Franz's invitation, Hermann following rumors of new and powerful music. Within hours of their first meeting, they had accurately assessed each other's skill and moved directly to mutual respect. And indeed, on most days and on most subjects they were very amicable and usually in agreement. There was one topic, however, on which both men had very strong opinions, and they were on different sides of the issue.

Just as Hermann opened his mouth to renew the verbal conflict, Marla Linder came walking in the door, books in arms. She stopped dead at the sight of Thomas and Hermann on their feet. "Not again!" She stalked over to the instructor's desk, dropped her books with a loud slam, and glared at Franz and Isaac. "Can't you keep them under control?"

"The battle was well under way ere they arrived, Fraulein Marla," Isaac said, holding up both hands in a placating gesture. "In truth, it were worth our lives to attempt to come between them." His inability to repress a grin garnered another glare from Marla.

"And I suppose that's your story as well." She shifted the adamantine gaze of her icy blue eyes to Franz.

"Well, as they had not progressed to the throwing stage yet, I had hopes that they would run out of energy soon." He twitched his shoulders; Marla was obviously in a testy mood today.

Marla snorted, turned to the other men and pointed at ranked chairs. "Take a seat!" Looking over her shoulder at Franz and Isaac, she added, "You, too!" They all wasted no time in obeying. As they did so, Franz propped his chin on his good hand, looked at them all through half-lowered eyelids, and smiled a little.

He remembered the day these discussions began. He and Thomas and their other close friend Friedrich Braun had met with the musicians that were going to participate in the music "sem-i-nar." In addition to Isaac, another of the newcomers was a man that he and Thomas and Friedrich had known in Mainz—Leopold Gruenwald, a maker of trumpets who was also a player of some skill. Leopold was the last of the musicians that Franz had invited to come to Grantville.

Of the others, there was Hermann, of course, and two brothers, Josef and Rudolf Tuchman. Hermann had come from Magdeburg, and the brothers Tuchman had followed the rumors all the way from Hanover to Grantville.

Leopold and Isaac were willing to accept the unanimous declaration of Franz, Friedrich and Thomas about Marla's knowledge, talent and musicianship. The other three, however, had come seeking the new music that was hinted at in the rumors, seeking with an odd mixture of skepticism and hope. Once they heard what they would have to do to learn it, the skepticism rose to the top and they expressed some serious reservations. The thought of sitting in a school room to learn music was unheard of, by all that was holy. Musicians learned by doing, by sitting with other musicians and copying technique until they made it their own. This sitting in a room and talking about it was nonsense!

Then they found out that the seminar leader was to be a woman, and hackles started rising. By all that was unholy, a woman had no place in music, or at least not in the serious work that they themselves were doing!

Franz remembered shuddering as he looked around to make sure that Marla was not in earshot. From the expressions on their faces, Thomas and Friedrich had been thinking much the same thing. Together they faced forward and glared at the Tuchmans, who had been the most outspoken in their opinions. Franz had started to speak, but Thomas held up his hand and Franz swallowed his words.

"I make allowances," Thomas had said sternly, "for the fact that you do not know Fraulein Marla. I also agree that a woman musician is most unusual, although perhaps not strictly unknown. However, I strongly urge you to keep the words you have just said behind your teeth in the future.

"Let me make it clear to you: you will accord to Fraulein Marla the minimum respect you would grant a visiting doyen or master. You will find that she is worthy of it."

"And what if we do not?" Josef had asked, almost sneering.

Three faces had glowered in return, and Josef's face went blank.

"You will not be allowed to learn from her," Franz had said finally. "And there is no one else to learn from, for Master Wendell has said that this is to be her work."

"Well, will she go all faint and quivery if I yell," Hermann had demanded, "or, God forbid," going falsetto, "I should be vulgar in her presence?" He had looked very nonplussed as Franz, Friedrich and Thomas had burst into laughter.

"No," Franz had choked, fighting down the mirth, "she is no wilting flower. She will assuredly deal with you as you are." Sobering quickly, he had reiterated, "She is worthy of your respect." Hermann looked at the brothers and shrugged, and they all nodded.

Franz felt Isaac nudge him, and he came back to the present quickly, noticing that the room had gone quiet. Marla's eyes were drilling into him. "Excuse me," he said.

"You with us now?" Marla asked sharply.

"Yes."

"English or German?"

She was asking what language this day's discussion would be held in. They had adopted the practice of alternating between the two to strengthen Marla's command of German and help the others improve their English.

"English," Franz said, and his heart beat faster as she rewarded him with one of her glorious smiles.

"Good," she said. "That's the first thing that's gone my way today." She glanced at the door, then back at the others. "We're going to have guests today. Elizabeth Jordan, one of my former voice teachers, has made contact with a couple of Italians who wish to join us today. One is a musician—a composer, I believe—and the other is a craftsman of some kind. They should be here any . . . ah, and here they are now."

The door to the choir room opened, and a short, slightly plump woman entered, followed by a short man in a black cassock. Franz didn't quite goggle at him, but was taken back a bit. One did not ordinarily expect that mode of dress in Grantville, or at least not in the high school. A Catholic cleric of some kind, obviously.

The third member of the party was somewhat larger, but definitely not of a size to stare Thomas eye to eye. Franz estimated he was about his own height. He moved with some grace, but was obviously not a courtier. He must be the artisan that Marla had mentioned.

"Elizabeth, you're just in time." Marla stepped forward and shook hands with her former teacher. "Please, introduce your guests."

"This is Maestro Giacomo Carissimi and Signor Girolamo Zenti, all the way from Rome." Each man nodded slightly when his name was called: Carissimi stiffly, as if he wasn't comfortable, and Zenti with a slight, crooked smile on his face. "The maestro has come in search of knowledge about our music, and Signor Zenti looks for knowledge about musical instruments. When you told me yesterday what you would be discussing today, I knew they would both find it of interest."

"Thank you for coming," Marla said, offering her hand. Carissimi hesitated, then reached out and shook it quickly, releasing it at once. Zenti in turn took her hand, and instead of shaking it raised it to his lips. Marla was obviously taken off guard, but kept her composure and retrieved her fingers as soon as he released them.

Marla turned and had the others introduce themselves. As they did so, Franz decided that the maestro was innocuous, but that he could find himself taking a dislike to Zenti without much effort.

Once the introductions were completed, Marla said, "Please be seated where you please. We were about to get started. And please, feel free to speak up at any time. This bunch certainly does."

With that, she shifted her focus again to Thomas and Hermann, who, despite their verbal combat, were sitting next to each other. "You two were arguing about tempering again, weren't you?" They nodded cheerfully. "And the rest of you," sweeping a hand motion to include Josef, Rudolf, Leopold and Friedrich, "were kibitzing and cheering them on from the peanut gallery, right?"

Smiles and nods were mixed with confusion over the figure of speech. "Meanwhile, the grinning gargoyle brothers over here"—she pointed to Isaac, who looked offended, and Franz, who just smiled—"were laughing at all of you. And you probably deserved it."

She sat down at the piano, and placed her hands on top of the cabinet. "I'm tired of all this argument, so I've spent the last couple of days researching this issue, and I'm ready to put a stake in it and bury it for good." The Italians looked very confused, but Elizabeth was whispering to them, explaining Marla's figure of speech.

As always when she started one of their sessions, Franz was a little nervous for her. He knew her heart, her desire: how she desperately wanted to succeed at this work; wanted to bring the glory of the music she knew to the time she was now in; how she wanted to midwife the birth of a glorious age of music. He knew how hard she studied and prepared. He knew how when she first started her stomach had ached before every class; knew, too, how she had castigated herself after each of those early sessions because she felt she had sounded uncertain and timid rather than assured and self-confident. The fact that he had detected nothing of the kind and repeatedly told her so was no comfort to her. But gradually, as she learned that she could teach them, that she could hold her own in discussions with them, that she could find answers to all their questions, she had indeed found assurance and self-confidence, and their sessions had become the joy that she had so wanted them to be.

Today, however, she was tackling head-on an issue that she had been dancing around for weeks, the issue of tunings and tempering systems. If she was feeling nervous, there was no evidence of it in her demeanor. She sat there calmly, smiling slightly, looking cool and collected in front of the eight of them.

"Hermann, how many tempering systems are you aware of?"

He sat in thought for a moment, then said, "The Just and the Pyth . . . Pytha . . ."

"Pythagorean," Thomas prompted.

"Pythagorean systems," he muttered under his breath.

"What did you say?" Marla looked at him with her head tilted to one side.

He squirmed a little, then said, "I have trouble wrapping my tongue around that name when I'm speaking good *Deutsche*. It is even harder with English."

"Continue."

"Just, Pythagorean, and Mean are the ones I know of, Fraulein Marla."

Franz looked at him out of the corner of his eye, checking his attitude, but he seemed totally serious.

"And of those, which are in common use?"

"Only the Mean."

"Why is that?"

Hermann thought for a moment, wanting to make sure he didn't trip up, then said, "Because the other two are too limited, are too discordant except in a few keys."

"Right. But, can't you say much the same thing for the Mean temperament as well?"

Hermann looked stubborn, while Thomas made no attempt to suppress a very wide smile as Marla made his case for him. Franz watched to see how Marla would handle this. He wanted her to do well, to bring Hermann around, because to be the power in music in the USE that he thought she should become, she had to be able to engage the stubborn peers of his musical generation in dialogue, reason with them and eventually bring them to see her positions. Hermann was perhaps her first serious test, as he himself, Friedrich and Thomas had been won over very easily.

"Hermann," she said, "you have to face the fact that the Mean system works okay with voices, strings and horns, all of which the musicians instinctively tune, usually without even being aware they're doing it. But with any kind of keyboard, it is just too limiting. You're basically limited to four or five tonalities, the simpler ones." She set her hands on the piano keys, saying, "Stay with me, Hermann. We're going for a ride."

Marla began playing "A Mighty Fortress Is Our God." Over the simple harmony, she said, "You know this hymn. Even in the time we came from, it's one of Luther's most famous works. It's in our hymnals in the key of C major—no sharps, no flats. Now listen, and listen carefully."

Franz saw an intent expression come over her face, one that he was coming to know very well. He nudged Isaac, and mouthed to him, "Get ready."

There was a brief pause, then Marla's hands began moving swiftly over the piano keyboard. Arpeggios were rolling up from the low end of the keyboard, and over it she began playing the melody and harmony of the old hymn in the traditional 4/4 time. At the end of the verse, she played a transitional phrase which modulated into a sustained chord, then suddenly began playing a light rendition of the song in 3/4 time, almost a dance, in a new key. Again, when she came to the end of the verse she played a transition, this time immediately modulating to a new key where once again she played in 4/4, this time playing the song as a canon of repeating lines over a constant bass note. Another modulation, another style—this time a quiet meditation, almost in the manner of an adagio.

Franz looked at the others, and saw on the faces of the newcomers the stupefaction he had expected. He, Thomas and Friedrich knew Marla's talent, but this was the first time she had unleashed its full potential before Isaac, Leopold, Hermann and the Tuchman brothers, and they were obviously stunned.

Once again she modulated, this time playing the old hymn in a hammering martial style, at once pompous yet regal. She brought it to a rousing close, playing the last line in a slow ritard that allowed her to alternate chords first in the treble keys, then in the bass, using the sustain pedal to let them ring and create an effect that almost rivaled an organ for richness and sonority. She allowed the final chord to resound in the room, then released the pedal and let the piano action damp the strings.

Franz saw a small smile play about the corners of her mouth as she took in the expressions of the others.

"Okay, guys," she said, "how many keys did I play in?"

Hermann shook himself, looked at the others, and said, "Five." They nodded in support.

"And what were they?"

"First was C."

"Right."

"Then the next was . . . G."

Hermann sounded a little reluctant, and Franz thought he knew why. When Marla smiled, he knew he was right.

"And what is G to C?" Marla asked.

"The dominant,"

"And in the Mean system," she said, "can those two keys sound consonant in the same piece of music?"

"Yes."

"Ah, but what about the next keys? Where did I go from G?"

"D?" Hermann sounded a little unsure of himself.

"Yes, D was next. I used an augmented sixth chord for the modulation, so it was a little tricky, but you got it, we landed in D. D is the dominant of G, right?"

Heads nodded all over the room.

"So now we have C, G and D. Is consonance possible in the same piece with those keys? Just possibly," she answered her own question, "just possibly. But where did we go from there?"

No one ventured a guess.

"Thomas, did you follow?" When he shook his head, she smiled again, and said, "Okay, I'll have mercy on you. I went from D to A, and ended in E. See the pattern in the modulations? Each time I modulated to the dominant of the previous key. I've now got five different keys in this piece, ranging from C major with no sharps or flats to E major with four sharps. Hermann," she looked at him seriously, "in the Mean system, can I have all five of those keys sound consonant *in the same piece of music*?"

Franz heard her emphasis, but was glad to note that her tone of voice and her expression were both serious, that there was no sense of mocking or humor. She was treating both the topic and Hermann with respect.

The room was quiet. No one said anything, no one even stirred until Hermann finally sighed, and said, "No, Fraulein Marla, you cannot. Your point is made."

"But don't you see, Hermann," Marla said, "don't you see that it's not *my* point? This is not some dictate that I'm trying to force upon you. It's not some up-time invention or standard that I'm trying to shove down your throat. The earliest mention I could find for equal temperament goes all the way back to some guy named Grammateus in 1518—that's over one hundred years before today, for heaven's sake! Equal temperament was something that generations—your predecessors in music, your peers now, and your successors in music—all worked toward. As composers and performers alike desired more tonal complexity and sophistication in their music, as they experimented and argued amongst themselves and with their patrons, they eventually hammered out a consensus for the equal temperament system."

Marla looked around at all of them, then said slowly, "And Hermann, it was the Germans who arrived at it first. By 1800, this was the standard in German music. It took the rest of the world at least another fifty years to catch up to you. So you see, I'm not trying to force the stream of music into an unnatural streambed, I'm not trying to force it to flow uphill. Instead, I'm trying to guide you into the natural bed for your stream, but I'm trying to guide you to it now instead of several generations later."

Hermann muttered again. Franz saw Marla lift an eyebrow, Hermann coughed, and said, "But it still sounds discordant."

"Of course it does," Marla laughed. "It's a result of musical diplomacy. I once heard a definition of diplomacy that goes something like this: diplomacy is the art of leaving all interested parties equally dissatisfied. That's a perfect definition of equal temperament. All keys are slightly less than consonant, but importantly, all keys are equally dissonant. Once we accept that compromise, then the full artist's palette of tonalities is available to us."

Franz smiled at her metaphor.

"Believe me," Marla added, "I know exactly how discordant equal temperament is. I have absolute perfect pitch, so anything less than pure consonance grates on my ear. But, I will accept the minor discomfort that equal temperament causes in order to play things like this."

She turned to the piano again, and began a piece in 3/4 time. It lilted and danced, almost like a stream flowing over rocks. The music flowed, with waterfall-like runs in it, broadened out to a more stately theme and treatment, then returned to the original style. Marla's fingers flew, the tempo ebbed and flowed, and finally began to move faster and faster until it trailed away under the right hand in the high treble keys.

Once again dead silence reigned in the room, until it was broken by a collective sigh from the men. Marla turned to them, and said, "That was the Waltz in C-sharp minor by Frederic Chopin, part of his Opus 64, one of the loveliest piano pieces ever written. The key has four sharps, and it probably couldn't be played in the Mean system."

Looking around the room, she asked, "Any questions? Any comments?"

"Excuse me, please, signorina," Maestro Carissimi said.

"Yes, sir?"

"I understand what you say, and it makes clear much that I did wonder about. But is there not a . . . how would you say . . . along side . . ."

"Parallel?"

"Yes! Thank you for the word. Is there not parallel issue, one of tuning, of intonation?"

"Oh, absolutely," Marla said. She pressed a key on the piano, and a tone sounded. "That is an A, the note defined by international agreement to be the tuning standard. And there are machines and tuning forks to exhibit that standard and to measure against. That standard was arrived at almost," she looked confused for a moment, "well, what would have been almost two hundred fify years from now. But between now and then, tuning was a local matter, usually determined by whoever built the organ in the local church or cathedral."

"Exactly my point!" said the Italian. "In Italy, the tuning is higher, brighter than in Germanies, but even within a province, is not the same from place to place. Until a standard for all of Europe can be devised, we musicians must still adjust tuning as from place to place we go. Music written for Italian churches transcribed to other keys must be to get same sound in northern German churches, and perhaps the same if northern music to Rome or Naples is brought."

"And that will change not so quickly," his companion said. "Musicians—especially Italians—will not like hearing that wrong are their tunings." There were murmurs of agreement from around the room, and Thomas and Hermann in particular nodded vigorously.

"Well," Marla said, "at least we all agree that developing a standard tuning is a problem, and that it probably won't be solved soon. But do you all understand why the equal temperament is so important?"

Heads nodded all around, and "Yes," was heard from every corner.

Marla looked down at her watch. "Yikes! I didn't realize it was that late! This is Wednesday night, and I've got choir rehearsal at church. Okay, we'll meet again on Friday here in the school choir room. We'll finish the discussion we started last time about modes and the changeover to major and minor keys. See you then!" And in a whirlwind, she grabbed her books and was gone. Elizabeth and her guests also rose, made their farewells, and left.

The eight young men sat quietly for a moment, as if drained of energy. Finally, Hermann looked up, and said to Franz, "Now I know what you meant. She is indeed worthy of our respect. It would be an insult to say she does not play like a woman, but when I close my eyes, all I hear is a musician of great skill and talent playing with vigor and authority."

He sighed. "Forced to discard another preconception. Two in one day. At this rate, in another month she will have me cleaned off like a blank slate, a *tabula rasa*."

"Well, I am tempted to ask if that would be such a bad thing." Thomas grinned, obviously restraining himself from crowing over Marla's victory. "But instead I will say that you at least had the advantage of knowing her first, and seeing that she did indeed posses some knowledge and skill before she unleashed the full fury of her arsenal on you. Friedrich and I, we were exposed to the full-bore power of her talent within hours of first meeting her."

"And do not forget the hangovers," Friedrich interjected.

"*Ach*, how could I forget? The memory of the thunder in my

skull being matched by the thunder of her piano playing still makes me shudder!" Thomas matched actions to words. "Some time, Hermann, have her play for you the 'Revolutionary Etude.' Then you will see the full scope of her power, and you will truly understand why I sit at her feet."

"But she is so young!" Josef said. "How can she be so strong, so assured, so . . . so . . ."

"Authoritative?" Thomas supplied.

"Yes, how can she be so authoritative? How can she be like a master at her age?"

Thomas looked to Franz. "How old is she?"

"She recently passed her twenty-first birthday, which is young but not so young. To us, she's of an age to be a journeyman. To the folk of Grantville, she's her own woman, to do as she pleases. Most of them know she is talented, but I believe that Master Wendell and perhaps Master Bledsoe are the only ones who truly appreciate her magnitude. Master Wendell says that if not for the Ring of Fire, he thinks she could have been one of the great ones of their time."

He stood and walked over to look out the window. "She is driven to mastery. Her spirit, her gifts drive her to rise above her origins, her womanhood, to become a master." He turned to face them. "She will not stop until she is either broken or is acclaimed by all."

"So if she is of age, why is she not married, as so many of the Grantvillers are?" asked Josef. "She is comely, and seems pleasant enough."

"Hah!" snorted Rudolf, surprising everyone, since he was the most taciturn individual most of them had ever met and never volunteered anything. "No, thank you. That *fraulein* has sword steel for a spine, and I suspect she could out-stubborn Gustav Adolf himself. She may be a muse incarnate, a very Calliope . . ."

"Take care," Friedrich warned.

"Nevertheless, I fear that most men would desire someone with at least some compliance in her soul. Fraulein Marla may be doomed to a spinster's life."

Friedrich and Thomas burst out in uproarious laughter. Friedrich actually slid out of his chair and rolled on the floor. Thomas bent over holding his stomach, howling.

The newcomers all stared, eyes wide and jaws agape. Finally Hermann collected himself. "What is the jest?" he demanded.

Thomas managed, by sheer willpower, to somewhat compose

himself. "The jest," he wheezed, "stands there." He waved a hand at Franz. Franz waved back, smiling slightly, as Thomas continued. "Our man Franz there woos her."

"Not just woos," Friedrich husked, levering himself into a sitting position on the floor. "Not just woos; for he has won her heart."

The astounded expressions returned, now focused on Franz. He shrugged and said, "'Tis true."

"Then why have you not wed, if you feel thus?" asked Hermann.

Franz lifted his left hand, and everyone sobered. They all knew the story by now. "When I can play again in public, when I can again make my way with my violin, then I will ask her." The fire in his heart at that moment was a match for Marla's, and enough of it showed that the others actually sat back a little.

"She assents to this? It seems somewhat unlike her," said Rudolf.

"She knows. She agrees."

They all looked at Franz soberly. He bore their gaze calmly, and they all saw the determination in his eyes. Finally Hermann spoke.

"Of all men, Franz, you may be most worthy of Fraulein Marla."

As the others nodded, Franz said quietly, "'Tis the challenge of the rest of my life, Hermann."

— *Gigue* —

Grantville
A few days later

"C'mon in, guys," Marla said to Franz and Isaac, holding open the door to her Aunt Susan's house. "The rest of the group is already here." She led them into the living room, where the only seats left open were the hard wooden chairs that had been brought in from the dining room. The sofa and easy chairs had already been claimed. Thomas, Hermann and the others grinned at them from the soft seats as Marla's aunt bustled around handing out glasses of apple cider and water. Cookies were evident all around, and Thomas was almost oblivious to their entry as he blissfully devoured a slice of apple pie that must have occupied a quarter of the pie pan it came from.

"Sit down, boys, sit down," Susan said, as she went by them on her way to the kitchen. She came back out with glasses of ice and pitchers of cider and water and set them down on the coffee table in front of them. "Fill up with whichever you like," came back over her shoulder as she returned to the kitchen once more.

She reappeared carrying another plate of cookies, which Isaac took from her with alacrity, fending off hands that reached toward it from those who had been there before him.

"Away with you, jackals," he mock-snarled, holding the plate out of their reach. "'Tis bad enough that you usurp the chief places, leaving poor Franz and myself to set our nether portions on the hardest seats. 'Tis not enough that you have already wreaked destruction upon good Frau Garrett's provisions. But when she takes pity on poor Franz and myself and brings forth the fruits of her labors to revive us, you attempt to acquire them as well. Nay," he laughed, leaning away from Hermann, "nay, you will not have them. Look to your own!"

"But there are only crumbs here," Hermann whined.

"Then lick the platters clean," Franz weighed in, taking a handful of cookies from Isaac's plate, "for you'll have none of ours."

He took a bite, and the expression that came over his face rivaled that on Thomas', who had finished his pie and was now diligently scraping his plate clean and licking the fork.

Franz stood and bowed to Susan. "Frau Garrett, once again you have demonstrated your command of the baker's art, and produced what might be a model for the ambrosia of Olympus."

"Enough of your foolishness, Franz Sylwester," Susan said, blushing slightly as she wiped her hands on her apron.

Marla's aunt was indeed one of the best bakers in town, but at this point in the post-Ring of Fire existence of Grantville, she had what some in town considered an unfair advantage. Her husband, Jim, had owned and managed Garrett's Super Market when the Ring fell. As soon as she had recovered from her shock and thought through the implications of that event, she had marched right down to the store and commandeered all the spices that were left on the shelves. As a result of her foresight and her sparing use of them, she had bottles of cinnamon, nutmeg and other spices hidden away long after most of the other households in town had run out. True, spices were now available from the down-time merchants that serviced Grantville's economy, but their supplies were low in quantity and erratic in availability, which kept the prices quite high. As a consequence, in the late summer of 1634, if a baking mood settled on her, children from all around could be seen gathered around the screen door to her kitchen inhaling the aromas, and it wasn't unknown for grown men to plead for the privilege of licking her mixer beaters and bowls.

Franz and Isaac gave testimony to Susan's skills as they wasted no time in reducing their plate to mere crumbs as well. There was silence as everyone was either chewing or chasing crumbs around their plates, obviously thinking hard about licking them, but resisting the temptation. Finally, Marla stood up.

"Okay, guys, let's get started. English or German?"

"English," several voices replied.

"Good," she said, "because I'm not sure I could discuss today's topic in German.

"I asked you to meet here today, because I needed access to a good stereo." She put her hand on a stack of black metal cabinets piled on a small table next to where she stood at the head of the room, and then pointed to some fairly large wooden boxes in the corners of the room. Franz noticed wires running from the metal cabinets to the boxes in the corners, and deduced that they must be some type of the "speakers" that were used elsewhere in Grantville to produce sound and music from the shiny silver discs called CDs. The speakers had the letters "JBL" on an emblem. He wondered what that stood for.

A sad expression crossed Marla's face, and she said quietly, "This was my brother Paul's stereo. Before the Ring fell, he spent hours listening to it. This is the first time it's been hooked up since then."

She fell silent for several moments, then sighed. The others waited patiently, knowing that her brother, along with her parents, had not been within the radius of the Ring when it fell. Franz in particular knew how hard she had been struck by the knowledge that she would never see them again.

She looked up and, with an obvious effort, said, "Anyway, I want to spend tonight talking about popular music.

"There has always been a difference between the music done for art's sake, and the music done to please the common man. You know that's true. The music you create for patrons, and I include the church in that category, is different from the music you create on street corners and in taverns. It may be related—you know as well as I do that melodies from the street and the taverns have a way of sneaking into even the music written for the churches—but there is a definite difference in complexity between the two. The more complex the music grows, the smaller it seems the audience is who can truly appreciate it.

"As I said, this has pretty much always been the case, but until the early 1900s, the music of the streets was more of an undercurrent in the stream of music. That changed with the invention of mechanical devices that could record music played in one place onto some kind of medium, such as wax or types of plastic—" They all nodded at the reference to the magic stuff that was so prevalent in Grantville. "—or even the CDs.

"What happened was that once the average citizen could own a device that would play whatever music he wanted whenever he wanted it, he began buying the music he liked. That changed the way music was created and performed. By the 1970s, it was becoming difficult for many orchestras to exist, partly because people were buying different music than what the orchestras played, and partly because even the music the orchestras did play could be recorded, bought and played anytime.

"The popular music, the outgrowth of the music of the streets, took many forms. Most people would like a few types. Very few people liked them all. But in almost every case, the popular musicians became like heroes, and it became a status symbol to people to have a lot of these recordings. The more you had, especially of rare or new or avant-garde musicians, the more status you had among your friends. By the time I was in high school, a ridiculously large amount of money was being spent every year by people all across our nation to purchase these recordings.

"The styles of music diverged for a while, but inevitably they began influencing each other again, both between different types of popular music and between the popular music and the art music."

Marla stopped here, took a drink of cider, then picked up a CD and began to turn all the equipment on. "We're going to listen to a number of different kinds of popular music tonight. Some of it you may like, most of it you will find discordant, some of it you will out and out hate. But this is part of what music was right before the Ring fell."

☆ ☆ ☆

Susan turned back into the kitchen from the door into the living room as music began to flow out of the speakers. She recognized the tune: "The Entertainer," by Scott Joplin. She was slightly pleased with herself that she knew it... Lord knew that music was not her strength, not like Marla and Paul and their mother Alison. Now that Marla was so involved with this bunch of boys—young men, rather—she had rather the feeling of the duck that had hatched a swan. Marla was growing and stretching her horizons, and Susan could only stand behind her and watch her go. It was good to see her living and laughing again, but it still was a little scary to see her surrounded by these young men all the time, talking about things that Susan didn't understand. If only John and Alison could have been with her. They would have been so proud of Marla, and Alison at least would have understood her and what was going on.

She dabbed at her eyes with her apron, then muttered, "Standing around leaking tears isn't going to get the dishes done, silly." She began running the water in the sink, added the soap, then gathered up the bowls, pans and plates and put them in the sink. As she was turning the water off, the outside screen door opened, and she looked around to see Ingram Bledsoe and Hans Riebeck coming in.

"Sorry we didn't knock, Susan," Ingram said, carefully closing the door, "but we didn't want to disturb anything."

"That's all right," she said, drying her hands on a towel. "You all want some water or cider? I'd offer you some cookies, but those two-legged vacuum cleaners in the other room have already Hoovered up everything I baked today."

Ingram chuckled, and said, "I'll take some cider, thank you kindly."

"I, too, *bitte*," Master Riebeck said. His English had rapidly improved since he had first come to Grantville back in March, but he was obviously still thinking in German and translating to English as he spoke. Occasionally, what came out sounded a little odd or stilted to American ears.

In the other room, the music had ceased, and there was a murmur of conversation. Ingram looked that way, then looked back at Susan and said, "How's she doing?"

She shrugged. "You're askin' the wrong person, Ingram. I'm a Linder born, and ain't no Linders been musicians before Paul and

Marla. Grandpa used to say that he was goin' to sing in Heaven, but it would take Heaven for him to do it. The Linder women all sound like rusty gates, and the men all sound like asthmatic bullfrogs. Even Marla's older sister Jonni takes after us. No, it was the Easterly blood that brought Paul and Marla their talents."

She picked up her glass of water and swirled it around. "Alison used to say that her great-grandmother was half Black Irish and half Cherokee and was what the old folks used to call a cunning woman, but that even in her eighties when Alison knew her, she could still sing the birds out of the trees onto her fingers. She said all the talent came from her."

She raised the glass and swallowed the water. "John was mystified by them two kids," she continued. "He didn't understand them at all. Called them his cuckoos sometimes. He was proud of them, though. He'd about bust his suspenders any time that Marla sang, and he just about couldn't keep his feet on the ground when Paul played that guitar." She set the glass in the sink, and she stared into the soapy water. "It about killed him when Paul got the cancer. He lost about as much weight watching Paul suffer through the chemotherapy for the leukemia as Paul did. That's why they weren't here when the Ring fell . . . they'd driven Paul to his next treatment. Oh, drat," she said matter of factly, wiping her eyes with her apron again. "It's been over three years. You'd think I could talk about them without crying."

She was surprised when Master Riebeck reached a gnarled hand over and patted her shoulder. "Frau Susan," he said, "those we love, we love forever, we miss forever. My brother was younger than me. He died years ago. I miss him still."

"Thanks," she said softly. "I miss them, I worry about how they felt and how they handled our being gone, but I think the worst is that we don't know what happened to Paul. Marla had a bad cold, so she'd been sleeping over here for several days so she wouldn't infect him. She didn't even get to say goodbye. She took it hard, real hard."

Ingram nodded in agreement. "The Bible says Hell is a place of fire, but I seem to remember readin' about some guy who said that there was a place of ice in Hell."

"Dante Alighieri," said Master Riebeck.

"Whoever. I could almost believe that, 'cause that's what Marla was like after the Ring fell," Susan said. "Her soul was frozen, and she was pure cutting edge. I thank God every night for Franz Sylwester. I mean, I'm sorry he got hurt and all, but I think it was purely the hand of God that brought him to Grantville and to Marla. Whether they marry or not, he's made her live again, and he'll always have a place in my heart and my home because of it."

"*Ja*, and we say *danke Gott* for Fraulein Marla, because she gave him life and worth again."

"Ain't it funny how God works?" The two men raised their glasses in a toast to that simple truth.

A long moment of quiet followed, and the music from the other room intruded. A man with a silky voice began singing. Ingram raised his eyebrows. "Frank Sinatra? What's she doing tonight?"

"She said she was going to walk them through one hundred years of popular music tonight."

"Well, it sounds like she's only up to about 1940. She's got a ways to go yet."

Franz's head seemed full to bursting, and he was very glad to hear Marla say, "Okay guys, we're almost done. Let's take a quick break, and then we'll wrap it up with one last song."

She disappeared down the hallway to the bathroom, and everyone else just seemed to slump in their chairs. Isaac leaned over, rested his elbows on his knees and put his head in his hands.

"Oooh," he moaned. "My head is spinning. Ragtime, Dixieland, jazz . . ."

"Southern gospel, black gospel . . ." Hermann added.

"Blues . . ." from Leopold.

"Country and western . . ." Josef and Rudolph said together.

"Rock and roll," finished Friedrich.

"Louis Armstrong . . ."

"Glenn Miller . . ."

"Harry James . . ."

"Billie Holiday . . ."

"Frank Sinatra . . ."

"Elvis Presley . . ."

"Brubeck . . ."

"Hank Williams . . ."

"The Beatles . . ."

"Johnny Cash!" several voices said at once, and they all started laughing.

After they regained their composure, Friedrich said, "How can so many different styles have developed so quickly? Our music develops slowly, changes slowly. Why did theirs change so rapidly?"

"We've already talked about the access to mechanical and electrical systems to play music," Marla said as she walked back into the room. "Another factor, though, is the changes in the place and authority of the church in society. For most of its existence, the church has been a conservative institution. That can be a good thing, at times. However, it can also be a drawback, for conservative organizations tend to be very slow to change. Ultraconservative organizations actively resist change. Hence the boiling pot of Europe that Luther and Calvin have lit a fire under."

She moved to the stereo, and continued speaking while she searched for a CD. "One of the areas where the church exerted its control was in the arts. Musical forms changed very slowly over the years. But as a result of the changes that occurred beginning with Luther, the influence of the church—whether Roman, Lutheran or Reformed—over music began to ebb, and musical evolutions began to cycle faster. By the 1800s, musical generations were occurring on a level with human generations. By my lifetime, musical generations were occurring every five to ten years.

"Ah, here it is!" She picked up a CD and turned to them with a smile so filled with mischievous glee that the hair on the back of Franz's neck prickled.

"Okay, guys, one last style, one last song. I've been promising Franz for weeks that I'd explain what 'heavy metal' means in our rock and roll music, and tonight's the night. You're all along for the ride. The song is 'For Whom the Bell Tolls.'" She loaded the CD player, pushed the play button, and turned the volume up.

Franz leaned back as a bell began to toll out of the speakers, and then the speakers erupted. After his exposure to what the local band Mountaintop played, he could call it music, but it was of a type that even Mountaintop had not produced. The sounds were harsh, discordant, but there was beat, there was rhythm, there was a recognizable harmony. What impressed him the most was the relentlessness of the music. There were lyrics—he heard them—but his whole focus was grabbed by the sounds produced by the musicians.

From the beginning, he was snared by the textures. The sounds that Marla had assured him before were produced by a type of guitar—somehow combined with the miracle of electricity—had an edge to them, and edge that was like both a saw blade that cut and a string of barbed fish hooks that caught and tore. There was no virtuosity, no showcasing of a musician's skill at ornamentation. There was only pure relentlessness, pure passion, pure drive, that reached deep inside him and struck a resonance that vibrated his entire being. The song was not performed, it was executed, and he was the target of it, caught up in it, feeling nothing but the angst of the music.

After an eternity, the song gradually faded away. Franz fell back in his chair, suddenly released from the tension, feeling more drained than if he had been performing for hours. He looked around, and the others looked even worse than he felt—pale, eyes wide, breathing hard.

Marla looked around, smiling slightly, and asked, "Well, what do you think?"

"I think I've heard the triumphal march of Hell," Hermann muttered. "Nothing could have prepared me for that."

"Was that really popular in your time?" Leopold asked.

"Oh, yes," Marla said. "Millions of people, including my brother, loved the stuff. If he had . . . Let's just say that his heart's desire was to play it, and he was well on his way when he got sick."

"I liked it," Rudolf said, which provided everyone with their first glimpse of a disconcerted Marla.

"You did?"

"Yes. Oh, do not mistake me! I would not choose it to listen to all day long, nor do I think it will ever be accepted by our people—definitely not by the church. But there was a passion to it, and once you get past the harsh metallic sound you can tell that it was crafted well. We could learn about the use of discord and tension from that music."

Marla had smiled in the middle of Rudolf's comments, then started to giggle, and finally started laughing when he was finished. She calmed down quickly, wiping her eyes, and said, "I'm sorry, Rudolf, I wasn't laughing at you. It's just that you were righter than you knew when you described the sound as metallic. The band's name was Metallica."

"Appropriate." He smiled in return.

Marla stood and stepped forward a step or two. Franz watched with pride as she effortlessly gathered their eyes and attention.

"There's a lot more that we could listen to, but the point of the evening was to give you an overview of what we called popular music to wrap up the seminar. Now, we've walked down a long road all these weeks, but you've been given a taste of what up-time music is like, the sonorities and techniques it can add to your musical palette. I don't want it to replace everything that you have. I don't want you to become imitation up-timers. I want you to be the musicians you are, but along the way I want you to incorporate what you find good and worthy from our music. Help preserve its master works, but produce your own as well. Regardless of what happens with the war, regardless of whether Gustavus Adolphus wins or loses, regardless of whether or not Grantville survives, don't let our music die."

Franz stared at Marla, standing straight and tall, eyes gleaming like blue torches, passion radiating from her like heat, and his eyes blurred as tears of pride welled up. Now she was coming into her own, now she was calling them, challenging them to follow her, to be more than they ever thought they could be.

Hermann was the first on his feet. He stepped forward, clasped her hand, stared up at her and swore, "By my name, Fraulein Marla, I am with you. If your cause is lost, it will not be for want of my best effort."

Swiftly the others joined them, hands joined with Marla's and Hermann's. "The music of Grantville must not, will not die!" Thomas thundered.

"Amen!"

— Coda —

Magdeburg
August 1633

Mary Simpson picked the letter up and read it once more.

From the Desk of Marcus Wendell
Dear Mrs. Simpson

I received your request that I come to Magdeburg and become involved in the establishment of an instrumental arts program. While I am very flattered that you think so highly of me, I must regretfully decline.

What you need is a virtuoso, and even in my best days, in my youth, I was never a virtuoso. I am definitely not one now. I am good at what I do, which is take children and turn them into well-rounded educated individuals who know something about the arts and music. Every few years, I am fortunate enough to have a student or two of talent sufficient that I can guide them into a life of music as a teacher or minor performer. But that experience does not equip me to do the work you are asking of me. Bluntly speaking, I have neither the temperament nor the tools to be what you are seeking.

Having turned you down for myself, however, now let me provide you with another possibility. I don't happen to have a virtuoso in my pocket, but I perhaps can point you to someone who can become a virtuoso.

Her name is Kristen Marlena Linder, although she prefers to go by Marla. She's young, about 21. Physically, she's rather striking. I wouldn't call her pretty—handsome is a better word. She's tall by our standards, about 5'10" or so, and she has that amazing Black Irish coloration that you sometimes see in the Appalachian hill families: coal black hair, skin so pale it's almost translucent, a dusting of freckles, and the bluest of eyes. There were girls in her class at school who were prettier, but if she was in the room, most of the boys preferred to talk to her. Marla is definitely a good example of that old cliché, the magnetic personality. And if she smiles, it's like switching on a floodlamp.

She was a senior the year of the Ring of Fire, almost ready to graduate. Musically, she was my drum major during marching season that year, and my student conductor and first chair flute player during concert season, but that's not why I'm bringing her to your attention. She is also an extremely talented pianist, easily the equal of many collegiate piano majors. But perhaps her greatest gift is as a vocalist. She can vocalize to about four and one-half octaves, maybe a little more, and has a usable range of almost four octaves. Her voice is unusual—she has the high range of a coloratura, but the timbre and power of a lyric soprano.

As an indication of just how good she is, the day before the Ring fell I heard from a college friend who is the brother of a woman on the faculty at Eastman School of Music in New York. He told me that Eastman was going to offer her a full scholarship in voice. She had scholarship offers from other universities, but as you know, Eastman is a conservatory to rank with Juilliard. The official notice never arrived, of course. I never had the heart to tell her, because she was pretty badly torn up by losing her parents and brother, and this would have made her grief just that much worse.

She finally came out of her shell after meeting some down-time musicians this year, and for the last several months has been leading what I would consider to be a graduate level multidiscipline seminar in music history, form and analysis, and piano and voice performance with several down-timers using nothing more than a couple of old college textbooks, encyclopedia entries and liner notes from classical music recordings. They're all young and arrogant, of course, but she has not only held her own with them, she's earned their respect, to the point that they have basically accepted her as their leader and mentor. I don't have to tell you just how unusual that would be in our time that was. I am almost in awe of it now.

Mrs. Simpson, if a music teacher in my position is very fortunate, perhaps once in his lifetime he finds a student who can soar to the highest heights, who can become one of the stars in the musical firmament. For me, that once-in-a-lifetime student is Marla Linder.

Allow me to present Marla to you as a virtuoso in development. I believe she is the best solution available for the situation you have described. I also believe that if you were to provide to her the guidance that I cannot, the guidance on how to be a virtuoso among virtuosi, then her potential will be realized, to the enrichment of the world we now live in and the joy of those who know her.

Sincerely,
Marcus Wendell

Mary put the letter down on her desk, and tapped her finger against her lips, thinking. Marla . . . a woman . . . She must be a truly remarkable young woman, to have brought forth such a paean from Marcus Wendell. She hadn't had much contact with the band director during the Simpsons' relatively short stay in Grantville, but he had impressed her as a direct, outspoken man who would usually call a spade a spade. If he judged her so, then she must be good.

One of the things that Mary had been wrestling with was how to get up-time music somehow disseminated among the down-timers. That was the cornerstone to the plans she was even now trying to formulate for building an arts program in Magdeburg. An imperial capital deserved the best: opera, ballet, a symphony. Spreading the musical knowledge that she knew was available in Grantville had to happen for any of those programs to be sustainable.

The irony did not escape Mary that, even as she struggled with how to begin such a process, it had happened without her. With a quirky smile, she reminded herself that the world did not revolve around her. In fact, she'd best pull up her stockings and hustle if she wanted to guide this particular parade.

Mary reread the portion of the letter where Marcus described what Marla had done. A bond between an up-timer and down-timers, based on nothing more than the common love of great music. How remarkable.

Marla . . . a woman . . . Her thoughts repeated themselves. Mary liked the thought. She had never considered herself a feminist. In her college days, she had known plenty of fem-libbers. Some of them had become very impressive women in their maturity—she'd allow, albeit a bit grudgingly, that Melissa Mailey was no one to sneer at. But many had later morphed into the types who seemed to do nothing but whine endlessly, fund litigations over every perceived slight, and extend "political correctness" into even trying to revise the Bible to remove gender references to God. She'd never had much sympathy for them.

On the other hand, she *had* quietly encouraged John to ensure equal pay for equal work in his industrial plants. She'd always been of the opinion that if they were given a level playing field, women of any ability would do well.

Mary laughed to herself, almost wishing that one of those

so-called radicals had been caught in the Ring of Fire. That would almost have made what had happened worth it, to see one of them caught up in the truly patriarchal societies of the seventeenth century. She would really have enjoyed seeing one of them square off against some of the down-time ministers. Melissa Mailey could stand her own against them, certainly, but most of the ones Mary had known in college would just run for cover.

Shaking her head, Mary returned to her thoughts about Marla. The more she thought about it, the more she liked the fact that a young woman had become the center around which this group revolved. Under her aegis, perhaps this young woman could serve as a dash of cold water in the face of the smug musicians she'd met so far, the ones who were just parasites on the coats of the *Hoch-Adel.*

There had been conflicts between up- and down-timers on many fronts. In the early days of the naval yard, John had more than once spent an evening raving about problems caused by hardheaded Grantvillers and hardheaded Germans both getting wrapped up in their pride and arrogance. She didn't delude herself that it would be any different between the court musicians and Marla and her young lions. But the fact that Marla was a woman would perhaps keep the "old school" off balance.

She sat up straight. Decision made—invite Marla here. Why not? If she was that good, she was worth bringing in as a performer. If she could in time become something more than that, well...

Telegram? No, too impersonal. This needed a human touch. She pulled open a drawer and took out a sheet of cream-colored paper—they did make such nice paper here-and-now—and uncapped her fountain pen.

Dear Miss Linder,

My name is Mary Simpson, and I am writing to offer you an opportunity...

Lost in Translation

Iver P. Cooper

Spring 1634
Grantville

"Hans, you fool, where are you!"

Hans hurriedly entered the room. The master's face was red, and his eyes were bulging, making him look rather like a choleric bullfrog.

Uh-oh, he thought. *What is it this time*? He lowered his eyes. "Yes, master?"

"You took a book to the translators today?" asked Bullfrog Eyes.

"Yes, master, I am sorry I didn't get around to it yesterday, but—"

"Which... book...." Each word was carefully enunciated.

"The one you had rebound recently. The octavo with red covers. In the locked bookcase."

"Moron. Imbecile. Idiot." Bullfrog Eyes hurled a book at Hans. "*That's* the book you were supposed to bring them. As you see, it has red covers. But I am missing a very valuable book, an octavo with *green* covers. Which was in the same bookcase."

"I am sure I took them a red book..."

"Enough. You must retrieve it at once."

"I humbly beg your pardon, master. I will go to the translator's office first thing Monday morning."

"At once, I say!"

"I am sorry, master, but they are certainly closed for the day. In fact, for the weekend."

"Closed." Bullfrog Eyes now looked as though he had swallowed something unpleasant. It did not enhance his appearance.

"On the weekend, one of the translators might come by, and start reading the book. That won't do. No, that won't do at all." He stared at Hans. "You will have to break inside and fetch it back. Tonight."

Federico Ballarino contemplated the pile on his bed. *I hate packing,* he thought.

But he had to do it. Tomorrow morning he would be off to Magdeburg, to give Princess Kristina her dance lessons. And the following week he would be back in Grantville, to teach down-time dances to the up-timers, and continue his research into up-timer dances.

Bitty, the petite director of the Grantville Ballet, had told Federico that thanks to the Ring of Fire, he was now the World's First Long-Distance Commuter. It was a distinction he would have gladly done without.

If that weren't enough, he had gotten roped into helping out "Words International," the translation company. It had started when a couple of the foreign language teachers at the high school were asked to translate a few documents. A few became many, and they decided to form a company to parcel out the translation work to whoever was willing and able to do the job. The foreign language teachers, trying to fit it in during the evening, on weekends, and over the summer, couldn't keep up with the demand.

It was all Nicole's fault. Nicole, the French teacher, knew that Federico had taught dance in France. Nicole pleaded that she was already teaching two adult sections of European History after the regular school day had ended. Could Federico please help with the translations into French? At least until the end of the regular school year? You said you like to read on the train, didn't you?

Sighing, Federico added the green-covered octavo to the pile.

Hans' employment with Bullfrog Eyes was not a matter of choice on Hans' part. It was the price for Bullfrog Eyes' silence about certain events in Hans' past. Hans wasn't entirely sure how

Bullfrog Eyes knew about his background. But he was sure that Bullfrog Eyes had deliberately sought out a servant with a secret.

Of course, there were secrets and secrets. Bullfrog Eyes didn't know, at least not yet, about Hans' other problem. The vision thing. Hans was afraid to tell him. Perhaps he would no longer be useful. Perhaps Hans would then be . . . disposable.

Hans stood in front of the Words International store. It was in an old, somewhat run-down commercial building, which had been divided up among several tenants. He looked up and down the street. For the first time in an hour, there was no one else in view. He gave the front door of Words International a swift hard kick.

"*Owww!*" He grabbed his injured foot and massaged it. He had assumed the door was ordinary wood. He now knew, the hard way, that it was just a wood veneer, with a metal core.

A few minutes later, the pain had eased enough for him to make a second attempt. This time one not involving forcing the door. There was a window he could climb through, once he dealt with the glass. He looked around, and while there was no shortage of pebbles, he wanted something with more heft. Hans sighed and hobbled down the street. He had to go several blocks before he found a likely place to hunt that was away from curious eyes. He picked up a suitable stone, and walked back.

He hefted it and . . . every time he even thought about throwing it, someone came down the street, or out of the tavern next door to Words International, and he had to hide it. Once, he actually dropped it, narrowly missing his injured foot.

Worse, he was starting to attract attention. The bouncer for the tavern was giving him the eye. Hans decided to move along, and come back later.

After walking a few blocks, he saw another drinking place. *Why not?* he thought. *I have to kill the time anyway.*

Sometime later, he staggered out. He returned to Words International, but its neighborhood was still hopping.

Then he had an inspiration. Perhaps he could try the roof?

But he had better collect some tools. The house which his master was renting came with an ax and saw, for cutting firewood. The ax had a blade on one side, and a pick point on the other. Hans approved. He also grabbed the hooded lantern he carried when he escorted the master on evening errands, and his "lighting kit." Flint, steel, and a tinderbox, that is.

It was a pity he didn't have one of those American "backpacks," so he could carry them with his hands free. No matter. He loaded them, and a rope, into a sack and carried them outside. Hans realized that it looked a little suspicious to be carrying a sack like that at night, but Hans figured that an ax and a saw would look even worse.

He sidled into an alley, and worked his way behind Words International. *Too bad. No windows on this side.* He tied one end of the rope around the mouth of the sack, tight as he could, and the other end around his waist. He struggled his way up a drainpipe, pulling himself at last onto the roof. He collected himself, let his breathing settle down. Then he gingerly hauled up the sack, hoping that neither the rope nor the sack would give way.

He took out his tools and, moving in a half-crouch, examined the roof, looking for a likely spot to begin. He couldn't waste time, it would be dawn soon enough. But had to work cautiously to minimize the noise he made.

Hans was equally worried about being seen. But there was a peculiar metal structure on top of the roof. He figured that he could use it to block any view of him from the street. And that would let him use a bit of light, which would make the search go faster.

Hans took out his lighting kit, and huddled over it. He tapped out the tinder into an untidy pile, and struck the steel with his flint. Sparks flew, and flitted into the tinder. There were glows here and there, which he blew on carefully. At last, he had a decent flame. He quickly lit the lantern, and snuffed out the tinder with his foot.

What was that? he thought. There was some kind of panel on the structure. He studied it more closely, bringing the lantern close up. Yes, there was a bit of separation on one edge. He forced the pick end of his ax into the crack, and started prying. His muscles strained—damn American technology—and then all at once it popped free. He almost dropped the ax.

There was an empty space beyond the opened panel, and beneath it, some kind of shaft. He stuck his head into the dark opening, and listened for a moment. He didn't hear anything suspicious, but he did feel warm air coming up. That was interesting. Was this a way inside? What was it, anyway? An up-timer would have recognized it as a rooftop air conditioning unit, but it was completely beyond Hans' experience.

Hans held the lantern inside the structure and tried to look down. Metal glinted but he couldn't really tell much. He carefully tied his rope around the handle of his saw, and gingerly lowered it down. After a few feet, he heard a *chink*, of metal against metal. He didn't know what to make of it.

Hans considered his options. It would be nice not to have to cut through the damn roof. But he didn't think he could take his lantern with him into the shaft, so any further exploration would be blind.

He shrugged. He tied one end of his rope around a pipe that came out of the roof just beside the RFU, and the other around his waist. It would keep him from falling, if there were something odd about the shaft, and also make it easier to back up if he had to.

Taking a deep breath, he leaned in. He pressed his hands and thighs outward against the sides of the shaft, to control his descent, and he started to snake down. The blood rushed to his head. After a few moments, his hair grazed the bottom of the shaft. He explored, first with one hand, then the other. It seemed like there were horizontal passages. Narrower, unfortunately, than the shaft he was hanging in. It all seemed very familiar all of a sudden, like something he had seen in an American movie at the Gardens, on their TV.

Hans wrinkled his nose. Mama didn't raise a boy stupid enough to try crawling through a passage that small in the dark, with no one to pull him back out if there was a problem, he decided. He would leave the vent-crawling to Bruce Willis.

Hans pushed himself off the bottom of the shaft, and laboriously worked his way back the way he had come. Outside, he untied himself with relief.

What was the American phrase? "On to 'Plan B.'" Hans spat on his palms, rubbed them together, and hefted the ax.

With a combination of axing and sawing, Hans had made a Hans-size hole in the roof. Well, a few feet across, at least. The lantern beam revealed a maze of cables and vents. Looking at the vents from this angle, Hans gave thanks that he hadn't gone any farther with his John McClane imitation.

Below the tangle was a peculiar checkerboard structure. It appeared that there were square panels of one of the peculiar American materials resting between, and perhaps on, metal strips. Ah, yes, he remembered now. The ceiling of the translator's shop had a square pattern. Hans had thought it was some kind of decoration, he hadn't realized that the squares were removable.

At least, Hans hoped they were removable. He looked for nails and screws, but didn't notice any. Then he started tapping the structure gingerly with the top of his ax. He wondered whether it would take his weight, let him crawl around and pick exactly where he dropped to the floor of the store.

Nicole Hawkins hadn't planned to stop by the Words International office that morning. But she hadn't been able to find her earring at home, or at her classroom, and she was getting desperate. The pair had been a gift from her second husband, Barry, who had been left up-time.

She opened the door, flicked on the lights, and locked the door behind her. A girl couldn't be too careful, even in Grantville. She headed over to the desk that she usually worked at. The earring wasn't on the desktop, or on the floor nearby. Sighing, she got down on hands and knees, and expanded her search area.

That's when she heard the noise. Rats, she wondered?

She heard a more pronounced thump. Definitely not rats, unless they were of the man-sized variety. It seemed to be coming from the ceiling. Somewhere above the ceiling, to be precise. It was a standard office-type suspended ceiling, with big two-by-two acoustic tiles.

She thought for a moment of running out the door. But if someone had somehow broken in above, he might have an accomplice waiting outside.

Nicole, moving as slowly as she could, unlocked the special drawer. A revolver had been kept there ever since the Croat Raid, just in case.

She readied the weapon, hid behind a desk, and waited.

She saw a side of a ceiling tile lift up, ever so slowly and the ceiling tile started to slide away.

Nicole fired at where she guessed the burglar would be perched.

There was an answering shriek.

Hans was lucky; Nicole wasn't a great shot.

But he didn't know that, and he wasn't eager to present the shooter more of a target.

Hans hadn't tried to crawl around on the suspended ceiling, he had just pulled up the tile directly under the hole he had made in the roof. So he was able to pull back quickly enough.

Nicole, still holding the revolver, and keeping her eye on the opening, picked up the phone. She took the receiver off the hook, and dialed the police station one handed. "Come quickly, someone is trying to break into Words International. From the ceiling. I shot at him. I don't know if I hit him."

"Help's on the way," said the dispatcher. "What the heck are you doing in the shop at this hour, Nicole?" The dispatcher was Jim Watteville, Nicole's cousin.

Hans made it safely away, leaving the tools behind him. Still, he could predict, well enough, how Bullfrog Eyes would react to the news of the bungled burglary.

He left his employer a brief note explaining what had happened, packed his bags, and hurried out of town.

Blackmail, he figured, worked only if the blackmailer could find the blackmailee.

The fireman came down from the roof. "I put back on the inspection panel for the RTU return air plenum. And I covered the hole with a tarp, to keep the rain out. But you're going to want to get a roofer out here, quick as you can."

Nicole nodded.

"Nice to know you can shoot when there's need," he added.

"I didn't hit the guy."

"You sure scared him," said Jim approvingly. He had hurried over as soon as he found someone to cover the phone. "Left all his stuff there. If he's been arrested in Grantville before, we'll have his fingerprints on file.

"After something like this, we need to give you a fitting nickname."

"Nickname?" Nicole sounded suspicious.

"Yep. How 'bout 'Raptor' Hawkins?"

"Raptor?" asked the fireman.

"Right. Remember *Jurassic Park*?"

"Oh, yeah. When everyone was hiding up in the suspended ceiling, and the raptor was leaping up at them."

"That's enough," said Nicole with raptorlike ferocity. "Out, both of you. I better call some roofers right now."

The men chuckled as they went out the door.

"*Grrr*," said Jim to no one in particular, one hand held in imitation of a claw, as the door swung shut.

"*Grrr* yourself," said Nicole.

Bullfrog Eyes crumpled the note and tossed it into the fire. Watching it burn, he wished the same fate upon Hans.

He felt his chest tighten, and forced himself to calm down. Well, he decided, he would have to visit Words International himself, this very day, and hope that someone was in. And that whoever was there had the book, and hadn't examined it too closely.

Just in case... he made sure his dirk was well concealed.

"What a day," Nicole muttered. Having gone to the trouble of going to the office, not to mention scaring off burglars and sweet-talking roofers, she had decided to stay there and get some work done. Not without an occasional nervous look at the ceiling. At least there were plenty of people on the street by now.

There was a knock at the door; she ignored it. The roofer had come and gone, the police had come and gone, she really, really didn't want to talk to anyone. Then came another knock.

Can't they read the sign? she thought. *It says* closed... *in ten different languages.*

The knocking became continuous.

She went to the window, saw that the intruder was a well-dressed, foreign looking gentleman. Presumably not the mysterious burglar.

She put the chain on the door and opened it cautiously. "The office is closed."

"I am so sorry, so sorry. My servant, he brought the wrong book to be translated. I have the correct one here. The book he brought, it was one I borrowed from an acquaintance, and I must return it before the owner leaves for Amsterdam later today."

"Did your servant give you a receipt?"

"Yes, yes, here it is." He stuck the paper into the gap, and Nicole took it from him.

"One moment, I'll check the ledger."

Nichole pulled the ledger out and ran her finger down the list. She walked back to the door. "It was one of the books we gave to Federico Ballarino to be translated."

"Where can I find this Federico?"

"At Cair Paravel."

Bullfrog Eyes raised his eyebrows. "Cair what?"

"I'm sorry. That's what Princess Kristina calls her official residence, the place she stays at when she visits Grantville."

"This Federico Ballarino, he is a member of the Swedish Court? But works for you as a translator?"

"He is the princess' dancing master, but he also teaches part-time at the high school. He speaks several languages.

"Anyway, I think he is on his way to Magdeburg today. He'll probably have the book with him. So he has reading matter for the train to Halle, and the barge ride afterward."

Bullfrog Eyes bowed slightly. "I will try to catch him at the train station, then. What does he look like? How does he usually dress for these trips?"

"Federico Ballarino? Yes, I know him," said the ticket clerk. "He's a regular. Got on the 9:30 to Halle."

Bullfrog Eyes cursed.

"Hey, don't work up a sweat. The 9:30 is a local. There's also a 1:10 express. If Federico is going to Magdeburg, he'll take the boat tomorrow morning."

"I have never met Signore Ballarino. Can you tell me what he was wearing?"

The clerk told him, then added. "Hey, I have a picture of him! He gave me a flyer for this dance exhibition he's doing in a few weeks. You want it?"

Bullfrog Eyes took it. There was just enough time, he figured, to go home and pack. Just the essentials. Like the Suhl-made rifle he was fond of.

The press at the dock was much greater than Bullfrog Eyes had expected. Every time he tried to move in the direction of Federico's distinctive hat, someone got in the way. He wished he had one of the Americans' machine guns. That would clear a path nicely.

The upshot was that Federico was on board, and Bullfrog Eyes was left watching the boat work its way into the main channel of the Saale.

Well, there were alternatives. The boat moved slowly, and there were several stops. Bullfrog Eyes would buy a horse, and get ahead of him.

☆ ☆ ☆

Federico shrugged off the backpack Nicole had lent him, and rummaged inside. It was time to read some more. He chose, by feel, the thinnest of the books. He pulled it out; it was a green-covered octavo.

He zipped up the backpack and put it back on. He had mixed feelings about the backpack. Yes, yes, it made it easier to carry things. But he didn't like what it did to his balance.

Bullfrog Eyes was in a clump of woods, not far from the landing at Bernberg. He still hadn't decided whether it was better to talk to Federico, find out what he knew, and, if he were ignorant, retrieve the book without arousing suspicion . . . or to just shoot him. The latter would silence him, but if the book couldn't be recovered, there was always the possibility that the police would take interest in it.

Federico was a bit puzzled. This book, it was interesting enough, he supposed, but not really the sort which down-timers were likely to pay to get translated. He inspected the inside covers, wondering whether there was anything written there which revealed the identity of the owner, and thus, perhaps, why he wanted the translation.

That's when Federico noticed the slit in the binding. He probed with his fingers. There was a letter there; he pulled it out. It was sealed. He wondered what it was doing there.

The boat came around the river bend, moving slowly as it made the turn. There was Federico, all right. But what was that in his hand?

Bullfrog Eyes raised the rifle, and took aim.

Federico had one hand on the letter, and the other on the book. When the shot rang out, he had no hand to spare for the boat.

On the dance floor, Federico was extremely graceful. He also didn't normally wear a backpack. Bullfrog Eyes' shot grazed Federico's cheek. Surprised, he lost his balance, and toppled backward into the water.

"Got him!" thought Bullfrog Eyes. He watched anxiously to see whether Federico resurfaced.

The other passengers on the barge had taken cover, as best they could. Still, it was only a matter of time before they spotted Bullfrog Eyes. While he was in disguise, that wouldn't help if he were caught before he had a chance to change back to his normal appearance.

The barge continued its ponderous movement downstream. In the riverbend, there was no sign of Federico. Or even his hat.

Bullfrog Eyes nodded with satisfaction. It had been a perfect assassination, Federico dead, and the book and letter lost forever. He worked his way back through the brush to his horse, pulled off the cloak he had been wearing, and rode off in the direction of Halle.

Federico had, somewhat to his surprise, managed, despite his unexpected dip, to hold on to both the letter and the book. They were somewhat the worse for wear, thanks to treading water briefly with them in hand. Once he had recovered from his shock, he had tucked them both inside his blouse and swum to the side of the boat.

Federico held on, using the hull to conceal himself from the shooter. "Could he really have been aiming at me?" he wondered. "And if so, why? Because I am Catholic, but am the dance instructor for a Lutheran princess? Because I told the shooter at some dance class that he had two left feet?"

It had been a lousy weekend for Federico. He had to give a statement to the dim-witted constable in Bernberg. Then another at the police station in Magdeburg. Once he got to the palace, the palace guard had more questions for him. Could this possibly be part of some plot against the Princess Kristina? More than a bit snappish by that point, Federico suggested that they interrogate the Ice Queen. He learned by this to never, ever, make a joke when questioned by the police. Their uniform entitles them to make all the jokes.

"Welcome back, Federico." The speaker was Jim Watteville, Nicole's cousin. He was still in uniform, having just come off duty.

"I could wish you weren't in uniform, Jim."

"Trouble with the police?"

"Trouble is too strong a word. 'Exasperation,' that will do." Federico explained.

"Weird," said Jim. "Care to join me for a drink? It is the least I can do, to make amends for the follies of policedom."

"That's fine. But I have an errand to run first, I want to drop off the last of the books I was supposed to translate on this trip. And explain to the owner what happened. He's about a five minute walk from here."

"I'll join you; we can go straight to the Gardens from there."

"You go in, Federico, I'll wait out here," Jim said.

Federico knocked. A servant answered. Not Hans, of course.

"Who may I say is calling?"

"Tell your master that it is a representative from Words International."

"Ah, he must be here to apologize for the loss of my book. I will let him grovel a bit, then tell him that I will waive my claim for the loss. Bring him in."

A moment later, Federico strode into Bullfrog Eyes' study.

"*Urkhh*," said the dumbfounded would-be murderer.

"I am Federico Ballarino, a translator in the employ of Words International. I regret to inform you that the volume you entrusted to us is a bit damaged." He held up the infamous green-bound octavo.

"And then there is the matter of the letter that was inside." Federico held that up; Bullfrog Eyes could see that it was no longer sealed. He moved his hand, very slowly, toward a drawer that held a small pistol.

Just then, Jim walked in. "What's taking so long?" Out of habit, his hand rested near his service revolver. Back in West Virginia, police dispatchers didn't go around armed, but since the Ring of Fire, it had become normal.

Bullfrog Eyes whitened. There were two of them. Federico had his sword; the hilt was visible through a fold in his cloak. Jim had a handgun and was primed to use it. Clearly, they were ready to arrest him. There were probably Swedish armsmen, in Princess Kristina's service, waiting outside.

Fighting didn't seem wise. And he couldn't flee easily, either; they blocked the only readily accessible exit from his study. They would hardly stand by while he broke a window.

Fight. Flight. Fight. Flight. His mind raced back and forth

between both unpromising alternatives, like an animal pacing inside a box trap.

Then his body selected a third choice. His chest tightened convulsively, his vision blurred, and the floor reached up to slug him.

The EMT shook his head. "Sorry. He's dead, Jim."

"I guess we'll have to notify his next of kin," the dispatcher said. "Federico, was that letter addressed to anybody that might qualify?"

"I couldn't say." Federico shrugged. "I was just about to apologize to the guy—the letter was probably a treasured love letter, or something of the sort—but after its swim in the Saale, all the writing was smeared beyond recognition."

"Lost in translation," Jim quipped.

Sailing Upwind

Kevin H. Evans & Karen C. Evans

Late September, 1633

"Sally, did Mr. Pridmore say where he was going?" Reva leaned toward the young receptionist, to keep the conversation a little more private. Reva worried about Marlon. He hadn't been eating or sleeping well for the last week. Just like he had last September, he'd gotten moody and irritated. And today, instead of finishing work, he just stood up and walked out of his office.

"No, Miz Pridmore. When he didn't see you, he told me to tell you he was feeling poorly, and then got his coat and left."

"Yeah. I guess he's got the flu, just like last year." Reva went back to her station behind the teller window. *No use going after him. I might as well finish work.*

"You sitting here moping again?" Reva came into the living room to hang her coat in the closet. While lights were on in other parts of the house, he was sitting alone in the dark. "I swear, you're gonna wear me out with your sour moods this time of year."

Marlon grumbled, "Tomorrow is October first. This weekend would be the beginning of the Albuquerque Balloon Fiesta. And I let Hilde down again."

"I know. I heard it all last year. Same old story. You were gonna help him get the money for an airship, and then you weren't there to hand it over. Nothing new. I thought you were over this."

She waited for him to respond, and when he didn't she continued. "I've worked at that bank with you for more than twenty years, and put up with your moods here at home. But you don't have an excuse to sit here and feel sorry for yourself. You don't need to be in here moping like this, Marlon Pridmore. Life goes on."

He glared at her. It was an old argument. "Reva, you just don't understand. I gave them my word and I failed. I've been adjusting, but when it starts to get to fall weather like this rain, it makes me long for the things we used to do. You enjoyed that balloon fiesta as much as I did, and you know it."

"Now, don't pull me into this mess, old man. Yes, I liked going to Albuquerque just fine. But that was then, this is now. We can't go back, and that's that."

He stood up and started walking toward the kitchen. "I'm going out to the barn. Don't wait up." He walked out the back door, hands shoved into his pockets.

Marlon sat out in the dark barn, drinking *kirshwasser* in memory of Hilde, mourning the loss of his friend once again. Marlon and Reva had both grown up in Grantville and most of their family still lived in the area. They had never had children, so there were no grandchildren left up-time. Now all that Marlon missed from West Virginia, besides getting a new computer once in a while, was Hilde and balloons.

Hilde and Marlon had planned to get some investors, including a loan from Marlon's bank, and buy the envelope and basket for a thermal airship. This wasn't just any balloon; it was a hot air blimp that could be steered against the wind. It was going to be their entry in the Gatineau Challenge, a thermal airship race with the prize of half a million dollars.

Reva found him in the barn later that night. She stepped under the single bare light bulb and put her hands on her hips. "Okay, I've had it!"

"You just don't understand! I gave my word I'd be there, and there's no way I can get there now."

"Listen here, Marlon Pridmore. You need to stop this pity party of yours, and go build yourself a balloon. You can do it. There ain't anyone here down-time that knows more about it than you do. But it ain't gonna happen with you out here drinking brandy, and feeling sorry—"

Marlon interrupted. "What did you say?"

"I said you need to stop this pity party—"

"No. The part about the balloon."

Reva stopped glaring, and laughed. "Swordfish, you're an idiot. What you miss isn't that silly airship project you set up in Leipzig. You miss spending time with balloonists. You miss flying. I just think that if you want a balloon so bad, there isn't anyone around here that knows more about building one than you, now is there?"

Marlon thought for a moment. He'd never considered building his own airship. Up-time, it was much easier and safer to have a professional company sew the envelope out of high tech materials, and just gather the money together to buy it. He took another sip of the brandy, then looked at his glass. He couldn't seem to remember why he was sitting out in this damp barn drinking in the first place.

Reva shook her head, then hurried back into the house. He sat for a moment more, then stood and ambled over to an old dresser at the back of the barn. He had always used it for plans and notes and such. Maybe there was still some of that graph paper in one of the drawers.

"Herr Pridmore, have you been out here all night?"

"Hmm? Is that you, Bernard? What time is it?"

"It is just before dawn, time for me to milk the cows. Can't you hear them calling me?"

"Oh, yes, so I can. Well, don't let me stop you." Marlon was busily drawing diagrams, figuring volume, referring to old ballooning magazines that had been stashed in the bottom drawer of his dresser.

Bernard Brenner, with his wife Agnes and his fifteen-year-old daughter, Hanna, had come to town as refugees in 1631. Bernard had been a distiller of cherry wine before the war destroyed his village. Now the Brenner family was woven in as part of the Pridmore family. By now, Bernard was accustomed to Marlon's eccentricities, like becoming obsessed with an idea, and forgetting to eat or sleep.

Marlon looked up from the paper. "Bernard, what do you

know about cloth? I think I have a new project that you can help me with."

It was late in the day when Marlon and Bernard came back from the barn. Agnes had peeked at them several times that day, and even taken lunch out when they didn't show any sign of stopping to eat.

"Reva, I think we can do it. Sure, Bernard and I have to do some more research, and it's anyone's guess what it's going to cost, but I think we can get the cloth we need and somehow make it hold hot air."

"Well, I kind of thought there would be a way. I'm sure that you can find someone either here in town or up in Magdeburg that can give you price estimates and such."

"That's what I'm thinking, hon. Look at these here figures, and tell me, do you think we can afford to do this? You know what we have, and what we need to keep going. What do you think?"

Reva sat down at the kitchen table and spread out the papers that Marlon handed her. Together they looked over the figures and diagrams. "Well, Marlon. I guess it depends on what you're willing to give up. You're probably going to have to sell some things. And it isn't going to happen all at once. We're going to have to take some time to raise some money. But I can see us doing this over the next couple of years. That is, if you're willing to give up some of your other toys and projects."

Marlon grinned like a ten-year-old boy who had caught his first fish. He pulled Reva to her feet and swept her into a big hug. "Sweetpea, we can sell whatever you say to get this done."

April 1635

It took almost two years, but finally it was coming together. The gondola, woven from wicker, was complete, and the last shipment of Indian muslin had been delivered. So this morning, Marlon and Bernard were busily working on their toy. Marlon was in the yard stirring a huge vat of brown smelly stuff.

"What is in that stuff?" asked Bernard.

"This, Bernard, is a modern miracle. It is a conglomeration of lacquer, gum Arabic, turpentine, and resin. It's gonna keep the hot air where it belongs."

"So you say, Herr Pridmore. But how do we get it on the envelope?"

"I'm glad you asked that, Bernard. We're going to soak each and every piece of cloth in this stuff and let it dry. Local weather wizards say we have about a week of clear weather, so we've got to jump on this."

"Oh, I see. Hmm. I think I've something to do in town..."

"No, you don't. You're my helper, and this is what you're helping with. Reva already bailed out on me, said she'd rather boil soap. Can you imagine that?"

Bernard looked as though he, too, would rather stir stinking soap over a hot fire than drag fifty-foot lengths of cloth through the vat and lay them out to dry. But there was no escape.

"Don't worry. I got more help coming. You remember them boy scouts over at the Methodist church? One of the boys won't let me alone with questions about hot air balloons. The Council has agreed to allow him to work on a hot air balloon merit badge, and named me as the local expert. He and about ten of his friends are headed over to learn how to build a balloon. With all those hands, and youthful enthusiasm, we should be able to get through this today."

The boy scouts arrived in good time, and all set to work with a will. The weather was fine and warm, and while it was uncomfortable standing by the fire, the breeze helped. By the end of the day, the muslin was coated and drying on every bush and clothes line in sight. Marlon, Bernard, and eleven boy scouts were coated with gummy brown stuff from head to toe.

September 1635

Ulrich Schwarz frequently felt like he wasn't a good choice for leadership of a scout troop. He had never been a boy scout, and wasn't always comfortable with all the customs of the troop. The boys knew much more about the requirements and the confusing paperwork for these merit badges. He had been methodically working through his first-class qualification, sharing one of the books they had for the group of new scouts.

He liked the idea of Boy Scouts. It really was a good idea to have training for young boys, and the uniforms and mottos were certainly uplifting. But he still didn't feel comfortable as the authority.

"Herr Schwarz, have you ever read *Tom Sawyer*?" The question brought Ulrich back to reality.

"No, I do not read English so good, yet. Do you like it?"

Fritz Metzger and J. D. Cunningham were bent over a book, trying to read it together. "Yeah. I think it's great," said J.D. He was an up-timer, and seemed inseparable from his friend Fritz. "See, there is this boy named Tom, and he's got a friend called Huck. And they go on adventures, and get into a lot of trouble."

Ulrich wasn't sure how advisable it was to give these boys a book about more trouble. They were well capable of finding their own.

"Boys, it is time to put the book aside. We must start our troop meeting." Ulrich watched as almost twenty boys ranging from ages eleven to fifteen settled into chairs. The meeting was held in a classroom at the Methodist church, and it was the first time that Ulrich had to run the meeting. Between the colds and flu that were going around, he was the only adult available today.

After the opening flag ceremony, and recitation of the motto, Ulrich nodded to Levi Carstairs, the oldest boy. Levi stood and walked to the front, carrying a small pocket notebook.

"Before we get to today's activities, I want to remind you about the Orienteering Hike we've got this weekend. We have permission to set up the course in the hunting preserve of the duke of Saxe-Weimar on the northeast of town. It's only a couple of miles away. How many of you need this for first class qualifications?"

Only the two youngest raised their hands. Levi nodded, and then looked at Ulrich. "Herr Schwarz is going with the Tenderfoots, so you two make sure you take good care of him. Mrs. Moss wouldn't take it too well if you let her handyman get lost."

"No, and neither would my platoon sergeant." Ulrich had been sworn into the army when he turned eighteen and was very proud of his rank of Private First Class. If only it was as easy to get a promotion in the scouts.

Levi looked sternly at the boys. "Now for the rest of you. We will meet here at the church on Saturday morning. Remember to be on time!"

☆ ☆ ☆

Everything for the balloon was ready. Reva and Agnes had worked hard to get the enormous envelope sewn together. It was a good thing that Reva owned one very good sewing machine, and the other older one she had kept after upgrading.

Bernard and Marlon were in the barn, gathering bits and pieces. Marlon grinned and asked his friend, "Where is Hanna today? She was up so early."

"She went with some of the girls from school. I don't know exactly what their plans are, but they have chaperones along. Agnes is with her. That soldier, Ulrich Schwarz, has been showing a little too much interest in her lately, and Agnes decided to put a stop to 'accidental meetings.'"

Marlon straightened from where he was laying out all his brand new instrumentation. "I think I've met that young man. He stays over there with Geneva Moss, doesn't he? I heard he was helping supervise a boy scout troop. Those boys get a mite rambunctious now and again. Ulrich seems to have a steady hand with them, without losing his temper. Good practice for him, I'd say."

"Ah, Marlon. You just don't understand. You don't have a daughter who is approaching womanhood. When I see all the young men in town follow her with their eyes, I just want to knock their heads together."

Marlon smiled and crouched to the ground. Along with the instruments he had built for the airship, he laid out the handheld radio that he and Reva had used on chase crews over the years. And Reva insisted that he add in the first-aid kit he had carried in his car for a couple of years.

"Herr Pridmore, those instruments are amazing. Do you think they will work?"

Marlon smiled and nodded. "Yes, I think they will. I've done all the tests on them that I can think of. Now we just need the field test."

Saturday morning arrived with clearing skies, which calmed one of Ulrich's fears. He had done maneuvers with the army in the rain, but he really didn't relish the thought of dealing with the boys in that weather.

Levi whistled for quiet, and stood on a stump that was there just for that purpose. "Okay, everybody. This hike today is for Orienteering. I want everyone to remember that as scouts, we leave a site better than we found it. We don't disturb the trees or animals, and only pick up deadwood if we need it. We want the duke to be glad he let us use his preserve again. And make sure that everyone stays with their group. Safety first, you know.

"Now, who has a compass?" Five of them held up their hands. Ulrich did also. "Right. There are seventeen of us here this morning. Let's break up into three- or four-man groups, and share the compasses. And we have a small prize for the first team that finishes the course and returns with the flag. Here are your instructions."

The boys sorted themselves into groups, and Ulrich found himself with Fritz and J.D. Fritz said, "Herr Scoutmeister, I have your compass, and a canteen. J.D. can carry lunch for us, and we will let you be in charge of the instructions. Is that okay?"

"*Ja*. That is good. We can trade later, so J.D. learns to use the compass also."

Levi held up his whistle and shouted to be heard over the tumult. "Everybody ready? On your marks! Get set! *Go!*" He blew a mighty blast on the whistle.

Like racehorses responding to the trumpet, the boys took off at a run. It had begun.

Marlon and Bernard spread the envelope out flat on the grass. Flattened, the envelope was more than one hundred fifty feet long, and sixty feet wide, and weighed four hundred fifty pounds. This airship was a monster! It had a gondola that would seat three and mounted two forty-horsepower ducted fan engines (robbed from two defunct dirt bikes). The frame had an inverted "V" tail. Lift was provided from a set of internal burners that blew hot air inside the sealed envelope. The gondola was hung from curtain catenaries.

"Bernard, the difference between this beast and a regular hot air balloon is the engines. If we didn't have them and the vector fans, we would be subject to the whim of the wind."

Bernard nodded as he listened to Marlon, but truly it didn't make much sense to him. He hadn't seen a "regular hot air balloon" to compare to this one. It would just have to wait until they got it up in the air.

Ulrich shook his head as he tried to make sense of the directions. They had been walking for two hours, and had not found point M, which was the second to last mark on the map before the flag. It had not been as long between any of the other locations, and he was sure that they were lost. It also didn't help that none of them had been here for other scout activities.

"J.D., hand me the map again." Ulrich had already examined it not five minutes before, and this time didn't change anything. They were still lost. He didn't recognize any of the landmarks.

Fritz held up the compass once again. "I think we have come too far north and not far enough east. What should we do?"

"Well, a scout should always be prepared. What did you bring for emergencies?"

"I brought a blanket in my pack, in case it rained again," J.D. said.

Fritz's eyes lit up. "I have some extra crackers and cheese."

"Good. You're both learning to be prepared. If we do not find our way home tonight, someone will come and find us. And I think we have enough to be okay tonight." Ulrich could tell that the boys tried hard to keep fear from their faces. It would not do to act like babies.

Ulrich looked around, and pointed to a hill southwest of them that seemed taller than the others around. "We will go to that hill, climb to the top, and see if we can spot something familiar from there. I think the sun has only two more hours before it sets, and we may have to be out here after dark."

Getting everything laid out, strapped on the gondola, and prepared for inflation took the men most of the daylight, with a short break for sandwiches and beer.

"Well, look at you two, smug as a cat with a mouse between his paws," said Reva.

"Darlin', I think this thing is really gonna run. You shoulda seen the fire-up on the burners before we set them in the envelope. Bernard just about burned off his left eyebrow." Marlon elbowed the tall, thin German in the ribs, and laughed.

Bernard grinned sheepishly. "One would think that I would remember to keep *mein* head away from it."

"I think you were mistrusting me about whether or not this thing would really burn."

Bernard frowned. "I've never seen something like this. How was I to know?"

Agnes hurried over to examine Bernard. Marlon stretched, and looked at the horizon west of his place. The sun had already passed behind them, and the sky was darkening. He shook his head. "I think it's too late to try this today. Don't want to be fiddling in the dark."

Reva put her hand on her hip, and got that same old belligerent look. "'Course not. Just get your tarps and whatnot, and cover it up till morning, and we can go in and have a nice supper."

She walked back into the house, shaking her head, and muttering to herself. Reva didn't always need others around to have a conversation, especially when she was irritated with Marlon.

Her husband grinned at her back, then turned to Hanna. "So, girl, you gonna be around in the morning to help with liftoff?"

Hanna's eyes glowed. "Yes, I think I will. But it doesn't look like it will fly. It looks like an auto with a very large cloth cover."

"Oh, it'll fly, all right. You just be here at five A.M. and see for yourself."

Ulrich and the boys neared the top of the ridge. There weren't too many trees, and bare rock jutted from the side of the trail they followed. At the crest, both boys sat on a large boulder to catch their breath. The walk uphill had been a little longer than Ulrich thought it would be.

He looked out over the landscape, and didn't see one thing that he could identify on the map. They were well and truly lost.

"All right. I cannot see a way to go, and it is almost dark. Right here by this rock will be a good place to shelter. J.D., you start gathering some wood. And remember to only pick up dead branches. We don't want to disturb this forest any more than we already have."

Ulrich and the two boys huddled together under J.D.'s blanket. They were burrowed into dead leaves between the roots of an oak tree.

It had gotten cold. Ulrich slipped out of the blanket to put more wood on the little fire, and then stepped out from under the branches of the tree. The night was very dark. No starlight, or even the moon, was visible through the clouds. At least it wasn't raining.

He turned at a small rustling sound behind him. "Who is there?" he whispered.

"It's me, Fritz. I've to go."

"Okay. Over there by that hazel bush. Be careful in the dark."

As Fritz scampered off toward the area they had decided was

their privy, Ulrich sat back down by the fire. The crackers and cheese they had eaten at dusk now seemed ages away. He was saving Frau Moss' oatmeal cookies for breakfast. Now he wished he had thought to carry more food. They had enough water, but not much else.

"Fritz, where are you? You have been gone so long. Are you all right?"

There was no answer. Ulrich checked the fire, and on J.D., snoring away in the pile of old leaves. Both could be alone for a few minutes. He stood for a moment outside the circle of firelight to let his eyes adjust, and then walked toward the bush.

"Fritz?" Ulrich listened for a moment, and then heard leaves rustling and the soft crack of a twig. It was coming off to his left. "Fritz, are you there? Fritz?"

Still he could hear nothing except rustling leaves. And he couldn't tell if it was Fritz, or a slight wind in the treetops.

Then a terrified scream split the night. It was ahead of him, and a little more to the left. "Fritz, answer me!"

"Ulrich? Can you hear me?"

"Yes, Fritz. Where are you?"

"I . . . I don't know."

"Just keep talking, and I will find you." Ulrich thought that Fritz's voice sounded strained and frightened.

"Ulrich, my leg really hurts. I thought I saw a light over here, but when I came toward it, the ground suddenly disappeared."

Ulrich was inching forward with his hands feeling the dark ground in front of him. "Keep talking, Fritz. I am close. I will help."

"I thought it was a lantern or something through the trees, and I thought I could find someone to help us. I guess it was a witch light, like in *Tom Sawyer*."

Ulrich felt bare rock, then nothing. He laid down on his belly, and inched forward until his head was hanging out over a chasm. In the darkness, it was difficult to tell how large it was. Fritz had fallen into a sinkhole. "Fritz, where are you hurt?"

"I don't know, Herr Scoutmeister. My arm isn't moving too well, and my leg really hurts." Ulrich could hear suppressed tears in the boy's voice.

"Don't move! I will get a light."

☆ ☆ ☆

Marlon rolled out of bed promptly at 4:30 A.M., as he had done every morning at any balloon rally he had attended. Balloonists know that in the hour right at dawn, the air is at its coolest—which aids in hot-air inflation—and the wind was usually still. He didn't want to inflate this monster in anything more than a one- to two-knot ground breeze.

"I'm going to go start breakfast," Reva said, a bit drowsily.

"Woman, don't bother with food right now. I got too much on my mind for that."

"I got something special planned for you, you old goat. I don't want no backtalk, either. You hear me?" The last was delivered with a stern expression, but the twinkling gray eyes and wry smile let Marlon know she was teasing him.

He grinned. "Yes, ma'am."

Bernard and Hanna were pulling on coats and work gloves. Marlon pulled his old leather gloves from his back pocket and did the same. "I'm kind of glad we don't have everyone in the neighborhood underfoot when we try to launch today."

Bernard nodded. "*Ja*, it is better to fail without an audience."

"What do you mean, fail? Don't you think we'll get it off the ground?" Marlon turned his grin on Hanna. "Maybe I shoulda had you get that young man to help us today. We've still got a lot of work ahead to get this beast off the ground." Marlon's eyes twinkled as he teased her. "What was his name? Oh, yeah, Ulrich. Maybe he could come over and help out. We could use another strong back."

"I think he does not like me now," Hanna said. "He said he would call last night when he got back from the hike. But he didn't."

"That's too bad. He'd have been a great help."

Bernard frowned. "I think we can do this without that man."

Marlon laughed out loud. "Well, Bernard, we're gonna have to, I guess."

They proceeded out to the meadow. The morning was crisp and cold, just like the weather guessers said it would be. In the pre-dawn, the wind still hadn't risen and that argued for little or no wind at dawn.

"We need to christen this ship before we launch," Marlon said. "And I think I know what to name her. Hanna, go ask Reva for something fizzy to launch this with."

Moments later, she returned carrying a beer bottle, and a strange paper contraption, followed by Reva and Agnes.

Laughing, Marlon took the items. "Looks like Reva anticipated what I'd want again."

They stood in a half-circle around the bow of the ship. Marlon didn't want to break a good bottle or leave glass in the meadow. So he opened the flip lid and said, "I hereby christen thee *Upwind*." He splashed about half the beer on the nose of the gondola, and then they shared sips of the rest of the brew.

"Okay, time to get this show on the road. I need to know wind speeds in the upper levels of atmosphere."

While Reva and Agnes went back to the house, Hanna picked up the paper construction she had carried from the kitchen. It was a small handmade balloon with a cup on the bottom that held a candle stub. She held the paper form from a string in the top.

Marlon went into the meadow to get a good clear view. From forty feet away, he shouted, "Light it up." Soon the paper balloon was filled with hot air, trying to escape skyward. The balloon had a white ribbon hanging from the cup.

"Let her go!" Marlon couldn't keep the excitement out of his voice.

The balloon rose gracefully upward. drifting a little away from town. At about two thousand feet, the candle guttered out. Even the ribbon wasn't visible.

"Almost no wind. It'll be a good flight," Marlon said. "Now be careful when we take up the tarps. The dew has settled, and we don't want the envelope wet. Pick the tarp up, and let the water pour off the side. And for heaven's sake, don't step on the envelope."

Bernard and Hanna lifted the tarps and poured the little rivulets of water to the side. Marlon stood for a moment, admiring the ship.

Reva came out of the house with a tray. Agnes followed behind her with a steaming pot of tea and four cups. "Marlon, before you go too far, it's time to eat."

"Woman, I don't have time for that. We need to get this thing off the ground!"

"Now, none of that, Swordfish." She motioned to Bernard, who took the small TV table from under her elbow and set it up. She set the tray on the table, whisked off the towel, and there, steaming invitingly, was a collection of bundles wrapped in napkins.

"What is it?" Marlon stepped closer, and got a whiff of beans and chili. "My favorite. When did you make breakfast burritos?"

"I put them together this morning. Went over to Monica's yesterday, and we made up a batch of refried beans and some of her *carne adovada*. What do you think I was doing all day, lollygagging?"

The envelope was inflated, and the engines were running. Hanna and Bernard had taken their seats in the gondola, and Marlon was doing final checks.

Reva nodded. "Nothing to worry about, Swordfish. Do everything by the numbers, and you'll be a winner."

Marlon wrapped his arms around his wife and leaned his cheek against the top of her head. "Woman, how could I have ever done anything without you?"

"You couldn't, of course." With that, Reva released Marlon, and then stepped back to the truck next to the bow line.

Marlon grinned and climbed into the gondola. He throttled up and looked to where his wife was waiting, next to the truck.

"Reva!" Marlon chopped his hand down, and she pulled the link. The bow line fell away from the truck. With another pull at full burner, the ground fell away just as the sun broke over the horizon.

Hanna let out a long sigh and stared at the ground. "Herr Pridmore, this is marvelous!"

"Yes, it is. I remember my first flight. Today's flight will be special for all of us. Where should we go first?"

Hanna shrugged and giggled like a little girl. "Oh, Herr Pridmore. Wherever you take us is fine. I just love the trip."

Leveling off at five hundred feet above ground level, Marlon gave the controls a work-out. He steered the airship to the left, then right, all the time drifting slowly backwards. This was definitely not something you could do in a balloon. He maneuvered the controls up and down, watching as small movements of the pitch wheel easily changed the attitude of the ship.

He looked over his shoulder at Bernard and Hanna. "So, what do you think?" He had to shout to make himself heard over the fan and the burners.

Bernard was gripping the back of Marlon's seat so hard that his knuckles were white. Hanna, on the other hand, was leaning across the edge of the gondola, and waving down at her mother and Reva. "Hello Mutti, hello Reva! Oh, Poppi, everything looks so small!"

Bernard nodded, and forced himself to look down at his wife, then closed his eyes, and continued holding on. Marlon hid a smile and remembered his first trip above the ground. There were a few moments of terror, but he couldn't even remember what that felt like.

The radio popped a short shot of static. "This is Sweetpea. Ya having fun?" Reva's voice had the same smile in it that he had heard on other balloon flights. She had gone up a couple of times, but enjoyed the chase crew more.

"Swordfish back at ya. This is great! Did you see me steer it in a circle? I've wanted to do this most of my life. For now, I'm gonna take her out about a mile or so. I'll stay in line of sight and radio range."

"Sounds about right to me. If you have to put it down, I'll run the truck out to find you."

"Roger. Swordfish out."

Ulrich sat at the top of the sinkhole and tried to comfort Fritz through the coldest part of the early morning. The darkness was easier for Fritz to bear when he knew he wasn't alone. Just before dawn, J.D. woke up alone and cold. Ulrich brought him over by the sinkhole and built another fire. They tossed the blanket down to Fritz, but could do nothing else.

Ulrich was still grateful for small miracles. He was certain that if it had really gotten cold last night, they would all be in very bad shape. Something nagged at the back of his brain, something about emergency situations. He couldn't remember what it might be. First, he decided, he would get the boys warm, attend to Fritz's wounds, and then try to remember.

Reva was changing into her Sunday best when the phone rang. "Hello?"

"Mrs. Pridmore?"

"Yes. Who is this?"

"Ma'am, this is Matt Prickett, from the police department."

"Oh, yes. I remember. Is there a problem, Officer Prickett?"

"Yes, ma'am, there is. Is Marlon around?"

"Oh, dear. I'm afraid he's out right now. Is there something I can do for you?"

"Well, Mrs. Pridmore, we got us a search and rescue situation here. The boy scouts had an activity yesterday out there at the duke's preserve, and three of the troop didn't come home last night. They searched as well as they could with torches and such most of the night, but didn't find any trace of them. So we need all the volunteers to report to their teams."

"Oh, my goodness. Which boys are they?"

There was a rustling as Officer Prickett turned pages. "I have the names Ulrich Schwarz, Fritz Metzger, and J.D. Cunningham. The first one is the assistant scout leader, and the other two are both eleven-year-olds."

"I'll go out and find Marlon, and call you back."

"Call the department and the dispatcher will know where we are. Let's just hope that they just got lost, and haven't run into some dangerous individuals."

"Okay, Officer. I'll have Marlon call back soon."

Agnes asked, "Something is wrong? What has happened?"

"I think Hanna's sweetheart, Ulrich, is in trouble. We've got to radio Marlon and Bernard."

Marlon didn't even notice the cold. The burners inside the envelope were keeping a lot of heat close, and it was almost uncomfortably hot when he pulled the burner controls.

Bernard was still clinging to the back of Marlon's seat, and had not quite gotten his eyes open. Hanna was reveling in the experience. When she saw Marlon looking, she laughed.

"Oh, Herr Pridmore, this is glorious! This is how I think that angels fly to the heavens."

"Yeah, Hanna. I think you got that just about right. Just like an angel." His musings were cut short by a static burst on the radio.

"Marlon, do you read me?"

"You're four by four. Are we late for church or something?"

"Now you quit your teasing and listen to me for a minute. The police department just called. Hanna's friend Ulrich is missing. He went out with two eleven-year-old boy scouts yesterday, and they haven't come back. They're putting together a search and rescue, and you need to get back down here and help."

"Don't you think that it would help if the search and rescue team had an eye in the sky? This is the perfect rescue machine."

There was silence from the radio. Marlon knew from long

experience that Reva was thinking about what he had said before answering.

"Maybe you're right. I'll find out where they think the boys might be."

Things were a little more cheerful in the daylight. Ulrich dug out the oatmeal cookies and they divided them for breakfast. Fritz didn't look good. He couldn't speak much, and his leg bent at an odd angle. Ulrich had not climbed down into the hole because the sides were narrow and unstable. Ulrich was afraid crumbling debris would fall on the boy. They could see that Fritz was pale and sweating, though. It was high time to find a way to get him home.

"J.D., you stay here and keep this fire going. Maybe someone will see the smoke and come to help. I will go back to the top of the hill. That reminds me of something." He had finally remembered what had been bothering him. It was from his army training. They told him that three of anything meant emergency, like three gunshots. Or three smoky fires.

At the top of the cliff, he carefully cleared and piled three bonfires. It would not be possible for him to carry Fritz home in his condition. They needed to be found.

Soon, three smoky fires were burning in the open glade. Ulrich went back to the sinkhole. "J.D., look there. Do you see those fires?"

J.D. stood up, and looked at the cliff. "Yeah, I see them."

"Okay. It is your job to take care of them. Don't let them go out, and don't let them get away from you. We don't want a brush fire, just a rescue signal. Keep putting wood on each one. This will help them find us, so they must keep burning and smoking. Can you do that?"

J.D. brightened at being given such a responsibility. "I sure can, Herr Schwarz." He hurried off to watch the fires.

Ulrich peered over the edge of the hole. Fritz still looked a little gray, and his eyes were not open. This wasn't good. "Fritz, can you hear me?"

The boy groaned and mumbled, but didn't open his eyes. Ulrich got the canteen, tied a cord to it, and lowered it to Fritz. The boy roused a little and sipped from the canteen. He seemed to come more awake, and drank a couple of sips of the water. Ulrich settled down to wait.

☆ ☆ ☆

Matt Prickett was just getting ready to assign grid squares to the twenty or thirty men in front of him when another officer stepped up and got his attention.

"Matt, I just got word from the dispatcher that Marlon Pridmore is on his way over and should be here in a minute or two."

"That was quick. Reva must have had a good idea where he was."

The other officer hesitated, and scratched his head. "Yeah, Matt, but you ain't heard the rest of it. The dispatcher said that Reva said to tell you that he's coming over here in a blimp."

"A what?"

"Matt, all I can tell you is what the dispatcher said to me. She said that Reva said that Marlon is coming over here in a blimp."

"I heard a rumor that he was working on a balloon. But I didn't believe it. We'll just have to see what he's got when he gets here."

With the engines running, it wasn't silent like a hot air balloon would be. Two motorcycle engines put out more noise than Marlon had thought they would. He watched the ground flow away underneath him. He didn't have radar, but he had a stopwatch and estimated they were doing about twenty-six knots. He was concentrating on where the boys might be and making contact with the search and rescue team. He hadn't even considered how the ground troops might react when they caught sight of him. His attention was pulled away from his instruments when he heard shouts from the ground.

Hanna was practically standing up in her seat, waving like a maniac. Bernard wasn't. "Hanna, sit down this instant, before you fall to your death," he said through clenched teeth.

"Oh Poppi, I'll be all right." A blazing smile lit her dark features, and her hazel eyes gleamed with enjoyment.

Down below, men and boys were running and pointing, and the babble of their voices wafted up to the airship in the eerie way they always do. Marlon spotted Matt Prickett standing in the bed of a pickup with his mouth open.

"Sweetpea, you catching me, darlin'?"

"I'm right here. And I'm gonna stay right here till you land."

"Good deal. Okay, tell me where they've been looking for the boys, and where they're gonna go today."

"Gotcha. I'll get back to you in a minute."

Marlon was again glad that the telephones still worked. His

radios were not wired quite the same as the others, because they were German, and used slightly different bandwidths. They had their own private channel, but he couldn't contact the team directly.

"Dispatcher says that the scouts searched the eastern side of the preserve last night, and the plan today was to try more to the south," Reva said.

"Sounds good, darlin'. I think we might circle the area and see what we find."

"I'll let the dispatcher know. You take care and don't fall out of that contraption."

"Don't you worry your pretty head about that. I got my seatbelt on. Besides, Bernard is doing enough worrying for the both of us. Hanna's having the time of her life, though."

The smile in Reva's voice was clear, even through the static. "I'll just bet she is. Most exciting thing that has happened to her in a blue moon."

J.D. wiped the smoke out of his eyes after sticking another branch on the middle fire. He felt lonely here away from Ulrich and Fritz. And hungry. Then he heard something.

It was like the chainsaw he had heard a long time ago. He looked at the trees around him, but didn't see anything. And then the day got a little darker, like when a cloud goes over the sun for a moment. J.D. looked up and saw something amazing. It wasn't an airplane, but something entirely different. It reminded him of the Goodyear blimp they used to have at football games when he was little.

"Herr Schwarz! Herr Schwarz, come quick!" J.D. waved his arms over his head to get the assistant scoutmaster's attention. "You have to come and see this. I don't know what it is exactly, but it's coming this way. Hurry!"

Ulrich dropped the stick he had been using to stir his small fire, and hurried up to the signal fires. J.D. sounded disturbed. It took him a few minutes to reach the boy. And when he did, J.D. stood staring up into the heavens.

Ulrich didn't wonder about that. It was unbelievable, all right. An egg-shaped thing colored in red, black and yellow. Like J.D., Ulrich stood staring with his mouth open. Then he noticed that it was coming toward them.

☆ ☆ ☆

"I see something. There to the left," Hanna shouted.

Good thing I brought her along, Marlon thought. "You got good eyes, girl. I see it. Three columns of smoke."

Marlon adjusted the yoke, crabbing sideways some. "Hanna, I'm gonna come in from downwind, keep a look out." Swinging the tail of the ship as it drifted by the signal, Marlon brought up the throttle as evenly as possible. The airship began to settle. Marlon helped it along with a degree or two of down-thrust from the engines. He picked up his radio handset, and thumbed the button a couple of times.

"Sweetpea, I think we got something. There are three columns of smoke over here. We're past the northwest corner of the preserve."

"All clear, Marlon. I'm relaying the info to the dispatcher now."

"Ulrich! Ulrich, can you hear me?"

He looked at the flying egg, and then saw a face, and an arm waving. "Hanna? Hanna, how are you up there?"

The egg came closer, and he saw that it was much bigger than he had thought at first. In fact, it was the largest vehicle he had ever seen, more than a hundred and thirty feet long, and at least forty feet high. And Hanna was in a small sort of cart at the bottom.

The ship came closer. Now he could see that not only Hanna, but her father, Herr Brenner, and their employer, Herr Pridmore were in the cart.

"Ulrich, where is Fritz? Where is the other boy?"

Ulrich shouted up, "Fritz fell in a hole over here. We were unable to move him. He has been hurt."

"Stay right there, we will swing around and see him."

The egg moved right overhead where they could look down the hole.

Marlon leaned over the edge, examining the sinkhole, the injured boy, and the path up and down. "Herr Schwarz, I think we can help get the boy out of there. You cut a couple of poles, and use that blanket to make a stretcher. Herr Brenner, here, will help you."

He directed the airship past the signal fires and into the open glade. "I'm gonna drop a rope. But don't touch it until I tell you." He was well aware of the dangers of static electricity. How many times had he seen that footage from the Hindenburg?

Ulrich and J.D. retreated to a large boulder, and watched. Marlon detached the bottom of the bow rope, and let it dangle. It dragged on the ground for a moment. "Okay, Ulrich. Run over here, and grab this rope. You can help steady us as we land. Herr Brenner is climbing out, and I don't want to overbalance."

Ulrich grabbed and held tight to the bow rope. Herr Brenner climbed out of the gondola, then leaned back in to retrieve something. But Ulrich didn't notice exactly what. He was looking into Hanna's eyes. Truly, she was the most beautiful woman he had ever seen. Her cheeks were red from the wind, and her hair was fly-away and tangled. But the look on her face was priceless. Her hazel eyes seemed to pull him into deep water. He hoped that she would continue to look at him like that forever.

"All right, you two." Marlon grinned when he saw the two young people gaze at each other as if they were seeing each other for the first time. "You'll have time for that later. Right now, we gotta get this rig back in the air."

Ulrich blushed and hurried backwards. He still didn't take his eyes from Hanna. He stepped backward until he ran into J.D., and they both watched the airship lift off the ground.

"You boys get that stretcher put together. I think that with Bernard's help, you will be able to get Fritz up here to the landing zone."

"Swordfish, you got info for me?"

"Reva, you got the prettiest voice." Reva could feel the blush. Here the man was saying things like that when there was an emergency going on.

"Enough of that. Have you got the boys?"

"Yeah, I got 'em spotted, but one is hurt. I need you to call the hospital and let them know."

"Who's hurt?"

"It's Fritz. He's in bad shape. We have to make this quick. Tell the hospital we have the boy, Tell 'em we're inbound. ETA about thirty minutes."

The men wrapped the blanket around two saplings, and pinned the ends down to create a rough stretcher. Ulrich and Bernard carried it to the side of the hole and examined the problem. They had to lift Fritz up out of the hole without hurting him more than they had to, and get him on the stretcher for the airship to carry.

Ulrich took the rope and tied a bowline on a bight, making a boson's chair. Then they lowered the chair down to the injured boy.

In his best fatherly voice, Bernard instructed Fritz. "Lad, when this rope comes down, slip it underneath you like a chair. Then Herr Schwarz and I will pull you up. Hang on tight."

Fritz whimpered a little as the rope lifted him. Tears were streaming from his eyes, and he was holding on the rope with the whitened knuckles of one hand as he came to ground level. Gently, the men took him by the shoulders and hips, and laid him on the stretcher. They splinted the injured leg to the other leg, and bound them both together.

Before picking up the stretcher for the trip back to the glade, Ulrich said, "J.D., you put out this fire, like they showed you in scouts. Use that stick as your shovel, and pour the rest of the water from the canteen on it. I don't want to see any smoke. We will keep the signal fires over there smoking until the others get here."

"Yes, sir."

Ulrich and Bernard carried Fritz to the large boulder. It was worrisome that with every bump and jolt, Fritz would groan a little.

They carefully put him on the ground, and signaled the airship. Not too long now, and everything would be all right.

"Hello, who is this?" The man's voice sounded almost as frustrated and harried as Reva had felt a few moments earlier.

"This is Reva Pridmore, and I'm trying to let someone over there know that you have a patient arriving in about fifteen minutes."

"Okay, I got that. How are they arriving?"

Reva hesitated a moment, then dove in. "They're coming in on an airship. You know, like a blimp?"

There were a couple of moments of silence, and then the man said, "You mean it's like a life flight? I think we can handle it. I'll get a gurney and a couple of men out into the parking lot to meet it. Don't worry, I'll take care of everything."

Hanna had not taken her eyes from Ulrich and her father. They were both busy taking care of the poor little boy. Then Ulrich looked up at her again, and began to wave his scout scarf.

"Herr Pridmore, I think they are ready. Ulrich is waving."

After settling the airship to the ground, Marlon had Hanna pull the pin from the middle seat, and it laid down flat, like a bed.

He waved Ulrich and Bernard over. They carefully placed Fritz and the stretcher into the gondola, and stepped back.

Marlon handed another canteen to Ulrich. "You take care, I've got to get this little fellow to the hospital double quick. The search and rescue team will get here as fast as they can." Marlon pulled both the handles to the burners, and pivoted the engines so they were thrusting straight down. Balancing on the thrust and with the heat in the balloon increasing, the airship rose rapidly into the air. Still at a full burn Marlon began pivoting the engines to thrust them forward.

He thought for a moment, then eased the throttles all the way to the stops. *Hilde always said that a ship like this could do fifty kph. I'm gonna call him on that.* He could feel the pull of acceleration, and the cold wind whipping past the windshield.

The parking lot at the hospital resembled a hill of ants that had been kicked open by a curious boy. People hurried everywhere, carrying supplies, watching the sky for the life flight, or just standing in the way gawking.

"All right, listen up!" It was the ER doctor, and as hospital protocol required, all personnel stopped for a moment to listen. "I want this area cleared of anyone who doesn't have a real job. The rest of you, stay over there on the grass. I don't need any rubber-neckers underfoot."

The crowd sorted itself out, and the tumult died down for a moment. The sound of a couple of trucks could be heard down the road, and a police car pulled into the parking lot.

"Albert, get that cop car out of our landing zone, then find out what he wants." All eyes looked into the sky. No one knew exactly what to expect. No description of the airship had been given to anyone.

"There it is! I see it!"

"Wow, it's beautiful!"

"*Coool.*"

"Okay, everybody. Just like we practiced it in the drill, only with a blimp instead of an ambulance."

Marlon looked down in frustration. "This thing needs a horn." The blimp was rapidly approaching the hospital. Pitching down, Marlon began to ease off the throttles.

He leaned over the side and shouted, "Grab the rope. Grab the rope!" The bowline was already dancing across the parking lot.

Luckily, they came to ground with a gentle thump. The gondola slid forward to a stop in the parking lot. As people swarmed over, he yelled, "Grab the sides of the car, so we can stay down." He ignored the furor that was going on behind him as the boy was removed, and people were already shouting orders in incomprehensible medical jargon.

Grinning, he picked up the radio again. "Reva, could you pack up some kind of picnic? I could run it back out to those boys in the bush, and let them have something to eat. They haven't had much since yesterday."

"That's a really good idea, Marlon. You wait there. I'll be there in two shakes of a lamb's tail. Then we'll go home for a proper celebration."

Marlon kept the burners going periodically to keep the envelope inflated, but not lift them off the ground. He had wrangled a couple of bystanders to hook their elbows over the edge of the gondola to keep it on the ground.

One of the men holding the basket grinned. "Marlon, when you gonna build one of these for me?" His jibe stirred laughter from those standing around doing nothing.

"Well, I guess that depends. I'm willing to advise any one of you who wants to build one, but you're gonna have to do the building of it. I'm outta the balloon-making business. Got more than enough on my plate right now."

Bernard, Ulrich and J.D. were sitting near one of the fires. With the rescue and the excitement over, they all felt just a little let down.

J.D. spoke first. "I wonder how long it will be until they find us?"

"Not so long. You will be home before supper." Seeing the worry in the boy's eyes, Bernard grinned and said, "And if you're hungry now, you can always have an extra drink of water."

Ulrich had been staring at the sky, the last place he had seen Hanna. He couldn't believe how wonderful she really was. He had been watching her, and thinking that in a couple of years he would like to settle down with someone like her. Now it seemed much more urgent. He needed a good job, and a bank account, and somewhere decent they could live. It would take at least that much for her father to consent to...

"There they are again!" J.D. was on his feet, jumping up and down and pointing. And sure enough, the flying egg had returned. As it came close, Hanna leaned out and waved again.

After the landing, Marlon called from the front of the gondola. "We came back to take J.D. home, if he thinks he can stand to fly in this thing."

J.D. hesitated for only a flicker of a moment, then darted to the gondola, jumped over the side, and snapped his seatbelt.

Marlon laughed. "I guess he really wants his mama's cooking. And speaking of food, Hanna's got something special."

She bent down and reappeared with a basket. "It is from Frau Pridmore and my mother. I hope you like it." The airship lifted off the ground again, and Ulrich still stood with the basket in hand, watching.

"And Ulrich, I expect you to call the moment you arrive home, so that we know you're all right."

"I will call, Hanna. As soon as I step foot in Frau Moss' house."

Bernard frowned at Ulrich's enthusiasm, and shook his head. It didn't seem as if he was going to be able to keep his daughter from this young man. Perhaps it was time to get used to the idea.

Marlon leaned over the edge of the gondola and waved. "You boys keep out of trouble. Reva says that search and rescue is already halfway here. Be good."

The sunset painted the sky before Bernard arrived back home. The clouds that had been threatening rain all afternoon cleared and the sun was glorious through the trees to the west. Reva and Agnes had prepared a sumptuous feast for the Sabbath, and everything was ready when Bernard came through the front door.

"Did J.D. get home? Will Fritz be all right? And Herr Schwarz?" Hanna tried to sound concerned with the scouts, but everyone could tell that she wanted to know about the scoutmaster.

"Yes, *Liebchen*, everything is good. The police tell me that Fritz didn't need surgery, and is conscious. His parents are at the hospital, and J.D. is home eating fried chicken and mashed potatoes." He frowned a little at his daughter, and didn't mention anyone else.

Marlon slapped Bernard's shoulder. "I'm glad you finally got home. You know, if you had stayed with me, you'd a been here a couple of hours ago."

Bernard held up his hands as if to stop any more such suggestions and began to take off his gloves. "No, my friend, I've had my first and last ride in your airship. If God had intended for me to fly, I would have been born with feathers."

"Oh, Poppi, I think it was wonderful. I can't wait to go again." Hanna's eyes still gleamed, and she seemed almost a different girl. She had more of a confident air about her as though she had seen what she wanted, and was going to do her best to get it.

"Now hold on there, Bernard. We still have some business to take care of."

"What is it that is so important? I've not had any decent food since this morning."

Agnes whirled around and put her fists on her hips. "Why, you terrible man. How could you say something like that, after the beautiful picnic Frau Reva and I sent to you? Now you just turn yourself around and go out to the barn. We have an important ceremony."

Bernard turned and walked back out into the night while the rest followed. Around back, near the barn, he could see a dark lantern standing on a small table, along with some papers, and a bottle of beer.

Marlon stepped up to the table and lit the lantern. He began in a sonorous voice. "As long as men have been flying in hot air contraptions, they have been honored with entry into the Society of Fire and Air. The tradition is ancient—or I guess it will be—so you must do as I say. Bernard, you stand here. Hanna, over here next to him."

Bernard and his daughter obediently lined up shoulder to shoulder, facing the table. Reva and Agnes stood behind Marlon, who was next to the card table.

"Mother Nature has taken you into the skies and returned you gently to Earth. So you become new creatures, that fly through the air.

"Now, both of you kneel on the ground." Marlon turned to the table, and picked up a long wooden match. He lit it in the lantern, picked up the beer bottle, and set a small piece of Bernard's hair on fire. Before the frightened man could jump up, Marlon poured beer on the flame and put it out. Not even an inch of hair was gone.

He reached over, and caught an end of Hanna's hair, but she knew what was coming and held still. The beer drenched her head as well.

"The fire symbolizes the power to reach the heavens, and the beer symbolizes the power to celebrate our return to Earth. Welcome to the ranks of the aeronauts!"

Agnes stepped up to Bernard, gave him a ceremonial kiss on the cheek and handed him a small towel. Reva held a towel for Hanna, but they could hear the telephone ringing.

"Oh, it must be for me!" Hanna grabbed the towel, and sprinted off for the back porch to answer the phone. Nobody had any doubts that the young scoutmaster was checking in as promised.

A Tinker's Progress

Terry Howard

Jack Jones made his way into the sleepy little town of Elstow, about a mile south of Bedford in Bedfordshire, home to perhaps five hundred souls—give or take half a hundred. There was a notable stone cross in the center of town where he stopped to survey for a tinker's shop. "A bloody tinker!" he muttered. "I'm carrying mail for a tinker? What next, a milkmaid? A bar wench? At least he's one of the better sort with a forge and a settled station." In a bit, when it was not obvious where he should go, he headed to the parish house next to the church of Saints Mary and Helen and approached to knock on the door. By chance the vicar himself answered.

Jack asked, in a slow voice, watching his word choice carefully to be better understood, knowing that his accent was often something of a bother, "Good morrow, good sir. Could you be directing me to the shop of one Thomas the son of Thomas, a tinker?"

"And you are?" the vicar asked.

"Jack Jones, dispatch rider, at your service. I'm up from London with a letter for Goodman Thomas, the tinker."

"A letter, you say?" The vicar looked skeptical. "And just who in London would be writing a letter to Thomas?"

"It was given me by the office of one Isaac Abrabanel just east of Temple Bar."

"Don't tell me Thomas has gone and borrowed money from a London Jew that he can't pay back?" The vicar let out a deep sigh. "That man will end in debtor's prison and his wife will be asking for charity. I knew it. I told her father not to let Margaret marry beneath herself. This is what comes of marrying for love."

"I wouldn't know anything about that, Vicar. I just have a letter to be delivered. Could you please tell me where I can find him?"

"Go to the cross. Face east. Take the middle of the three streets. When it forks, go left and the shop will be on your right. There is a shingle of a mended pot hanging over the door." The vicar started to close the door.

"One more question of your grace, please. Would you know if Thomas has his letters or do I need to take a reader with me?"

"No, he does not. But his wife, poor woman, does." And with that the vicar did indeed close the door.

Jack led his horse through the town. When he entered the front door of the tinker's shop he was promptly addressed.

"What can I do for you?"

"Are you Thomas the Tinker?"

"No. Thomas is my brother. We share the shop. What can we do for you?"

"Does Thomas have a son named John? The lad would be not yet seven years of age."

"That's right. What is this about?"

"Could I have a few words with his wife, Margaret?"

"You could . . . if I have a mind to call her from the kitchen, which I am not about to do until you tell me what this is all about!" By this time the tinker had put down his tools and stood up from the bench, quietly picking up the heaviest of his hammers.

Jack decided he'd better answer quickly. "I have a letter for your brother. I suppose it will be all right if I give it to his wife, seeing as Thomas hasn't his letters and she will have to be the one reading it, anyway."

"A letter, you say?"

Jack lifted the flap on the pouch over his shoulder and brought forth a folded parchment, sewn with a string, set with wax and sealed with a stamp.

"Maggie?" the tinker called out.

"Yes?" The answer came from the back of the house.

"Can you come out to the shop, please?"

Margaret pushed open the door that separated the shop from the living area. She was drying her hands on her apron as she did.

"This fellow says he has a letter for your husband."

"How very odd," she replied. "Are you sure?"

"The letter is for one Thomas, the son of Thomas, a tinker in Elstow, who has a son named John," Jack said.

"That would indeed be my Thomas. But why, in the name of all that is holy, would anyone be sending Thomas a letter?"

"Goodwife, could you tell me your father's family name?"

"What an odd thing to ask."

"True enough. I've never been instructed to asked the likes of it before but—" Jack put the letter back in the shoulder pouch and lifted a small bag of coins. He tossed it up and down in his hand, causing it to clink with the distinct sound of large silver coins. "I was told to ask and if I didn't get the right answer, the letter and the money are to go back to London."

The tinker promptly answered. "Bentley. The family name is Bentley."

Jack set the bag down and dug a stoppered inkwell out of his shoulder pouch along with a quill and a bit of paper. "Goodwife, would you please assure yourself that the seal on the coin bag is unbroken and then sign a receipt?"

"What is the money for? What is all this about?"

"Now, how would the likes of Jack Jones be knowing that?"

"Perhaps I had better read the letter before I sign anything."

Jack shrugged and handed her the missive.

As she read it, her lips moving silently as if in prayer, her face became increasingly contorted by puzzlement. The tinker's face held ever more curiosity until it erupted like a spit melon seed. "Well? What does it say?"

"The money is to pay Thomas' expenses to go to London to discuss a business matter with one Isaac Abrabanel. Thomas is to see him three doors east of Temple Bar."

"A London Jew? What business does Thomas have with the likes of that?"

"You would know better than I, as tight-lipped as the two of you are about money matters."

"You and Rose don't need to be worrying about how much is on hand and what is coming in."

"No. We're just supposed to figure out how to feed the lot of us when there isn't anything left to buy food with."

"Times are hard, woman. Thomas and I are doing the best we can. If you are so all-fired concerned, we could save the cost of sending John to get his lettering."

"For sure, and then he could go through his life at the mercy of whoever it is that is reading to him. If he doesn't go now, he'll not go later when he's old enough to be of some use."

Jack was growing more and more uncomfortable. These were family matters that should not be discussed in front of a stranger.

The tinker opened his mouth and shut it. Jack suspected that he wanted to say "it never hurt me any," as many men would have. But Jack could well imagine many disputes—had even had some himself—that would not have happened if people had written the agreement down to begin with. It was a common enough problem in life.

Jack cleared his throat, "Gentlefolk, if you could, I need a signed receipt. Then I can be getting on my way."

"What can you tell us about this?" the tinker demanded.

"I'm naught but a dispatch rider. I just need you to sign the bloody paper."

"Well, I'm nothing but a tinker and I don't give a damn what you need. She isn't signing anything until you tell us all you know."

Jack reached for the money but the tinker was faster. He held the bag out of reach. "All I know is what I've told you already."

"Well, tell us about this Abrabanel man."

"I never set eyes on him. I talked to a clerk in the front room of a fancy office with a big brass handle on the front door and an even bigger glass window. Now, either sign the bloody paper or give me the money and the letter to take back to London!"

"Sign it," the tinker told his sister-in-law.

Later that day Thomas came back from making the rounds. He walked through the door and before he could put the new lot of pots to be mended down he was hit by a question. "Brother, what business do you have in London?"

"What are you talking about?"

"Why does a man in London, and a Jew at that, want to see you in his office at 'your earliest convenience'?"

"Have you lost your head?" Thomas asked. "You know I don't know any Jew in London or anywhere else."

"Margaret, bring that letter out here and read it to your husband."

"Letter? What letter?" Thomas was puzzled.

"The one that came from London today while you were out. The one that came with more money than we've had at one time in years. Enough for you to take a coach to London and dine in fancy inns along the way."

Margaret pushed open the door. The total puzzlement on her husband's face told her all she needed to know. He obviously didn't know one iota more about what was going on than she did. She held up the letter for him to see, then she began to read it aloud.

Thomas listened to the end without saying a word. "So all I've got to do for this money is go down to London and talk to this man?"

"I read you the letter, Thomas. You can ferret out the meaning as easily as I can."

"I know, but it doesn't make any sense. What does he want with me? They've got tinkers aplenty in London."

"Well, Brother, I guess you'll just have to go down there and find out."

"You say there's enough money to take a coach?"

"Don't go getting any fancy ideas, brother of mine. There *was* enough. After I pay off what we owe the tin man—and pay for the next round up front to get the discount we never have been able to afford—then there's enough left to take care of you, there and back. As long as you start out with a cheese and a loaf and don't dally along the way."

Margaret met her husband at the door with a satchel holding a small cheese about the size of a good cabbage, and two loaves of bread about the same size. "The cheese should see you there and back. You can buy more bread before you leave London." Two loaves, two days walk, fresh enough, but there was no point in Thomas eating stale bread when it could be had for a fair price. She gave him a peck on the cheek.

"Margaret, please. What will the neighbors think?"

"Thomas, the day I can't send my husband off to London with a kiss because the neighbors are Puritans is the day we will move to Rome. I still think you should have hired a horse, or taken the coach."

"No. My brother is right. The money is better spent. I'd walk twice that for a lot less. Besides, I probably couldn't stay on a horse anyway, then it would run off and how would we ever pay for it? I've got my walking stick. I'll see you in five days."

"Thomas, when you get there call yourself a brasier instead of a tinker. It sounds better."

With these words of advice from his wife, Thomas set off for Temple Bar in London, wondering each step of the way what it was all about.

While munching the last of his bread in the last of the daylight Thomas found Temple Bar. He asked where he could find the office of Isaac Abrabanel, thinking to locate where he would go in the morning.

"It's right there. That's his shingle hanging over his door, just three down. The one that reads Isaac Abrabanel, Importer. Didn't you look, or can't you read?"

Thomas suspected that the fellow he asked couldn't read either, but wasn't about to admit that to some bumpkin just in from the country. To his surprise, the window spilled lamplight out onto the street. A glance through the glass made it clear that people were about.

"Well, the sooner begun, the sooner it's finished." Thomas pushed the door open and walked in.

The clerk summed up the man in front of him with a glance. "It's after hours. Come back tomorrow."

"Is this the office of Isaac Abrabanel?"

"Yes. We open at eight in the morning."

"He wants to see me."

"I'm sure he does! Tomorrow."

"Tell him Thomas Bunyan was here, then. I'll be back tomorrow."

"Thomas Bunyan? The tinker from Elstow?"

"I prefer to think of myself as a brasier."

As Thomas turned to leave, the clerk realized he had just made a big mistake. "Please, wait a moment, sir. Let me check with Mr. Abrabanel. I know he is anxious to speak with you."

The clerk came back in short order. On the one hand, he was vindicated. His boss would see the ragged scarecrow tomorrow. He was in a conference at the moment and it would run late. On the other hand, he was unhappy. Yes, he could lock up and leave, but he was to buy the dusty countryman a good dinner and settle him into a decent lodging. And he was to see the fellow back to the office in the morning. It wasn't the way he'd intended to spend his evening.

"Mister Abrabanel is tied up right now. He will see you in the morning. Join me for dinner and then—"

The tinker brushed at his shirt. "I've eaten."

"Are you sure? There is a very nice dining establishment just around the corner."

"I'm sure."

Avram, the clerk, was annoyed again. There went the paid-for dinner he was looking forward to, even if it meant being seen with a tinker. "Well, then. Let me get you settled into your lodging for the night."

Thomas took one look at the hired room. It was, without question, the finest room he had ever even seen, and he would be spending tonight here. There was a huge bed, a fireplace laid but unlit on an August night. The wash stand, sink and pitcher, along with an actual bathtub, were absolute luxuries. "I can't afford this."

"Oh, but it's at our expense."

"You're sure?"

"Of course." The clerk hesitated a moment. "Dinner is at our expense also . . . if you would care to change your mind?"

Later, Thomas, smiling, stuffed and bathed, settled into bed with the knowledge that his laundered clothes would be returned in the morning. "A fellow could get used to this if he wasn't careful."

"Master Bunyan, it is good to meet you. Please be seated. How was the coach ride down from Elstow?"

"I walked."

"Oh, I see. Your wife and young John, they are in good health?"

"Yes."

"Well, Thomas . . . do you mind if I call you Thomas?"

"Most do."

"Yes, well . . . Thomas, I have been instructed to pay all of your expenses if you will relocate your family to the town of Grantville in the Germanies."

"Grantville?"

"You've heard of it, I'm sure."

"Yes. I've heard of the city from the future... and I've heard of the sea monsters that dwell in the lakes of Scotland. You might as well pay my way to the New World so I can move into one of the Spanish cities of gold and start making golden pots and kettles."

"I assure you, Grantville is real. I have a cousin there. He wrote me concerning you and your family. You are wanted in Grantville. All expenses are to be paid. A complete shop will be provided and there will be more than enough work—at a sufficient rate of pay to more than provide a good living for your family and a good education for your son."

"Why?"

"What?"

"Why? They have tinkers in Germany. Why docs someone want me?"

"Well, as you have heard, Grantville is from the future." Isaac held up a hand to forestall Thomas' objection. "I assure you it is true. So, while you may have lived a very ordinary life up till now, it would seem that you will do something extraordinary in the future and someone wants that to happen in Grantville."

"What?"

"I have no idea. Perhaps you will invent something or create some notable works. Perhaps it is young John who is to do something of note, or a child yet to be born? I wasn't informed and I don't know. What I do know is that you are wanted there and I am to see to it that you get there if you are willing to go."

Thomas' mind raced. The bag of coins in his brother's keeping, the room and the meal last night, the bath and the clean clothes, the fancy office. Someone was willing to spend money like Thomas had never had and never dreamed of having. Still... "There is a war in Germany."

"Yes, but not in Grantville. It will be quite safe, I assure you."

"This is beyond belief!"

"Yes, I imagine it is. But it is quite true. Master Bunyan... Thomas... there is a ship leaving in six days. I would like it very much if you and your family were to be on it."

Thomas sat in silence.

"You will want to discuss this with your wife." Isaac brought a small bag of coins out of his desk drawer. It had been prepared for just this point in the conversation. He let it drop several inches, in a spot Thomas could reach. It made the sound that only comes when gold meets gold. "Take a coach home. Think about the offer, and then bring your family back to London by coach. At least, let your wife sit in on the discussion." Isaac had laid the bait. Now it was time to set the hook. "I am authorized to tell you that money for a return trip will be on deposit with us until you use it or it is released to your heirs at the time of your death."

Secure in the belief that the Abrabanels would be successful, and looking to the patent and copyright laws in the books he'd read, an attorney in an office in Grantville was quietly preparing a brief to claim the royalties for *Pilgrim's Progress* for young John Bunyan. True, John hadn't written it or any of his other works yet. But he was undeniably the author. It was a fine point. A very fine point of law. He would have to argue it in court, of course. But he thought he had quite a good case.

Elsewhere in Grantville, an old Free and Approved Mason was wondering what John Bunyan's output would be when he had received a first class education. The expense to find out was well worth it.

Jenny and the King's Men

Mark H. Huston

And thus a mighty deed was done by Jenny's valiant hand,
Black Prelacy and Popery she drove from Scottish land;
King Charles he was a shuffling knave, priest Laud a meddling fool,
But Jenny was a woman wise, who beat them with a stool!

The column of soldiers advanced down High Street from Edinburgh castle. They parted the market-day crowd like a trout swimming upstream. Young boys ran up and down the column of soldiers, reveling in the novelty of having a troop of King Charles' men marching through their market.

Ahead of the boys flew the rumors. By the time the squad of soldiers and their officer reached the corner of St. Giles Street and High Street, where the greengrocers and fishmongers were selling their wares in the shadow of St. Giles Cathedral, the rumors had raced ahead of them like wildfire.

Jenny Geddes, the greengrocer in the second stand from the end, had one eye on the soldiers and the other on the vegetables in her cart. When there was a distraction in the street, someone, usually one of the street urchins, would dart up and try to run off with a carrot or two. Not today. She had been doing this for over twenty years, taking the stand over from her father when he died. And if her two daughters were lucky, maybe one of them could do the same.

The officer bellowed out his halt order, and the soldiers stopped in front of the cathedral.

Jenny took a moment and sucked on her pipe, put her hand on her hip and glared at the soldiers. *Ever since Charles*, she thought, *that dirty papist-leaning king with a Catholic wife, arrested a whole lot of young lords over talk of a rebellion, things have been unsettled.*

But there was nothing that required this sort of armed display down the middle of High Street. She shook her head at the nonsense, and went back to keeping one eye on her stand and one eye on the troops in the street. *Besides, that mess was over weeks ago; they were past this sort of thing. Bad for business, it is.*

The troops stopped at the other end of the square, and she could hear the murmur of the crowd around them. She grabbed her little three-legged stool and stood on it to get a better view, still keeping one eye on the cart. She thought she heard her name and raised her hand to shield her eyes from the glare of the sun. She shifted her pipe to the other side of her mouth. It fit well on both sides, as she had teeth missing on the right and left. She squinted against the sunlight with her not-so-perfect thirty-five-year-old eyes, and listened again.

"They be alooking fer Jenny?" someone said. "Jenny Geddes?"

"What on earth has she done?" said another.

An old man spit on the ground. "These are t'king's men. Why would they be looking fer Jenny Geddes? That makes not a wit o' sense."

Heads and eyes began to swivel toward Jenny. She stepped off the stool as inconspicuously as possible, and knocked the fire out of her pipe on the heel of her shoe. The pipe went into her pocket. She could see the soldiers advancing through the crowd to her left and to her right. They were surrounding her.

She had a decision to make. Stay or flee. In all of her years in Edinburgh, she had never seen anyone who was arrested in this manner live to tell the tale. She thought of her daughters, her small plots of land outside the city gates, and made her decision. It was a simple and practical decision. There would be certain torture or death in the hands of the king's men. She had done nothing wrong—at least nothing wrong enough to send more than the sheriff after her. Whatever the reason that they were coming for her—guilty, innocent, mistaken identity—it was a sure thing that no good would come of it.

Flee.

She'd had a talent for evading pursuit since she was a girl.

The twists and turns and dead ends of the medieval streets of Edinburgh were a playground to her as a child. She knew she could evade them, but then what?

Jenny scooped up the few coins she had made this morning, moved back from the oncoming soldiers, and headed for the church courtyard directly behind her. There was a small passage that led to Candlemaker's way, and then to Cowpath Street. She took Cowpath Street into town every morning at dawn. It was one of the few streets on the south side of the town that had its own gate, one of only a handful into the walled city. She'd make for that gate.

Troops were hollering for her to stop, and she sprinted to a narrow opening in the corner of the courtyard. She wasn't quite as skinny as she had been as a girl, but she still fit. Her tattered clothing caught on the bricks, but she kept moving.

The opening became a long passageway between two buildings, with just enough room to slip sideways between them. The bright sunlight abruptly changed to shadow as she shuffled sideways into the musty passageway. It smelled of urine. She tried not to think about what was happening to her shoes.

She glanced behind her and could see the soldiers gathering at the opening. She kept shuffling as fast as she could.

"Where does this come out?" growled the officer. "You four stay here, you two follow her in the passage, the rest of you come with me."

She glanced back again, and saw two men begin to squeeze into the passage. She knew her pursuers would have to work their way back through the dense market-day crowd still clustered in the church courtyard. They would then have to backtrack up the hill to another street that cut through, and then race back. By then, she should be long gone.

"If I wasn't so afraid, this would almost be funny," she muttered when she popped out of the passageway a moment later. Her pair of pursuers had gotten stuck.

"Cowpath Road is where I need t'be," she thought. "If I can get there, I'll go home and get the bairns, and then I'll..." The thought trailed off as she continued to walk quickly through the maze of the city. Then what? She had no savings, no money, and no immediate family. Since her husband had died five years ago, she had been just holding on. There was some help from the church, but charity always irritated her. "One thing at a time, Jenny me girl, one thing at a time."

The terrain turned dramatically downhill as she continued to slip between buildings, and she knew she was close to the road. Just a few more yards and she would be in view of the gate. She slowed to a walk and caught her breath. Soldiers were nowhere in sight, far behind and limited to the streets.

"Attract no attention to yerself, lass," she thought, "just walk around this corner and be calm. Say g'day just like always."

She peered out from around the corner, looking straight at Cowgate. She took a moment and looked carefully. Everything seemed normal. She waited, and watched. She was about to step around the corner when a young woman carrying a basket approached the gate to leave the city. As the girl reached the open gate, soldiers appeared from outside the gate. With their swords drawn.

"Well, now. That's a bit odd." Jenny kept watching. The soldiers questioned the girl, inspecting her basket carefully. They then started leering, and grabbed at her. She complained and pulled away. McNulty, the regular gatekeeper and toll collector, stepped in and spoke to the men. McNulty was over fifty years old, and in no shape to take on two soldiers. But his commanding demeanor, roughly honed by three decades at Cowgate, convinced the men to let the girl through the gate without further molestation. He continued to talk to them after she had gone on her way. He then began to talk very animatedly to the men, who responded in kind. The argument continued. McNulty was one of the few honest gatekeepers in the city, and he had known Jenny all of her life. He was the gatekeeper when her father had his stand.

Jenny leaned back against the wall, out of sight of the gate and tried to think. Were they searching for her at the gate? She had to find out before she tried to go through. She frantically tried to think of a way to find out what was going on; how could she get home without being discovered?

"Dear Lord Jesus, please give me a way t'git home wi' me bairns," she whispered softly with her hands folded. "Take me if ye needs, but leave them be, please." She would need to act quickly; the other soldiers would be coming soon.

She heard footsteps approach from the direction of the gate. She eased farther away from the street and pressed against the building. She watched McNulty pass on his way up the street.

He was muttering to himself, still upset from his encounter with the soldiers.

Jenny took a sharp breath as he walked past her, and made another quick decision. "Oy. McNulty. It's me, Jenny Geddes. What be happening? Are they looking for me?"

McNulty stopped suddenly, and did not respond. He casually eased toward the corner where Jenny was hiding, and leaned his back to the wall facing the street. He did not look at her. He looked up and down the street, and then spoke quietly over his shoulder. "Jenny Geddes, wa' in Gods name did ye do, lass? They got the king's men out after ye. I ain't seen the likes of this fer many a year." He paused and pulled his cap down lower on his face. "Aye, they be looking fer ye. They got orders to kill ye. W'a di' ye do, lass?"

"Nothing. I swear it on my mother's grave, McNulty. Ye knows me, knows I go t'kirk always. I don't cheat folks. I am a god-fearing woman and I have a business. I didn't do nothing." She paused to think. "I don't like the papists, ye know that. But who does?"

"Then why are they looking fer ye, lass?"

Finally the frustration welled up in her, as the adrenaline melted away. She began to cry. "I swear that I hae done nothing! I just want to get back to me bairns and hug 'em and make sure they are well." She sniffed, and regained control. No time to cry. "I hae got to get home, McNulty. Wa' cannae do?"

"They will be a waiting fer ye at home, Jenny. You got to hide. All the gates be manned like this one, with English soldiers. You got to hide."

"But me bairns..." The tears welled up again.

"Have you heard of the 'Committees of Correspondence'?"

"Aye." She sniffed. "The ones with the speeches and the place on Little's Close." She sniffed again.

"Go there. Ask for the German. His name is Otto. He will be able to help ye. I will send word through him aboot the bairns. Go and stay outta sight. If they catch you, they will kill you. That much I do know from these lads at me gate. Ye may want to hide until it's dark; there will be just a sliver of moon tonight. I will find out about the bairns." He glanced toward the gate. "Get away from here. The bloody English lads at the gate are starting to notice me here. So git."

"There will be more soldiers coming soon. They will be looking fer me."

"Lord, girl. What could they want with you? Now git on w'ye, before they get suspicious."

"God bless ye, McNulty."

"Git, woman!"

Otto Artmann sat in the back room of the tiny CoC building in near perfect darkness and listened. He could hear the rats moving in the dark alley behind. Most of Edinburgh had gone home for the night. Soldiers had stopped patrolling the streets looking for Jenny.

Carefully, so as not to make any noise, he shifted positions in his chair. He had been sitting for two hours, waiting, and his leg was falling asleep. He had caught a bad pike wound in his calf while fighting in the Germanies four years ago. After his capture by the Americans, he was released into a new world. A world he was determined to make better. He had spent a lot of his life making the world worse. He pushed the old thoughts out of his head, and focused on listening again. He was rewarded with a new sound. Silence. The rats had stopped moving in the alley. Silently, as he rose from the chair, he slid his dagger out of the sheath in his boot, and moved to the back door. It was so quiet that he could hear someone breathing and the movement of fabric from behind the door.

"Otto? Are ye there? Otto?" The voice was low, quiet, tense.

He paused before answering. "Aye. Who is this? Who sent you?"

"McNulty. I'm Jenny. Jenny Geddes."

"I'm going to open the door. Jenny, please step forward and I'll close it behind you."

"Aye."

Still in darkness, he opened the door and allowed the person to walk in. "Step in and stop."

The dim light that came in from the alley gave him a silhouette, nothing more, but he thought she fit the description.

She whispered, "Are you Otto? You sound German."

"I'm Otto," he said and closed the door. "Wait and I'll uncover a candle."

He looked at her when he uncovered the candle. Her face was plain, he decided. Worn, tired. She had a large frame for a Scot, tall, sturdy. Her nose had been broken once or twice. She was dirty from her ordeal and her clothing was soiled and dank. When she smiled back at him, he could see that she was missing teeth. He had lost a few teeth over the years himself, so who was he to judge?

"I'm a bit of boggin, I am." She looked away. "Thank ye. I'm no' used to charity, an I don't know if I kin repay ye the kindness." She straightened, as if realizing what she said, and looked him in the face. "I'm no' a girl who would be repaying ye wit, well, ye knows." She looked down at her body and smoothed her dirty dress. "I don't do that, nere will. Ye ken that?"

"I understand, Jenny. I don't expect anything in return, at least not now. And when I do, it will not be that sort of thing. Do you want something to drink or eat?"

"Aye. Both please."

Otto handed her a mug of beer, turned and began to prepare her food. "What do you know of the Committees, Jenny?"

"No' a lot. Ye just do braw for people. Guilds nae like ye. Ye have something to do with the strange people from Germany. S'posed to be from the future. That's all."

"The Americans."

"Aye, them's the ones." She paused and looked up at him. "What de ye hear 'bout me bairns? Are they safe? Do ye know? I ha' been worried to death. I dunno what I'd do if something happened—"

"They are safe with some people who are with the Committee. The soldiers came to your home looking for you, and the girls hid. We found them later in the afternoon when they went to the Dunnes. They are safe."

He watched as she bowed her head, and prayed a quiet thanks. She looked up at him. "The Dunnes be good people. When can I see them?"

"We need to get you safe first. Do you have any idea why they are trying to hurt you?"

"No. I have been thinking on that all night; I cannae come up with an answer. I don't know what I have done. Ye think they have me mixed with another Jenny of some sort?"

"We don't know. But we are trying to find out. We think the order may have come from London. The timing is right. You were wise to run away when you did. Damn that King Charles."

"I not like words like that if it's not in the kirk." She grinned mischievously. "But I did run, didn't I?" She smiled again. Otto liked the way her face lit up when it smiled, even with the missing teeth.

"Your food is ready. It's not warm, I don't want to risk a cooking fire and draw attention to us. This room has no windows, and we fixed it so there is no danger of someone seeing the light from the candle."

"I see." She bowed her head and offered a short prayer over the food, and then she wolfed the small meal down.

"We don't understand what is happening, Jenny. But something tells me that you're part of it. Or will be in the future. We'll have to find out which part you play. Or will play. You can stay upstairs here, and out of sight till tomorrow. Then we will move you to a safe house, and possibly out of the city in a few days when things settle down a little."

"And me bairns?"

"After we move you, we will get you together with your children."

She nodded and smiled. As he watched, he saw the energy drain out of her. The tension of not knowing about her children must have been a huge strain. *And now that she knows they are safe, she probably wants to sleep.* He picked up the candle.

"Take this, Jenny. There's a loft above this room; the ladder is over there. There is some clean bedding; we will get you some clean clothes tomorrow. And don't worry, I will be down here all night."

He watched her slowly climb the ladder to the loft. When the candle went out, he sat back down in his chair and listened for the rats to return outside.

"What do you mean, they failed to capture her?" John Lauder was not a happy man, and his high-pitched voice squeaked higher than usual. He coughed to bring it under control. "I wanted her head, dammit."

Lieutenant William Hignall shifted his weight from foot to foot. He was clearly uncomfortable. Lauder liked him to be uncomfortable. "Sir, the troop and I did exactly as ye requested. We thought we had her trapped in the churchyard during the market, but she escaped down a passageway we couldn't follow."

"Is she still in the city?"

"We don't know for sure." Lauder shot his best glare at the man, and watched him with satisfaction as he carefully considered the rest of his answer. "But . . . we believe she is. Her children have also disappeared. She is hiding somewhere—"

"You have a keen grasp of the obvious for one in your position, Lieutenant," snapped Lauder.

Hignall inhaled, exhaled, and tried to relax. "Sir, she is probably in one of the tenements somewhere in town. She has no family to speak of, although she is well thought of with the lower class of people in the city. She sits at church as a placeholder on the Sabbath for some of the more devout families. I am certain we will find her."

Lauder stood up. "That is what I am paying you and your men for, Lieutenant. To find her. If she is hiding, then let it be known that there is a reward." He crossed his arms and looked coldy at the lieutenant. "This reward is an investment for me, Hignall. A substantial investment, in my future. Go now and do your duty as I have requested. In the king's name, of course."

Lauder watched as the lieutenant retreated through the door of his study. He smiled. John Lauder knew something that not many men could say. He knew the future. He repeated it to himself. The phrase seemed so unnatural.

He knew what had happened to him in that other future, and he was going to improve it. In his old future, he had achieved one of the goals of his life. Peerage. Nobility.

He was a merchant. Wildly successful, and rich. Richer than most of the so-called nobility. He huffed at the irony. He was a commoner, who could buy and sell many of them.

In that other future, he achieved only the lowest ranks of nobility. He smiled coldly as he looked at the papers in front of him. The conclusion to be drawn from them was obvious, even if it was not written as such. During the war with Scotland, which now might not be fought, he had supported King Charles. That much was clear. He was rewarded with lands taken from those who opposed the king. Which increased his vast fortune even further. He was given the opportunity to buy a baronetcy, the lowest of the ranks of the noble class.

This time, it would be far more than a baronet of Nova Scotia. Far more. *Lord* Lauder had a very nice ring to it, he decided. And taking the head of Jenny Geddes was one step along that road.

The king would be pleased.

He rubbed his hands together, placed them on his skinny hips, and called to his servants for lunch.

☆ ☆ ☆

Jenny was not a happy person, nor was her seven-year-old daughter who stood in front of her. The girl, Dolina, was on the verge of tears, and was holding her butt where it had just been swatted.

"I told ye you couldn't go outside. It's not safe for us here. I been worried sick about ye. Where ye been, girl? Tell me now."

Dolina's lip quivered. "Just playing, Mum."

"And where is your sis, Elspeth? She's supposed t'be watching ye."

"Elspeth's playing too, Mum."

"Where is she, then?"

"In the alley, Mum. Couple houses over."

"Sit down there, and stay. Do you understand me, lassie? So help me, I'll tan your hide if ye do this again."

"Yes, Mum." The lower lip continued to quiver.

Jenny went to the front door, and opened it a crack. Otto had been explicit in his instructions. Do not go outside, not for anything. Stay away from the windows. She had fallen asleep for just a moment and Elspeth, who was ten and should have known better, slipped away. Jenny was going to tan her hide when she got her back. She peered out the slightly open door, and looked up and down the street. There was nobody in sight. The street was a small one, no more than a dead-end alleyway, with three-story townhouses on either side of the narrow way. The homes were run down and gritty looking, and the street was filthy with garbage, both human and otherwise. The strong odor of it struck her nose. She crept out and quietly closed the door behind her.

Jenny knew that Otto would be back soon, and she wanted to get Elspeth back into the safe house before he returned. Otto had gone to the market to buy something so she could prepare the evening meal. She glanced up and down the deserted street again. Nobody seemed to be out, so she headed down the street toward the end. From there she could see a small gangway between two houses and could hear children's voices from behind the house. She walked quickly and quietly down the alleyway, and stopped before she rounded the corner behind the dwelling. The area was a typical hodge-podge of crumbling and propped-up buildings. Behind two of the buildings, there was a junk-strewn open area. Something was probably there years ago, but she guessed that it had burned down.

She listened at the end of the alleyway, until she could hear Elspeth's voice. She glanced behind her once again, and seeing nobody, she peered around the corner. She could see the girls playing on a trash pile, using sticks for dolls and burned wood for their doll cribs. There were three girls, along with Elspeth, all of then between ten and twelve years old, she figured. She could see no one else in the alley. She stepped out and called quietly to her daughter.

"Elspeth. Elspeth. Oy, girl. Come here."

Elspeth looked up and saw her mother. Jenny could see the emotions flowing across her face. She could tell that the first thought was momentary confusion. The second was the realization of where she was, third the realization that she was in trouble, and the fourth thought, Jenny saw, was her daughter looking for her little sister, who was nowhere in sight. Elspeth turned and looked at her mother with panic in her eyes. Jenny stepped further around the corner and waved to the girl to come to her.

She saw Elspeth glance at her new friends, then back at her mother. Elspeth said goodbye and hustled toward her. As she ran up, she began with the excuses. "Mum, I am sorry, I lost track of Dolina. She can't have gone far, Mum. She was right here a second ago, and when you was sleeping, I thought that it would be all right to go out and play. I heard the girls outside and—"

All of this came out in a rush of apology, fear, anxiety, and the terrible understanding that she had made a big mistake. She braced for a slap. Instead, Jenny shushed her. "It's all right, Elspeth. Be quiet. Now."

Jenny looked around the back alley to see if there was anyone there except for the other children. She saw nobody else. She sighed with relief. She knelt in front of her older daughter, and looked at her face. It was flushed with embarrassment. She whispered to her. "Lassie, did ye tell anyone your name?"

Elspeth looked at her mother with fear. "Umm. Sort of. I told them I was Elspeth, and that I usually live outside the walls, and that we were staying down the street. I didn't see the harm in it, Mum, they are just kids like me." As the girl finished the sentence, her eyes went beyond her mother and focused on someone else. Her eyes then flicked back to her mother, and she swallowed. Jenny tensed at her daughter's reaction. Someone was coming up behind her. She quickly stood up, turned around, and pushed her daughter behind her, facing whoever was coming down the alleyway.

They were two large men, who were dressed as if they were stonemasons, dirty and dusty from a day at work. She tried to control her fear, but her face must have given her away. She watched as they became suspicious, reacting to her fear. The two men looked at each other, and then turned back to her. The older one spoke.

"Who might you be?"

"We are just a visiting, down the street a bit." Jenny smiled at them, hoping to charm the burly stonemasons.

The younger man called to the other girls in the alleyway. "Alice, Mary. Get ye home, and be quick about it. Now!" The girls ran off, looking back at Elspeth as they went by. One of them waved. The younger man took a halfhearted and somewhat playful kick at the last one, and landed it on her rump. Jenny and Elspeth both smiled at him, and he smiled back. The younger one took a step forward, as if to introduce himself. The older man held him back.

"Just a moment, Andrew. I asked this lady a question, and she hasn't answered me yet."

Andrew looked confused, and turned to the older man. "Da, she is just a new lass from down the street. We're not the papist inquisition, fer heaven's sake." He turned to Jenny and smiled. "My name is Andrew, and this is me da, Bill. We live up there on the third floor, and my sister's kids and my daughter live below. Nice to meet you."

Jenny was still holding Elspeth behind her. She smiled and curtsied. " 'Tis nice to meet you, Andrew. You too, Bill." She grabbed Elspeth's hand. "I am afraid it's time for us to be heading back home—"

"Not so fast. What did ye say your name was?"

Andrew once again looked at his father in surprise. "Da—"

"Quiet, boy. I am asking a question. Now what did ye say your name was, lass?"

"I don't believe that I have said it, kind sir. Now if you will excuse me, we need to be getting home..." Jenny grabbed her daughter by the hand and tried to work her way past the men in the narrow passage. The older man put his arm out against the wall and blocked her way.

"Da—"

"Quiet, boy!" he bellowed. Andrew backed away, and Jenny flinched at the power in his voice. "Your sister said there was two girls playing out here with the kiddies. And now here is the mum. Think, boy. What was everyone talking about at work today?"

Andrew looked perplexed. "I dunno, Da. What was it?"

"If I said, 'reward money,' would that ring a bell?"

"Oy. D'ye think this is her?" Andrew asked.

Jenny couldn't help the stammer. She was never very good at lying. "Oh, I'm not that woman, the one they are after. Oh, no. That be someone else. My name is Mary. Yes. Mary, that's it. Mary Dunne. So we will be getting along now, kind sirs . . ."

Bill looked at Elspeth. He took a small step and loomed over her. "What be your name, now, lassie?" Jenny felt her daughter's hand tighten in hers.

"I . . . It is . . . Els— I mean, Mary. It be Mary, too, sir." Jenny squeezed her hand back.

Bill unexpectedly reached out with his calloused hand and clamped onto Jenny's wrist. She winced in pain. Andrew stepped back again, away from his father. "Da, do you think this is her?"

Bill looked at his son, and then back at Jenny. He held her arm up. "She not be crying out now, is she, boy? I would think if she wanted to be rescued, she would cry out now, don't ye?"

Andrew smiled. "Where are we supposed to take her for the reward? Lord, Da. The reward. We'll be rich!"

"Aye, boy." Bill turned around and started. Otto Artman was calmly standing in the narrow alleyway, arms folded, leaning against the wall.

Otto's voice was quiet and even, and with his German accent, it sounded all the more menacing. "This lady is under the protection of the Committee of Correspondence for Edinburgh. Nobody is going to turn anyone in for reward. Let her be." He smiled. "Please."

Jenny could see Bill and his son exchange a glance, measuring up the man in front of them. He was armed with a sword; they had no weapons. But together they were three times his size.

Bill smiled at Otto. "Four years of work is what it might take me, if I was lucky, to make that reward money. Neither you or your Committee scare me." With no more than a flick of his wrist, he pushed Jenny aside and back down the alley. She heard Otto's blade come out of its scabbard.

She yelled. "No! Otto, don't hurt them." The two stonemasons stopped and glanced at her in surprise. When they turned back to Otto, they were looking at his blade held level at their throats. He was faster than they ever thought possible. Jenny, too, blinked at the speed. She knew he was a soldier at one time, that was obvious, but she had no idea...

Otto looked at them grimly. "It is not the policy of the Committee to cut men down like dogs in the street. Someday, maybe, but not now. Not today."

"Otto, they have children and live in this building," Jenny said.

Otto looked at her and smiled faintly. He stepped back very slightly and addressed the father and son. "If you were to collect any reward, you would not live to profit from it." He stepped forward, and pushed his blade closer to their necks, one at a time. "Do you understand what that means?"

Andrew and Bill looked at each other. Andrew quickly shook his head at Bill, and Bill nodded back. They turned to Otto. "Aye, sir."

Otto took a step back. "The CoC takes care of their own, gentlemen. There are more besides me who would make sure there would be no profit in it."

Andrew and Bill nodded again. "Aye, sir."

Otto motioned Jenny to move behind him. He smiled broadly at the two stonemasons, stepped back again, and sheathed his blade. "I invite you to stop by the CoC building. We are just off the Mile, up from St. Giles High Kirk. We can always use help, especially when the help is the size of you two. There is much you could do." His smile went wider, and he bowed slightly.

As Jenny looked back over her shoulder, she saw the two men still standing in the alleyway. She waved at them, and after a moment's hesitation, they waved back. And smiled.

"Otto, ye haven't told me where we are goin?"

"We are almost there, Jenny."

"These new shoes hurt my feet. And I feel like some sort of a fancy bird in these clothes."

"Almost there."

"'Ave you ever tried walking in new shoes the first time? It's murder till they get broke in. There was a man I knew that all he did was walk around in rich people's new shoes so they would be broken in when they wore them for the first time. He was a cousin to the shoemaker over in Harper Lane. I used to think, 'that would be a life, why he's got it made, he does.' But hiking over the cobblestones and the shite in the street in new shoes is not the easiest job in the world."

Otto smiled at her with that strange smile of his. He spoke quietly so nobody in the street could overhear him. "Jenny Geddes, you are the only woman I ever met who would complain about new clothes and shoes."

She leaned toward him to whisper. "I ain't complaining about the clothes and the shoes. Not at all. I'm complaining about having to walk across the whole of Edinburgh city in new shoes. That's all."

When he first gave the shoes and dress to her, she was confused by what she thought was a gift, and an expensive one at that. He explained to her that it was a disguise.

She was still not sure what to make of this taciturn German. Jenny had spent most of her life being practical. Nothing more. Her mind put any other thoughts completely away. "One thing is for certain. Nobody will recognize me in this, even if I was behind me own cart in the market."

"Aye, Jenny. You do clean up rather well."

She laughed and turned to look at her daughters, who were following. They too, had been given "new" used clothes by Otto. Both girls were dressed in something nicer than they had ever hoped to wear in their lives. She looked at the happy expressions on their faces and felt guilty. Guilty that she could never have provided for them in this way. As a greengrocer and a widow, she lived precariously. It was not that much different an existence than most of the city, granted. But as a mother, she had always hoped for something better for her children.

While they continued to walk, she went over the last few days in her mind. Chased by soldiers, finding Otto and the Committee of Correspondence, nearly being caught for the reward money, and the tedium of hiding in the house for several days. And now, here she was, dressed in finery as a disguise, hiking across town to places unknown. She shook her head. Strange times indeed. Her practical mind told her that she shouldn't get used to the finery, because that was going to change. She didn't know when or how. But she knew it was true. She sighed and trudged on.

"Here we are."

She looked up and felt her jaw drop in amazement. "Is this the house where we be going?"

"Yes."

"By the front door, not the back door?"

"Yes."

"Oy. You're sure?"

He mounted the three steps to the heavy oaken front door and knocked. "Quite sure."

There had been no change of neighborhood to get to where the rich people lived. Edinburgh was so crammed together that everyone lived on top of one another. The members of the privy council, judges, lawyers and clerks lived alongside tenements and the shops of candle makers and smiths. The door opened, revealing a large man dressed as a servant. Jenny knew just by looking at the fellow that this was not your typical servant. He looked like he should be on a battlefield, not an Edinburgh townhouse, and a new house at that.

The large servant spoke. "Hello, Otto."

"Thomas. Good to see you again. I believe we have an appointment with Robert and his visitors?"

"Please come in; be seated in the library. I will let them know that you are here. Right this way." He led them down a hall and into a large room. There were more books there than Jenny had ever seen in her life. She was good with figures. She counted at a glance maybe twenty-five bound books, along with another dozen or so unbound ones. She turned to the children. "If either of you touch anything, I will swat your arses all the way back across town. Do ye hear me?"

Elspeth looked as overwhelmed as Jenny felt. She nodded. "Yes, Mum." She nudged her sister who was looking at a cabinet of curiosities standing in the corner. The cabinet had one of the most interesting dolls they had ever seen, with silky blond hair, and fancy clothes, and funny pointed shoes with a tall thin heel.

"Don't touch a thing," Jenny reminded them. She turned to Otto. "Will you now tell me where we are? And how do you know these people?"

"Jenny, you are impatient sometimes, do you know that?"

"Aye, I can be. And you can be frustrating at times."

"I know these people from Thuringia, in Germany. That's where I met them."

"These don't look like the type of people that the Committees are interested in, Otto." She glanced over at the girls, who were staring into the cabinet. She reminded them in a stage whisper,

"All the way across town, that's how far I will be tanning your little hides. No touching! Do ye hear me?"

"Yes, Mum." The girls tore their eyes off the strange doll, and put their hands in front of them.

"That's more like it."

The door opened and in walked a short man with red hair and whiskers. He was smiling through curiously good teeth. Otto recognized him instantly. "Alex! Good to see you. You are looking well."

The two men embraced briefly, and Alex turned his attention to Jenny. "So this is the famous Jenny Geddes, eh?"

Jenny could feel herself blushing. "Umm. Aye, sir, I am Jenny Geddes. I don't know about the famous part. Sir."

The man in front of her got a twinkle in his eye, and she found him instantly likeable. "Ah, but I do. Please sit down."

Otto spoke first. "How is the 'baroness,' Alex?" They laughed together. Jenny felt bewildered by the reference.

"Aye, she is fine. She is putting the baby down to nap, and will be here shortly."

Jenny leaned forward to catch Otto's eye. She raised her eyebrows, and said "A baroness?" very quietly, almost mouthing the words.

Otto smiled at her, and back at Alex. "Suppose you tell Jenny here how your wife was elevated to the Swedish nobility."

"Well, it's a long story, but basically it was due to her valor in combat." Alex smiled. Jenny decided it was an honest smile. She believed he was telling her the truth. She just didn't believe what she was hearing. The surprise must have shown on her face.

"Jenny," Otto said, "you really need to close your mouth. You look like a codfish."

She snapped her mouth shut. And immediately opened it again. "Oy! In b-battle?"

"Aye. My wife, Julie. But she didn't do nearly what you did, all on one Sunday morning."

Jenny got a little defensive. "I am at the kirk every Sunday morning. I get there early and save a place for the Dunnes, usually right in the front. I save them spots, and then I sit down on me stool, and listen to the preacher. So there's nothing I could have done in a battle or anything else on a Sunday morning. And when did I do this thing? Is that why the soldiers are after me? I swear, it never happened, whatever it was. You got the wrong woman."

Otto said, "It is not what you did, but what you will do. Or at least would have done." He looked at Alex. "Our language needs a new tense for this. A 'future that may not happen' tense. It's not past tense, it's not future tense, so perhaps we should call it 'maybe' tense. It would make this so much easier."

Jenny cut him off. "I have no idea what you are talking about. Otto, if this is some kind of joke, then I—"

"Wait a moment, Jenny." Otto paused. "I brought you here because you are so practical, and so hardheaded, there was no way you would believe me if I just told you. So I have to show you."

"Show me what?" This had been a difficult week for Jenny, and she decided she was no longer in mood for games.

Otto looked her in the eyes. "The future that might have happened, but didn't."

"Aye. And I'm the bloody queen of England." She crossed her arms and sat back in the chair, quite unladylike.

Alex jumped in. "What he's telling you is true, Jenny. I have never known Otto to speak aught but the truth. You can depend on that with your life." Jenny thought she saw a look pass between the men, as if recalling a specific incident.

She sighed, exasperated. "All right, what was it I was supposed to have done but didn't and still may or may not do?"

From behind her, a youthful female voice with a very strange accent answered. "You started the English Civil War. It eventually led to the beheading of King Charles."

Jenny found herself standing and looking at the woman who had answered the question. She was dressed in a most outlandish fashion, with a pullover shirt with writing on the front, which Jenny couldn't read, but it was very colorful. It was also stained with what looked like baby spittle. For an instant she thought she was meeting the wet nurse. But this girl was far too small of build for that. Slim in an athletic sort of way, like a circus performer she remembered from her childhood. Her pants, too, were outlandish. For one thing, they were *pants*, for heaven's sake. Women did not wear pants. Especially pants that showed her female figure to an advantage. Snug, like Jenny had never seen.

But it was the girl's eyes that Jenny noticed. The face was young, a little tired. Pretty in a girlish sort of way. Nice teeth. But the eyes, they were so... she grasped for the right word... wise? Experienced? They weren't old eyes, but Jenny felt that they

had seen far too much in her short life, and she instantly felt her heart go out to the girl.

"Oy. King Charles' head! I did that?"

Alex rose from his chair and went to the girl. His kiss made the cloud go from her eyes, and only the girl was visible again. Jenny marveled while Alex made the introductions.

"Jenny Geddes, may I present to you Mrs. Julie Mackay, Baroness of Sweden, formerly of Grantville, West Virginia, in America, and the absolute best shot in the entire world, without compare. Julie, this is Jenny Geddes. Jenny, Julie—Julie, Jenny."

The two women stared at each other for an awkward moment, then smiled. Julie's eyes landed on Jenny's daughters, and she smiled again. "Who are these fine young ladies?"

"The older one is Elspeth, and the little one is Dolina."

"What pretty names."

"Elspeth was my mother, and my husband was Donald, so we named the little one Dolina after him."

Dolina spoke up. "Is that your doll in the cabinet?"

Julie crouched to her level. "It used to be. But we gave it to Alex's father, Robert, as a present."

"Can I play with it?"

"I don't see why not. That's what it's for." With that, Julie opened the cabinet and gave the girls the doll. At first they were tentative, and then began to examine it closely. They really fixated on the strange shoes, Jenny noticed, as she wiggled her sore feet.

Julie leaned over to Jenny conspiratorially. "That ought to keep them occupied for a while." She paused while she looked at the girls. "You have lovely children, Jenny."

"I suppose. They are a bit of all right. Strong and sturdy, they will make fine wives someday. They are old enough to do their chores, and they do them well. Elspeth is learning some letters from the Dunnes; they have a fine house up the way from us and our cottage." Jenny paused while she thought of her cottage. "I don't suppose we will ever be able to go back there again."

Julie looked sympathetically into Jenny's eyes, then took her hand and set her down on the couch. "Jenny, I'm from the future, from the town of Grantville. Do you believe me?"

Jenny leaned back and looked at the girl again. There was just something so different about her. Jenny couldn't quite place it. A radiance, health, something subtle that she could not put a name to. She thought about what they could possibly gain by lying to her, with some elaborate ruse. But she was just Jenny Geddes, greengrocer. And they had protected her from the king's men.

She decided. "Aye. I do believe you. Not sure why. But I do."

Julie smiled warmly. "Have you heard of Grantville, and the Ring of Fire?"

"Aye, the preacher was talking to it the other day. I figure the church don't know what to do about it, but they say it is real enough. That's all I know. Is that where you got that funny accent?"

"Doesn't sound funny to me, Jenny." Julie smiled, and both women laughed nervously. "Would you like to know how you did all of this? What you did?"

Otto leaned forward. "Girls, we are going to visit with Robert for a few minutes." Jenny gave him a "please don't leave me" look. He just smiled that odd smile of his, and patted her hand. "You're in good hands, Jenny. I'll be back in a moment. Julie will explain it all."

When the men filed out of the room, Jenny turned to Julie. "How in the world does someone like me manage to bring down that bloody papist, Charles?"

"Do you have a stool that you sit on in church?"

"Aye."

"Well, to start the war off, you threw the stool at a bishop. He was starting to read from a new liturgy that was put in place by Archbishop Laud. You are reported to have said something about 'preaching papist something or other to your lugs.'"

"Me?"

"And after that, the whole place went up for grabs, and a riot started. Then the riots spread, and the whole thing went on from there. This is supposed to happen about three years from now."

"Me?"

"It's what *that* history remembered you for."

"*That* history?"

"Well, Jenny, I say that history because it is the history I knew, in my world."

"I caused the whole thing to start? Me. Jenny Geddes, the widowed greengrocer."

Julie just nodded. "It is a little hard to believe." She sighed and sat back on the couch. "Sometimes I don't think it's real myself. Before the Ring of Fire, I was a high school senior, head

cheerleader, looking forward to graduation, college. And today, I'm in the seventeenth century, married to a fine man, with a new baby. That man's father, Robert, whose house this is, has a broken back, and he is dying. In my world, there was so much we could do to make him well—be able to live a full life. And we are trying to do so much..."

Jenny took Julie's hand, and gave it a squeeze. That odd look had come back into Julie's eyes, the one she saw a flash of when she first came into the room. Jenny tried to imagine what this girl must have gone through. She just squeezed a little harder.

They stayed like that for a moment, and Jenny began to think, trying to assimilate all that she had learned in the past few minutes. She knew in her gut it was true, and she knew that Otto was right. Without meeting Julie, she never would have believed it. A thought came to her. "Now I understand why the king's men were after me. They wanted to kill me so that I wouldn't throw my stool, and then there would be no war. That is it, isn't it?"

Julie pulled her hand back and brushed a bit of hair out of her face. "Well, no. At least we don't think so. Laud and Stafford have agreed to leave Scotland alone, so Charles can deal with all the people who overthrew him, or at least might have. But that history is not going to happen. It's impossible. So what's the point of coming after you? It makes no sense. They have agreed to leave the Scots alone. There are any number of stupid shit royals up here who helped Charles to the block, why pick on you?"

Jenny shrugged. "Heaven knows, I have no idea..." She paused for a moment. "Baroness?"

"Please. Call me Julie."

"Aye. Julie it shall be."

Otto half-staggered and was half-carried out of the pub by three soldiers. One was a sergeant, and the other two were regulars. He had gone to the bar with the goal of trying to find out who was behind the attempt to capture Jenny Geddes. He was leaving in a state of semi-consciousness.

Sergeant Thatcher had overheard the conversation, and could tell his men were being pumped for information by the German fellow, under cover of old warrior's tales. The German talked a big game, fighting with Tilly on the continent, Magdeburg, White Mountain. Trading stories. Garrison life must be dull, what do you men do to stay sharp? Chase greengrocer women? Who paid you to do that? How much does that sort of a job go for here? Can I buy you another beer?

It was at that point that Thatcher walked quietly up behind the man, and rapped him on the side of the head with the pommel of his sword. Not enough to kill him, certainly. Just enough to render him senseless for a while. There was a skill to hitting someone that way, and it took considerable practice over the years to get it right. As well as a few fatal and near-fatal errors. He'd gotten good at it by practicing on Irish prisoners five years ago.

They dragged him out of the pub, and waved at the concerned barkeep and the serving girls. "He's had a bit too much. We'll take care of him . . ." They dragged him toward an alley not far across the lane. There, Thatcher would find out who he was working for and report it to his lieutenant. Should be a bonus in it for him, he figured.

"Take him over there, lads, and sit him down against the wall." Thatcher knelt before the semi-conscious Otto. "Well, well, well. What have we here? A German asking questions about a worthless greengrocer woman. I wonder why that is." He stood up, turned to his men, and smiled. "Right, lads. This is where I'm going to teach you a little about interrogation. Pay attention and learn from your sergeant." The two regulars grinned at each other expectantly.

"First, we need to wake this lad up." He squatted back down and began to slap Otto hard about the face, first one way and then the other. Otto moaned as he began to regain consciousness.

"Next, we need to make sure he is not going to go anywhere."

The first soldier spoke up. "Do you want us to tie him up so he won't run away?"

"No. Not necessary." Thatcher pulled his dagger and ran it through Otto's calf, just below the knee. Otto screamed. Thatcher twisted the dagger so he could pull it out. Otto screamed again. "Wakes them up and keeps them from moving, it does."

The regulars nodded at the wisdom and efficiency of their sergeant. He squatted down next to Otto again.

"I know that a man such as yourself, who has been in so many illustrious battles, won't tell me anything because you are so tough." Thatcher grinned up at the two regulars. "But let me ask this. And you should answer, otherwise, I run you through on the other calf. Then your thighs, then the wrists, the arms,

and finally your dick. You won't be dead. You will then tell me what I want to know, so that I kill you to stop the pain. Let's get started, shall we? Who are you working for?"

"Fuck off, you shithead." The three soldiers laughed.

"Well, at least you aren't like some of those damned Irish, begging for your life right away. There will be some sport in this, lads. Pay attention and learn from the master." All three men were smiling. The man on the ground in front of them was helpless, bleeding and holding his calf with both hands. They didn't see his right hand slipping into the top of his boot.

Sergeant Thatcher turned to smile at his two pupils. "Now, lads, the next cut will be to the opposite calf."

They were just beginning to grin when Otto's dagger went deep into Thatcher's neck at the base of his skull.

Otto left the dagger where it struck and pulled the sergeant's sword from its sheath, launching a desperate lunge at the vulnerable neck of the closest soldier before either of them could react to his savage assault. Otto's lunge caught the man through the carotid artery. Blood sprayed from the wound as the man gurgled and stumbled backwards before falling to the cobblestones.

The third soldier had his sword out. He surprised Otto by attacking immediately instead of running. Otto barely parried the lunge, and stepped back defensively. His calf gave out and he fell to the ground. He cursed his incompetence as he fell, cursed himself for not remembering the wound. He made a mental note to remember wounds—if there was ever another.

"You bloody bastard," the remaining English soldier growled. Otto lay on his back with his blade raised ineffectively.

"*Probably won't be a next time*," thought Otto.

The soldier batted aside Otto's sword and stepped up to deliver a fatal thrust. Suddenly he froze. He looked confused, then reached behind him. His hand returned stained with blood.

Otto saw the light go from the man's still-confused eyes. Then the soldier fell.

"About goddamn time, Mackay."

"Aye, Otto, sorry. I had to piss."

"Well, hold it next time."

"How's the leg?"

"What do you think? It bloody hurts. I just hope the damage isn't too bad."

Alex surveyed the carnage in the alleyway. "After all of this, have we learned anything?"

"The soldiers in the tavern said it was some rich bastard by the name of Lauder. No idea why, just who."

"And just what is a Committee of Communication?"

"The Committee of Correspondence, Mr. Lauder." Lieutenant William Hignall sighed inwardly. His bosses in the privy council had told him to give this man whatever he wanted. Hignall was trying to accommodate, but he was not happy about it. He would be respectful, polite, and try very hard not to kill the idiot where he stood. He took a breath and continued. "The people hiding Jenny Geddes are called the Committees of Correspondence. There are a couple of Germans involved, as well as many Scots. My men apparently escorted a German out of the pub last night. According to the barkeep, this man is a known organizer with the committee."

"I thought they were killed due to your men quarreling among themselves, Hignall. As competent as they seem to be, it would not surprise me at all."

Hignall bit his tongue at the clumsy sarcasm. It was either bite, or run the man through right then and there. "Sir, the fact that we can get no information from our informants in the city is also typical of the Committee's methods. They are as bad as the worst criminal gangs, sir. And they are political. They are linked to the Americans in Thuringia. We have been unable to get a spy into their inner council."

"My God, you do have the excuses, Hignall!" Lauder's sharp and thin face looked as if it were about to burst. "All I wanted was a simple arrest and killing of one greengrocer, a woman at that. And this one German, who was dragged unconscious out of the pub, is possibly part of this correspondence committee and lethal enough to kill three of your men in an alley. It is far more likely your men were fighting over who was going to steal this German's boots, or whatever else he might have on him. Although I can't imagine anything he could have that was so valuable." The rich businessman stopped and wagged his finger, and Hignall had the briefest fantasy of snapping it off and shoving it up his ass. "This is simple incompetence, and I will have words with my friends on the privy council. You know what the council does, don't you, Hignall?"

Hignall felt his tongue bleeding in his mouth. "Yes, sir, I do. But—"

"The council is the group that advises the king on all matters regarding Scotland. They have the direct ear of the king. Most of them are my friends, Hignall. You would do well to remember that. It seems you need constant reminding."

Hignall swallowed some more blood, and replied. "Yes, sir."

"There's a limit to my patience, Hignall. Get the job done, soon. Otherwise we might embarrass the privy council, and that would be very—how should I say it?—awkward for you. So. You have two more days. Otherwise . . ." Lauder paused, and tugged on his goatee, and waved his hand. "Otherwise, there will be severe consequences for you. Do you understand?"

"Aye, sir. I understand."

"And Hignall, how many Germans do you think are in Edinburgh?"

"Can't be that many, sir. Less than a hundred maybe."

"Find that German from the pub. He should lead you to the woman."

Hignall bit his tongue even harder, if that was possible. "We are working on that now, sir. Looking for the German."

"You are? Wonderful. It seems you do have a brain, Lieutenant. You have two days. Any more than that, I will have to stop looking, and you will stop . . ." He smiled a great officious, oily and false smile. ". . . stop doing whatever it is you do."

Outside Lauder's fortified house, Hignall took the reins from his man, and they mounted the horses for the nine-mile ride back to the walls of Edinburgh. He spat the blood out of his mouth onto the ground. "This asshole wants to be a bloody damn Lord-dumbshit-royal-bastard." He spit more blood. "He don't need to work very hard at it, he already has the stupid-asshole-bitch-like-a-woman part down. He will fit right in with the rest of those pricks."

The soldier next to him nodded. "Aye, sir."

"We got to find us a German or two." Hignall spurred his mount harshly, and rode off toward the town. His man followed.

Julie Mackay rapped the proper code on the door of the safe house, with Thomas, the Mackays' bodyguard servant, in tow. The door opened cautiously, and then was immediately thrown open.

"Julie! This be a surprise, lass. What brings ye here? Hello, Thomas." The large man nodded. "Well, come in, come in, don't stand out there like a couple of beggars, come on in. It's not too fancy, but it's clean." Jenny closed the door behind them after a quick glance up the empty street.

"I've come to bring you a little present, Jenny. Is there somewhere a little more private that we can talk?" Jenny looked about the small first floor, and then at the staircase.

"Up here. But mind the seventh step."

"Why the seventh step, Jenny?"

As Jenny bounded up the stairs, she pointed to the seventh step. "This one here is a stumble step. It's different than all of the other stairs, so if ye be creeping up the stairs in the dark, and ye don't know the house, you are going to stumble and fall, and wake us up."

As Julie walked up the stairs, she smiled. "Well, son of a gun. Seventeenth-century burglar alarm. You have to step up another couple inches to clear it."

"Aye. Your Otto is a clever one, Julie."

"My Otto?" Julie giggled. "I sorta thought he was your Otto." She walked into one of the larger bedrooms on the second floor.

"Very funny. I got no time for that nonsense. Men can be a pain in the arse."

Julie sat on the side of the bed and motioned for Jenny to sit down beside her. "What do you mean, Jenny? Haven't you seen the way he looks at you? And smiles? In all the time I have known Otto, I have never seen him smile that way. And it is always at you. Nobody else I've ever seen."

Jenny remained standing, and fiercely shook her head. "I ain't seen nothing of the sort. You're imagining things, you are." She popped her pipe in her mouth with a frown. "I be too long in the tooth for that sort of thing, girl. No time, no money. Men can be a pain in the arse."

"Jenny. Please sit down."

"I am fine where I am, lass."

Julie snickered a little under her breath. "You know that Otto is a very busy man. He runs what we hope will become a real Committee in Edinburgh. Have you seen anyone else come and take care of you? Have you noticed the way he looks at you? The way he smiles? I noticed as soon as I saw him with you in Robert Mackay's home the other day. He likes you, Jenny."

"That be children's play, that is." She crossed her arms and pulled on the unlit pipe. "I ain't got the time nor the inclination for that sort of foolishness."

Julie laughed out loud. "I hear you saying it, Jenny. I'm not buying it."

"Suit yerself."

Julie grinned. "I am glad I met you, Jenny Geddes. I didn't realize how long it had been since I talked openly to another female about anything. I really needed to. We must have gone on for three hours."

Jenny cleared her throat, and put her pipe away to stall for some time. "Well, I think ye needed it too, Julie Mackay. Even if you are some sort of duchess or baroness, or whatever it is. And that little Alexi is a cutie. I'll be here for you if you need to talk, anytime. Providing that the king's men finally give up on me someday."

"Do you want to see your present?"

After Julie and Thomas had left, Jenny showed the present to the girls. "This tiny little thing is a revolver. It is a gun, like a great gun a cavalryman wears, so don't you girls go messing with it. It looks like a toy, but she says that it will kill a man right quick. It's a twenty-two caliber, the smallest of the guns she has. I'm going to hide it under my bed and I don't want you two touching it. Ye hear me?"

"Yes, Mum."

She didn't tell them that Julie had shown her how to use it. It was to be used up close and personal. And she was to keep pulling the trigger until it stopped firing.

William Hignall knew that he had made a mistake the first time he did what that idiot Lauder had told him to do. Take the troops out and capture the woman. It didn't feel right the first time, and sure enough, it went to shite. He should have taken a small squad, just a few men, and picked her up at her home. No fancy show, just get the job done. This time, he was not going to make the same mistake. He broke the men up into three- and four-man teams, each one tracking one German or another. He took three of his better men with him, and went after any Germans that might be involved with the Committee of Correspondence. Those were the most promising leads. And one of those, a fellow named Otto, was the most likely prospect.

They tracked him, through the word of some street urchins, to a small, out of the way street that appeared to dead end. The urchins said he was there often. Hignall surveyed the short street. "We'll start on this side. Bang on the doors, break 'em down if you have to. We're looking for the German and Jenny Geddes."

The first decrepit townhouse they came to had a large family with six or seven kids living in two rooms, and another family upstairs. When the door was answered, they forced their way in, and there was a lot of screaming by children and adults.

Hignall grabbed one of the kids—she looked maybe nine or ten—and held her by the hair. His men kept the others at bay with drawn swords. "Quiet," he roared. "I am going to make this very simple. I am looking for a German, or a woman with two children. They might be on this piece of shite street. Who in here does this filth belong to?" He presented the child in front of him, still holding her by the hair, his dagger pulled and pointing at her neck. "I want an answer now, you ignorant Scottish bitch." He raised the blade as if to strike, and a woman came screaming and sobbing out of the gaggle of ragged people. She was halted at the points of the drawn swords of his men.

The woman sobbed, pacing in front of Hignall's men like a caged animal. Agitated, but harmless, thought Hignall. Like some bitch of a dog. "She be my child, sir. What do you want to know? Please don't hurt her. I'll tell you what you want to know." The rest of the children were cowering in the corners, and a few had run off. Hignall didn't care much where they went; it didn't matter. He was going to find out what he needed right now.

He pressed the blade to the back of the child's neck. "Answer me, woman. Is there a German living on this street?"

She glanced with apprehension over her shoulder at her other children and what looked to be her husband, then turned nervously back to Hignall. "Aye. Please sir, let her go."

"Which dwelling?" The woman hesitated, and Hignall pressed the blade tighter to the little girl's neck. She began to whimper. "Which dwelling, woman?"

"He be three doors down, sir. Clean house it is, good house, with windows in it. Please sir, let her go."

"Anyone living with him?"

"He don't live there, sir, he just visits. Every day." She was struggling to be calm, fighting to stay rational. "Please, sir."

"Is there a woman and two kids living there, two girls about this one's size?" He nodded toward his hostage.

The woman dropped to her knees. "Please, sir, do not harm my little girl. I beseech ye, please."

"Answer the dammed question, woman, or I will run her though in the name of the king. A woman and two children?"

"Aye, sir, she be the one you are looking for. Three doors down. Please, sir, I beg ye."

Hignall snapped, "You know this is the one we have been looking for? Why didn't you come forward?"

"I don't know, sir."

Hignall almost whispered. "The next time your king, through his men, tells you to do something, you *do* it, woman!" With that, he pulled back his dagger and neatly sliced off one of the girl's ears. She screamed, the mother screamed, and Hignall threw the bleeding child toward her. "You will be reminded of your duty to your king every day now. All of you."

He turned and stalked out of the room and into the street, wiping the blade of his dagger between his fingers to clean it. "Damn these Scots. They are almost as bad as the Irish." He turned to his men. "Let's get this over with. I need a drink." He sheathed his dagger and strode to the third door down, leaving the screams behind him.

"Prime your wheel locks, lads."

"Aye, sir."

"Shoot the German if he's there, and run everyone else through. We'll just take the heads, don't need the whole thing."

Jenny heard the screaming from down the street, and tried to see from the window what was happening. Outlaws usually don't go into homes like that one with the screaming children, and seldom in the daylight. Nothing there to steal. They must be searching, she thought, searching for me. She saw a couple of children run away in panic from the house, then turn with their hands on their heads and start sobbing, walk a couple of paces back to the house, and run away again. Helpless in their agony and fear. Jenny bit her lip.

"Elspeth, Dolina. We are going to run out the back and through the alley. Can you find the Mackay house if we get separated?"

"Aye, Mum," replied Elspeth.

Dolina began to sniffle. "I'm scared, Mum."

"Don't be scared. Your big sister will take care of you. Listen and obey her. But you must run like the wind, my little lassies, like the wind. I need to get something from upstairs. I will be right back." As she turned and sprinted up the stairs, the first thuds of men trying to batter the door could be heard. The girls screamed.

"Run *now*!"

Jenny darted out of the bedroom with the revolver. Her hands were shaking, and she felt naked with this little weapon. The door exploded inward, and the men stormed into the room downstairs.

Jenny drew back into the bedroom as quietly as possible, looking at the small weapon in her hands. She stepped up onto a stool, looked out the tiny window, and watched the girls running, hand in hand, as fast as they could go.

Hignall entered the room and stood still, listening. He saw an open door at the back of the house, and sprinted to look through the door.

"This place has a back door. These places never have goddamn back doors. Smith. Get after them kids."

"Aye, sir, what about the mother?"

"Never mind her. She's still here."

"How do you know that, sir?" one of the men asked.

"Because no mother would run in front of her children. They are always behind. She's still here." Hignall looked around the two rooms that made up the first floor. He could see no cellar, only a staircase going up. He smiled, and nodded to his remaining men. "Follow me, men."

"Aye, sir."

Otto Artman was bleeding from his calf as he limped at a furious pace toward the safe house. He had avoided a group of soldiers once, and he was worried. As he rounded the corner, he realized he needed to be worried. He had seriously misjudged the amount of effort Lauder was putting into finding Jenny. The first house he came to was in chaos. No time for that. He continued down the street, now leaving frequent drops of his own blood as he walked. When he saw the door to the safe house off of its hinges his heart went dark. Knowing what might be happening beyond the open doorway made him angry at a primal level. He drew his sword and dagger and charged through the open door.

He came face to face with three soldiers, one of them an officer. English regulars. The king's men. His face drew back into a snarl, and he attacked. Otto went low, hoping to score a quick hit on the officer, but the man was already poised for combat before Otto came through the doorway and easily parried Otto's thrusting sword.

"Shoot this son of a bitch." The officer called as he stepped out of the line of fire.

Wheel-lock pistols came out of the belts. Otto dove blindly to the side, landing on the bottom of the stairway as one of the guns discharged. The noise was deafening, and the smoke that formed was thick and acrid.

The soldier who had fired dropped his pistol, drew his sword, and charged Otto.

In Otto's mind the man was dead already. He easily parried the soldier's thrusting sword before closing to thrust his dagger into the man's belly.

The soldier dropped his sword, both hands felt for the wound in his belly. "You've killed me, you bastard!" he hissed, falling and rolling into the path of the other two men.

Otto's eyes turned to the second wheel lock. He backed up the stairs as the officer came after him. The soldier with the wheel lock followed, trying to get a clear shot from his position behind the officer on the narrow stairway. Smoke filled the air and rose up the stairway, stinging everybody's eyes.

Sergeant Robert Smith felt a little foolish chasing a couple of kids with a drawn sword. They had ducked down a gangway between two buildings and run into an opening beyond. As he was about to round the corner, a dusty arm the size of a tree branch suddenly extended across his path. He could feel his head stay stationary, and the rest of his body move forward. He had a curious sensation in his neck. His feet swung out and he fell onto his back, breathless. As he was lying on the ground, looking up at the sky, two giants appeared. Their rock-hard hands picked him up as if he was a rag doll.

"Da," one of them said. "Don't kill him in front of the children."

Robert wanted to agree, but he found he could not speak. As a matter of fact, he noticed he was very short of breath. His limbs dangled at his side, and he couldn't move. As the giants carried him away, he heard another popping noise come from his neck, and then there was merciful blackness.

Otto continued to back up the stairs, thrusting at the officer, attempting to keep the officer between him and the remaining wheel lock while also preventing the officer drawing his own pistol. They moved from side to side, always moving, going up the stairs one at a time. Otto felt the stumble stair, and stepped up. He planned his attack.

But the officer was good. He had seen the adjustment that Otto made for the stairs, despite the smoke, and cleared the step easily. He easily parried Otto's attack, and drove him back another step. Otto lost his balance, and had to hop up another stair to keep upright. Finally a safe distance from Otto's deadly sword the officer dropped out of the line of fire. "Shoot, goddammit, *shoot*!"

Otto found himself staring down the length of the stairway into the barrel of a wheel-lock pistol. Time seemed to slow down. Otto watched the soldier jerk the trigger. He saw the wheel rotate at the side of the weapon, creating a shower of sparks. As he tried to dive out of the way he saw the flash of the pan igniting.

Otto felt pressure in his head, and his vision went black. He was angry at his failure.

Hignall's ears were ringing; the German—Hignall assumed he was the German—was sprawled across the stairway. Hignall rose to his knees and looked up the stairs. There was a woman standing at the top. He smiled through the smoke. "Hello, Jenny Geddes."

The voice that came back to him was hard as steel on a midwinter's night. "You have the advantage, sir. I don't believe we have met."

"Lieutenant William Hignall, the King's Men."

"Aren't you supposed to say, 'at your service,' or something like that?"

"Normally I would, but in this circumstance... Well, I'm sure you understand." He smiled, and started to stand.

A heavy footstool raced toward his head. He dropped to the stairs again, and the soldier behind him caught the stool hard in the face. He saw the man stumble and fall. Hignall pursed his lips as he saw the angle of the man's neck. Broken.

He got up again and looked to the top of the stairs. "You bitch. I've had enough out of you." Sword in hand, he kicked the sprawled body of Otto to check for signs of life before continuing up the stairs.

The woman was waiting at the top. She had her arms extended, and in her hands was what had to be a pocket pistol of some kind. Arrogantly he reached out with the blade to slap it out of her hand, but it fired. Something tore along his cheek. He felt the wound with his left hand. Something had gouged a gully through the flesh of his cheek and torn up his ear. He tried to curse her, but it hurt. He shook his head to clear the fog and the pain. He went for her again, a lunge with the blade. The gun popped again and the side of his neck stung. His hand went to it. *What the hell is happening?*

He took another step up the stairs. She backed up. He thrust at her with his sword.

The gun popped a third time and his shoulder exploded with pain. He dropped his sword.

She now took a step toward him. He raised his other arm to tell her to stop. There was another pop, louder this time, and his hand, wrist, and forearm exploded in pain. He felt pieces of bone and blood and tissue splatter his face.

She came closer. He could see it clearly now. It was like no gun he'd ever seen before. Something buzzed by his ear, like an angry insect. He could not believe what was happening to him. *It wasn't supposed to be like this, not in some run-down building by some bitch of a wo—*

He never finished the thought. A bullet went into his right eye and tore through his brain.

Jenny sat in the library at the Mackay house, with her daughters. They huddled together on a sofa, but Elspeth and Dolina were both asleep. Julie entered the room and quietly closed the door behind her. She sat across from them, and looked at the girls.

"You have a nice family, Jenny."

Jenny had a far-off look in her eyes. She shook her head slightly.

"What is it, Jenny?"

Jenny glanced down at the girls, then back up at Julie. "You didn't tell me what it would do to him. I kept going until it was empty. At his face."

"Jenny. I know it is hard to kill someone. But if they are going to hurt you, or someone you love, you need to—"

"No, lass. You don't understand. His face, that man's face. I want to remember it for a long time. That wee gun of yours made it look like a slab of meat with holes in it."

Julie's eyebrow arched in surprise. "What?"

Jenny smiled. "That man and his men were bastards. Deserved what they got. I know that, and God knows that too. That don't bother me none at all. That is simply doing the right thing. I want to remember that face, because of what it means to me. Bloody tyranny, that is what it represents. Just bloody tyranny. That is gonna be a face I remember for a long time."

"You're sounding like a Committee of Correspondence recruiter."

"Aye, and maybe that is what I should be adoing with my time, instead of greengrocer. Something better for my kids, better world."

"You are not sounding like a stubborn and hardheaded Scotswoman, Jenny," Julie said.

"Aye, that's true. But that don't mean I can't go doing that in a hardheaded and stubborn way." She giggled quietly. "And I throw a mean stool."

"Did you really get one of those guys with a stool?"

"I certainly did. The one that shot Otto. The bastard."

The door opened and Alex stuck his head in. "He's awake."

Jenny got up as quickly as she could, extracting herself from her sleeping daughters, and dashed over to Alex. "Can I see him?"

Julie came up behind her. "He has a nasty concussion. The bullet grazed his skull. So be very quiet, he is still a little out of it." They went down the hall, past Robert Mackay's room, and into another room on the first floor. The curtains were drawn, keeping the light to a minimum, and in the bed was Otto, his eyes open. Somewhat glazed, to be sure, but still open.

When Jenny walked into the room, he smiled. "I am glad to find you alive, Jenny Geddes."

She walked quickly to his bedside, smiling back at him. "I'm glad to find you alive too, Otto. How are ye feeling?"

"Not too bad, considering the circumstances. So, I guess we won, then?"

"Aye, we did at that. We have taken the liberty of using your newly arrived printing press to put up posters, explaining who was behind the attempt to capture me. The king's men have been asked to leave Edinburgh by the privy council, and our Mr. Lauder is not likely to be a lord of anything. He lost a few friends on the council, but nobody is willing to come out and say he was behind it. And the mood of the city is—interesting." She moved closer to Otto, and now held his hand. "Ain't that something?"

Otto smiled that curious smile, and squeezed her hand.

Jenny froze. She looked at her hand. She looked at Julie, who was smiling at her with an overtone of smugness. She looked at Alex, who was pretending not to see anything except the ceiling. Jenny snapped her hand back and glared at Julie and Alex. "Just because I held his hand, don't mean a thing. Don't you go supposing what I be thinking. We've got a world to change. No time for nonsense. There be a whole world of no-good lords and ladies that will need a stool thrown at them now and again. That's what I'm gonna do."

She dug her pipe from her pocket, popped it in her mouth and folded her arms in front of her. "Men can just be a pain in the arse."

Cinco de Mayo...er, Der Fünfte Mai

Edith Wild

"So what the heck is a taco, really?" asked Maria, David's girlfriend.

It was with great fanfare that the owners of the Thuringen Gardens added real honest-to-God tacos to their menu in May of 1634. May 5th, *Cinco de Mayo*, was to be celebrated with a mariachi band, Mexican food, piñatas, Mexican-style candies, cotton candy and German beer. Of course, the Gardens was packed with anyone in Grantville who was addicted to tacos. This included David Dominic Villareal and company.

"They're...well, they're just good," David said. "I've missed them, missed them a lot. The fast food kind, that is. Mom does great spaghetti, but her tacos...well, never mind. It's nice to be able to go to a restaurant and order what you want, don't you think?"

Maria held on to David's hand. They were the usual party of twelve, David, Maria, some of his friends and their girlfriends. They were normally in the Gardens at least twice a week, often more, drinking beer and eating typical Gardens food. Maria did like sauerkraut and sausages, so why not tacos? David had gotten her to agree to try them, even though she still had her doubts.

"May fifth will be forever different," David said. "It's time to celebrate our heritage as Mexican Americans, not just Thanksgiving and Fourth of July."

The platters of tacos were rolled out and set on the tables. David's eyes lit up like two roman candles at a fireworks show.

"Tacos! Tacos!" he said. "Look, Maria!"

She did. Hugely layered, with beef, spring greens, baby tomatoes, shredded cheddar cheese, sour cream and hot sauce on tortillas the size of dinner plates.

"Pico de gallo!" David exclaimed. "I sure miss guacamole, though. But you can't ship in avocados yet."

David looked like he'd died and gone to heaven. The beer steins, enormous things, were all loaded with a local pilsner. Maria felt aghast at the mound of food and could not for the life of her figure out why David liked the tacos so much. They smelled funny. There was a burning sensation in the air, but no flames. David was sweating profusely and appeared to be in pain but washed it away with more pilsner.

Maria picked at her taco, rolled her eyes and shuddered at the thought of eating anything strange looking. It was not ladylike, nor particularly practical. *We had tacos for dinner and I couldn't eat them,* she thought.

The music was another element; it was so different. The mariachi band was really not Mexican but they played the music, fast and sweet and romantic, or so David whispered into her ear. The band was even dressed authentically, in Jalisco costumes, David called them. They wore huge sombreros, and silver-embroidered velvet suits and the band even had a *viheula* and a *guitarron.* Maria could see that David recognized all of the men who played so fast and furiously.

David was grinning ear to ear at her like the silly ass he was.

Then he was poking Maria in her side a tad, encouraging her to try the stupid taco. Well, maybe it wouldn't be so bad. No sour cream, she'd stick with that. A little of the beef, perhaps some greens and some cheese. Pico de gallo... Maria hesitated. It had tomatoes in it. She was still not sure exactly how she felt about those, either.

Hesitant, Maria lifted the taco to her lips. There were waves and waves of fire emanating from it or seeming to... she took one small bite. At first there was not any sensation other than maybe it was really warm in the Gardens. Then the fire hit and Maria gasped, grasped her stein of pilsner and swallowed. She thought that half of the stein's contents had gone down her throat. She was coughing a bit and sputtering... but found herself reaching for more taco.

David was laughing and singing and clapping in time with the mariachi band. Then when the song was over, David, on bended knee, grasped her hand and slid a sparkling diamond ring on her left-hand ring finger... "White gold—" she heard him say "—so as not to compete with your beauty."

David smiled. He got up and slid back into his seat, then picked up his fork and started eating more taco. Another band was playing a song, "The Cherry Tree," with a hard rhythm, a line of thirty pairs of men and women were on the dance floor dancing the *Seguidilla*...

Maria thought, *Oh my God. I'm going to get married!*

There was so much going on at the same moment. Stein after stein was filled with beer. One group of men was trying to sing "Eine Prosit" to the mariachi band's tunes. Two down-timer men in their group still didn't want more than a bite of taco; their faces said "no way ever again." It was one thing to bite your food; it was another to have it bite back.

Arthur Esslies had actually spat it out and had stomped out of the Gardens and was chased after by another down-timer, Felix Brandt, who yelled, "Coward! It is good food! You dolt!"

The whole building was almost vibrating with music and dancing and singing.

A whole bunch of construction folk wandered in wanting the usual meal. They were rapidly converted to the idea that tacos were king. Then it was time for the piñatas to be beaten open and for the karaoke contest to begin. So the DJ set up and a contest got going. There was more beer and flan for dessert.

Maria thought, *I have a fiancé.* She looked at David intently: handsome, smart and silly and up-timer. "Do you want to dance, darling?"

He smiled. "Why not, babe?"

Conversion to American ways and food was an interesting process, Maria decided. She looked at her ring again. Maybe it was a step in the right direction.

A Matter of Unehrlichkeit

Kim Mackey

The breeze along the Rhine was beginning to freshen again when Philipp Hainhofer glanced once more towards the gates of Cologne. *Where are you, Georg? It's been over an hour!*

His youngest daughter, Sophie, noticed his look. "He's probably in a beer tavern somewhere with Magnus," Sophie said, nodding her blond head towards the walls of Cologne. "You really should have sent me with him, Father."

"Too bad you didn't mention that at the time, Sophie," Augusta, his next eldest daughter, said. "Advice comes too late when a thing is done."

Sophie's blue eyes narrowed. "Is that a challenge, my dear sister?" Sophie thought for a moment. "Good advice never comes too late."

Philipp Hainhofer sighed. As a way to get his sons and daughters to read and learn other languages, he had often practiced what he called "the proverb game" with them. His eldest daughters, Barbara and Judith, had enjoyed it so much that he had continued the game with his younger children as well. But with them, especially with Sophie and Augusta, it had turned more into a competitive struggle than a learning game. Sophie had the better memory, but Augusta had inherited both her mother's (God rest her soul) ability to get by with little sleep and her father's knack for languages. While Sophie could often respond in Latin, English or French, Augusta could often reply in Spanish, Dutch, Italian and Hebrew as well.

"Now daughters, please..."

Augusta smiled sweetly. "This won't take long, Papa, I promise." She looked at Sophie. "*Non dare consigli a chi non li chiede.* Would you like a translation, dear?"

Sophie shook her head. "Italian, of course."

Augusta nodded. "You've been studying. Good."

Sophie glared. "I'm not a complete ignoramus. Nor are you..."

A powerful gust of wind came from the north and all three of the Hainhofers grabbed their hats or caps to keep them from blowing away. Sophie's eyes widened and her hand flew to her mouth to stifle a scream as the crane transporting the last, large crate from their ship swayed dangerously.

All three watched anxiously. *Please*, thought Philipp, *not the writing desk too!* The first crate, which contained the small curiosity cabinet for Rentmeister Cronenburg, had crashed hard on the dock and Philipp knew that he would have to have repairs done to it before delivery. But the writing desk for Hardenrat would be much harder to repair if it broke, given its unique construction.

For several seconds the Hardenrat desk continued to sway in its net, and then the stevedores got it under control.

"That was fortunate," Augusta said. "And look, here comes Georg. That is the fastest I've seen him move in years." Like Augusta, Georg Hainhofer had inherited Philipp's tendency towards plumpness.

A trickle of apprehension ran down Philipp's spine. Why was Georg running?

Georg Hainhofer stopped in front of his father, gasping for breath.

"What's wrong, Georg?" Philipp asked. "Where is Magnus?"

Georg shook his head. "I... couldn't... find... him." He took a deep breath. "So I went to the city council house. He's been arrested! At the request of his own father!"

The next morning it took almost an hour for Philipp and Augusta Hainhofer to walk from the Inn of the Golden Grape in the parish of Saint Kunibert to the intersection of Schildergasse and High Street. To Augusta, Cologne seemed much like Augsburg except for the black slate roofs and more level streets. Like Augsburg, artisans and shoppers filled the streets and women washed clothes near bridges across the streams. But unlike Augsburg, the Catholic cathedral and churches dominated the skylines.

"How many parishes are there again father? Twenty?"

"Nineteen. But Cologne is also a destination for pilgrims. There are over three hundred religious institutions if you count all of the convents, stifts, hospitals, cloisters and abbeys in addition to the typical parish churches."

"But no Lutheran?"

Hainhofer grimaced. "No. Or at least, none that are publicly acknowledged. There are 'secret' congregations of Lutherans and Calvinists in Cave Lane, however. But that will probably change now that Cologne has negotiated an agreement with Gustav Adolph and his allies. According to Hardenrat, the next election in June should see the Pragmatists take control of the city council." Philipp stopped and pointed across the street. "Here we are. Noah's Ark."

Augusta's eyes widened. The store known as Noah's Ark took up two entire floors of the building on the southeast corner of Schildergasse and High.

"It's huge!"

Her father laughed. "Indeed. Herr Fetzer started it originally as a supply house for apothecaries and physicians, but branched out early in the century to indulge his own interest in curiosities. He was able to take advantage of Cologne's location and trade connections to provide items for all the naturalists and curiosity seekers in Germany, including my own cabinets. I've purchased many an extravagance from him."

As they entered the shop Augusta shook her head in amazement. She had been involved with her father's affairs for almost five years, including assisting him with the *Kunstschrank* that had been presented to Gustavus Adolphus in Magdeburg in December 1632. Gustavus Adolphus had been delighted to receive the curiosity cabinet and had given her father a substantial bonus. But never had she seen such a wide variety of strange and unusual artifacts as she saw in Noah's Ark. The lower shelves in the shop were filled with shells, porcelain, and aromatic woods. Overhead dried and stuffed fish and mammals hung from the rafters while birds of every color and description lined the top shelf.

"This is truly splendid, Father!"

Philipp smiled. "It's as nothing compared to the *Kunstskammer* in Munich. Perhaps someday I can show it to you. It is truly a magnificent chamber of arts." He frowned. "If Maximilian of Bavaria can ever be convinced to deal with me again. He's not feeling particularly friendly towards those who seek the favor of Gustavus Adolphus."

Augusta pointed to a shelf off to her left. "And what is that? And why does it seem familiar?"

Philipp chuckled as he and Augusta approached the object. The stuffed animal seemed wildly improbable. There were seven catlike heads on long scaled necks connected to a scaled body with large claws underneath. "A hydra. You've probably seen one in the broadsheet I have of Durer's 'Whore of Babylon.'"

"Philipp! Is that really you? Have you come to drop off a copy of the Hainhofer Report in person? I always look forward to your insights into European politics." An older, white-haired man with sharp blue eyes and a large smile approached them from the darker recesses of the shop.

Philipp clasped the man's arm. "Unfortunately not, Paul. We are just stopping over in Cologne to deliver some cabinets and desks on our way to Essen. I've been offered a position with Louis de Geer. This is my daughter, Augusta."

Paul smiled as Augusta curtsied. "A pleasure to meet you, Augusta."

"And for me as well, Herr Fetzer. Your shop is wonderful."

Paul beamed. "It is, isn't it? So is this just a social visit then? Or have you brought me some more of those interesting artifacts you sent me from Grantville?"

Philipp shook his head and then peered into the face of Paul Fetzer intently. "We were also delivering my son, Georg, to serve his time as a journeyman clockmaker with Magnus, now that Magnus has had his own masterpiece approved, according to his letters. The question is, Paul, why have you had your son arrested?"

Paul scowled and then motioned them to follow him into the back of the shop. They passed several young men and Paul stopped to motion one towards the front of the store. "Take care of the shop, Caspar, while I talk with Herr Hainhofer and his daughter. Don't disturb me unless it is an emergency."

At the back of the shop, Paul motioned them into a small office, and then toward several chairs placed across from a small desk. He sighed as the Hainhofers seated themselves.

"I'm sorry you had to come now, Philipp. But Magnus has gone insane. My wife and I had no choice but to put him in prison. He absolutely refused to change his mind." He scowled again. "And the girl was no better."

"What are you talking about, Paul?" Philipp asked.

"You know that while journeymen are prohibited from marriage, masters are required to marry?"

Philipp nodded.

"Well, Magnus' inspection master, Johann Felwinger, has several eligible daughters and Johann and I had arranged to have Magnus marry his eldest daughter, Elisabeth. It wasn't a perfect match, but Johann has no sons and wanted to provide for his daughter while at the same time easing Magnus' entry into the business side of Cologne clockmaking. Johann's health hasn't been good, so this would ease several concerns and provide Magnus with a ready clientele."

"He decided to marry someone else, didn't he?" Augusta interrupted.

"Exactly," Herr Fetzer said. "But that wasn't the worst of it. It was who he decided to marry that has caused all the trouble."

"Who?" Philipp asked.

Paul grimaced in distaste. "Barbara Leichnam, the skinner's daughter. As you can imagine, the clockmaker's guild is in an uproar and are threatening to expel Magnus from the guild. They have petitioned the city council to block the marriage. Johann is scandalized and on the warpath and as for his daughter... well... she never wants to see or be near Magnus again. My own business was beginning to suffer, so Maria and I thought it best to have Magnus put in prison for disregarding the wishes of his parents. He is still underage at twenty-four."

Augusta nodded. The skinner trade was among the most dishonorable in Germany, even worse than executioners. No father in an honorable trade would want to see his son or daughter married into a family of skinners. No wonder Herr Fetzer was upset.

"How long has he been in prison?" Augusta asked.

"Three weeks. He's a stubborn boy. He refuses to reconsider. So tomorrow we try a different tactic. After considerable discussion with the Leichnams, it was decided to imprison the girl instead." Subconsciously Paul wiped his hands on his shirt. Clearly he was uncomfortable even talking with members of a trade like the skinners.

"Will that work?" Augusta asked.

Paul shrugged. "Who knows? Right now both are refusing to listen to reason, despite all the threats and cajoling that has been done. *Insania filia amoris.*"

☆ ☆ ☆

"Love is blind," Philipp muttered as they walked back towards the Inn of the Golden Grape.

Augusta smiled. "*Azah camabet ahava*," she said in Hebrew.

Philipp shook his head. "Hopefully not. If love is as strong as death in this case, Georg will have to find another master to work for. And Magnus, despite his talent, will never work for the clockmaker's guild in Cologne, or any other city in southern Germany. The journeymen's associations will see to that."

"Then we'll just have to talk him out of it," Augusta said.

Peter von Hardenrat walked around his new writing desk again. Perfect. It was perfect for an *Amtmeister* of the *Eisenmarket Gaffel*, the political guild dominated by the iron merchants. Made of ebony, dark leather and cast iron, the desk stretched most of the width of his office. It had taken two days for Philipp Hainhofer and the two cabinet makers he had brought with him from Augsburg to put it together. But now...

"So where are the artifacts from Grantville you mentioned? You can be so mysterious, Philipp!"

Philipp smiled at the cabinet maker next to him, Ulrich Baumgartner. "Show him, Ulrich." With a flourish Ulrich reached under the desk on the left side and manipulated a lever. Several wooden doors on the drawers at the front of the desk clicked open. Philipp motioned for Hardenrat to inspect them. The first drawer contained a clear rectangular container with five coins.

"Is this the plastic we heard so much about?"

Philipp nodded. "The coins are part of what is called a 'proof set.' These are the first five state quarters minted in the up-time year of 1999, roughly a year before the Ring of Fire. It's difficult to believe, but these were minted in the millions. The detail is really quite exquisite. And to see that more clearly..." Hainhofer reached into the second drawer, narrower than the first, "A viewing device with lenses."

Von Hardenrat took the red and black cylinder and then rotated the black portion. Two lenses labeled "5" and "10" rotated into view. Peter took the coins and lenses to the window for better viewing.

"My God, you are right, the detail really is amazing! Have you looked at this horse on the Delaware quarter?"

Philipp laughed. "A number of times. But what really convinced me to purchase this for your desk, despite the cost, was the motto on the Georgia coin. Very appropriate for a political leader in Germany right now, don't you think?"

Peter peered more closely at the Georgia coin. "Wisdom, Justice, Moderation." He smiled. "Quite appropriate."

For the next hour Ulrich and Philipp demonstrated the intricacies of Hardenrat's new writing desk. When they began to leave, Peter drew Philipp back into his office. Philipp motioned for Ulrich to continue and then shut the office door.

"Yes, Peter?"

"I have some news about the Magnus Fetzer problem," Peter said. "The city council will allow the marriage to go forward, assuming the parents give their permission. But if the marriage does go forward, then they will also support the clockmaker's guild threat to expel him." Peter shook his head in exasperation. "No honorable guild will employ him here in Cologne. So if he decides to stay, he will have to work as a day laborer."

Philipp sighed. Then what would his son do? He supposed he could send Georg back to Augsburg. But Georg and Magnus had been friends for years and had worked well together.

Peter held up his hand. "There is another possibility, however, if Magnus would be willing to relocate."

Philipp cocked his head. "Relocate?"

Peter nodded. "Have you heard of Jost Buergi?"

"Of course. But isn't he dead?"

Peter laughed. "Not yet, although he must be close to or over eighty years old. Apparently he was returning to Cassel from Vienna in late 1631, intending to live out the rest of his days close to home and kin. And guess where he happened to stop over for a visit on the way."

"Grantville?"

"Exactly. He helped restore the clock on the middle school to working order. That job and all the new knowledge he discovered there seemed to invigorate him. He and an up-timer named Phil Reardon are helping set up the Essen Instrument Company for Louis de Geer."

Jost Buergi was as famous as Tycho Brahe and Johannes Kepler. All three had been invited to Vienna by Emperor Rudolf II. Because of Jost's mechanical ingenuity and mathematical abilities, the landgrave of Hesse-Kassel had even declared him to be "a second Archimedes."

"Are you saying that Magnus and Georg could get work with Buergi in Essen?"

Peter shrugged. "Why not? Magnus has a lot of talent, from what you've told me, and Georg is very precise in his work. De Geer asked me to be on the watch for men with mechanical ability. And the Dutch don't have the same kinds of problems with honor and dishonor as the German guilds do, especially in Essen." He smiled. "Now you just have to convince Magnus and take care of the marriage issue."

"Ah yes, the marriage issue. Or more precisely, the parental permission aspect of the marriage issue." Philipp shook his head. Perhaps his children had come up with something.

"You really aren't helping very much," Magnus Fetzer complained, looking around the table at Sophie, Augusta and Georg Hainhofer. "I want to marry Barbara. I'm going to marry Barbara. I love her, and she loves me." He sighed. "She is my soul mate. My stomach hurts just thinking about her."

The public room of the Inn of the Golden Grape was beginning to fill as the businessmen staying there came down from their rooms for dinner and merchants stopped by to indulge in a glass of wine before heading home. There were many fewer wine taverns in Cologne in 1633 than had been true in the late sixteenth century as beer became more popular. The few higher class businessmen's hostels that still served wine did a thriving business.

"Hunger pangs are no problem," Georg said. "The cook here serves an excellent roast pig."

Sophie hit her brother on the arm. "It's not hunger, silly. It's love pain." She smiled. "It's so romantic."

Augusta laughed. "You've been reading too many of those novels from Grantville . . . again." She turned to Magnus. "How did you meet Barbara, Magnus? You never did tell us. Given that her family has been involved with skinners for three generations, she obviously must live outside the city."

Magnus nodded. "Yes, their house is north of the city, on the Rhine. You remember how much I like eel?"

Augusta nodded.

"Well, several sons of fishermen I grew up with and who are

now guild members themselves used to stop by the skinner's house for a drink during bad weather along the river. A little gambling takes place and..."

Sophie laughed. "I remember. You always were interested in dice and strap jump-off."

Magnus nodded. "And you don't want to get involved with the sharper's rings here in Cologne." He shuddered. "They steal you blind and if you complain too loud you wind up in a brook with your head crushed. The council tries to outlaw them, but they move around a lot. So finding a friendly game is worth it, even if it is in the skinner's house."

Magnus held his hands out. "So..."

Sophie snickered. "Love at first sight."

Magnus nodded again, this time in misery. "Yes. My one true love." He put his face in his hands. "What am I going to do?" He moaned.

"*Trop aimer est amer*," Sophie said.

Georg nodded in agreement. "Full of trouble indeed."

"*Men verdrinkt zowel in de liefde als in een rivier*," Augusta said.

"Oh, stop showing off, Augusta," Sophie said crossly. "None of us understand Dutch except for you."

Augusta pouted. "I was just agreeing with you. It translates as 'One can drown in love as well as in a river.'"

Sophie suddenly sat upright. "That's it!"

"What?" Georg asked.

Sophie motioned her siblings in to the center of the table. "Remember *Romeo and Juliet*?"

Augusta smiled. Georg looked puzzled. Magnus took his face out of his hands with a clueless expression on his face. Sophie looked over at her sister. Men were so dense.

Barbara Leichnam listened for the towermaster's footsteps to fade away before returning to her task. She had her doubts about the plan that Augusta Hainhofer had come up with. But if this was the only way to be with her beloved...

It took over an hour to sharpen the metal spoon Augusta had slipped to her. Then she had to wait for just the right time. When that time came, Barbara reminded herself that the cuts had to be just right.

☆ ☆ ☆

Towermaster Hans Schreck was making his usual rounds when he came to Barbara Leichnam's cell. He was a bit nervous about this prisoner. It wasn't just her size, although she was one of the tallest women he had ever met. It was also the reputation of her father, Martin Leichnam. Not a man to make angry, not at all.

Hans glanced into the cell, expecting to see Barbara kneeling in prayer. Instead he saw her body on the floor in a pool of blood.

"Dietrich, get the physician! Barbara Leichnam has committed suicide!"

Magnus looked at the fast-flowing Rhine, buried in his own thoughts. Was this really the only way to be with his one true love?

Courage, Magnus, courage. Barbara was courageous. Now it is your turn.

"I'm coming, sweetheart."

Magnus jumped into the swift moving waters of the Rhine.

Martin Leichnam glared across the room at Paul Fetzer.

"This is your fault, Fetzer. I should never have listened to your drivel about my daughter. If you had had more control of your son . . ."

"My son would never have met your daughter if you didn't allow honorable men into your home for gambling and drinking!" Paul responded. "Your kind are an abomination!"

"My kind?" Leichnam said softly. "My kind are the ones keeping you from drowning in your own filth, shopkeeper. Perhaps it's time for my dagger to bury itself in your doorpost."

Fetzer blanched. Such an act would be terrible for business. And he would be unable to remove the dagger without incurring an honor offense himself. His own *gaffel* might expel him as the clockmakers had expelled Magnus.

"Please, gentlemen, please," Philipp said. "Clearly the suicide attempts by both Barbara and Magnus show the depth of their affection for each other. Perhaps they are indeed both insane with love. But unless you want to jeopardize their souls . . ."

Martin nodded. "I've done what I could. Barbara will be expelled from my house, but to preserve her soul I give my permission for her marriage to Magnus Fetzer."

Philipp looked over at Paul. "Paul?"

For a moment it looked as if Paul Fetzer would maintain his

obstinacy. His will crumbled when he saw Leichnam place his hand on his dagger.

"All right! I agree. I give my permission for Magnus to marry Barbara. We have done all that we can. But what will he do for a living? The clockmakers have expelled him and the city council has upheld them!" He looked over at Martin.

Martin shook his head. "Don't look at me! I won't have him!"

Philipp smiled. "I think I have found just the position for Magnus. In Essen."

"They look so cute," Sophie said.

"Cute is not quite how I would describe them," Georg said slowly. Barbara and Magnus were arm-in-arm waving to the few friends they left behind in Cologne as the ship moved away from the dock. Both were tall, over six feet. But where Magnus was thin to the point of emaciation, Barbara was solid and broad as a warhorse.

"Oh come on, Georg, where is your sense of romance?" Augusta said. "I remember you being all goo goo eyes over Sybilla Waiblinger."

"That was different." Georg said.

"Oh right, different," Sophie said. She looked at Augusta. "*Amantes sunt amentes.*"

Augusta smiled. "Latin. Lovers are lunatics." She thought for a few seconds. "Try this one…"

Letters of Trade

David Dingwall

October 1630
Downham Market, Norfolk

To John Paulet, Winchester

To my good friend John, and to your lady wife Jane, we congratulate you at the glad news of the birth of your first son, Charles. We hope both mother and child are well, and his auspices are favourable.

John, Mary and I have heard of last year's Parliament from my lord Francis Russell, earl of Bedford. From the problems in your last note in June, we have been concerned for you both, it is hoped that outgoing expenses during your attendance as a Member in London were not extreme, and recovery of your estates continue. We had not expected your father's past entertainments would be covered by the banks to such an extent, nor the reports in the London papers to bring such unwelcome public revelations on his death.

On a happier note, I must let you know your visit to London has also caused trouble in the Weasenham house. We hear an ode to your wife's presence and beauty at Court is published by that Cambridge upstart John Milton, and is available in his latest collection from publishers in the Strand. Mary has asked, in jest hopefully, how I might commission one for her. No trips to London for us I think, but now must take her with us to Hamburg to shop whilst my uncle and I arrange future trade.

However, mainly I write of the King's Commission at Lynn this past week. Attending on behalf of our family's trading and estate interests, my brother and I heard that the proposal from the king's embankment engineer, Sir Cornelius Vermuyden, to drain the Great Fen has finally been agreed at the Privy Council, but in detail I have some surprising news.

Lacking capital to the satisfaction of the Drainage Commissioners, Vermuyden is no longer undertaker of the venture. Representations (and, we are sure, some monies) from attending landowners persuaded the commissioners that further capital is required to complete the works.

After the deaths and riots at the works at Aldeney Island and Hatfield Chase, the cases still in the Lincoln court against the king rumble on. We witnessed at the meeting many, including a spectacular oration from a Cambridgeshire squire, Cromwell, ranting on for an age about the "ancient rights of pasture and hunting on common land by God-fearing fen-men being denied and ignored by land hungry foreigners." Much upset was displayed during the meeting, and the commissioners adjourned for a third day for overnight discussions with the major landholders and the bishop of Ely.

In reaching agreement, and to avoid further legal complaints, the Cambridge and Norfolk shire lords and landowners must now lead the enterprise. Francis Russell is now the undertaker, his holding of Thorney being the largest property affected by the scheme. He has promised ten thousand pounds capital to the corporation, with the expectation of retaining forty thousand acres to improve his holdings and a further ninety thousand pounds promised for the corporation from the other investors.

As you know Francis' estates in the east have not returned well without direct access to the king's highways or to port. With the new land, and an open aspect, he has boasted he now retains the architect Jones to rebuild

Woburn Abbey as his family seat, and from whence he may manage his holdings and travel to London as needed.

For my family, a new great drain for the River Ouse from St. Ives to Downham Market shall cut somewhat through our lands at Hilgay, but we expect equal replacement, and are promised in writing an addition of five hundred acres from reclaimed sections for assistance in canvassing parish landholders and using our family links with the town council at Lynn to agree the plans.

Vermuyden shall continue in the syndicate as works director, and other English and Zeeland connections are also promised their own land grants at the end of the task, to the satisfaction of the commission. Ten thousand men to labor are expected, preference now offered to local men, then Protestants from the Spanish Netherlands and lastly from the Dutch Provinces.

The Commissioners shall sponsor an Act of Parliament, "The Lynn Measure." If the works can keep the designated land clear for two consecutive summer growing seasons by 1638, then parcels and land grants shall be allocated. If not, the Company must bear the brunt of all capital costs, with no recourse to the courts or the king. Let us hope this is an end to open envy speculation, and with a clear relationship between a man's effort (or capital) over seven years, and the resultant land assigned to him.

At market, the grain harvest is good and fine this year, however prices are still depressed below last. In our eastern counties landowners are attempting other alternatives from the Gardeners' Company. Grain is hardly profitable, and in many places in Norfolk is grown only to feed the families idling on estates. We understand in the southern counties you have similar experiments, with George Bedford working to producing the dye madder for the first time outside the Low Countries.

Baltic grain does not land; most is diverted to the Germanies via Hamburg, and we expect none for some time. Our farmers with small plots are now completely dependent on any local surplus from market in good harvest years. We expect hunger, suffering and death when the dice rolls the other way, which it must.

Sufficient timber arrives from Sweden and the Pole's lands at our yards at both Lynn and Wisbech before the winter gales. I shall include this note and packet with the final shipment of Polish oak beams to the Cathedral School at Winchester, via Southampton, and hope it reaches you before the end of the year.

Lastly, my father has asked to enclose samples of good seed on trial from the Gardeners' Company in London, with directions on handling. He asked that you attempt them on your lime soil at your estate in Southamptonshire, as we do not think of them well in our peat, nor do we have space apart from our part of the ongoing woad experiments for the Dyers Company.

Be well with God my friend, and do let us know if there is anything further we can do to assist in balancing your estate debts. As usual, we shall keep an ear to the news coming our way from London, from the Germanies and Baltics, and shall share anything to our mutual advantage.

Your Servant,
Robert Weasenham

November 1632
A Road near Heidelberg

"Can you remind me again why I'm freezing my arse off on this God-forsaken mission of yours?" grumbled a faint voice through the driving sleet, from under a wet fur hat.

"Oh, the usual when dealing with the London Companies—connections, bribery and profit, especially the bribery and connections," Rob shouted back through the wind.

Tom Cotton was a city boy in his late thirties, and not a great traveler. "*I'd rather be in a gaming house in London at this time of year, not plonked on the back of a bony nag in bad weather. Or at least give me a coach with soft pillows, and a curtain to keep off the wind.*"

As the mission leader, Rob Weasenham, was enjoying his cousin's discomfort, watching his companion hunched unhappily on the horse in front. Tom had always been a bit of a fashionist, too much time dressing up at Court, not enough in the fresh air. Their small trade party was well covered with guards, but they needed to move quickly to avoid the worst of the winter.

"Let us hope the next change of horses is an improvement," Tom muttered.

"Take Tom; you'll need someone who knows books," a friend in London had suggested. "He's been a miserable git, moping about town since his father died." Well, Rob had him now, but he could have done without the constant whining about the weather, mud on his fine clothes, traveler's rations, rotgut wine, and a hundred other complaints through Dover, Calais, Paris, and parts east. And now diverting farther south was wasting valuable time, and costing more than Rob had expected, the Swedish armies had taken the Rhine/Main junction at Mainz last year, and that route was reported as still not safe.

"Another hour, we should find the inn. Soon, Tom; another hour and you can drink yourself silly with some hot wine." Rob resigned himself to another bad night shepherding his investment, and an expectation of another thumping head in the morning. His cousin's drinking had always been a bit free in Oxford, but he'd settled down when he'd married Margaret, and running the estate at Connington. Taking on his father's responsibilities last year had been a bit of a shock, but what could you expect when the king put the old man in the Tower over winter? Rob had not spent time with Tom for a few years, and was tired of dealing with a relation continually looking for answers in the bottom of a glass.

But the bulge under Rob's coat with the packet of letters from London was a constant reminder of the opportunities for, at least, some major favors awaiting back home.

Most of the letters and lists were due to connections in the City, mainly flapping tongues in trade halls and the Exchange in the City. The Apothecaries had started it—"Dr. Harvey has promised some seeds to a Master Little for a physic garden, and we must have some cannabis from Mr. Stoner."

It went from there to the Mercers—"find any almanacs, especially information on harvests and the weather."

"Riiiight," Rob thought. *"Try to fix the price of grain for the next twenty years."* Rob and his uncle didn't believe those London pedants had thought through that more could be made playing

the European shipping insurance market to best advantage with the same information.

Next, the Gardeners' Company chimed in—"we have heard Grantville plants cabbage, squashes and other Dutch crops in the way of our market gardeners. Record growing methods, and any seed varieties. We also have been unable to grow potatoes well, unlike Ireland. Do they have some that would suit England?"

And the Silk Makers—"if this place is truly from Virginia in the Americas, search for Red Mulberry trees, as the seeds and cuttings from Jamestown have not served us well from long ocean voyages. Mayhap seed available closer to and planted earlier shall be more palatable to our silk worms."

And the rest. Rob carried wish lists from all the other London Companies wanting an English merchant with active trade contacts in Thuringia.

The court was in quiet turmoil, but for once the palace birds were not squawking and little of the king's intentions were known. Concerned at the rumors, his worship, the mayor of London, had arranged a secret Companies meeting in the Guildhall, along with the professors from Gresham College, for advice on what to do next. London's trade must not suffer, and when money was at stake, when did the City and its merchants wait for guidance from any king?

His old Oxford college friend—now a professor—John Greaves had therefore suggested the Weasenhams at Lynn for an off-the-books visit. The Dyers Company also had connections to Erfurt from ten years before because of Rob's uncle William supplying German woad plants and extraction methods to various landowners in an attempt to make England self-sufficient in the blue dye.

So here Rob was. October and November in the rain with a grumpy cousin, the license to travel to Grantville that had been much harder to obtain than anyone would believe, and a pocket full of wild expectations. He had hoped to use the existing relationship with Erfurt as an excuse to travel, but the French were having none of it. He and Tom were both taking a calculated risk to get to Grantville before winter set in, and get out before any more roving armies attempt to flatten it when the following spring arrived.

Another note that had caused them to be on their horses in filthy weather was sitting safely in a desk at home. Stark bribery!

Uncle William had judged the risk and that had tipped the balance. Rob and Tom were to go to Grantville.

To Master William and Journeyman Robert Weasenham, Hilgay, Norfolk
Most Private and Confidential
Sirs,

Professor Greaves was kind to mention you have agreed to visit Thuringia and Grantville for his worship, the mayor. May I also ask to add a charge of my own, and to your family's benefit?

With the new tasks in the Great Fen, and developing Covent Garden in West London, I have secured against all capital and a percentage of my rents for next years. My fellow investors must know if our intended endeavors succeed, and what troubles to avoid on the way.

There have been mentions of a great "English Encyclopedia," and other history books in the Grantville Library that is open to all that come. It is hoped that somewhere an indication of the result of the Lynn Measure in six years shall be recorded.

As for Covent Garden, I continue to be exasperated. Our king demands beauty in design and form, but it is not his monies at risk if I may not find tenants. Acquire a selection of some building designs from Grantville suitable for his majesty's approval, and any plans that shall help my agents in London to keep my bankers at bay.

If you can find what you may before summer next, the Levels Corporation shall add five thousand acres to your family's allotment at the Isle of Southery from Mr. Lien's piece.

Robert, I have also contacted your cousin Thomas, and in confidence have encouraged him to travel with you. He is still not attending to business and is continually in his cups in town, and gambling heavily since your godfather, Sir Robert, passed. Thomas now holds the largest library in England and should be certain to sift information wanted by the London Companies and myself, for you were never one inclined for the books unless it contains a column of numbers. If we can include him a part of this mission and under your direction, mayhap the cloud may be lifted from his countenance.

In your debt,
Francis, Baron Russell, Earl of Bedford

December 1632
Grantville

Thomas removed his hat and strode into the double doorway of the Grantville Public Library. His cousin was off doing more deals for the day, but Tom had reassured him this was not yet the right time to be exploring through the book collections in this wonderful place. Tom knew that when visiting another's library he should arrange to impress the owner or sponsor first with a few gifts.

"My bailiwick, I think," he had assured Rob, and then left their lodgings at the schloss above the "power plant" on his new horse earlier this morning. He then headed back down the new road into Grantville in the snow.

Rob and Tom had tried the previous day to negotiate with the town council, but it seemed that in Grantville the Milady Head Librarian was God Almighty in her bailiwick, and the governor of this town had little to do with arrangements and policies for access to the book collection.

Once inside the building, Tom handed his cloak, hat, and silver tipped walking staff to the elderly guard inside the library doorway. Some things might change, but some were reassuringly familiar. A sharp-eyed pensioner watching the comings and goings like a hawk in the entrance was exactly what he had expected.

Cecelia Calafano was standing behind the main desk, sorting—not very enthusiastically—through today's batch of newspapers and magazines from the recycling ferrets. Most of the textbooks had moved to the high school, and the deep reference section shelves were just the right depth to be stacked flat with newspapers and magazines by year, month, and edition.

She looked up when the door opened and suppressed a groan. The approaching well-dressed figure was unwelcome. Nearly all the new library visitors were directed to the high school, and Cecelia was not in the mood to deal with anyone.

"Chandler Bing in black velvet, a lace shawl, and pointy shoes." That was the first thing that came to her mind. She suppressed a snort, attempted a straight face, wiped her nose with a handkerchief, then began to put a flea in his ear using her improving German. "You will want to go to the school . . ."

He cut her off in perfect, formal English. "Good day, madam. I have come to make introductions and would arrange a meeting with Milady Marietta Fielder."

The man placed what looked like a map roll case on the counter, and handed over a parchment envelope with a finely gloved right hand. "I wish to converse with Milady Fielder urgently. Can you tell me when her duties may allow her to be next available?" he insisted.

Cecelia sniffed, blew her nose loudly into her cotton handkerchief, and wished someone would hurry up and reinvent a decent, fast-acting, twenty-four-hour cold remedy. "Mrs. Fielder is off sick with the flu, and can't be disturbed. I'm in charge. What do you want?" She knew she growled at him; her headache, sore joints, and wheezy chest were beginning to really piss her off.

His unexpected response was, "In that case, good lady, may I view your index?"

The question jarred her into her fuddled head, making her concentrate. Her librarian's instinct started flashing little red stars—no, it wasn't just because she'd blown too hard into her hanky. Most of the visitors dived straight to the history books, technical manuals, and political novels. No one asked about the index first. It usually took at least three visits to begin to civilize them.

Cecelia, still not mentally quite there yet, thought of a question from college, which popped out. "And which cataloging and indexing methods are you familiar with?"

His answer had her and her new guest sitting in a chair in the back office ten minutes later, with some tea brewing on her small hot plate. Cecelia grabbed the phone and started dialing.

Marietta Fielder wished she were dead. Dead would be easy, dead would be warm and less painful. Every winter since she was a child she had caught the latest sniffle, cold, or exotic flu. Regular as clockwork for the past ten years, she'd made a point of getting her flu shot early November, either at the mall in Fairmont, or from the doctor in town. Most of the time it had worked, and winter wasn't as bad as it could have been.

This year was worse than 1969. This time it *hurt*. No shots, no Advil for the migraines, precious little lemon juice. But she was mobile—just enough that she could be left safely at home alone during the day.

Shuffle to the toilet wrapped in an old dressing gown and bunny slippers, cough and splutter back to bed. All that was available was Gribbleflotz aspirin and some peppermints. Yuck!

Shaking her head in disgust while standing was a visceral mistake. Marietta gasped, held onto the rail at the top of the stairs waiting for her vision to return and carefully worked her way back to bed, levering herself back slowly under the quilt.

A thrash metal rock band erupted from the phone next to her head. More vision loss in an attempt to grab the handset. "What'cha want? No respect for the dead?" the corpse moaned down the line.

Cecelia was gabbling at her. Marietta could hear her also coughing, spluttering, and the odd sneeze, but still gabbling.

"Marietta, we have a visitor, from England, insisting that he wants to meet you, *sniff*," Cecelia chattered away. "He has presents and everything."

Marietta was sure there was a combined chortle, giggle and a wet snort in the middle of that sentence.

Cecelia looked down at the map roll emptied onto the desk between her and their visitor. She ran her hand over "A Mappe of Massachusetts Bay Colony for His Worship Governor John Winthrop" and a package of papers marked "Inventories and Maps of Plymouth Colony, 1621" that were signed by a Captain Christopher Jones.

"He's a walking, talking librarian's Christmas present." This time Cecelia lost it completely, and barked out a laugh. *Oooohhhh!* More sore ribs, but worth it.

Her guest stared, frozen, with goggle eyes, perhaps wondering what had gotten into this sniffling, grumpy lady with the stupid smile. She waved one hand, mouthed, "Wait."

"Marietta, do you remember your first term taking your M.A.? Indexing and Classification Systems . . . Middle Ages to Victorian?"

Now she was enjoying herself. Life at the libraries had been a hell for the past couple of years. It seemed that God was having a little joke with the last two qualified librarians (or was that first?) in this universe. "You have someone here who uses the Caesarean Library Index—ACCCDEFGJJNOTTVV."

Getting into it (and being a smarty pants to boot), Cecelia quoted by rote from her college days, "Augustus, Caligula, Claudius, Cleopatra, Domitian, Faustina, Galba, Julius, Justinius, Nero, Otho, Tiberius, Titus, Vespasian, and Vitellius."

Tom nodded sharply, a grudging smile on his face.

A short garbled mutter from down the line, Cecelia answered sharply, "No chance, the British Library won't exist for another one hundred and twenty years, *before that*... where did the British Library get the Caesars' Index?"

More waiting, and then Cecelia heard a particularly painful sounding exclamation from the handset. Finally, Marietta was getting very close.

"No, not him. His son. Yup! His father died over a year ago." Looking directly into Tom's sad eyes, Cecelia proclaimed, "I have Sir Thomas Cotton from London right in front of me, proposing some kind of library exchange program with the Guildhall in London, the Bodleian Library in Oxford, and Sir Robert Cotton's Antiquarian Library at Connington Manor."

Tom was satisfied that his family's reputation for preserving books and manuscripts had survived.

June 1633
Woburn Abbey, Bedfordshire

Francis Russell opened the shutters of his reception room window, looking down on the fallow deer grazing on the lawn in the late afternoon sunshine. He tossed his satchel with the paperwork from London onto his oak desk, and sat back to light his favorite pipe; smoke curling gently to the ceiling.

The now not-so-secret mission to Thuringia had not yet returned when Francis was summoned to Blackfriars Palace in April. Wentworth had informed him he had traded all of the king's twelve-thousand-acre interest in the Levels Corporation to others: selected landowners, merchants, minor lords and barons.

A condition was that Francis was to keep the "New Men" closely involved in the project, out of London and away from court. No doubt Wentworth was playing chess games with information from the history books. And Vermuyden—him too: no speculating on the London market, no crazy ventures in mining, keep him and his out from under the king's feet.

At the time the offer was a gift from heaven. Real investors with capital were always preferable to King Charles Stuart, who was always glad to spend other people's money with the slash of a pen. After the ham-fisted affair at St. Ives with Squire Cromwell's family, the king's boast that he could govern well without Parliament was going very sour, and Francis was pleased he had severed all current financial ties with the court. His bankers had also indicated with an improved rate of interest, and had also accelerated payments for the building work on Covent Garden Square on improved terms.

Now his old childhood playmate, Robert Weasenham, had come back—alone. To be fair, he had delivered everything Francis had commissioned, and more. Tom Cotton had died in Grantville from a hot winter fever; however, his bookwork had mainly been completed with precise collation of information that indicated that the Lynn Measure would fail.

"Whilst clear on certain details, the histories indicate the Measure will fail due to bad weather, thus some of the ditches and dykes must fail during some winter storm in 1636 or 1637. The other landowners also complain that the drainage is insufficient."

Francis' own encyclopedia entries had recorded that King Charles had assumed the project after the failure in 1638, and the impetus to complete the works had been lost until after a civil war. It also suggested that in that other history Cromwell was the coming man, and he had supported the completion of the project during the 1640s. Cromwell was a prickly subject for Wentworth and the king. Francis knew well enough to stay away from that subject in London.

A page from a 1994 road map of England (What was a "rental car"?) and encyclopedia entries for the towns in the Fen area showed the revised works during the late 1640s and thereafter for the next three hundred years. Francis now knew that they needed another parallel drainage canal for the Ouse, changes to the outflows of both the Nene and Ouse, high tide retaining gates at the river mouths, flood relief reservoirs. The list went on and on and on. This warranted more capital, more men, and he still had only five years to finish. Francis shook his head in wonder. The existing investors and the New Men would certainly have enough to keep them full occupied, and Francis had decided to delegate the financial arrangements more than he usually liked.

And for himself—only eight years left to manage his affairs. God! Seeing your own life history written down would sear any man's soul. Robert had assured him that these "Americans" believed God had changed what was written by bringing Grantville to this time. Francis had huffed and puffed at Robert, especially not understanding the story about the butterfly, and dismissed it as a piece of whimsy. Francis was a practical sort of man, what was written is written. He had immediately updated the will and inheritance clearly onto his children.

He now had had only two available options to attempt to square his debts before his potential death in 1641. He played the arguments again through his mind:

Point the First: Covent Garden.

Here the information was very, very good, especially for a developer. His original plans had finally turned out well it seemed, and his descendants had prospered as a result. Francis had leaked a little of this information to the London market, and waited for offers to assist in bringing his plans to completion.

The keys to early success were not housing and tenants as originally thought, but shops, arcades, and the concentration of specific trades. Booksellers and map makers on one street, tailors of high fashion on another and the vegetable and flower sellers concentrated in a single square. He would be damned if he would give them Covent Garden Square, and preferred its more profitable later use as a fashionable covered arcade for shops and dining. More work for Inigo Jones, after he finished the church on the west side.

He also enjoyed the idea of a sober theatre with large columns and retiring rooms on the north side. That would please the king, and his agents had already been approached with offers to fund and build it by the Mercers Company.

As far as Francis knew, Rob had bought the only copy of the "Central London A-Z" map. Therefore he had only changed one thing on his original street plan, renaming the newly assigned tailors street "Saville Rowe." No one would ever know the difference.

Covent Garden should bring in about three-quarters of what was needed, especially the idea of the nine hundred and ninety-nine year leases, and recurring land rents. *Cobnuts to the duke of Westminster, whoever he was!*

Point the Second: The Great Level.

This was going to be a little trickier. There was an obvious new source of capital: Dutch landowners and merchants salting their monies outside the United Provinces. Robert had similar concerns about the introduction of a flood of new residents to the Fen. So they had decided on a two-pronged approach:

Set land aside near the existing towns for housing, to generate more land rents and increase the tithe returns for the towns and surrounding areas. Use the American style of building in "divisions," using a local developer to build townhouses, shops, schools and amenities, and releasing them for sale in stages. In these ways new families, their retainers, and the merchants they depended on could be introduced gradually. If possible, grease the palms of councilors, and co-opt the Gardeners' Company to the scheme. The seed of this idea came from Tom Cotton's copies of 1930s encyclopedia entries on English towns that did not yet exist: Letchworth and Welwyn Garden Cities, "planned in advance and surrounded by a permanent belt of agricultural land." And they now knew which crops would thrive on the new level so there was no need for experimentation. Francis liked the sound of "Wisbech Garden City."

Lastly, apprentice the children of prominent Dutch merchants to the corporation. The war on the continent was not going well for the United Provinces; it would allow fathers to get their sons and daughters safely out of the way of Spanish armies for a time. An example had come from a "Second World War" picture book; it had described English children being fostered abroad to escape war's ravages and hunger. The effort was to be circulated in the press and churches as "true Christian charity." The children would continue to learn their trades, and many would probably stay and make a life, thus tying their families' fortunes to the area. Let any man tell the Dutch children's accents from a fen man after five years, and Francis would pay him twenty pounds.

There was a lot still to think about. Francis quenched his pipe and reopened his account book. The bankers' meeting was next Thursday and the numbers seemed to total up quite well, but

Vermuyden was coming over to be briefed tomorrow. Francis was unsure how that second meeting would go, on one hand his Director's name was still known in the future; "Vermuyden's Plans" had its own place in the encyclopedia entry for the Great Fen. On the other, immediately thereafter the plan's shortcomings, losses to intentional flooding in a war, and how others had tried to resolve his flawed design might bruise a touchy ego.

October 1633
A Wednesday, Englefield House, Reading, Berkshire

Rob and the other groomsman knocked on the door of Englefield House, and then returned down to the bottom step. The white double doors opened, and two Irish lads waited; one in green and the other brown and blue corduroy jerkins, both decorated with blue flowers and green herbs.

"The brothers, I suppose," he speculated, not that he cared at this point.

"Will she come, lads? Tell us if your lady will come?" Rob's fellow groomsman asked the bridesmen barring the doorway.

The brothers turned inside the house, and returned escorting the bride. Her hair hung to her waist, her dress was all blue satin, pearls, flowers and mixed ribbons as she stood between their linked arms. "Aye, here she comes. We go to St. Mark's to see her wed, do ye come?" they said in unison.

A large cheer from the villagers behind the groom's party responded favorably, and a few dirty suggestions volleyed over the back of Rob's head. *A country wedding indeed!*

The two groomsmen returned to their own party and watched as the bride's family and friends funneled through the front door and down the lane after the bride and her two brothers. Two bridesmaids tailed their group, as usual checking out the potential young bucks in both parties.

The bride's father nodded to Rob on the way past. They had negotiated the match between them in Dublin last month. After John Paulet's first wife, Jane, had died suddenly; the pressure to marry him off again as quickly as possible had been, for a well-landed English nobleman, immense. The line must have more children;

new alliances should be forged, and others quietly forgotten. The tight Roman Catholic community in England all had opinions on who John should marry, why, and for how much money.

Although not a Catholic, Robert had offered to take the pressure off. John had still not cared at that point, still missing his "bonnie Jane," and fretting after his only son.

Even though Grantville was said to change this world's story, Rob wasn't in the mood to push John's fate further. Milton's poem had been revived and revised for the funeral. John had been lost in his grief.

This girl was recorded in the histories as giving John healthy sons and daughters in the Other Place, so Rob had resigned himself to his task. If God pleased this to be, so would it be again. From John's biography, and knowing her given name, "Honoura," it had not been hard; the history books had said she was Irish, obviously Roman Catholic, and titled. Her father owning Englefield clinched it, he was sure it was the right family.

Rob had pressed his friend's case, and showed the information to the earl of Clanricarde, but the two had still tussled the terms between them this weekend past to settle for a dowry. Only then had the intended couple been allowed to meet for a short walk and conversation at Aldermaston on Monday.

The house, estate and rents of Englefield House would transfer to the groom's family. In return John and his new bride must follow the Irish tradition—thirty days in this house between wedding and returning to John's own home near Basingstoke. The estate workers had the traditional Irish wedding mead and the feast waiting in the main barn for after the ceremony.

Rob gathered the groom in his finery, and called the rest of the visiting party to order. His wife Mary held onto young Charles Paulet's hand on the half-mile walk to the church with the lad's nurse. Ellen Margaret Cotton, her first outing since her mourning period was completed, gathered the children to her, with the first signs of a tear in her eye. It was nice to see some color in her dress at last; yellow mourning clothes had not suited her at all the past year.

"Hmm, I'll ask Mary about seeing for Margaret also. All alone in a draughty house is not safe for a widow," Rob mused. In some part of his mind, he could have done without the additional paperwork of Connington on his plate. When he'd offered to stand witness to Tom's will in all the haste before traveling to Thuringia, he'd forgotten that there were no other Cotton men of age to be the prime executor.

"Ah, well." Robert smiled. He, too, could make best use of the next thirty days. At his request, John's estate steward had already been exchanging letters with his family at Hilgay in secret. Rob's recollection from years before, visiting between terms at Oxford, of John's main estate land and facilities had not been off course. Between them they had ventured that the happy couple's wedding present from the Weasenhams might help clear John's debts in three or four years, and set the family up for life.

In Grantville last year, Rob had been held in "isolation" for three weeks, whilst his cousin had suffered and died of his fever. The doctors had explained that the hot fever changes its mood periodically, and a few hundred years of changes had hit Tom's drink-weakened humours, or "immune system," hard. Tom had so wanted to meet the two ladies, and in his short happiness of seeing a new library, it had killed him.

While waiting to be allowed to leave Grantville, Rob had finally, with reluctance, turned to the books himself but naturally wanted to follow up on his family's specialty: the future trade market in the Germanies. He had bought or borrowed every book and pamphlet he could, including those from the Grange, the libraries, and the personal collections of the history "buffs" he had been introduced to.

The typical crops described from the encyclopedias in the twentieth century for Norfolk and Lincolnshire areas had led to the making of some positive notes by Tom for the Gardeners. Rob had laughed that the Dutch methods of vegetable farming were later called "The Norfolk method."

Back in England Rob's family and other landowners were interested in introducing all the crop varieties to the Level when the works completed. But in the meantime, they needed somewhere to try out some of the planting and refining methods described in the 1911 Encyclopedia Britannica for one crop in particular.

In his last week Rob had delved into an enjoyable and entertaining read of some of the series of books following the character "Hornblower," some which mentioned the closing of European ports by the English during the Napoleonic War. It had had drawn parallels in Rob's mind to England's current trade gap. At the moment the most expensive international commodities went first to Amsterdam, Hamburg, Venice, or Istanbul. Without a strong English trade fleet, London, Southampton, Lynn, Boston, and Bristol were at best secondary markets for some products, with all the appropriate mark-ups.

Excited, he had asked for other story and history books on the same period. Finally one had described, in some detail, a dinner in a future German province of "Prussia," in honor of Emperor Napoleon himself. It had shown an example of how some of the same Fen crops from the encyclopedia could replace the most expensive of this world's delicacies in the right market conditions. In Prussia and Silesia mills had made great profits in the early 1800s until that war ended. Rob thought there was a chance this could be done again; England now was just like the closed Continental ports during that other war. The venture would not work in Amsterdam or Hamburg, but with a Crown License, just might produce at home.

The groom's party entered the Norman church of St. Mark's, and the organ music changed to a more somber tone.

Back on the estate, a gilded box lay on the top table in the barn. The usual flowers and herbs garlanded all the walls, windows and table surfaces. Uniquely, two root crops lay next to the present. Mary still didn't quite believe he'd put a sample of red and white beetroots—Silesian winter cattle feed and sea kale—on a wedding table, but since there was no superstition to forbid him, she'd kept her mouth shut for once. Unknown to everyone but Robert, instructions on how to make sugar from these plants was locked in the box.

March 1634
Wisbech, Lincolnshire

Rob took the small oilskin-wrapped parcel from the shipmaster, and stepped carefully down the gangplank to the new wharf. God's teeth, the weather was awful! The parcel went under his arm as he strode back to town, the rain bouncing off his large brimmed hat and overcoat.

"Filthy day, sir," said Mr. Bell, the customs man, from the porch of his office at the entrance to the new timber dock. "Settle up tomorrow?"

Robert swept past, trying to keep the rain from his eyes. "Noon? We should get her unloaded by then," he called back.

Not waiting for a reply, he turned the corner onto Norwich Street, then through the puddles onto West Street, and on to his in-laws' house near the church.

Wisbech streets had changed somewhat in the past two years. The Bedford Levels Corporation had contracted with the town council to land supplies, fish, and additional laborers from the war-torn United Provinces, and to rent marshaling yards and build warehouses. Three new wharfs had been built recently, and the Weasenham family had taken a larger interest in the timber dock. His men were now to fulfill the contract for the new lock gates to be installed on the Nene and Ouse Rivers to hold back the high tides.

He passed a bustle of Dutch merchants in the churchyard, including Vermuyden and his young staff. Obviously they were heading to the Nene Ditch cutting through the town, and the engineer was extolling the new land opportunities of the next phase of drainage to potential investors. The decision of naming the first section of new town houses "Meadowlands" was great press.

"You had to admire the man," Robert thought. His plans had been savaged by information from Grantville, but with copies of other books from the libraries procured by Robert, he had taken to new engineering forms like "built-in redundancy" and "risk management" like a salmon going upriver to spawn. There might have been God's hand at work in the Germanies, war in the United Provinces, and a fickle king at home, but never try and keep a Zeelander from making money, or getting his hands on more land.

He winked at the very wet lad at the back of the Dutch contingent, Vermuyden's new apprentice, young van Rosevelt. Rob had served his time following his uncle in much the same way, lagging behind unnoticed in all weathers.

Master Mercer Robert Weasenham laughed at the cycle of life, and opened the side door. "Mary, I'm back!" he called, while brushing off his hat and hanging up his overcoat on the door peg. Shoes were dropped in the box by the door. No mud through the house, or there would be hell to pay.

"Captain Williams has your fabrics and packages from Hamburg. We'll get them offloaded tomorrow morning." Rob placed the package he carried on the kitchen table, and added, "And here's the naming present for John and Honoura."

Getting books and other printed material past the king's customsmen and censors was so much easier in Wisbech than the main port in Lynn, he thought with a wry smile.

Mary smiled back, and shooed him out of the kitchen fussing over flour and pastries.

Robert hurriedly took the parcel and went upstairs to his office. Better to get this done now, so the boy could take the post before the day was done. He sat down at his desk, and wrote a short note to John Paulet on fresh paper to go with the present.

To John and Honoura,

To you both, a short missive with another package from my agents in Hamburg. We would like you both to accept this storybook as a naming present in advance of the occasion of our godchild's birth.

Mary has a German copy of this book, and suggested we procure an original "Up-time" edition in English. Note the printers are the "Oxford University Press." Ironic, John, considering our labors cleaning presses and scraping parchment as punishments for failing the Rule at Exeter College.

In the Germanies and United Provinces, a fashion has taken for Ladies to read "Romantic Fiction." Publishers are spending a fortune translating hundreds of storybooks from the Grantville libraries, and they are in wide circulation. Most involve a formula following various trials and tribulations of a young Lady, and how she finds "Eternal Love with the Man of Her Dreams." Another American phrase you will have to get used to if the London publishers are ever allowed to print this kind of thing. Unfortunately for my purse, Mary has developed a taste for these and every three months receives parcels from a "Book Club" in Magdeburg. I have learned to pace my business trips to be away the week they arrive.

Mary tells me this book was seen in the might-have-been future as the most important and influential romantic fiction "novel" ever produced and to note it is written by a gentlewoman of quality, the daughter of a Church of England incumbent. No one may reproach Honoura to read it during her confinement.

The "Romance Appreciation Society" in Magdeburg has circulated a short biography of the author, which we also include. She was (would have been?) born in your county of Southamptonshire, or "Hampshire" as it will later be named, two hundred years from now. It may be interesting to inquire to see if the Austen family has as yet any association in society near Basingstoke.

Mary and I have selected this particular book as entertainment and for your interest as there is mention of your wife's family, although as a protagonist to the main character. If the sketch is true of the future, Honoura's family continues to be well connected at court, has prospered in London, and holds large estates in England (and I assume continue still in Ireland, although there is no mention of that).

However we must also include a "Glossary of Terms" as our English language has subtly changed in the next two hundred years. The researchers at the Grantville libraries were most helpful in collating the changed words, and alternate meanings. We must trouble you both to keep it at hand whilst reading.

A simple example of misunderstanding in the use of our mother tongue comes from my visit to Grantville two years ago. I was named a "Gentleman" in the first person singular during a conversation at dinner at a beer garden in town. I instantly lost my temper and of course tried to hit the man who called me thus, and needs must to be restrained by my colleagues.

A priest, a new visitor from Rome also dining that evening, stepped in and cleared up the confusion. He explained to me I was truly being described as a man of breeding and quality, and that the word had moved later in meaning back to the Old English form. To the surprised Americans at the table at my violent reaction, he added that to a Stuart Englishman they had unknowingly insinuated I was a court ponce or a pimp.

Obviously, the German or Dutch editions of these books do not have such confusions; the publishers take care to use local phrases to pass on the intended meaning during translation. A printer in Hamburg later explained it to me using another of these attractive American terms: "No point upsetting the target audience."

Gladly, Mary and I shall be happy to stand up for the child, and we thank you both for your kind offer. We hope and expect to be with you before the end of June in time for the birth.

However she believes we have found a way to decide the argument between you both on a name for the little one, and a suggestion.

Mary speculates using Honoura's family's future Christian names, as shown in the book.

She suggests naming the child "Darcy" if a boy, or a girl "Catherine."

Yours,
Robert and Mary Weasenham

Robert folded the paper, unfolded one side of the parcel, and slid the note inside next to the exquisite up-time book and the glossary. Resealing the parcel, he wrote an address on a scrap piece of paper to give to the boy to send by messenger.

To: The Marquis of Winchester Lord John Paulet,
and his Wife, Lady Honoura De Berg
Basing House
Southamptonshire

Notes for the Reader

All the English characters are historical. The Englishmen attended or were around Exeter College, Oxford between 1610 and 1620. The Russell and Paulet families were heavily involved in developing the English woad experiments in their western estates in Cornwall and Dorset respectively.

The Weasenhams had been trading from Bishops Lynn (Renamed

Kings Lynn in Tudor times) since the 1330s. The family was one of the four strongest English trading families with links to the Hanseatic League, "The Hansa," until Queen Elizabeth expelled foreigners from England during her reign. By the time of this story, they have three hundred years of trade links with Hamburg and the other Baltic ports. There is still a fine example of Hansa building and a trade yard in Kings Lynn, behind a later Georgian fronting.

The Cottons were descended from a Weasenham branch that needed to marry a son off quickly to a rich heiress in the 1380s to avoid bankruptcy. They chose a girl from the Scots noble family "de Bruc," who included in her family tree a Scottish king, "Robert the Bruce," as we now call him. Tom's father, Sir Robert Cotton, meddled in politics frequently, and sidled up to the new King James when he came down from Scotland to take the English throne. Robert flashed his family tree, added "Bruce" as a middle name and ingratiated himself to the point that King James was later persuaded to call him "Cousin." Apart from a few short stays in the Tower of London, (a time-out zone for many a Privy Councilor) Sir Robert is famous for his Antiquarian Library, which became the one of the seeds of the British Library in the 1750s, and inventing his own peculiar Caesarean classification system.

Sir Thomas Cotton stayed out of the limelight and lived out his life at Connington Manor maintaining his father's library and adding to the family collection with contemporary architectural building plans, copies of navigation and colonial maps, and other ephemera, most of which was lost during a fire in the 1730s. There seems to have been an open deal in London where second copies of plans, log books, and anything else "useful" that they could get their hands on ended in the Library. "Fashionist" is a real word, and was first recorded in 1616 in London, then died from use within twenty years.

Sir Cornelius Vermuyden also "sucked up big time" to King James and King Charles, finally getting into land reclamation for wealthy Englishmen and the crown. Originally from Zeeland, he started as a tax collector in the United Provinces, became a naturalized Englishman in 1626, and persuaded fourteen other Dutch "adventurers" to fund the Bedford Level Corporation scheme. There is a disputed portrait of him in a private collection, but none available online.

Cornelius' new apprentice, Claes van Rosevelt, in this version of events has been diverted from going later to Nieuw Amsterdam, and buying the famous farm in what is now Midtown Manhattan. The Vermuyden and van Rosevelt families were from the same area in Zeeland, and were friends and business associates. As a Brit I felt had to have one small change in a piece of Americana.

The fourth earl of Bedford, Francis Russell, did not expect to inherit his title. Some cousins in the main line died in quick succession, and he was landed with diverse estates and the family title. Recorded as a details man in politics, he enjoyed the fussy work of Parliament in 1628/9, and in his projects to make money. He spent most of the 1630s working on the Great Fen project and as a property developer laying out the whole of Covent Garden in London from the Strand to what is now Russell and Bedford Squares.

The fifth marquis of Winchester, John Paulet, was expected to inherit, but what he got were massive debts in 1628/9. His father died after twenty years of exorbitant dining, pleasures, and entertainments for guests at his home: Basing House, a larger and grander example of a Tudor mansion-style brick building than Hampton Court. John was no politician, and as his was a Roman Catholic family in trouble, decided to retire from court and quietly rebuild his family wealth. He did not appear again at court until 1639 when his second wife Honoura and the queen became friends. He is most famous for a holding action in the English Civil War, where Basing House was under siege by Parliamentarians for over two years. Eventually Cromwell himself had to come and finish the job, not surprisingly winning the day, and had the house flattened to the ground. John and family ended up in the Tower, but after the Restoration the Paulets retrieved all their estates. Lord John Paulet and his second wife Honoura are buried under the new, Victorian St. Mark's church in Englefield. The local post office and nearby farm shop still sell honey.

The ruins of Basing House have been a tourist attraction on the road between London and Winchester for three hundred and fifty-odd years. Every year in late August there is a reenactment of the siege, with the "Sealed Knot" regiment on hand to show off Civil War military tactics.

Gresham College, located in Bishopsgate, was founded to be the M.I.T. of London in 1597, paid for by the new Stock Exchange and the London Companies and Guilds. Its original charter was to provide public lectures, and apply the new knowledge becoming available from abroad to England in projects that made the city money. It has no students and awards no degrees. They were probably most successful in using mathematics to refine English shipbuilding methods, and improving magnetic compasses, giving rise to the new English trade fleet and Royal Navy. After the Restoration, Gresham College became the founding place of The Royal Society. The college still provides public lectures on science, history, culture, and finance.

Professor John Greaves, Chair of Geometry (Mathematics) 1631–32 at Gresham College specialized in Arabic Studies; he collected many science books from Turkey, and traveled to Egypt. His was the first modern description of the pyramids' dimensions and astronomical alignments in the mid-1640s. I was never quite sure where Dr. Phil's fascination with pyramids came from, as information in the 1630s was almost impossible to find. Maybe he needs to talk to Professor Greaves, and arrange an expedition get the revised astral alignments needed ten years earlier to get his models to work?

The English silk maker's trials in the first half of the seventeenth century with red mulberry from the Americas failed; those pesky worms still preferred the white variety to everything else. That's also why white mulberry trees are scattered over the east coast of America.

During the Continental Campaigns, Napoleon was presented with large sugar loaves made with processed sugar from sugar beet. After the Napoleonic Wars ended, Britain (and Portugal) flooded the European market with cane sugar from its newly extended Caribbean island holdings, killing the price support mechanisms in place on the continent, with the result of holding back major sugar beet processing until the next Franco-Prussian war in the 1870s, and finally expanding worldwide after World War One. Prussia and Silesia continued to make sugar locally on a smaller scale, but at a profit.

Starting up a pilot sugar extraction and processing facility is going to be very possible, even with a seventeenth-century technology base. The 1911 Encyclopedia Britannica is very specific on each step, and the machinery needed for the method of sugar extraction from sugar beet (typically a cross between wild fodder beet and sea kale, but common beetroot will also do to start). There are only three logistical essentials—plentiful fresh water supplies, a ready supply of rock lime, and lots of wood or coal to heat the water and extract carbonic gasses from the lime. Old Basing village has the first two: the river Lodden passes fifty meters from Basing House, and the modern parish is studded with features like Lychpit Farm, and The Lime Pits Play Area (400 meters from the House). Lord John Paulet also owned Pamber Forest nearby, over five square miles in size. A Paulet family survey of their lands after the Restoration in the 1660s recorded the forest had been neglected for many years and had such poor quality mature timber and significant underwood that was all only fit for burning. Manpower is not going to be a problem; unlike the continent at war, England is awash with farm laborers with hungry mouths to feed.

Why bother with homegrown sugar? In Tudor and Stuart times England sourced most of its fine quality sugar from the prisoner island of Madiera, the rest from Amsterdam. Interestingly, there was no sugar or molasses excise tax in England; this would not happen until over 120 years later. The price was set on the Venetian and Amsterdam markets, and tied to the inflation rate of gold. The English prices varied, but in general transportation costs using English merchant ships added around thirty percent to the Amsterdam wholesale price. (Punishing taxes were laden on cargoes from foreign vessels as a matter of state policy, in place since the 1380s to protect English merchants, and there was a fair amount of "flagging" of ships for much the same reasons we do it today). A general import tariff of around twenty percent was added when the cargo landed in port, as the product was not English, nor had it come from an English colony. If you had a townhouse in a port that traded in sugar, and could afford it, you bought it there. If you were in the country or an inland town or city, because of the weight and bulk of sugar loaves or lumps, the price could easily double again.

Thanks to British Sugar for rules of thumb for the historic sugar price well before they were formed, and the Guildhall library, and the City Companies' archivists for helping me through the trade journals and exchange rates.

Can English sugar make a profit? Well, that's another story for another day.

Breakthroughs

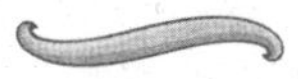

Jack Carroll

General Electronics laboratories
March 1634

Something didn't fit.

Else Berding had gone to the break room for a cup of coffee. She came out to see Jennifer Hanson in the hallway, carrying on a conversation through a ham walkie-talkie. It was a little bit of a thing, no more than four inches high, with an eight-inch flex antenna sticking out the top.

"Far as I could tell from the phone message slip, it sounded like he was talking about some old CW transmitter that he hasn't used in years. Nothing high powered, but for sure a way to get on the air."

The other station came back. "That sounds pretty good, Jennifer. You think we could afford it for the club station?"

"Good chance of it. I'll be seeing him tonight, and we'll find out one way or the other."

"Okay, and if it don't work out, maybe we can build something up from junk box parts. Well, I've got a class in a few minutes, so I'll sign off with you now. W1PK, W8AAG."

"See you later. W8AAG, W1PK."

Else stopped dead. "A class? I've heard you talk to him before, but I thought he was someone here in the plant. Where is he?"

"Oh, that's Rolf Kreuzer. He's a junior at the high school. We've been scrounging around for some gear to put together a club station over there. The kids need it, if they're going to actually do anything with ham radio."

Else looked confused. "He's at the high school? What band were you using?"

"Two meters."

"I thought everybody said all those high frequency bands are line-of-sight, until the sky wave skip finally comes back."

"Well, it pretty much is."

"But, there's a hill between here and the high school! There isn't a line of sight between here and there."

"It's pretty close to one, though."

"Pretty close isn't the same thing at all. There has to be some other physical effect involved. *Does Professor Müller know about this?"*

Without waiting for an answer, Else charged off to her boss's office.

John Grover was just getting up to leave. Müller waved her in.

"Conrad, you asked us all to report any unexpected observations that have anything to do with the project . . ." Grover turned back, listening alertly.

Else described what she'd just seen. ". . . so you see, line-of-sight can't explain that. There must be another physical effect, to make that happen. It might be something we can use." Else stopped. She saw how Grover was standing. He was no longer poised like some prospector looking at gold dust on the bottom of a creek. Now he was leaning back against the door frame, and smiling slightly, like—a teacher listening to a favorite student? "You know about this." It was a statement, not a question.

"Uh, yeah, we do. There are several effects that can make a radio wave go around terrain obstructions. The army is making good use of them, too. Thing is, we don't think the Ostenders and the Austrians have figured it out yet, and we want to keep it that way as long as we can. So keep it quiet outside our group, okay?"

"Oh. All right. Well, I'd better go back to my desk, then."

By this time Jennifer had caught up, and they walked down the hall together. Else asked, "Did I do something foolish?"

"No, you did what they asked you to. I was about to tell you, but I didn't get my mouth open fast enough. I'm sooorrry. Forgive me?"

Else burst out laughing at the sight of a thirty-four-year-old wife and mother pouting like a penitent little girl.

After they left, Grover stayed a moment longer. He shook his head. "Damn, that was brilliant."

Müller looked up at him. "Oh, yes. If we had two or three more like her, this project would move faster."

"You know why she spotted that so quick? Chuck Fielder and the rest of them teach their students to think like scientists."

The invitation to an interview at General Electronics had come as a complete surprise. John Grover had been honest, and so had Else.

"You understand, Mr. Grover, I've finished only about half the courses I planned. And even that is from study groups, not school courses."

"Yes, I do understand that, Fraulein Berding. But Conrad and I think the ones you've finished are the ones you need to do this job. Your last study group adviser thinks you have what it takes to learn the material.

"Of course, it would be better for you and us if you had the rest of the courses and an experienced electronics engineer to work with on the job. But not much about the Ring of Fire was fair. There isn't anybody like that. What we have is a really good collection of books on vacuum tube theory in Gayle Mason's library. What we don't have is somebody who can put them to work. You're the first person to come in here who has the math and physics to really understand the electrical insides of a tube."

"Wouldn't it work better if I went further with physics before taking up something like this?"

"Probably. But let me lay out the situation. VOA runs on tubes, and they don't last forever. We only have a few. When the last ones burn out, we're off the air unless we figure out how to repair them by then. Most of the long-range transmitters for military and diplomatic radio are in the same situation, and some of them don't have any spares at all. And then there's a lot of transistor gear the army is using. They don't need tubes, but when something breaks, we don't have parts to fix them with. Before too many of them wear out or break down, we need to be building replacements. And once we run out of up-time parts we can salvage, that takes tubes. We're already behind schedule. You can imagine what could happen if we let too much more time slip away. Battles can be won or lost in seconds. Better something they can use in time than a perfect solution too late."

"I see. I'm still not sure. Could I look at these books, and see how well I can understand them?"

"Sure. I can't let them out of the building, but I'll take you up to the library. And there's one other thing. You won't be stuck completely on your own. You know Charnock Fielder? He has a lot of other demands on his time, but he does some consulting for us. He can help you figure things out if something doesn't make sense."

"That might make a great difference. I had one of his physics classes. He explains things very well."

The next day Else was back.

"Mr. Grover, I've thought very hard about what you said. I probably wouldn't be alive if the Emergency Committee hadn't taken me in three years ago. They offered me citizenship and school. Now, it seems, it's time to pay back. I believe I can learn what is in those books. I will join you and do my best." She reached her hand across the desk to shake. She looked very serious and very young at that moment.

That night she prayed. *Lord, help me do what they ask of me.* Research engineer...

She lay down to sleep, wondering whether she'd ever hear anything of her family again.

Else had studied hard before, but not like this. But the principles were starting to make sense. The vacuum wasn't quite good enough yet, and it would be a while before the materials people could give her group what they'd need to build a test model, but they had some idea of what they'd be able to get within the next few months. Meanwhile, she was working out a couple of trial designs on paper.

Late in the morning Else went out to the lab. She called across the room to Heinz Bennemann, "I need to study the pieces of that dead tube you took apart some more. Where do you keep them?"

"Third shelf in the cabinet, in the little red felt-lined box."

"Felt-lined, is it? Still the fine jeweler?"

"I was only a jeweler's apprentice. Now they call me a general technician. It means I'll never be done learning things. There's no such thing as mastering this trade."

"No? What do you think a research engineer is?" Else took the box over to a bench where there was a microscope and a precision mechanical stage, and settled down on a tall wooden stool. A flapping belt drive under another bench caught her eye.

"Heinz, shouldn't there be a guard over that belt?"

"We'll put it on when we're done. You know Marius Fleischer, here? No? He's a mechanic from the vacuum group. He just brought over a better roughing pump, and we're trying it out."

Fleischer put in, "It seems to need a few adjustments yet."

He and Heinz turned back to the assembly drawing.

Marieke Kettering was a good-natured woman in her mid-forties, with the gift of maintaining her good nature regardless of what kind of deadline pressure and turmoil were erupting around her. Being in charge of personnel and purchasing for both VOA and GE, she needed it. She heard the front door close, and then footsteps coming to her office.

"Gertrud! What a pleasant surprise! What brings you here? Sit."

"Oh, Marieke, we were just passing by. We're going into town for a little shopping."

"And who is this fine fellow in your lap?"

"This is my little nephew Erwin Spiegelhoff. Erwin, say hello to Frau Kettering."

"Gwathm!" exclaimed Erwin, with the sunniest of smiles.

Gertrud continued, "So, have you seen the new Brillo play yet?"

"No, but I want to. My cousin says it's insane, with them saying one thing in English, and then not exactly the same thing in German."

"Well, why don't I see if I can get us some tickets? Do you think Hermann would want to come too?"

Erwin slipped off his aunt's lap and started playing with his wooden duck on the floor. After a few moments of conversation, Gertrud noticed the silence. "Erwin?" She looked around the office. No Erwin. She stepped out into the hall, just in time to see the toddler disappearing through a doorway.

"*Nein, Erwin! Komm zu Tante!*"

Erwin didn't feel like coming to Auntie just then. What he heard was the interesting rhythmic *blup-blup-blup* coming from under a bench. He saw the shiny things going round and round, and the long thin black thing bouncing energetically up and down between them. He made a beeline for the vacuum pump.

Else was just taking a quick stretch. Something was moving down low...

"Heinz! Look out!" She pointed at the little boy, and scrambled off the tall wooden stool, sending it flying.

Heinz dove for the floor, trying to get between the child and the moving parts. Else flew toward the spot. They got in each other's way for just a moment. Just as Heinz got an arm in front of the boy and started to push him back, and Else got one hand on the edge of the bench to brace herself and the other hand on the boy's shoulder, he grabbed the drive belt. It whipped his left hand under the idler wheel.

Marius yanked the power cord out of the wall and started cranking the roughing valve shut to keep the diffusion pump from coming up to air.

It was never clear afterward whether the child had grabbed at the test leads dangling over the edge of the bench, or whether Heinz snagged them with his foot as he hit the floor. Else saw something start to slide toward the edge of the bench, and tried to stick out a foot to cushion its fall. There was no time. It hit the floor with a sickening crack.

Marieke and another woman came running full-tilt into the lab just as the boy let out his first deafening scream. Else cradled the child in her arms, blood on them both.

"Erwin," the strange woman cried. "Erwin!"

Else called, "Frau Kettering! The first aid kit!" She held Erwin as still as she could, while Heinz took a fast look at the injury and got a bandage on it to control the bleeding.

Heinz looked up with a sober expression. "It doesn't look good. His hand is all cut up. He needs the hospital."

Marieke swallowed. "I'll get the ambulance." She picked up the telephone.

The other woman took Erwin in her lap and wrapped her arms around him. "Erwin, Erwin, it will be all right. There are good people coming to make it stop hurting." Erwin screamed.

After the ambulance left, Else and Heinz finally had a chance to look at what had hit the floor. It was Gayle Mason's Simpson 260 multimeter. The case was smashed to fragments, the glass had a crack all the way across, and the needle was bent. Heinz delicately picked the pieces off the floor to prevent any more damage, and collected them in a box. About then, John Grover arrived in the lab to see Else glumly sizing up the remains. She showed him.

"It's a mess, all right. I'm a lot more concerned about that little kid, though. We've got other meters in the lab."

"Yes, John, but this is the only one with a calibration sticker from up-time. We've been using it to standardize all the other electrical measurements."

"Oh, boy. Well, we'd try to fix it anyway, but it looks like we have a real incentive here, huh? Heinz, you're about the best tech here for fine work. What do you think?"

Heinz shrugged. "I haven't worked on meters before. This is different from the other little parts I've made. I wouldn't like to take a chance with this, if there's anyone else in town who knows more about these things."

"Well, there's always AEW. They make meters. Fine, let's see what they think."

The accident investigation took up most of the afternoon. Jacob Cokeroff, the head of the vacuum group, doubled as the company's safety officer. He had barely started interviewing everybody involved when the city fire marshal showed up. Between the interruptions and the staff's state of mind, there wasn't a lot of useful work done for the rest of the day.

Late in the afternoon Cokeroff and the marshal were wrapping up in John Grover's office, and discussing what would go in the report. The phone rang.

"That was Marieke. She just heard from the hospital. Erwin is out of surgery. It's not great, but it could have been a lot worse. They had to pin two bones back together, and he's lost one joint off his middle finger. There'll be some scarring. Outside of that, they think he'll be able to use the hand all right."

Cokeroff nodded. "We should be thankful."

"Oh, yeah. I was really worried. All the effort we put into safety, and this comes out of the blue. We don't want anything like this to happen again. So, recommendations..."

The next morning, Frau Kettering started working through a handful of signed requisitions. Her first visitor of the day was a carpenter.

"Right here, in the hall, between the offices and the workshops—I'll show you. A divided door, with fire exit hardware, locked on the outside. All right? How much, and how soon can you put it in?"

Next, she called in a sign painter.

"We need a sign on each of the doors going into the lab and shop area. 'Danger, Escort Required,' in big black letters on a yellow background. German and English. Latin too, I think."

Then things got harder. She called the sales department at American Electric Works. "Hello, I understand you make meters. We have a damaged multimeter from up-time that needs repair. Can you help with that?"

"What exactly is that? Something we make?"

"No, it's from up-time. It's irreplaceable, and it was calibrated. We need it for a defense project. My engineers think you're the only company that would know anything about it."

The president of the company came on the line.

"This is Landon Reardon. What can I do for you?"

"This is Marieke Kettering at General Electronics. We have a damaged Simpson 260 multimeter. It was broken in a fall. I understand you make meters, and I wonder if your company could repair it."

"A 260? Yeah, I know what that is. I used one when I worked at the power plant. How bad is it?"

"Well, the case is in pieces, and some of the parts inside are bent. They're not sure what else might be wrong."

"Oh, brother." He sighed. "I can't promise anything, but send it over with the manual. I'll ask the guys to go over it, and we'll let you know whether there's anything we can do."

The man who sometimes called himself Johann Schmidt was intrigued. He'd passed this building before. *Those locks on the doors look new. Yes, the metal isn't weathered. Nobody to be allowed inside without being watched? Danger? What a naive ruse! There are secrets behind those doors. Obviously. Perhaps useful ones.*

He continued to observe the building at intervals, but now he came no closer than a block, and never faced it directly. His patience was rewarded after three days. Several people left work, and one of them didn't show the alertness and purposeful stride of someone in charge. This man was dressed a little more cheaply than some of the others. "Schmidt" followed, half a block behind and on the other side of the street. The man went into a drinking establishment, a nondescript working man's place. "Schmidt" went in after a few minutes. He found a seat across the room, ordered a beer, and sat down to sip it, speaking to nobody but the barman. He continued to observe, without looking directly. After a while, the plain-looking man joined a card game at a table. *This looks interesting. Yes, an indifferent player.* The play of expression on his face as he lost very small sums showed it. *Here's a man who can use a little money.*

The next night, "Schmidt" arrived first. The room was fairly crowded, but there were two neighboring unoccupied places at the bar. He took one of them and waited.

The pace at GE was back to normal. Normal meant frantic. Else was constantly dealing with things she'd never studied, reading up herself, sending queries to Father Nicholas and the other researchers, answering questions, supervising experiments, taking measurements herself, or conferring with specialists in other groups.

One time it would be Heinz asking, "Else, do these results make any sense to you?"

Cokeroff wondered, "There's a kind of high vacuum gauge that looks something like a tube. Do you know anything about that? Could we make it?"

Another time: "Else, do you think we'd be better off modeling the electric fields around the control grid by computer, or in an old-fashioned electrolytic tank?"

"I'm not sure, Conrad, I'll give that some thought and get back to you. Maybe they'd both have a place. Do you know a good computer programmer? But maybe an analytic solution might be possible."

At least she didn't have to worry about vacuum-tight electrical feedthroughs for the tube bases. That was mostly mechanical engineering, and Conrad Müller was working away at it. Even so, it was hard to keep up with everything.

One morning she planned to write a technical paper on receiver tuning capacitors. She'd solved the math the day before, and now she was going to reduce it to a procedure a high school–trained electronic designer could manage. She reached for her notebook without looking, and felt—nothing. She looked up. There it was on her desk, but a foot to the left of where she was certain she'd left it the night before.

Her boss came in while the befuddled look was still on her face. "Is something the matter, Else?"

"Nothing, really. I just misremembered where this was. I almost always put it over here. I was sure..."

For a moment Professor Müller didn't speak. She looked up to see dismay plain on his face. "You look exhausted, Else. How much sleep have you been getting?"

"Well, I was up late last night studying. There's so much to understand, to be ready to move right away when we have a good vacuum."

"Hrmm. And unless I'm mistaken, there have been a few nights when you fell asleep right here in your chair, and never went home at all."

"Well, yes, a couple of times." She rubbed her eyes. "This work is so important."

He sat down in the visitor chair and laid one hand on her desk. "Else, Else, you can't keep this up. You'll ruin your health."

"But there are so many people depending on us!" It came out as a half-moan. "You heard John Grover last week. The good transmitters and receivers are wearing out from so much use, and there never were enough of them. What if we can't make tubes in time? What will happen to all of us? And there's nobody but me to design them!"

"I know. It's on everyone's mind every day, but burning yourself out won't help. I'm learning faster than I ever have in my life, to work out how to make the glass seals and the welds and so many other things. It's just so different from teaching at the university."

"That's right, you weren't here when the Croats came, were you? One phone call made all the difference. And then those radio messages from Amsterdam saved Wismar and Lübeck.

"But I'll never forget the soldiers roaring into our town up north. We had no warning, no warning at all. I was just far enough away to run into the forest. All I could do was keep running, and I found Grantville. Maybe some of my family got away, I don't know. The Red Cross could never find out." She shuddered. "We can't let that happen again. That's why I agreed to take this job."

"So many awful things in this war. But, this isn't the way. Let me give you a lesson now on how to be a student. You're what, twenty years old?"

She leaned down with her elbows on her desk and massaged her forehead for a moment. "Nineteen, Conrad. My birthday is in May."

"Listen, then. When you're too tired to think, you make no

progress. I learned that the hard way in my undergraduate days. And it helps nobody if you have to do work over because you were too exhausted to do it right the first time. You know what an optimum is? The optimum amount of sleep is what you need, so you can keep going as fast as you possibly can."

"But . . ." She gestured openhanded at the piece of paper she'd started to write on.

He nodded. "Yes. I can see you have your teeth into something and your mind won't let you rest until you write it down. All right. But then go home and sleep. And stay out of the lab today. You're so tired, you're swaying in your chair! The last thing I'd ever want is for you to get hurt like that poor Spiegelhoff boy."

The tube group found workarounds for the missing meter, but it was tedious and inefficient. Finally, the wizards at AEW pulled off a small, expensive miracle.

Heinz showed it off to the group. "See here? Somebody in the cabinet maker's shop at Kudzu Werke made this oak case to replace the broken one. And there's a padded leather outer cover. I might tie it to the bench the next time we use it, though. You can hardly tell that the needle was ever bent. They said there was a wire torn off a range resistor inside, and fixing that was the most delicate repair."

Conrad asked, "So it's good as new?"

"Well, not quite. There was some damage to the jeweled pivots they couldn't do anything about. We have to tap it lightly with a finger to get the needle to settle to the final position. But I've compared it with readings from some other meters before it fell, and it doesn't seem to have changed."

Heinz went back to putting together an experimental vacuum gauge he'd been working on the night before. He went to pick up his little Phillips screwdriver, but it wasn't in sight. *Maybe somebody borrowed it?* He looked at the nearby benches, but didn't see it there. Then he saw it from two benches away. It was behind his toolbox. *Hm. Must have rolled there somehow.*

Else kept tearing away at the theoretical work. It wasn't always tubes. It would have done GE little good to develop tubes if they weren't ready to make all the other parts for receivers and transmitters.

So it might be, "Else, Jennifer has taken apart an old coupling capacitor. It's made of tinfoil, paper, and beeswax. That, we could make, if we substitute copper foil for the tin. Could you work out the design equations, and help the manufacturing engineer figure out what kind of paper to use?"

On another day it was, "Else, Jennifer is asking for help. The *Radio Amateur's Handbook* has equations and charts for the inductance of an air-wound coil, but there's nothing about sizing it according to the power level. Can you come up with some recommendations? The techs can run any tests you need to confirm it."

Or Grover asking, "Else, we have a new high school graduate coming in tomorrow to apply for an electronic designer job. Would you help us interview him?"

Some nights they'd go up to the comm station to pick Gayle Mason's brains. John Grover was a fast hand at the key, but conversing in Morse code was slow going compared to talking face-to-face, especially on the nights they had to relay through Amsterdam. Still, Gayle saved them a lot of wasted effort.

While all that was going on, Else continued studying more advanced math. She could see that she was going to need the convenient but conceptually challenging theory of Laplace transforms even to understand the cookbook manuals, once she started in on the receiving filters that picked out just one incoming signal. So, she was currently participating in a group studying differential equations. It got together a couple of times a week. There was just so much to learn, and so little time before it would all be needed.

The family she boarded with had three small boys. She didn't exactly mind the noise, but sometimes it was too much even with her door closed, when she was trying to grasp really difficult material. Besides, her office was a comfortable place to study, and she could always get a cup of coffee from the break room. It was a much-appreciated benefit the company provided.

One night she was working through a textbook problem, with only her desk light turned on. The floor creaked briefly. *Somebody in the lab?* She looked out, but there was nobody there. Maybe it was the building settling after the heat of the day.

John Grover happened by while a couple of techs were joking about the haunted laboratory. "Oh, yeah, my dad used to tell stories like that. He worked on bombers in England during the

Second World War. Stuff would go haywire for no obvious reason. They blamed it on the gremlins."

"What are gremlins?"

"Little people you never see. Kind of like fairies."

Jacob Cokeroff growled, "*Gut*, but we are in Germany, not England. If we are to have imaginary friends, they should be called kobolds."

"Sure, Jacob. On another subject, how's the vacuum looking?"

"Almost good enough to do something useful with. I have hopes of something usable for lab work in another week or two."

"Glad to hear it. The materials folks have been poking into some pretty strange places and come up with little bits of scrap to try out. Thanks to Father Nick for the clues again."

The experimental work was about to start.

Else decided she needed a change from her difficult math studies. She decided to attempt something not quite so demanding for the moment. She could see that with the stage the project had reached, she'd need to operate transmitters herself before very long. So she decided to get her license now, rather than later. After two evenings with the study guides, she felt ready. And so, one Saturday morning, she showed up for the test session put on by the Grantville Amateur Radio Club's volunteer examiners. Typically for Else, she passed on the first try. They issued her a ham license and a station call sign—W8AAQ. Then they invited her to the club meetings.

On the last Friday afternoon before Labor Day, there was a set of cathode coating samples Else wanted to test herself. Near the end of the day she finished taking the data, and shut everything down but the vacuum pump. The tech who'd stayed as safety observer while she had the high voltage on went to finish up some other work. Else wanted to think about the results over the long weekend, so she took her notebook along in her canvas bag, along with some reference material.

After she left the building, she happened to glance back. *What on earth? I'm sure I turned off the bench light.* She mentally cringed. *If I hadn't looked back, three days of that bulb's life would have been used up for no reason.*

Else stepped into the lab, and stopped. What she saw made

absolutely no sense. Somebody was sitting in front of her bench, writing on a piece of paper. She could see by the warning lights that the power was on. *Why is somebody else repeating my experiment? It's that mechanic from the vacuum group—why would they be interested in this? Why would Conrad let somebody else run my setup, and not tell me? And there's nobody else here, this is an awful safety violation.*

She spoke hesitantly, just loud enough to be heard over the noise from the vacuum pump. "Marius? What are you doing?"

The color drained out of Marius Fleischer's face, and he came up off the stool with a squawk, unbalancing it and knocking it over. He tried to dodge around Else to get out the door, but one foot caught in the stool's rungs, and it pulled him to one side.

Else saw him coming straight at her. She took a half-step back to get a firmer stance, and reached out to fend him off. The shove unbalanced him further. He shot out his hand to one side for support. It came down on the power supply.

"*Conrad! Heinz! Anybody! Help!*" Else shouted.

When Conrad Müller and two techs came running into the lab half a minute later, they found Else on her knees, one hand on top of the other, pumping rhythmically on the center of Fleischer's chest.

Müller called, "Heinz! Call for an ambulance! Electric shock." He knelt beside Else and said, "I'll take over the CPR. Turn off anything dangerous before the ambulance gets here."

Between emergency treatment and getting the lab into a safe condition, things were busy and confused for the next few minutes. After the ambulance crew got through with the defibrillator and it looked like the patient would probably live, Conrad finally had time to ask, "What happened?"

Else shook her head. "He was re-running the experiment I just finished. Did you tell him he could do that?"

"No, of course not. There was nobody else here? He didn't want anybody else to know. Now, why? He wasn't taking that data for our benefit..."

Heinz put in, "Kobolds."

"What?"

"All those times things weren't where they were supposed to be. Maybe some of the time it was us being absentminded. Maybe some of the time it was him looking at stuff, and not remembering just where it was before he picked it up."

Conrad called John Grover. Grover called army intelligence. Two agents had a long discussion with Marius Fleischer.

"Fleischer talked, no problem," the intelligence officer said. "He didn't even try to clam up. Unfortunately, he doesn't know anything useful. He has no idea who he was working for. It was dead drops in both directions, money and instructions in, reports out. The only time he met anybody face-to-face was when he was recruited, and he didn't get a name—which would have been fake anyway. The guy spoke perfect high German, like some local burgher. Maybe he *was* a local burgher, or had been."

Grover sat back in his chair. "Wow. Tradecraft like that? Sounds like some Russian faction."

"Not necessarily. Could just as easily be somebody who read a bunch of spy novels. Maybe a foreign spy, maybe just a freelancer selling secrets to anybody who'll pay."

"You catch anybody else?"

"No. By the time we got to talk to him, he was overdue to shift the position of a half-brick underneath a mailbox someplace. Whoever was servicing his drop quit doing it. So. What did Fleischer get?"

"Well, the general scope of what we're working on. Building all the radio gear we can with the parts we can find, developing tubes and new components, and all our vacuum work right up to the minute. Writing up the vacuum work was part of his job—he didn't even have to hide that. We've been asking everybody about their kobold experiences, and it looks like he was poking into just about everything around here that gives clues to what we're doing and how we're doing it—if we're not all being paranoid now. If he got some of Jen's antenna designs, a good analyst might be able to figure out what we're really doing with radio, but that cat got out of the bag, anyway. One big thing he didn't get is a workable formulation for a good cathode coating and a process to make it, because we don't have that yet ourselves. And we don't have any complete tube designs. But it looks like we're getting close, and he probably reported that."

"Kind of careless, wasn't he? Weird, sitting down and running that lab test. I don't see why he took the chance."

"Probably because Else took her notebook home that night, so he couldn't just copy the data. He must have thought there was something important in those results. There wasn't. Well, I doubt anybody else can put together the industrial base to use what he got for a long time."

The officer's face grew grim. "Don't be too sure. Those machine tool factories have been running three shifts for a couple years now, and not everything they've shipped has turned up where it was supposed to go. There's an industrial buildup starting somewhere. Still, you stopped him before he got the real goods."

The only thing to do was keep the work going as fast as they could sustain it.

They had to order parts to repair some of the equipment Fleischer had dragged to the floor when he fell. At least this time, it was all down-time equipment they'd built themselves. It took four days to get everything working again.

Meanwhile, the materials group delivered a new batch of samples. Else hooked up the test gear. "Let's see what they've given us today. Maybe we'll be lucky." She turned up the voltage while Conrad and Heinz watched over her shoulder. Ten minutes later, the numbers in her notebook told the story. "There's emission, Conrad, but not enough to be useful for a tube. We aren't there yet."

"Well, you know what they say. Any experiment that produces data is successful."

"I keep telling myself that," she said with a rueful smile. "I'd better go show them these results."

Heinz interjected, "This is much better than last time, though. It feels like we're close."

It took two more batches of samples, and three more weeks. This time one of the samples was twenty times better than the rest. Still nothing like the best up-time cathode coatings, but marginally usable. Else said the magic words: "Conrad, I think it's good enough. Just barely, but good enough. With this, I can design an amplifier tube."

Müller straightened up and smiled. "How long, do you think?"

"Probably a day or two. I'll do the calculations, and give Heinz the drawings for the parts. Then we'll see."

Things happened fast after that. Near the end of the week, Else and Heinz were mounting the delicate assembly in the vacuum chamber and starting the pump-down. The next morning it was baked out and ready. Else finished connecting the test setup. She turned to Heinz with a nervous smile. "You'd better check it, too. We've come so far, I don't want to risk burning something out now."

He started comparing the connections on the bench against the diagram in the notebook, lead by lead. Finally, Heinz said, "I agree, Else. It's correct."

Else looked at the bench with a little frown. There was so much test equipment spread across it, that there was no room for her notebook. She settled herself on a lab stool, with the notebook in her lap. "Heinz, you'll have to work the knobs this time. To start with, load resistance to maximum. Grid voltage . . ."

He began stepping the voltage and load controls through the test conditions as she called them out, while she took down the meter readings. By the time they were halfway through, it was obvious. Müller was already on the phone to John Grover. In some mysterious way, word started to spread through the building, and heads began popping out of offices and shops. Finally, the test run was complete. Müller took one long look at the columns of numbers. Then he stepped out into the corridor grinning like a seven-year-old on his birthday, and held out both hands above his head thumbs-up. Cheers erupted.

When he came back into the lab, there was a serene look on Else's face that he'd never seen before. She was gazing out the window at the brilliant reds and golds of the sugar maple outside. One arm was draped casually along the edge of the bench, and the other rested on the notebook in her lap, the pen still in her hand. She looked up at him, and spoke quietly. "Now we know, Conrad. We can do this."

Heinz was still shutting down the power supplies. Without looking up, he said, "Now we got to figure out how to turn this into something we can put in a glass shell and seal it up. We still got work to do."

The push was on for the payoff. The former jewelers and glassblowers were working the kinks out of their new techniques, getting ready to cut open the precious burned-out up-time tubes.

The test samples from the materials group kept getting better. Else was continually revising her repair part designs and performance estimates.

The engineering contingent was starting to look ahead to pilot production tooling for the new tube designs. Conrad and Else walked down to Marcantonio's machine shop one afternoon, to have a brainstorming session with the machine designers there.

"Well, what do you think, Else? Is the job a little less intimidating now?"

"Oh, I still have days when I wonder whether I know what I'm doing. But, yes, this is the most fascinating thing I can imagine. I've decided. This is my career. There's a lot of studying left before I can finish the curriculum, but I intend to be an electronics engineer for real. What about you, Conrad? It still feels strange to be calling a full professor 'Conrad.' Are you going back to teaching?"

"When the right time comes, I will. Yes."

"So. We'll all miss you, when you do."

"Maybe not. I might be teaching right here. There's starting to be a little loose talk of a college, for engineers, like us. Maybe we'll get you teaching, too. I hear you've been doing some lecturing."

She blushed. "What? Those little talks at the radio club? They're nothing. Nothing at all."

Toward the end of the year the power lines reached Schwarza Castle. Five months later the Schwarza Castle two-meter repeater went on the air. It was the most ramshackle collection of obsolete junk imaginable. Higher hills a few miles away limited its useful coverage. But it worked. Rolf Kreuzer spearheaded the effort, and the automatic Morse code identifier carried his call sign. And Rolf made his own career plans and signed up for calculus in the spring term. But that's another story.

Duty Calls

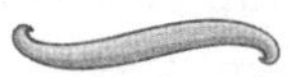

Karen Bergstralh

March 1634

The room was packed with villagers happy to see visitors and hear the latest news and gossip. Rob Clark, stretching his legs, found two young boys under the table. It seemed to him that every inch of space was crammed with people. Some youngsters sat at the edge of an unfinished staircase, legs hanging, eyes and ears wide open. One boy, after losing his balance, had literally hung from the rafters.

It was a party and a feast with the villagers bringing out what food they had. The town mayor and his son-in-law squeezed through the door, each carrying a keg of beer. Rob and his friends had food presented to them from all quarters. Now, after three winters in the seventeenth century, Rob understood how little food must remain in the village larders. When Dieter Wiesskamp reached for his pack, Rob whispered, "Can we give 'em everything except what we need to get home?" Dieter nodded and began emptying his pack. Sausages hit the tabletop and were followed by a sack of rutabagas and carrots.

When Dieter hauled out the two slabs of bacon Wilf Jones winced. With the bacon gone the group's rations were down to a couple of slabs of salt pork and a handful of sausages. Rob smiled back and mouthed "Hearts and Minds" at Wilf. That got him a grimace in return. Reichard Blucher smiled from the far end of the table, obviously distracted by the two young women hovering over him.

Rob realized that Wilf had been right to insist that they not wear their militia uniforms or tell anyone what their real purpose was. This area was just regaining population and rebuilding the villages. These people had little reason to trust any military—both sides had pillaged them and burned their villages while foraging.

"We're a small party," Wilf had stated. "If we go up there in uniform we're more likely to wake up one morning with our throats slit than find the bandits Major Stieff wants us to look for. Best go as a simple group of horse traders checking out the market for our stock. Naturally we're interested in any rumors about robbers."

The previous fall a Grange-sponsored group came up here to help the villages with their harvest. Rob had come with them. The army platoon that came along to guard the machines had been forced to camp outside the villages. Even those of the soldiers who joined in the heavy labor had been greeted with silence and suspicion.

Rob reached into his pack and took out a Walkman radio. He brought out a pair of battery driven speakers and plugged them in. When Wilf nodded Rob turned the radio on and found the Voice of Luther radio station. The party went from raucous to solemn as he dialed in the broadcast. It was the Vespers service from Madgeburg cathedral. Scratchy and static-filled as it was, the choir's "Glory be to the Father and to the Son and to the Holy Ghost" filled the room. Pastor Borstorf nodded thoughtfully; stroking his chin and mustache while the service rolled on. The miracle of hearing what was being said and sung in that distant city even quieted the children. When the Benediction and the last "Amen" had been said, the villagers slipped out into the cold to their houses and bed. Pastor Borstorf remained behind.

"Many thanks, Herren, many thanks for that. It was fifteen years ago when I last heard that choir. Perhaps, should this year's harvests be good, it may be that the village can afford such a machine. Of course, Mayor Bishoff has his eyes on one of the new manure spreaders and so it may come to making a choice between the practical and the uplifting." With a sly grin the pastor added, "I may vote for the manure spreader myself to save my sermons being compared to those from the cathedral."

"Ah, but Pastor, *you* know it was little Hans that threw his sister's doll in the well and Old Klaus who drinks too much . . ." Dieter teased gently.

"Oh, yes! I know my flock well enough." Pastor Borstorf grew grave, his voice dropping to a near whisper. "You go to Oberschwartzwald next, don't you?"

"Yes, that is our plan," Wilf replied as softly.

"Do not play your radio for them, especially not a Lutheran service," Borstorf whispered grimly.

"Are they papists, then? I'd not thought around here . . ." Wilf asked.

"Heretics! Would that they were only deluded papists. No, those left in Oberschwartzwald have corrupted Christ's teachings beyond even the papists' heresies. Beware your souls in such a place. At least the Good Lord has seen that those sons of Satan do not prosper. Would that He removed them from the face of the Earth. We would be well done with Groenwald and his thieving 'cousins.' "

"We've heard others complain about thieves . . . are the men from Oberschwartzwald the ones who have committed these thefts?" Wilf asked.

"They've stolen anything that wasn't chained down or held in hand. Three sows, a horse, and two cows in the last month have wondered off toward the Devil's village. Die Weltzin's freshly washed blankets and the Donners' two casks of sauerkraut walked off with the animals. Others have lost tools. My own good ax went from the chapel entrance."

The pastor's pained look reminded Rob of how precious the stolen items were to the villagers. It prompted him to ask, "You said something about Herr Groenwald's cousins? I take it you think they are the thieves?"

"Young man, for centuries my family and the Groenwald family have known each other and yet none have ever heard of these cousins nor their supposed ancestors. Devils in disguise they may well be, visited on Groenwald for his heresy. Keep good watch at night."

The Grantville quartet exchanged glances. Rob felt a twinge of conscience. His first feeling had been one of glee. If these strangers in Oberschwartzwald were their bandits, he and his friends might be on their way home in a day or two.

☆ ☆ ☆

Yesterday's snowstorm had turned to sleet around dusk. Just past midnight the wind slackened, the temperature dropped, and the sleet turned to ice. As the sun rose over the hills the village took the appearance of a landscape carved from ice. Sunbeams danced from icicle to icicle, shimmering brightly.

The beauty of the scene was lost to the men huddled around the small fire. The room that had been stuffy and over-warm last night now was frigid. The walls and roof had kept them dry but the wind found every crack.

"What curse follows us that the very weather turns against us?" murmured Reichard as he delicately added a small branch to the fire. "As cold as it is, it's well Christian didn't come with us."

"Yeah, two weeks riding in snow and sleet after recovering from pneumonia isn't too smart," Rob agreed. He missed the lanky man and his acerbic wit.

"Come, now, Reichard. It isn't that bad. At least it isn't sleeting anymore," Wilf teased. "And look there, our young friend Rob seems as comfortable as can be."

Rob, shivering on the other side of the fire, took one hand out of his pocket long enough to give Wilf a single-digit salute. "Yeah, just like I'm at home in front of my own fireplace. All that's missing is the popcorn and beer." Despite his up-time parka, fur-lined pants, and heavy boots Rob was cold—down to the bone cold. He wondered again how the others managed. Wilf was wearing an old faded-blue parka neatly patched at the elbows and too long in the sleeves. The parka had once belonged to one of Rob's older brothers. Under the parka Wilf wore a wool shirt, wool pants and a pair of western style boots. His hands sported a pair of rabbit skin gloves. To Rob's eyes the oddest part of the older man's ensemble was the plaid wool scarf tied around his head. Dieter was similarly attired, save his parka was newer, bright orange, and fit him better. Reichard, as big as he was, hadn't found an up-time parka that fit him. Instead the man wore a sheepskin jacket that left Rob idly wondering how many sheep had died to make it. All of the men wore Stetsons. Somehow the sight made Rob think of a Saturday Night Live take-off on *Bonanza*. Wilf would be cast as Papa Cartwright, Dieter as the smooth-talking Adam, and Reichard, of course, as the oversized Hoss. That left Rob himself as Little Joe. The thought tickled him and he found himself laughing.

"Ah, now you prove my point. You *are* just as comfortable here as at home." Wilf grinned back at him.

"More so, I think," Dieter chimed in. "Here he doesn't have to listen to all the women chattering."

"Aye, or get dragged off to see the tailor 'just one more time.' Frau O'Reilly is a level headed, practical woman, or so I thought." Dieter shook his head mournfully. "Now, with your wedding at hand, she has gone as mad as the rest."

"Come now, Dieter." Wilf chuckled. "I'd say that 'tis Liz and JoAnn who are wildest about the wedding. Frau O'Reilly's daughters, too. If anyone gives Frau O'Reilly trouble it is her girls. Fraulein Lannie, she stays calm."

"Well, yes . . ." Rob replied. "Grandpa Ev has been running interference for us. He's declared his house a 'wedding free zone.' Even JoAnn shuts up when he reminds her that it's not *her* wedding. The trouble starts when they get to my house and run into their cousins . . ." He drifted off in memory, then heaved a sigh and grinned back at the other men. "Lannie and I have talked about eloping, except there's no Las Vegas to run to."

Rob tossed a burning branch back on the fire. The guys had it right; he'd come along because he couldn't deal with any more wedding plans, wedding talk, wedding decorations, or sly digs about the wedding night. A week after Christmas, Maggie O'Reilly moved into the housekeeper's quarters in Rob's house. She'd rented out her own house to Christian du Champ and his family. Rob had been in favor of the move as it meant that he got Mrs. O'Reilly's cooking for all his meals. However, he also got the three O'Reilly girls—and their enthusiasms over his upcoming wedding.

Over the last two years he'd had trouble getting used to being alone. Having the O'Reillys in the house helped and in less than a month things would change again. He would officially be a part of a family. A large, noisy, boisterous, alive family.

"Yeah," Rob answered, keeping his eyes down so the others wouldn't see the hint of tears in his eyes. "Yeah, I came along to get away from all the wedding craziness. Besides, someone's got to keep you guys out of trouble." Ducking, Rob almost avoided Dieter's rolled up sleeping bag.

"We need to eat and get moving. Oberschwartzwald is just a couple of miles up the road. Even if there are no bandits it is the last village on our list," Reichard announced. He picked up the frying pan and offered it around. "From what the pastor said it sounds like our bandits might be in residence there."

"Aye, we'd better move or we'll freeze our asses off. Until last night Major Stieff's odd stories about bandits from the villages out here appeared to be no more than noises in the night," Dieter commented while eagerly spearing a piece of meat from the pan.

"Well, the good major did say he didn't think there was much to them. Just that he wanted us to check them out. All that we've heard about in the other villages were a missing cow here, a couple of sacks of onions gone there, a horse that didn't come in from the pasture, and so on. But the pastor's concerns about Oberschwartzwald also make me think there is something more to the stories than random chance and the odd thief," came Wilf's calm reply. He, too, readily speared his share of meat from the pan.

"Don't forget the missing girl," Reichard said. "I don't think she just wandered off on her own to admire the snowdrifts. That scared boy two villages back said he saw four or five riders trying not to be noticed. These mysteriously appearing relatives could be deserters. The Good Lord knows there are enough of them wandering about. The tracks we saw the other day, they looked like five ridden horses and they were heading toward Oberschwartzwald." He extended the frying pan to Rob.

Rob flipped open his Buck knife and gingerly speared the smallest piece. Fried salt pork was one down-time food he didn't like.

"We'll check out the village, spend tonight under cover, and head home tomorrow. If we push and the weather holds we'll be back in Grantville by Wednesday." Reichard's share of the fried salt pork disappeared in two large bites and he continued, "We can report to Major Stieff and be done with our militia duty for another year." A broad grin split the big man's face.

The men exchanged puzzled looks. They were just coming into the village of Oberschwartzwald, past a pair of half-ruined barns. Ahead they could hear a man yelling.

"Sounds like someone is calling someone else a 'dirty little thief,'" commented Dieter.

"Aye, and I think I know that voice," Reichard said. "If it is him, he dies today." Suiting actions to words, the big man reached down and pulled his rifle from its scabbard.

"Yes, and any of the mangy crew he runs with," Wilf added

in agreement as he also readied his rifle. "That pastor last night had the right of it—devils in disguise."

"Who are you talking about? Do you think these are the thieves Major Stieff was worried about?" Rob asked in confusion. He reached under his coat for his own revolver.

"Stay out of the line of fire, Rob. This is old business—dangerous business," a grim-faced Wilf warned. "Not your business nor that of Grantville . . ."

"It's old mercenary business, Rob, with as bloody-handed a mercenary as you'd find. Made the Spaniard look like a saint." Even Dieter, usually smiling and laughing, had a grim look. "The tracks said five men."

"Don't assume that's all. This place may hold others. Spread out. We don't want to give anyone a massed target." Wilf grinned, his face looking wolflike. "Against wheel locks or snaphances we've a good chance. Pray they've not gotten their hands on up-time weapons. Rob, your eyes are good, watch the upper stories and our backs."

Rob nodded in agreement and started to turn his horse around. Art Deco, the Spanish stallion Rob was riding, quivered and refused to turn. Shoving his revolver into a coat pocket, he reached down to stroke the stallion's neck. "Easy, Deco, easy, fellow."

The shouting was coming closer and now Rob could hear hoofbeats on cobbles. Deco suddenly rocked back on his haunches and rose into a levade. Rob took both sets of reins in his hands, automatically separating curb and snaffle reins. He took a solid hold on the snaffle as Art Deco's forefeet landed and the horse arched his neck with a snort. "Hey, silly, ease off," he told the horse and again turned him; thankful that he had the pelham on the stallion instead of the plain snaffle he usually rode with. With the stallion this restive the curb would come in handy.

"Get a good hold, Rob. That's a warhorse. When the fight starts he'll be ready to move fast—very fast." Wilf started forward into the village square.

Rob managed to hold the stallion back until the rest of the group had cleared the road. He eased up on the bit. A pair of prancing steps brought horse and rider far enough forward to see what was happening.

In the open area a mounted man was chasing a small boy around the well. The child darted frantically back and forth while the horseman cursed and threatened to trample him. A couple of men standing in a doorway yelled bets back and forth on how long the boy would live after the "captain" caught him. Two other men were restraining a woman against the wall of a house.

When Rob leaned forward to see better, the stallion grabbed the bit and leapt out, hitting a full gallop on the third stride. Without veering the warhorse ran at the other horseman. Rob sawed on the reins and finally managed to put Deco into a sliding stop, somehow ending up next to the child. Rob leaned down and scooped the boy up. He tried to spin the stallion away, thinking to dodge back the way he'd come. Instead, Deco spun to face the other horseman. Rob managed, barely, to stay on.

His game spoiled, the horseman spurred straight at Rob, his hand fighting with his bulky cloak to reach his saber. Deco leapt forward again, colliding with the other horse. The lighter mount went down.

The downed horseman screamed, "You bastard! You'll die a long, painful death for this!"

Rob recognized several shots from at least two up-time rifles and the boom of a wheel lock. His attention was focused on the horse under him. Deco didn't quiver with excitement now—he radiated rage. The stallion half-reared and smashed his hooves down at the fallen horseman. None of Rob's efforts to control him made it past Deco's pinned ears.

The stallion screamed, high-pitched and eerie, his head snaked forward and grabbed the downed man's face. The crack of splintering bone followed. The fallen horse struggled, blocking Deco from his prey, and the stallion stepped back a pace.

Rob slid off and, still clutching the child, stumbled backward until a wall stopped him. He set the child down behind him and turned back to watch the monster that two minutes before had been his favorite horse.

Deco's backward steps gave the other horse room enough to stand and limp off. The rider lay unmoving, his face an unrecognizable mass of raw flesh and blood. Rob was certain that the man was dead. The stallion circled the body, his nose nearly touching it, sniffing and snorting. Then Deco squealed, reared again and brought both front hooves down on the body. Again and again the horse reared and brought those steel-shod hooves down, trampling the body.

Movement on Rob's left resolved into a man with a sword and pistol. Rob ducked away from the sword and pulled his revolver from his pocket. He danced far enough away to bring the revolver up and fire a quick shot. The attacker hesitated, dropped his sword and pointed his pistol at Rob. Rob took aim and squeezed off another shot. The wheel-lock pistol in his attacker's hand wavered and dropped, followed by the man's body. Belatedly Rob remembered to check for other bandits.

Against the wall, where the woman had been held, two bodies lay crumpled. Another body convulsed in a doorway. Rob heard Reichard yell "Clear!" off to his right and Wilf's reply from the left. Dieter's voice seemed to come from the house with the open door. The man Rob had shot gave a sighing groan and was still. Blood was everywhere—a shocking red highlight to the brilliant white snow. After one last check for other bandits, Rob turned, dropped to his knees, and lost his breakfast.

"Are you hurt, lad?"

Rob looked up to find Reichard standing over him. "No, I'm okay. But Deco . . . God, Reichard, I've got to shoot him! He's gone nuts!"

"Ah, lad, no. He's a warhorse, doing what warhorses are taught to do. Now, if horses have souls I might worry that Deco is enjoying his revenge a bit too much." The element of satisfaction in Reichard's voice caught Rob's attention.

"Revenge?" Climbing to his feet, Rob made himself look again at the stallion and the bloody bundle of rags under the horse's hooves.

"Few of your horse's scars came from battle. That miserable excuse for a man . . ." He sneered, pointing to the body Deco was still pounding. ". . . put the rest there with spur and whip. Especially the whip." Reichard spat and continued. "I, for one, would say this is a fitting end to Captain von Schor."

"Aye, and he had no right to either the 'von' or the 'captain,' " Wilf said as he approached. A look of satisfaction spread across his face. "It was just the five of them. Old Jacob's still alive, for now at least. Dieter is with him so he may not last long. Joachem and Pigears had the boy's mother. They'll not bother anyone again."

Struggling to hold himself upright and steady, Rob mechanically reloaded his revolver. He looked around and saw a few heads peering out of doorways and windows. "I reckon we've saved the town from the outlaws, Marshall," he drawled in English.

Both Reichard and Wilf laughed. Most Saturday nights found

the former mercenaries at Rob's house watching old movies. Westerns were their favorites. The movies were generally accompanied by cackles of laughter and loud exclamations of the number of ways various villains and heroes would have died in a real battle.

Wilf added thoughtfully, "Watch yourselves with the villagers. I don't think we've earned ourselves any welcome here. To them we are just another set of armed scum. Be careful of catching a knife in your backs."

"Or a shot from across the square," Reichard added.

"Maybe not. From the quick glance I got, the village's guns are all in the house these swine were using." Wilf grimaced. "I suppose we'll have to play nice and give them back."

That brought Rob's mind around again to the stallion snorting and pawing in front of them. "Wilf, I've got to put Deco down—before he turns on someone else."

"What? No, Rob, just wait. Once the horse is certain his torturer is well and truly dead, he'll calm down. No need to destroy such a magnificent warhorse. That bastard Schor taught him too well. And Schor knew it. That's why he sold Deco off. Now the horse has found his old master and taught him a lesson." Wilf's laugh was as satisfied as Reichard's had been earlier.

"Are we going to have any kind of legal hassles over killing these guys?" Rob asked. His head was still full of sounds and sights from the brief fight and his hands shook slightly. He carefully cleaned each part of his disassembled revolver. Beside him sat his rifle, ready and easily at hand.

Wilf had "played nice" and returned the villagers' guns to the villagers. But he had first separated powder and shot from the weapons and handed those over only after all the guns had been claimed. Rob fully understood the earlier warning about watching his back after that little exchange. The looks the villagers gave the Grantvillers made it clear that there would be no thanks. Wilf didn't think the villagers would openly attack them but everyone had weapons at hand just in case.

"I don't think so. Each of them was on the old Grantville 'Kill if found' list. I doubt that anyone from our present government will complain," Wilf replied as he patiently and thoroughly cleaned his rifle. "These black powder reloads work well save for the mess they leave."

"The ones who have to bury them might complain," Dieter joked. "The ground is still frozen." He was cleaning out several deep scratches and scrapes on the boy Rob had rescued. The boy's mother, Marta Altbotersin, sat holding him on her lap. Her bruised face was stolid but her blackened eyes darted from man to man.

Reichard sat to one side, his attention on the doorway and Rob's extra pump shotgun across his knees. "We've done the world a service this day by ridding it of those scum. *Faw!* Look at this place! I swear it looks like a pig was slaughtered in here."

"No, not a pig . . ." Marta sobbed softly. She looked around fearfully and clasped Mattias tightly.

"Come, now, Frau Altboters." Dieter smiled warmly at mother and child. "We'll not harm you. No need to hold your son so tight. He's been a good boy and not fussed or squirmed. I'm almost finished with him."

Wilf was looking at the young mother, an odd expression on his face. Reichard began to curse under his breath. Rob smiled at her, trying for "trust me" and fearing he looked instead like he was sneering. "None of us will harm you. You and your boy are safe with us. As safe as in your father's house." Her reaction surprised him.

"Safe as my father's house, eh! My father—" She spat into the fire. "—was the one who shoved me in here to keep you satisfied and away from the other women."

"Ah, that explains it. I thought he said something about sacrificing. He's made you the sacrifice. Your son, too, were we that sort of men." Wilf shook his head and frowned. "Whether you believe it or not we will not harm you or your son in any way, Frau. Perhaps we should introduce ourselves. I am Wilfram Jones, a reasonably respectable horse dealer from Grantville. The overly large man concerned with the former tenants' housekeeping is Reichard Blucher. He is a partner of mine, as is Dieter Wiesskamp. Dieter acts as our surgeon as needed and is very good at it. Lastly, this young man is Robert Clark, horse breeder, trainer, and good friend. He has eyes and thoughts only for his betrothed back in Grantville."

"Aye, Rob's thoughts won't stray—he knows what his Lannie would do to him if they did!" Dieter jibed.

"Come on, Dieter!" Rob found himself blushing.

It might have been the blush or maybe the polite nods from

each of the men that took the wild fright out of Marta's eyes. She looked down at her son and lightly fingered each bandage. Finally her head came up and she stared at the men. "What manner of men are you?"

"Not the likes of Schor and his gang," Wilf bit off. "You said something . . . I'm half-afraid of the answer . . . You said 'No, not a pig.' "

"A girl. About twelve or so. They brought her here a week ago. When they were done with her they had me take the body out."

Reichard spit out one last long and vehement curse. "Pigears liked them young. He died too fast. I should have ripped his balls off." Reichard eyed the woman. "They've been bashing you around, too, haven't they? Bastards!"

Marta nodded and sobbed out, "Yes. Father handed me over to them when the woman they brought with them disappeared."

"And your husband didn't object?" Rob asked.

"How could he? He's been dead these last three years."

"The woman disappeared as in 'under a convenient snowbank'?" Wilf asked. "Oh, woman, what kind of monster is your father to do such a thing?" His hand gently brushed her loose hair back, exposing a large, raw abrasion on her jaw. "These wounds need to be cleaned out or they will fester. Will you allow Dieter to attend to them?"

She looked around at all of them then slowly nodded. Leaning down, she whispered something to her son and he slid off her lap. Rob motioned the boy over. "Let's get something on you, Matthias, before you freeze." Rob reached into his pack and pulled out first a flannel shirt and then a T-shirt. Grinning, he tossed the tee to Matthias. "Put this on." The boy smiled shyly back and pulled the T-shirt over his head. The result brought smiles to other men as Matthias stood draped from neck to toes in the black shirt with gold lettering. "Here, wrap yourself up in this shirt and slide down inside my sleeping bag." Rob handed the flannel shirt to the boy.

Matthias wound the flannel shirt twice around himself and, with a few anxious looks at his mother, wiggled down into the sleeping bag. Seeing the boy settled down gave Rob a warm feeling and he turned back to cleaning his revolver. Wilf hummed to himself as he reassembled his rifle. With a final click he slipped the clip in place and carefully set the rifle aside. Rob looked up. He realized that the tension in the little house had lifted a bit.

"Frau Altboters, did von Schor or any of the others ever talk about why they were here in Oberschwartzwald?" Wilf asked suddenly. "This village seems an unlikely place for them to spend any time."

"No, they didn't talk—they argued. Constantly. The one called Jacob was always complaining about staying here. The captain hit the one called Pigears over the head with a chunk of firewood once. He kept saying that they would stay until they had finished their job. Until the job was done they wouldn't get paid." Marta winced as Dieter swabbed out an abrasion.

"Ah, now that sounds like our late and unlamented acquaintances!" rumbled Reichard. "Money, or at least the chance for money, was all that mattered to that crew."

"Aye, but money for what? Who was paying? Mayhap we should have tried to keep old Jakob alive a bit longer," Wilf replied. "As it is we have an answer to Major Stieff's puzzle. We know who and how many 'bandits' were causing trouble. However, I'm certain he'll want us to find the answer to this new puzzle."

Rob nodded. A thought struck him. "Frau, did you ever see or hear talk about their paymaster? How did he contact them?"

Marta Altboters sat silently for a few moments. Rob thought he saw fear cross her face. After a long look down at her sleeping son, she grasped Dieter's hand and pushed it away. "There was a man they spoke of. A man who met them outside of town, on the other side of the woodlot. When they came back from that meeting Schor had a satchel. He hid it behind the bed." There was a sly, defiant look on her face as she spoke the last. She looked around at all of them as if waiting for blows to fall.

"Oh! Clever woman! I bet that those swine never thought of you beyond their dinners and the bed! Stupid of them." Wilf bowed to Marta. "Gallant woman. Your trust in us is well founded." He looked around the room. "Rob," he commanded quietly, "take the shotgun and guard position."

Rob nearly tipped his stool over in his haste to comply. He thought he knew what was coming. Reichard grinned, arose, and handed over the shotgun.

"You worry about the door, we'll worry about keeping out of your line of fire," Reichard said, a wide grin on his face.

Rob sat in the chair, keeping the shotgun pointed at the door. The first time he'd gone horse-trading with Wilf and the others he'd considered a barred door and shutters sufficient safety precautions. Now he found comfort in Wilf's paranoia as expressed by the shotgun and the unobstructed line of fire. The shutters could be pried open from the outside but it would take time, make noise, and neither window was big enough for a man to slip through. As well, Reichard had driven nails through the shutters and it would take a sledgehammer or ax to open them. The chair he sat in was carefully placed. Should someone break down the door the intruder would find the shotgun on his unprotected side. Also, a gun stuck through either of the windows would be hard put to line up on the chair.

The table sat in front of the door, just close enough that a group of men trying to force their way through the door would be stopped by it. On one side the door's swing would be stopped by a large trunk, on the other side sat the shotgun and guard. Up in Poland the previous year there had been a band of men who had decided to relieve the horse traders of their gold. Five of the thieves died before getting off a single shot and the sixth managed only to put his shot into the thatching. There had been no further trouble with thieves on that trip.

"Shall I?" Reichard's voice rumbled as he stood beside the bed.

"Aye, pull it out and while you're at it get rid of those bloody blankets," Wilf directed. "Might as well chuck the mattress out, too. I'm not so fond of lice anymore. Especially not lice who've been dining on Schor and his band."

Reichard grabbed the bed frame and pulled it away from the walls. He reached down and produced a leather satchel of the kind the Thurn and Taxis post riders used. It landed on the table with a solid thunk. Reichard turned back to the bed, and gathered the blankets and straw stuffed mattress into one large bundle. He carefully stepped around the table and waited while Wilf snuffed the candles and opened the door. A quick step outside, a heave and the filthy mess disappeared into the night. Another step, back this time, and Reichard was inside and the door closed. The bar dropped into place.

Wilf lit the candles, then grinned and drew the satchel toward him. "Mayhap now we'll see what Schor was up to." Papers spilled out, several letters and two large vellum rolls when he upended the satchel. There was a single clink announcing the presence of a large silver coin. Wilf held the coin up and showed it around.

It was only half a coin with a jagged edge. Wilf set it aside and started scanning the letters.

"Reichard, as you've finished with the bed, take over guard again. Most of these are in French." Wilf indicated the letters on the table. "Here, Rob, you read French. See what you make of this."

The exchange was quickly made and Rob sat again at the table. After squinting at the first letter in the candlelight he grabbed up his pack and unzipped a side pocket. The small battery-powered lamp lit up the interior of the house remarkably. Behind him he heard Marta gasp but his attention was on the letter. What he read made him reach for the rolls. "Maps, that's what this is about. Maps of the roads around here and on up toward Magdeburg." Rob unrolled one vellum and held it open. Wilf and Dieter crowded around.

"Maps with notes on roads, road conditions, fords, and military patrols." Wilf's voice was tight.

"Here and here, notes about the villages—supplies of food, livestock numbers, details about the town militias, how many guns, how much gunpowder and shot . . . Just what a raiding party needs to move quickly." Dieter's face was grim. "Or is it to be more than a raiding party?"

Rob scanned two more of the letters. "I can't tell. Some kind of raiding party. That's my guess from the information asked for—the letters don't say. Nor do they give a time. From what you've said the fact that they are in French doesn't tell us anything, either."

"No," Wilf replied. "Schor read French but none of the others did so it could just be his way of keeping them ignorant. He wasn't the most trusting soul." Pausing, Wilf looked around the room. "I think that this package belongs on Major Stieff's desk as soon as possible. Moonrise should be late tonight but the road is clear. We'll leave before it's up. Two hours, men. Rest and eat."

"My son and I will go with you." Marta's voice was firm, her chin was up and from the look on her face she was expecting to fight for her decision.

Reichard chuckled. "The lass has more spine than her father. Certainly you can come along. I'll don't think any of us want to leave you to be 'sacrificed' again."

"Aye, Reichard," Wilf declared flatly. He looked at her for a moment and then nodded. "Right. By rights Schor and his band's horses are yours. They aren't much but selling them and their tack in Grantville will give you some money. There are several places you can stay—safe places." He stared into the candle flames for a moment and continued. "Reichard and I will ride with you. Dieter and Rob, you two will take the satchel along to Major Stieff as quickly as you safely can."

"You will not need to wait on us. I can ride as well as any man." The voice was proud but wavered a little at the end. Marta stood and began rummaging through a pile of clothing on a bench. She pulled out a man's shirt and a pair of long trousers that were obviously much too large.

"Frau Altboters, I have no doubt about that. The fact is that Dieter and Rob are light riders and have the two fastest horses amongst us. They will make the trip quicker and I confess that I'm getting too old for the kind of breakneck riding those two delight in. We four will follow at a slower pace. Rob, I'd like to keep your sleeping bag with me—for the boy and his mother." A smile played across Wilf's face as he looked down at the sleeping child.

"Sure, Wilf. There's an extra pair of jeans in my pack that should fit you, Frau Altboters, and some socks. My extra boots are probably too big . . ." Rob grabbed his pack and dug out the promised items. His mind was busily planning how to make the fastest time back to Grantville. A stray thought bubbled up and he glanced at Wilf. What was the man up to? Wilf was usually the one who set a fast pace. He glanced at Reichard and when their eyes met Reichard winked slowly and tilted his head toward Wilf. Wilf was speaking softly to Marta Altboters while helping her find a warm cloak.

"Well," muttered Rob under his breath, "this should be interesting. The man who is impervious to women's charms . . ."

"Looks to have found a winter rose," Reichard whispered softly.

Major Stieff settled back in his chair. The wondrous warmth of central heating rapidly thawed his frigid feet and hands. The mug of coffee and three of Frau O'Reilly's oatmeal cookies served to warm his insides as well. One of the other men seated in the room coughed and that brought Stieff back to the reason he'd ridden out to the Clark house.

"Don Francisco has your maps and letters. He's set his people puzzling over them. So far the conclusions are that your bandits might have been working for Turenne. Given the number of factions interested in military information in that area the number of possible 'paymasters' is quite large. Still, I was asked to pass on thanks to you. First for removing Schor and his friends, second for recognizing that he must have had a compelling reason to stay in the Oberschwartzwald area, and third for bringing the maps and letters back so promptly." Stieff sipped his coffee and nibbled on a cookie, enjoying the moment.

"We accept Don Francisco's thanks," Wilf answered. "There's more, isn't there?"

"Ah, yes." Stieff smiled. "One of the up-time sayings I find so charming is 'No good deed goes unpunished.' It sums up life's little quirks so nicely."

"So, Major, what will be our punishment?" Reichard asked.

"Nothing specific at this time." Stieff paused. "However, I did get the impression that Don Francisco may have the odd job for you from time to time. Not," he added hastily, "before Rob's wedding. Definitely not."

"So Don Francisco is afraid of Fraulein Lannie's temper, too?" Dieter laughed.

"More likely of Herr Parker's. He would not like to see his granddaughter's big day spoiled."

Major Stieff decided to take his leave on that light note.

The Galloping Goose

Herbert & William Sakalaucks

"Okay, guys, very carefully, peel the logo stencils and coverings off the doors and I'll get the big one on the back end," Arlen instructed. The sharp smell of drying paint hung in the air, a fine mist shrouding the gathered crowd, as Mike and Martin peeled off the new door logos for the Grantville, Rudolstadt, and Saalfeld Railway and Tram Line; the rays of light glistening off the black logo. A capital G above the R and S looked like they were ready to fly with their speed lettering extensions.

"You know, Arlen, this new logo really makes it look like it *is* ready for speed," Martin commented. "How's the rear logo look? You've kept it a real tight secret, I'm not even sure Don Francisco's spies could have gotten any hint about its design."

"Come on back and see," Arlen said, with a smirk on his face. Everybody crowded around in the tight space behind the engine. There on the back door was a picture of a goose running flat out, neck parallel to the ground, feet in mid-stride. "I'm calling this new engine the 'Galloping Goose' class railbus after its Colorado narrow gauge ancestors up-time."

Resplendent in its silver and black paint scheme was an old Ford truck cab and frame with a hand-crafted wooden passenger compartment that Martin had built. Martin's prior experience as a boatwright showed in the smooth sweeping lines of the body. It could seat twenty-four passengers and could carry luggage and freight in the back. Arlen had scrounged the glass and seats from an old Blue Bird bus that was being scrapped. The interior looked like a Black Forest cuckoo clock–maker's dream. Every possible inch was carved black walnut and polished to a high sheen. A small propane stove for heat was also in the rear of the car. Underneath the Goose, Arlen had installed a small set of lead wheels with a large drive wheel set in back, powered by a chain drive. The Ford's frame still had a hydraulic lift in front for machinery.

"How fast do you think it can go?" asked one of the workers in the crowd.

"On a good, flat track and no load, probably forty miles per hour. Around here in the hills, and with the rail we've got, maybe twenty to twenty-five with a good tail wind." Most of the GRS's current freight trains averaged around ten miles per hour. "That's still twice as fast as our freight trains can do." Arlen was grinning from ear to ear.

"So, has the railroad bought it already?" Mike tried to prick Arlen's ego a little. They'd been friends since grade school and were always trying to upstage each other. "Last I heard, they wanted to run trials with it to make sure it really worked, and see if passenger demand would support its cost."

"They're still looking at a trial. I've painted this one as a demonstrator. I had to scrounge up just about all the silver auto paint that was left in town. Hopefully, seeing it in railroad colors will help seal the deal." Arlen had put a lot of his own time in on designing and building the Goose, but his enthusiasm still had a bit of doubt clouding it. Mike sensed the hesitation and waited for Arlen to continue. Arlen sighed and went on, "It's probably got the same problem the original Geese had. They tended to gallop from side to side at higher speeds. We've got an upgrade planned for the production model to improve the springs and weight distribution that should solve that problem if it crops up. We just need to get the first one sold. We even have a larger steam-powered version with a wooden body on the drawing board, but first, we have to sell the railroad investors on the idea that passenger business can be a paying proposition."

Passenger service in November 1634 was very austere, expensive, and slow. The Goose showed potential to provide a quick way to overcome many of the objections that had been raised about improving passenger service. Arlen knew that the best-engineered equipment still had to be sold to be successful.

The whole crew proceeded to board the Goose while Arlen started the engine. “Mike, since you’re a trainee engineer, I thought I’d let you be the one to back her out of the shop and show her to the world.”

Mike slipped into the seat that Arlen vacated for him. He turned on the music system and inserted a CD. “I thought this might be appropriate for the occasion.” Strains of John Denver singing “Jenny Dreamed of Trains” filled the Goose. Slowly, Mike backed the Goose out into the rail yard and then parked it on the service track. Everybody piled out, many commenting on how beautiful the interior was and how comfortable the seats were. Mike muttered under his breath, “Not if you ever had to ride two hours on a field trip on them.”

After a while, the excitement died down and Mike nudged Arlen in the ribs to gently remind him of the passing time. “Don’t forget our evening plans. You know that Dee and Mimi are waiting for us to take them to Tyler’s Restaurant tonight and we both need to clean up before we meet them. What time are the reservations for?”

The deer in the headlights look that Arlen got told him everything he ever needed to know. “Move! I’ll help Martin check that everything’s cleaned up with the paint sprayer. He can lock up and I’ll meet you at your house.”

The shop crew hurried to clear the shop before the boys’ girlfriends ended their short, yet exciting lives. Tonight was the informal rehearsal dinner for Arlen and Mimi, who were getting married on Sunday. Mike had gotten leave to be there as the best man and Deirdre Hardy was going to be Mimi’s maid of honor. All the workers razzed Arlen for his forgetfulness as he hurried off, but they were also proud of what they and Arlen had built. Martin was the proudest of all.

When Arlen arrived at his parents’ home, out of breath, his mother greeted him at the door. “You make sure you don’t get any of that grease and paint on the bed. Last time you were late, you just tossed everything and you almost ruined the comforter!”

“I’ll be careful, Mom.” Arlen responded light-headedly. “Can you call Tyler’s and make sure everything is set for the dinner, please?”

“I already did. I also called Mimi and Dee at the new apartment and told them that you and Mike were working at finishing the Goose. I called her back when you came in and they'll meet you at Tyler's in forty five minutes."

Arlen called out, "Thanks, Mom! I've got the coveralls in the basket. I'll start the laundry before I go."

Just as Arlen finished dressing after his shower, Mike arrived and the whole process was repeated. He and Mike checked each other's appearance, flattened Arlen's cowlick for about the fifth time, put on their best winter coats, and walked to Tyler's.

On the way, Mike went over the plans for Sunday's upcoming nuptials. "Just remember, Arlen," Mike started his lecture, "You've got the easiest part in the whole thing. Make sure you're there by noon. Then, you stand at the front of the church, smile from ear to ear as Mimi walks down the aisle, turn around, say 'I do,' put the ring on her hand, kiss her, turn around and walk down the aisle without tripping. Got that?"

Arlen chuckled, "I think so. Just don't forget the ring, okay?"

"Right."

The friendly banter on wedding plans continued. As they approached Tyler's Mike asked apprehensively, "Are we on time? Dee said she'd skin me if I got you here late."

"Funny, Mimi told me the same thing about you! We've still got five minutes. Wouldn't it be funny if they were late this time?"

"Not a snowball's chance. Speaking of snowballs, I think we're in for some snow. You can almost taste it in the air." Mike loved snow. He'd spent quite a bit of his winter breaks skiing at Snowshoe Mountain before the Ring of Fire and had a knack for sensing when snow conditions would be good.

"I just hope if it does, that it doesn't spoil the service on Sunday. Mimi and I don't have a lot of family that can be here." The thoughts of just what the Ring of Fire had cost them carried Arlen and Mike into Tyler's. Once across the threshold, the aromas from the kitchen woke them from their reverie. They looked anxiously for their dates.

Herman Bartig, the doorman, greeted them as they walked in. "Mimi and Dee are waiting in the bar area for you. They just got here five minutes ago. Don't let them tease you that they've been waiting. They sounded mischievous as they came in!"

When they entered the bar, Mimi spotted Arlen and made a beeline for him. The unladylike, full-body kiss drew a round of applause from the regulars at the bar. After the wolf whistles died down and Arlen got his breath back, he asked, "Do I know you, ma'am? My fiancée is supposed to be around here somewhere and she's the really jealous type."

"Just wait 'til Sunday night!" she said with a sly grin. "You ain't seen nothing yet!"

"I hope I'll see nothing on Sunday night. The wait since our betrothal in June has been killing me. Cold showers only work so long!"

Dee came up and greeted Mike with only a slightly more demure kiss. "Maybe next year, Mike?" she asked with a wiggle of her eyebrows. Dee and Mike had been going together since their junior year in high school and were starting to get serious. All four young people had been friends since they were in grade school and the last three years had brought them even closer together. Mimi and Dee were both starting teaching careers and Mike and Arlen had worked on trains since their volunteer days at the Cass Scenic Railway.

The maitre d' came up at that point and interrupted to tell them that their table was ready. The table they approached was covered with a crisply ironed white tablecloth, elegant porcelain plates, stainless steel flatware, crystal glasses and a silk rose in a vase. As they sat down, a waiter arrived with a tray of appetizers. "Compliments of the management, Thuringerwald Oysters, for the bride and groom."

Mike responded with laughter. "After the earlier demonstration, I don't think Arlen will need them, but please, give the chef our thanks!"

The rest of the evening was a complete success. Arlen and Mimi had a chance to have an evening to relax after all the preparations of the past few weeks. When Arlen started to try to talk shop with Mike, Dee fixed him with a withering glare and the subject quickly changed. Around midnight, the celebration broke up and Mike and Arlen escorted the girls back to the new apartment, each couple pausing frequently to embrace and warm up.

The snow started falling softly in large, fluffy flakes. The world seemed to narrow down to just them as the snow muffled the sounds of the evening and visibility decreased.

Arlen sighed. "Looks like I'll have to stop by in the morning and shovel."

"I'll have something to warm you up when you're done."

"You'll probably still be asleep. I've got some paperwork to finish if I'm going to get next week free. We've got one engine in for a major repair and I need to show Joachim and his crew how to braze and refinish the broken part. I should be done by noon. I'll stop by afterward to help get the last of my stuff moved into the new place."

They were covered by a light white blanket by the time they finally said good night. Mike and Arlen hurried back to Arlen's parent's home because the snow was now starting to come down in earnest.

Saturday morning dawned gray, cold and snowy. Even though it was only late November, it looked like the storm was going to dump a lot of snow. Arlen and Mike shoveled out his parents' house and the new apartment. Mimi and Dee had a big breakfast ready for them and then shoved them off to work.

"We've got a ton of stuff to finish up today and it's looking like we'll have to fight the snow as well as time. You guys go do what you need to at the shop and we'll see you later this afternoon." Dee looked like she would brook no argument, so Arlen and Mike set out for the shops.

After trudging through ankle deep snows for fifteen minutes, they were huffing and puffing, just like the engines they worked with. They weren't the first to arrive that morning. They were greeted by a toasty fire in the office's pot belly stove and the aroma from a large pot of coffee warming on top.

"Everybody in?" called Arlen as he walked out to the repair bay. The steam engine sitting there had its piston rods out. The rod from the engineer's side was on the work bench due to a stress crack that had been found during routine maintenance. An instructor from the tech school was coming by to show Arlen and three of his senior down-time shop machinists how to handle the brazing and heat treating. The informal class was set to start at ten. Over the next hour, Arlen was planning to finish his reports to Hugh Lowe, the GRS president, on the Goose and develop a plan for testing the railbus.

As Arlen was putting the finishing touches on the plan, Martin Erlanger came in the front door of the shop, shook off his coat and stamped his boots clear of snow. "Such a day, not even a wild pig would go out!"

"Any word on how long they think this will last?" Arlen was starting to get worried that the weather could ruin the next day's wedding festivities. He knew everyone coming was already in town, but trudging through snow was not his ideal of how a wedding party should leave the church. He didn't want Mimi to be disappointed.

"I just stopped by the radio station and what reports they could get from the west and north show a wide area of snow. They think it will probably go through tonight or maybe tomorrow morning. They also had just gotten an emergency signal from Saalfeld. There's been another industrial accident, this time at the steel works, with some serious injuries. They had to use the radio because the telegraph line was out. They think there was a snow slide or a tree down somewhere along the rail line. I hope they are able to handle the injuries at the steel works' clinic. The hospital's full and this storm has all the roads closed between here and Saalfeld."

The phone rang. Martin answered, "Hello."

Everyone could hear his end of the conversation and watch his body language. Immediately, they all could tell it wasn't good news. "No, the engine's not ready. You'll have to talk to Arlen about that." Martin held out the receiver. "Arlen, Mr. Lowe from the railroad. He has some questions I can't answer."

Arlen had a bad feeling about what was coming. "Arlen Goss here. What can I do for you, Mr. Lowe?"

"Arlen." Mr. Lowe sounded rushed. "We've had a serious accident at the Saalfeld steelworks. We need to transport two serious burn cases. I've talked to Dr. Adams at the hospital, and he has some real concerns about where best to treat these cases. They've still got a number of people they're treating for that chemical spill and they've got a heavy load of flu cases. Two of their staff members who have some burn experience are at Jena right now working with the university to set up a new trauma unit. Jena hasn't been hit with the flu yet, and this snow should slow down travel enough that it shouldn't spread there too soon. The big question is, can we get them there? Is Number Four done with its rebuild? It's the only engine with a plow that's big enough. We don't have anything else that could get through heavy snow."

"Number Four has a cracked rod. We won't be able to get it rebuilt before Monday."

All Arlen heard was a deep sigh on the other end as Hugh thought back to his conversation with Dr. Adams. The doctor had gotten on his soapbox about all the world's medical problems always having to come to Grantville to be cured. The current overload at the hospital made this an ideal opportunity to showcase what other facilities could do. Hugh decided to see if there was any other way to get the patients safely to Jena. "Is there any way to accelerate the work? The men that got injured were doing some experimental test castings for the railroad and I really want to help."

Arlen saw his chance. "We just finished that railbus I was telling you about last week. It's got enough power to buck the snow and we can put a plow on it. Should take us half an hour to hook up and by the time the medics are ready and get here, we should be ready."

"Great! I'll call the hospital and tell them to have their EMTs meet you at the shop. Just be ready to roll as soon as you can. The reports I've gotten indicate at least two serious burn cases and one fatality already. I'll also send a track crew along, in case there's any trouble on the line."

"We'll be ready, Mr. Lowe." Arlen hung up and motioned the staff to gather round. "Martin, call the county road shop and tell them they need to bring over the old wedge plow truck so that we can use the plow. Vardy Rowland, the foreman, will know which one we need. Julius, get the Goose fueled and make sure we've got extra fuel for the motor and the stove. Stefan and Joachim, take off the arm rests on the last four sets of seats. Put boards between them and get some sleeping bags so that we can use them as beds. Mike, give Mimi a call and tell her what's happening. Also, I'll need an engineer, can you handle it?"

"Sure, but don't you want someone with more experience than I've got running the Goose?"

"You *are* the most experienced engineer we've got for it. Nobody outside the shop has even been in it and Martin and I will be along if any problems crop up." Mike's eyes went wide, but his military training kicked in and he just saluted and went to finish his tasks.

Arlen took a deep breath and started going through a mental checklist on what else might be needed. This would be the Goose's shakedown run and there were a lot of things that could go wrong, especially with the amount of snow they had already gotten and what was still coming.

"Spare drive chain, extra sand for traction, rerailer, bars, shovels and jacks in case of derailment, track bars and spike mauls in case of track problems, two chainsaws, extra blankets, food and water in case we're stranded and a rabbit's foot for luck." As he thought of each item, Arlen called out to the shop crew and they located and loaded the item into the freight compartment. Martin got two of the shop crew to help him top off the sandboxes on the Goose and then added four fifty-pound bags of sand in the back. By the time he'd finished his loading, the truck had arrived with the plow. Mason Sizemore came in, shaking off snow like a small bear and sputtering about proper channels for requisitioning government property.

"Mason, please, we've got an emergency. Just help us get the plow switched over to the railbus."

Mason looked like he wanted to say some more but then acquiesced. "The snow is breaking branches and trees that are blocking the roads. Where did you say you want the plow set?"

Arlen pointed out towards the yard. "We've cleared a space on one of the crossings out front. If you can set the plow on the tracks so we can just hook up and go, that would be great. It'll save us time and that's the most important thing right now."

Mase went out at the fastest jog Arlen had ever seen him do. The sound of gears meshing told him that the truck was being positioned. Then, brakes squealing brought Arlen to the window to see what had happened. It was the ambulance from the hospital pulling in. Walter Allen and Frieda Zimmerman, both EMTs from the Fire Department, got out and unloaded their gear from the back.

"Come on in here and tell us what more you need!" Arlen called. "We're getting the plow installed now and should be ready to go in five minutes."

"Has anyone called with an update?" Walt seemed extremely concerned. "The last radio call we got was that there was one definite fatality and two serious burn cases." While Walt was talking to Arlen, Frieda and Martin were transferring additional supplies from the ambulance into the Goose. Just then, three more figures came high-stepping through the snow in the yard. The snow swirled in through the door as they entered. Lucas Chehab from the VoA radio station was followed by Mimi and Dee.

"Walt, I've got the status update for you. Michael Koester and Fredrich Klein have got second degree burns on their arms and upper bodies. Their team leader, Gustav Arndt, received third degree burns over most of his body and died shortly after the accident. They're not sure exactly what happened. Mr. Pierce sent word that he thinks they have enough pain killers to hold the two for about two hours. You'll need to get there before then or they may lose both of them to shock."

Walt took a moment to digest the news. His conversation with Dr. Adams when the call came in had been short and to the point. The hospital was full. If the patients could be transported to Jena safely then it was Walt's responsibility to make the call and get them there. This was a golden opportunity to start expanding medical care expectations to other sites. It looked like the parameters were a go for transporting to Jena unless something came up while they were enroute to Saalfeld. "Arlen, how long will the trip from Saalfeld to Jena take?"

"A normal run would be Saalfeld, Rudolstadt, and then to Jena. With the regular trains, that would be almost three hours in clear conditions, four in the snow, if at all. If the Goose works as well as our plans say she should, we should be in Saalfeld in less than half an hour and in Jena by mid-afternoon. Say about two hours, including the time to load the patients," Arlen said.

Frieda slipped in from the rail yard. "All the supplies are loaded. We're set. Are we ready to go?"

The shop entrance door swung open again and a group of five track workers from the railroad congregated around the entrance.

"Were you all raised in a barn?!" someone yelled from the shop. A chorus of good natured "*ja*'s!" came from the group, who were mostly down-timers. "Well, shut the door before you let all the hot air out!"

"*Jawohl*, we wouldn't want Julius to wander out into the snow." The old joke drew a sharp elbow to the ribs of the joker from Martin.

Julius quickly shot back, "At least they let me in the house now. You, they still keep in the barn." That drew another round of laughter from the track crew.

"If you are all done with your jokes, let's get loaded. Two men are waiting on our arrival. We've got a long day ahead of us. Anybody have anything else they need?" Silence greeted Arlen's question. "*Los gehts*!" They all filed out into the swirling show in the shop's switching yard and started to board the Goose.

Mike settled into the engineer's seat. Martin took the conductor's seat in front of the passenger area. Mike commented, "You know, without the steering wheel, there's a lot more space here than you would think."

"I sure hope we're in time for those guys in Saalfeld," Arlen muttered.

The only sound as they worked their way through the tracks in Grantville was the hum of the Ford's engine and the clickety-clack of the wheels on the rail joints. The Goose was a ghost through the snow as they approached the station. The Goose slowed and Mark O'Reilly got out and threw the harp switch to move the Goose to the main track. He signaled with his kerosene lantern to have the Goose move onto the station main track. The Goose moved slowly over the switch and picked up Mark as they went by. Arlen then had Mike stop and Martin went into the station to get the train orders for the first leg of the trip. Mr. Nisbet, the railroad's general manager, was waiting inside to personally deliver the train orders.

"You're the only thing on the line today. We've cleared anything that might slow the run. You're authorized to run at whatever speed you feel is safe. Show me what the Goose can do and I'll decide how to present it to Mr. Lowe and to the board, but get those guys there safely. Remember," Mr. Nisbet added sternly, "the trip from Rudolstadt to Jena, it's all older strap rail. You'll have to watch the rail in case the weather has caused any problems." With that, he handed Martin his Form 19. Nisbet's fervor surprised Martin. The railroad manager was known as a cold fish, but maybe he had a heart after all. Martin turned and headed out the door into the blowing snow.

When he reached the Goose, he looked up to check the sky. It was still snowing, and the sky was a uniform gray. The wind had started to blow the fallen snow into drifts in the yards around the station. Martin opened the door and got in quickly, shaking the snow off as he entered. "Here's the Train Order. We're the only one on the line. We need to watch the strap rail on the Jena line. They're not sure what this type of weather might do to it." He felt a little pompous repeating what the written orders said, but railroad regulations required that the engineer verbally acknowledge the orders from the conductor. Since he was acting as the conductor on this run, Martin wanted no questions that he had followed procedures.

Mike acknowledged the orders. Grinning, he added, "At least we don't have to watch for snake-heads like the old-timers did. With the welding and the short sections of real rail at the joints, it's a big improvement over the old style strap rail." Mike then let off the brake and the Goose started trotting its way to Saalfeld.

The silver paint scheme on the Goose blended in well with the falling snow. Only the headlights and red markers on the rear highlighted its departure through the Grantville yard. As it hauntingly glided out of town, the chatter inside the passenger area slowly died down. Everyone knew this was a mercy mission and thoughts of what lay ahead weighed heavily on them.

Mike asked, "What's the speed limit on this short section to Schwarza? The plow seemed to handle the snow in the yard pretty well."

"Hold it down to twenty-five. The wye at Schwarza's not too far and we may have to pick up updated orders there. I'll be glad when the signaling is upgraded and we don't have to get orders at every station." Arlen was concentrating intently on the track and the sounds and movement of the Goose, so Mike just nodded and went back to watching the track for snowdrifts.

Five minutes of waddling later, the small whistlestop station at Schwarza loomed up on their left. It was positioned inside the wye where the three tracks from Grantville, Saalfeld, and Rudolstadt joined together. Mike slowed down, but the station master was standing on the platform with a wooden hoop outstretched for Mike to grab. Mike rolled down the window, stuck his arm out and snagged the hoop. He handed it to Arlen and then rolled up the window. As he brushed off the snow that had come in, Arlen took off the flimsy paper and read it quickly. "Mike, there's a track crew located a telegraph break just south of Mile Post 3. Top speed five miles per hour between Mile Posts 2 and 4. Watch for workers and new rail along track. Saalfeld is expecting us in twenty minutes."

"You've got it, Arlen. If you see anything, let me know."

Walt called out from the back, "Any new word on the patients?"

Arlen yelled, "Nope, just slow orders for a crew fixing the telegraph. We should be in Saalfeld in fifteen or twenty minutes. Looks like the track's okay to there."

The track crew was relieved. They hadn't looked forward to working in the snow, if they could help it. As cold and blustery as it was, hands would freeze to rails or tools in minutes if they weren't careful. The news that they would reach the patients in Saalfeld quickly lifted everyone's spirits. As they passed Mile Post 2, Mike slowed down. The spray from the plow subsided and the Goose's waddle dissipated. Everyone got a good look at where a tree had taken out the telegraph line as they drifted past. There was a bundled up figure with a lantern that waved the Goose through. As they passed, the three telegraph workers gave a muffled cheer that could be heard inside the Goose.

Arlen got up and walked back into the passenger area. "Walt, Frieda, we're about five minutes out. If there's anything you need to do before we arrive, now would be a good time to do it."

Frieda nodded, "Your guys did a great job and got everything set before we left Grantville. We just need our patients now." Arlen accepted the praise quietly and turned back for the cab. He gave Martin a pat on the back. "We'll have to let the shop crew know what a good job they did when we get back. You've really gotten them working together as a team." Martin smiled. In the guild, only a master might ever be thanked for a job well done.

The normal scene inside the foundry was like a vision from *Dante's Inferno*. Heat and smoke left everyone who wasn't acclimated gasping. The sparks and noise left visitors on edge.

The morning had started out quietly enough. It was Saturday and they were working a light shift. The railroad's experimental casting work was the only major job scheduled. Susan Swisher had hoped to get caught up on paperwork when the scream of the steam whistle alerted her to an emergency. As she bolted out of her office she could see the workers starting to gather in the casting area. There were three groups, each gathered around an injured worker. Thadeus Zakrewicz, the shift EMT, came jogging out of his office, emergency gear in hand, and yelled "What's happened?"

"I don't know, but it looks like it's in the casting area."

They got their first good view of the situation when they turned the corner between the open tool racks. Gustave Arndt was on the floor in the pour area with a small group gathered around his still body. It took Thad only a glance to tell that, if

Gus wasn't already dead, he soon would be. He'd been burned severely over the top half of his body and his leather protective gear was covered with slowly cooling steel that still popped and sizzled. Susan did a quick pulse check, shook her head and they headed over to the other two burn victims.

"Susan, take these keys and go back to my office. I'll need the full emergency kit and what morphine that's there. You know the drill. Anything else you might find that could help, bring it along." Knowing that there would be questions later about what had happened, Thad decided to ask while the events were still fresh in everyone's minds. "Anybody see what happened here?"

"I did, Mr. Zakrewicz," one of the men said. "They were all set up to try the test casting for the new turntable support ring. Gus was supervising the work and Michael and Friedrich were making sure the mold was secure. The crane operator called out to ask if they were set. It sounded like Gus said, 'Go,' gave a hand signal to start, and then he was lying across the mold. Michael and Friedrich tried to pull him back but all they got for their efforts were burns. Gus didn't make a sound at all."

"Anybody else?"

"Just like he said. I saw Gus wave his hand like Jaimie should start pouring. Gus had an odd expression on his face, took two steps forward, and seemed to be reaching for something in the pattern area. Then the pour started and Michael and Friedrich were trying to help him."

There were other nods of agreement but no more comments. Thad was starting to get a suspicion about what had happened. The lack of response to the initial burn and the collapse were key indicators. "It sounds like Gus may have had a stroke or a heart attack."

He was interrupted by the sound of someone getting violently sick across the room. The crane operator, Jaimie, was down on his hands and knees, trying to stop what were now dry heaves.

"Jaimie, are you all right?" Thad asked. He knew he would probably need to send Jaimie to see a counselor after this was all over. Thankfully, someone had found a blanket to cover Gus.

"It was my fault, Thad. I thought Gus signaled to start."

"He probably did, Jaimie. It looks like he may have had a stroke and was gone before he even started to reach for the pattern box." The dazed look in his eyes lifted a bit. Jaimie was young and, with help, should recover. Thad turned back to his two surviving burn patients as Susan and Gunther returned with the needed supplies.

"Michael, Friedrich, we're going to get you to a hospital as fast as this weather permits. Right now, you're not feeling much pain because you're in shock. I'm going to have to get your leather gear off so that I can assess the extent of your injuries. Before I do that, I'm going to give you some morphine and you'll be out like a light in a few minutes. You won't feel the pain when I start to work. Your families have been called." He looked at the crowd and got an affirmative nod from Jim Pierce, who had just arrived. "And they'll be here shortly," he continued. "Anything you want me to tell them when they arrive?"

Michael whispered, "Tell my wife, I love her and to take care of herself. The safe box is . . ."

Susan interrupted. "You can tell her that yourself tomorrow at the hospital. This looks bad and will hurt like hell for a while, but you definitely aren't going to die."

An hour later, after the two men had been freed of their protective gear and the wounds cleaned as well as conditions allowed, Thad turned to Mr. Pierce, and asked, "What's the word on transportation? Can we get them to Grantville okay?"

"I talked to Dr. Adams. He wants us to send the two burn cases to Jena if we can. The trauma folks with burn training are in Jena for a meeting on the new trauma center and he's worried that all the flu cases they've got right now could hurt their long-term survival chances."

Susan turned white and looked like she might faint. Jim Pierce hurried to add, "It's not as bad as it sounds, the railroad's been contacted and is sending a special train that will take them directly to Jena and should be here anytime. Grantville's sending their two EMTs with burn experience and a fresh supply of morphine. They think they can get everyone to Jena before nightfall. Can we move them to the station now?"

Thad considered the situation for a moment. "We're set here. They're both stabilized and the morphine has them out. I'll need eight strong, steady carriers to get them transferred to stretchers and carried to the station. If we cover them with enough blankets, the five minute trek shouldn't be too hard on them."

Mr. Pierce called out, "I need eight volunteers to move the injured!" Twenty hands shot up and in two minutes the two injured had been gently placed on stretchers and the carriers were ready for the trip to the station. Just then, a strange noise startled everyone. In the ensuing quiet, Mr. Pierce said softly, "I think your ride's here now!"

On the outskirts of Saalfeld, Mike hit the button on the electric horn Arlen had installed. The loud blasts of "*aahhOOOOOgah*" startled the crew in back and announced their arrival to the whole town. As soon as Mike slowed down for the red approach signal, one of the track crew jumped off and slogged through the snow and tried to throw the switch for the depot's turnaround wye. It wouldn't budge.

"Damn blue ice's frozen the switch!" Somebody else jumped out with a sledgehammer and broom and between the two of them, they had the switch cleared in less than a minute. Mike brought the Goose up and they reboarded on the fly. They repeated the process at the next leg of the wye and then backed down the track to the depot. They were greeted by a procession from the foundry. A figure broke out of the crowd and stumbled through the snow to the Goose. When she got closer, Walt and Frieda both recognized Susan Swisher. Even with all her winter gear on, nobody else in Saalfeld was that short.

"Walt, Frieda, you have superb timing. We were just bringing the two patients to the depot to wait for you. Are you ready to board them now?" Susan asked.

"We're all set," answered Walt, "We've got four sets of seats set up to be temporary berths. We can just set the stretchers across and not have to transfer them at all. Are there just the two?"

Susan nodded. "Yeah, we lost Gus before the accident. Thad says it looks like he may have had a stroke and was dead before Michael and Friedrich tried to save him."

The next minutes were spent in organized chaos trying to get the stretchers in without jarring the patients. Once in, they secured them to the improvised berths with rope.

Mr. Pierce approached the railbus. "I don't know what this thing is but it's the prettiest thing I've seen since my wife had our last kid. Who's in charge?" Arlen pointed at Mike, Mike at Arlen, and then they both looked at Martin.

After a short, pregnant pause, Arlen said, "I designed it, Mike's running it, and Martin built it."

"Well, thank you. All of you. I don't know how I'll ever be able to repay you, but please, get these guys safely to Jena. They've both got families that are depending on them. Will you have room to carry five other passengers? Susan promised them she'd try to have the families there at the hospital when they woke up. I'd also like to send Thad and Susan along to help care for the injured. Can the—what did you call it—the Goose handle that big a load?"

"No problem. I know Walt was a little concerned that he and Frieda might be hard pressed to handle two serious burn cases by themselves."

"How soon can you get them to Jena?"

"If all goes well, we should be there in less than two hours." Arlen was confident. "The Goose is running well and we've brought along tools and help in case we run into any unexpected problems."

"Under two hours to Jena in this weather? I didn't know the railroad had anything like this. Where's Hugh been hiding it?"

"This is her shakedown trial. We finished with the plow this morning after your call came in."

"Just keep up the miracles, and again, thanks." After shaking their hands, he turned and started to clear the crowd back from the tracks.

Since he'd been appointed as the conductor for this trip, Martin went into the station. There were orders waiting for them as far as Rudolstadt. All they said was, "Track now clear, proceed at best safe speed to Rudolstadt. Pick up new orders there. Signed, Nisbet." When he got back to the Goose, the crowd had grown, but Mr. Pierce was keeping them back at a safe distance. Martin boarded, gave Mike the orders and checked with the medical team.

"Are you and your patients set?"

Walt and Thad answered together, "All secure. Ready for you."

"Mike, signal the crowd and let's go." The Goose let out with a raucous *aahhOOOOgah* and started waddling down the track. A couple of kids in the crowd imitated the horn and started flapping their arms as the Goose left the station, with the gathered people waving and cheering. As they left the well wishers behind, Thad asked, "Where did you get that horn, Arlen?"

"On the bottom of a shelf over at the old auto parts store. They had a dozen of them and I bought all of them. If the Goose is successful, I wanted all the railbuses to have a distinctive warning horn."

"I don't think anyone here will ever forget it," chimed in Susan. "I jumped three inches when you announced your arrival with it."

Everyone settled down for the ride to Rudolstadt. In ten minutes, they were passing the Schwarza station again and the signal was green for the track to Rudolstadt. Mike hit the horn to announce their arrival but the stationmaster just waved them through. As the Goose waddled through the switches for the wye, Friedrich tried to roll over and moaned when the blankets restraining him rubbed his arms. Thad checked the dressings and drip bags. "I think we better break out the morphine you brought, Frieda. These doses are starting to wear off. They're both in better shape than we originally thought." After a bit more morphine, Friedrich settled into a light sleep.

Once they were past Schwarza, the grade started a slight rise for the route to Rudolstadt. The plow was throwing a bow wave of snow to each side as the Goose waddled along at a steady twenty-five miles per hour.

"Everything's working fine, Arlen. If I keep it at the high end of each gear, it seems to cut back on the side to side motion. I think you've got enough power to even pull a trailer for freight." Mike was smiling. "I've hardly had to use any sand so far!"

"Don't jinx it, Mike. The worst stretch is on the far side of Rudolstadt." Even though he was trying to sound pessimistic, Arlen could not help but feel optimistic. The Goose was performing far better than he had hoped.

Mike concentrated on potential snow drifts. They were almost in sight of Rudolstadt before the first serious problem area was encountered. The track crossed the corner of an open field where the wind was being funneled to the opening. Mike geared down and started spreading sand. As they hit the drifts, the Goose shuddered as it carved the drift and then broke into the clear fifty feet later.

"That wasn't bad at all," remarked Arlen. "Any problems in the back?" Martin gave a thumbs up after checking with the EMTs. "We're just about at Rudolstadt. We'll stop for orders and a quick break. Facilities are outside, behind the station. The last stretch will be the toughest, so use the opportunity if you need it."

Ten minutes later, the semaphore signal for Rudolstadt station shone bright red through the swirling snow. Mike pulled up in front of the station and set the parking brake. Walt and Thad quickly busied themselves checking that the ropes holding the stretchers hadn't loosened.

Arlen called out, "Rudolstadt, two minute break!" He turned to Mike, "I've always wanted to do that since I was a kid. I'll be back in a minute if you can hold it that long."

Mike had a quick comeback, "I wasn't the one who drank two cups of coffee before we left. I'll mind the store until you get back. Make sure you remember to pick up the train orders!"

Arlen headed out behind the station. By down-time standards, the facilities were luxurious, with ventilation and varnished seats. While the cold kept the odors down, they were unheated, so no one lingered. Arlen was quickly back inside the station to get the orders for the remainder of the run but Martin had gotten there before him.

"What have you got for us, Thomas?"

"You aren't going to like them. We've had two breaks in the telegraph line between Jena and here. Before the wires went down, the track crew at Rothenstein signaled that they had ten inches of snow, with drifting. They were patrolling the tracks on horseback but they haven't reported back yet. I'm giving you cautionary orders to proceed at best safe speed with a danger warning for snow and debris beyond Mile Post Twenty-Two. There are some deep cuts beyond Kahla and Rothenstein and you could get some serious drifting there. The wind's in just the right direction for problems on that stretch. Good luck and Godspeed." With that, he shook their hands and went on to change the signal to green.

When Arlen and Martin got back into the Goose, they were covered with a light dusting of fine snowflakes.

Martin went into the Goose to check on the passengers. "How're they doing?" Thad was just checking their vital signs. "Michael is stable and in remarkably good shape, everything considered. Friedrich got a deep burn on the back of his neck and his blood pressure's been fluctuating a little, but if we get them to Jena soon, they both should be okay. How's the situation looking?"

"This last stretch will be the most difficult. Once we reach Rothenstein, the tracks appear to have some problems but the track crews haven't been able to reach the trouble area. At best, we may have a tree or two down, more likely, the tracks are drifted over." Mike was climbing back in the cab. He looked like a miniature polar bear with all the snow covering his winter gear.

"All aboard!" called Martin as Mike shifted the Goose into first gear.

Arlen climbed into the fireman's seat, rechecked the passenger compartment and then told Mike, "Let's roll! I've got a wedding to get back for tomorrow."

The track was aligned for departure. As they rolled out of town, Mike and Arlen both felt a change in the Goose's performance. After a few moments their worried looks slowly changed to comprehension. "We're on the older strap rail now! You can hear the different clatter as we cross the joints."

"I just hope we don't have a problem with this rail, Arlen. The snow looks to be slowing down, but they've had more here than we had in Grantville." The window wipers were laboring to keep the windows marginally clear. Mike rolled his driver's side window down and tried to clear the buildup he could reach. "At least this is easier than a regular truck. I don't have to worry that I'll swerve into the next lane." Just then, the plow of the Goose found a small drift and Mike got a face full of snow.

"Looks like I'll have a simply abominable best man if you keep that up!" roared Arlen.

Sputtering and cleaning snow from his eyes, Mike groaned at the miserable pun. "Just wait until that first kid arrives, Arlen. Paybacks are hell."

The Goose made steady progress. Before they knew it, the station at Kahla was in sight. It was just a whistlestop station and the signal was green so Mike didn't even slow down. The problem areas were beyond Rothenstein. Mike was a study in concentration as he tried to watch for any drifting and gauge when the use of sand was needed for traction. The passenger compartment was staying nice and toasty with the passengers' body heat and the stove putting out its share of heat, too. Both patients were quiet. Their families were still in a daze from what had happened, but were starting to ask Walt and Susan questions about the future.

"When will my Friedrich be back to work? We don't have much money to pay the hospital," pleaded the injured man's wife.

"Don't worry, Anna, the company's paying all the bills. Mr. Pierce told me so before we left, and his pay's continuing, too."

The smile Susan got from her seemed to light up the whole compartment. "Friedrich told me this was a good job, but now I know it has good people too. *Danke!*"

The Goose rounded a curve and the mounted track crew came into view at the Rothenstein station. Mike slowed to a stop to let Martin check on the track's status.

Two minutes later, Martin climbed back in looking grim. "The crews were able to locate the breaks in the wire. The snow had broken off some overhanging limbs. They're going to wait until the weather clears before fixing them. Our problem is that about four miles outside Jena, there are a series of three cuts that are starting to drift shut. We may have to do some serious snow bucking to open the route."

"Well, that's why we waited for the plow," said Mike. "I'll watch the speed and we can have the boys in back get out and check each cut before we try to break through. Anything else?"

Martin shook his head no, sending snow all over the cab.

"Then let's roll!"

Arlen got up and went to discuss the situation with Walt, Thad, and the track crew. "Martin says we're about thirty-five minutes running time from Jena, but we're probably going to have to plow through some big drifts. Walt, Thad, I'll need you to make sure the patients are braced securely. Mark, you and the rest of the crew will need to get out to check the drifts for any debris that might have come down the sides of the cuts and let Mike know how big a drift he's facing. We'll probably need to take a couple of shots to get through each one if the track crew's description was accurate. Take all the shovels and picks out and pass them out when you get off. We'll need to clear the rails after each shot to reduce the chance the Goose jumps the track from the snow build up."

The entire track crew looked like they were dealing with a befuddled spinster. "We'll handle it, Arlen. We've done this before. Don't try to teach us how to suck eggs!" The good natured laughter that followed helped quiet Arlen's nerves.

About ten minutes later, the first cut came into view. The drift was as high as the top of the plow. Mike slowed down, shifted into first gear and inched up to the drift.

"Time to earn our pay, boys!" Mark called.

The track crew piled out to get their tools and start checking the drift. Inside a minute, Mark was back in the Goose grinning from ear to ear. "It's just a narrow wall, taller than it is wide. You should be able to bust right through. We'll stay outside, just in case you need a second shot, but it should go on the first try." Mark got out and waved the crew back up the track so they wouldn't get showered with snow.

Mike let out the clutch, applied sand, and nudged the drift. He almost broke through on the first try. He backed up fifty yards, waited for the crew to clear the rails, and then came at the drift again, a little faster than before. With hardly a shudder, the Goose broke through in a cloud of snow. As he stopped a hundred feet past the drift, Mark and the track crew hustled down the cleared track to reboard the Goose.

"That was easy," remarked Thad.

"Don't count your chickens yet," said Arlen. "We've still got two more to go." Within a half mile, the next cut appeared and the drift was definitely more formidable. Mike made a halfhearted attempt at the drift and actually cleared five feet before he was forced to stop. The track crew got out and repeated the drill. No debris was found, but this time, the drift was almost thirty feet wide. After the rails were cleared, Mike backed up and made a run at the drift. There was a jolt as the plow struck, but neither patient was disturbed. When the cloud of snow from the impact cleared, almost twenty feet of track was cleared. The Goose pulled away from the snow bank it had created and the track crew fell to with gusto to clear the rails and the packed snow at the front of the pile.

After five minutes, the crew cleared out and Mark signaled for Mike to try again. When the plow hit the snow this time, a huge pile of snow flew up and landed on the roof and behind the railbus, but the Goose broke through to the other side. The track crew scrambled over the snow left on the tracks and reboarded.

Inside, thermoses of hot coffee were passed around. Everyone was tired, but cheered by the fact that only one cut was left.

The last cut appeared and someone in the back choked and sprayed coffee everywhere. A whispered "*Gott in Himmel*" was the only comment as the extent of the drift became visible. The cut was more of a ledge cut into the side of the slope. The track was on a shelf extending for a hundred yards with a steep drop off on the left and a thirty-foot-high stone face on the right. Amazingly, the tracks were clear, but for almost the full length of the shelf, a ten-foot ledge of snow overhung the rail bed. The snowfall had slowed to just flurries and the smoke from Jena was visible about two miles in the distance.

"What now, Arlen?" asked Walt.

"I don't think we have a choice. Everybody unloads and, quietly, walks to the far end of the cut. If we can, Mike and I will try to get the Goose past. If we don't, Martin can send someone to Jena for horse litters for the patients. That may take an extra hour, but they'll get there. The track crew can work at digging us out. If we make it, we reload and are in town in five minutes. If anybody else has any better idea, I'm open to suggestions."

Silence greeted his request.

Thad broke the silence. "Okay, then. Let's get our two patients bundled up again, just like we did for the trip to the station. While we're doing that, Mark, why don't you have your crew carry their tools down past the drift? Then come back and we'll all help get the patients moved."

The next minutes went quickly as the passengers and patients were all walked or carried past the drift. Once they were safely set on the other end of the cut with Martin, Mike turned to Arlen and asked, "Shall we do it fast or slow?"

"If we do it slowly, it's just about sure that we'll get trapped and they'll have to send for the horses. If we go quickly, we may stay ahead of the snow as it falls. Either way, I don't think we're getting back to Grantville tonight."

"Fast it is, then. Hold onto your hat, and buckle in. This could get hairy!" Mike tapped the horn once to let the passengers know he was ready. Mark signaled back with his lantern to come ahead. Luckily, the track was straight here, so Mike backed up the Goose for a running start. One more tap on the horn and the Goose was off.

As it picked up speed, Arlen read off the speed for Mike, "Ten, fifteen, twenty, thirty, thirty-five..." They passed the start of the overhang and almost immediately snow started to spray in all directions. The plow struck a column of snow when they were about a third of the way through the cut. The ensuing snow cloud hid the Goose from the view of the small group huddled beside the tracks. The snow ledge started to collapse from the far end. Just then the Goose broke into the clear, and, like a surfer riding the Banzai Pipeline, the Goose stayed just ahead of the falling snow and cleared the cut.

Mike lay into the horn and the call of "*aahhOOOOgah*" resounded across the hillside. About three hundred yards past the group, the

Goose finally stopped in a cloud of snow and sparks from the braking wheels. As the screech stopped, Arlen could be seen pounding Mike on his back in celebration. The Goose then backed up and the group jumped back on board as quickly as they could with two litters. Five minutes later, with the horn echoing off the city walls, the Goose entered Jena with its patients.

The Goose was greeted by a cheering crowd assembled around two waiting ambulances. A space had been cleared of people from the station platform to the vehicles and had been shoveled and swept clear of snow. There were two gurneys with attendants waiting for the patients. A group of very important looking people were off to the side. As Walt and Thad got out to make arrangements to transfer their patients to the gurneys, Beulah McDonald and Patrick Onofrio hurried forward to meet them. It had been Beulah's call that the center could handle the burn patients. She wanted to make sure that they got the best care right from the start. The transfers to the ambulances from the Goose went smoothly. Patrick rode in the back of one with Thad and Walt and Frieda rode in the other. Susan stayed with the families to help get them lodgings at a local inn before they went to the medical center. As soon as the ambulances left, the crowd poured into the cleared area to get a better view of the Goose and its crew.

A tremendous cheer went up when Mike, Arlen and Martin got out and the group of dignitaries descended on them. The mayor started in with a speech immediately. "Congratulations on a magnificent accomplishment. Your efforts to . . ." Arlen smiled and waved and tuned out the rhetoric to check on what was happening with the rest of his passengers. The stationmaster was leading the track crew over to a nearby *Brauhaus* for some serious toasting. The ambulances had departed and Beulah and Susan were shepherding the families onto a wagon to take them to the local inn. Beulah caught Arlen's eye and pantomimed for him to wait and that she'd be back in thirty minutes. The crowd noise drowned out whatever she might have tried to yell.

Thirty minutes later, the speeches were still going strong. Every dignitary in town wanted to be heard and each speech was an agonizing rehash of the previous one. At one point, Arlen caught himself starting to nod off and looked over at Mike. Mike seemed to have perfected the art of sleeping with his eyes open. Arlen started searching the crowd and finally saw Beulah approaching. When the current speaker paused to draw a deep breath, Arlen quickly broke in, "I'd like to thank all the wonderful people of Jena for this magnificent reception. I see my contact from the medical center coming and I must check with her on my passengers. My associates, Michael Lund, who was the engineer for the trip, and Martin Erlanger, who helped build the Goose, will be able to stay, but I must make my farewell."

Mike turned to Arlen and muttered under his breath, "I'll get even!" Martin just stood back quietly and enjoyed his fifteen minutes of fame.

Arlen chuckled and turned to meet Beulah. She gave him a huge hug. "They both should recover. Walt and Thad did a great job stabilizing them for the trip. I know we could have gotten them to Grantville faster, but after we heard Gus had died and the others were not as serious, Dr. Adams and I felt that all the flu cases at Grantville were the more serious threat to their survival. This also gives us a chance to show the world that Grantville isn't the only place to get medical care."

Just then, a roar from the crowd caught their attention. Mike was just finishing his short speech with ". . . he got betrothed in June and his bride-to-be is tired of waiting. So just be here at dawn with your shovels!" He turned to Arlen with the biggest grin possible.

Arlen told Beulah, "I think I'm in trouble. I better get back to see what Mike's done to me now. I'll stop by the medical center as soon as we're done here." As he made his way through the crowd, all the men were shaking his hand or slapping his back. "What did you do to me now, Mike?"

"Paybacks! I told them about you wanting to get back for your wedding. There's no way to get the track cleared so that we can return tonight. The students have volunteered to start out early in the morning to hand shovel the tracks as your wedding present from the school. Now smile and accept your bachelor party!"

As the crowd started to lift Arlen and Mike on their shoulders, Martin waved them off and yelled to Arlen, "I'll take care of the Goose. I'll stop by the medical center when I'm done." All Arlen could do was give him a thumbs up. As the crowd headed for the street Arlen yelled to Beulah, "Radio my fiancée! Tell her I'll be there tomorrow. I'll stop by the medical center before I go!"

His voice raised in pitch as the wave of people moved him away from Beulah.

"Good luck! I'll make sure she gets the full story!" Beulah walked slowly away, chuckling as she went.

Arlen let out a groan. "She's gonna kill me!"

One of his supporters informed him, just loud enough to be heard over the crowd, "Only if the hangover from our party for you doesn't get you first!"

Early the next morning, still dressed in his shop coveralls, Arlen slogged through the snow up to the medical center front door, bleary eyed and with a day-old beard on his chin. Mary Pat Flanagan spotted him first and came over with a sympathetic grin. "You look like you could use a good cleaning up and a gallon of coffee. Follow me. We've got a small shower facility for the staff down the hall. Leave the dirty clothes on the bench and I'll have one of the orderlies freshen them up while you're cleaning up."

Thirty minutes later, after a shower, shave, and a change of clothes, Arlen came back to the main reception area. "Thanks, Mary Pat. That sure makes my morning! How are Michael and Friedrich doing?"

"Their prognosis looks good. Thad did a great job on the initial response. Walt and Frieda will be returning with you but Thad and Susan are planning to stay over an extra day or two to help the families. You might want to go get Mike and Martin and get the Goose ready for your return trip. The half of town that wasn't celebrating with you boys last night left two hours ago to start clearing the tracks."

"Any idea where my best man and my conductor might be hiding?"

"Try the lounge. Mike came in an hour before you, got cleaned up, said something about 'needing to drive,' and curled up on an old sofa in there. His snores have been shaking the walls since then. Martin came in late in the evening. He got a good night's sleep and left about the time Mike arrived. He said something about getting the Goose turned around and ready for the return trip this morning."

"I'll take you up on that offer of coffee. Two cups, black, please, so I can get Sleeping Beauty in there moving. I've got a wedding to get to."

"Coming right up! I'll meet you in the lounge with them."

After their morning coffee roused them a little, Mike and Arlen went to see the patients. Walt and Frieda were in the room when Arlen and Mike arrived. The families crowded around to thank them again for helping save their loved ones. Pleading the pressing urgency to get back for the wedding, Mike and Arlen gathered up Walt and Frieda, took their leave and headed for the station. The ten-minute walk in the brisk morning did as much as the coffee to wake them up.

"I must have sipped that same beer for two hours last night. I'm tired but not hung over," said Mike, disgustingly clear-eyed.

Arlen groaned holding his head. "I wasn't so lucky. Everyone kept insisting on buying a round for the hero and groom. If I don't see another stein of beer, it will be too soon."

"You can sleep it off on the ride back. With a little luck, the anesthesia won't have worn off before Mimi kills you for missing the wedding."

When they reached the station, the stationmaster said, "The Goose is all preened, fueled, and ready to go. Herr Erlanger took care of that when he showed it to Count von Sommersburg last night."

At the mention of the count's name, Arlen swung around, "Who did you say was here?!"

"Count von Sommersburg. He was here for a meeting with some engineers at the University and he was all over the Goose with Herr Erlanger after you left yesterday. He gave strict orders that everything possible be done to get you back to Grantville in time. The tracks should be clear inside the hour. Your track crew will go back on the regular freight tomorrow. Herr Erlanger is with the Goose now."

Arlen went to smack himself on the forehead but thought better of it. "How could I let a chance like that to promote the Goose slip by?"

"Don't worry, Herr Goss. There were a lot of telegraph messages going north after he was done last night to someone very important. The count looked very pleased when he left. I think Herr Erlanger did a very good job. He seemed very pleased too, when he left."

"Wait and see, Arlen. I think the run we made was promotion enough. Martin's tour may be the clincher. He knows the Goose as well as you do."

"I hope you're right." The previous day's adventures and the evening's festivities were starting to tell on Arlen. He looked like a feather could knock him over. With a visible shake, he cleared his mind to organize his thoughts and changed the subject. "You said we have about an hour yet until the tracks are cleared?"

"*Ja*. The crew has a portable telegraph with them and they've sent back reports on their progress. Everything is going smoothly."

Walt interrupted. "Frieda and I have to secure some gear we left with the ambulance. We'll go get that and be back in half an hour."

Mike and Arlen were left standing on the platform with the stationmaster. The quiet was then broken by a noisy rumble. After a few seconds, Arlen asked, "Anyplace a person could get a light breakfast nearby?"

"I live here above the station. My wife would be happy to fix you gentlemen breakfast. We serve food for any passengers the train might have when it stops and we feed the crews. Herr Erlanger ate earlier. Just follow me!" Hurrying inside and up the stairs he yelled, "Gertrude! I need two more breakfasts for *Herren* Goss and Lund. *Mach' schnell, bitte!*"

Gertrude came into the common room twenty minutes later beaming and carrying an armload of dishes heaped with eggs, bread, and sausage, and two beers in her free hand.

"You eat! You have a big day ahead!"

"And hopefully a bigger night," quipped Mike.

Mike and Arlen set to with an unexpected gusto. Sixteen hours between meals required some serious eating. As they mopped up the last of the eggs with bread slices, Arlen asked, "How much do we owe?"

"*Nein, nein!* The railroad will cover for your help."

"*Danke*, Frau Schimmel! That's the best wedding breakfast a person could hope for." As they pushed away from the table, Mike glanced out the window. Martin had the Goose parked in front of the station warming up, shining like a new silver dollar in the early morning sun. Walt, Frieda, and Martin were already waiting in the passenger compartment.

Mike got an ice cold splash of water down his back from an icicle hanging from the station's overhang. He let out a yelp when it landed. "Hey, Arlen, the sun's out. Maybe we can get back in time!"

The stationmaster came running up and gave Arlen his train orders. "Must not forget these!"

All the orders said was, "Highball it! Signed, Curtis."

"I think she's anxious, Arlen."

"No kidding. Let's go!"

They climbed into the Goose, Mike hit the horn and headed for Grantville. As they approached the cuts outside of town, Mike sounded the horn again. A cheer greeted them as they reached the first cut. A group of shovelers was returning from farther up the track with shovels over their shoulders. The students in the group were singing a bawdy song and Arlen blushed beet red when he finally caught what the song said. Mike slowed down and rolled down the window as the track boss came up to the Goose.

"All clear to Rudolstadt. Just watch this last group. After them, you're clear."

"Okay, tell everyone thanks. I'll get him there on time." Mike rolled up the window and with a strident *aahhOOOOgah*, the Goose continued its journey. While Mike ran the Goose, Arlen talked to Martin about the meeting with the count.

"He wanted to know everything we have planned. He was especially interested in the plans for a steam-powered Goose. I told him that the Steam Engine Company should have the new steam design ready by the time we move to the new shop in Saalfeld. He also wanted to know if we could make the car body larger. Something about living quarters during campaigns. I told him the new steam design should be able to handle that. I've already drawn plans up as you asked."

Arlen sat there for a minute and digested the information. "It sounds like we've got someone very interested. When I get back after the honeymoon, we'll start building the new steam power plant prototype. Right now, I need some shut-eye." He got up and headed back to the empty seat next to Mike. Inside a minute, he was asleep.

The ride back was through a winter wonderland. The trees were all draped in a thick blanket of snowy boughs and the countryside sparkled with its clean white coat. There was some light drifting, but the plow blew through it, leaving silver clouds of snow. The sun had some warmth to it and was already starting to melt the early snowfall. As they rolled along, Mike had a chance to watch the scenery more than he had the day before.

The tree branches were hanging low with all the snow that had fallen. "Looks like the AT&L linemen will be busy the next few days repairing wire." The only comment he got from Arlen was a change in the timbre of his snoring. Mike settled in to make sure he got back to Grantville in time.

The wedding was scheduled to start at one in the afternoon. The Goose arrived in Grantville at a quarter to twelve.

The cheers were deafening as everyone got out. Martin got the keys, and told them he would bed the Goose down. Ed Piazza and some other town notables headed the reception committee.

Ed pulled Arlen aside, "The truck will get you to your folks' house so you can clean up and change and then it'll take you to the church. I'll see you later at the reception. Good job!" With a solid pat on the shoulder, he propelled Arlen towards the truck with Mike Lund following close behind.

The next hour went by in a haze, but at five minutes to one, Arlen and Mike were delivered by their driver to the front door of the Church of Christ. The minister, Douglas Curtis, came out to chivy them inside. "Are you all set? Got the ring?" he asked.

Mike's face looked like he'd been struck by club. Arlen choked and turned white, "After all the warnings!" He was hardly able to get the words out.

Mike laughed. "Gotcha! I told you about paybacks. I've got them right here." He pulled the matched rings from his pocket.

The church was packed. Then the music started. Dee was first through the door in her peach-colored bridesmaid outfit. After she reached the front of the church, she smiled at Mike, turned to the other side of the altar and took her place.

Then the "Wedding March" began. Mimi entered. She had on her mother's white silk wedding dress. She had added a knitted white shawl that Antanette Tranis had made especially for the occasion. Antanette had recently arrived with her family from Lithuania. Her husband was one of the machinists at Vulcan. Arlen's heart felt ready to burst; the soft colored glow from the stained glass windows only enhanced the glow from Mimi. The pride and love in her eyes told him everything was right with the world.

Afterward, Arlen swore that was all he saw until the minister said, "I now pronounce you husband and wife. Ladies and gentlemen, I present Arlen and Mimi Goss. You may kiss the bride!"

As they started to walk down the aisle, the organist started to play the recessional march. As they reached the front doors, Mike turned to Dee, "What's that tune?"

"It's something one of the Stone boys suggested. Mimi and I had him play it for us and it sounded very good. Some march from Ralph Bakshi's movie *Lord of the Rings*."

The crowd started to file by, Ed Piazza shook Dee's hand. "Good choice of music, gets the crowd out quickly!" Chuckling, he congratulated Arlen and turned to Mimi, "Good man you've got there. He's really going places!"

Hugh Lowe was next and also added his well wishes. "See me after the reception!"

Later that evening as the reception was winding down and the presents were being readied for opening, Ed Piazza and Hugh Lowe took Arlen aside. "You sure showed what that Goose can do," said Hugh. Ed nodded agreement and grinned. "A lot of questions came up after you got to Jena. I've got a message from the Transportation Minister. They want a special Goose for Gustavus. It was a good thing that message came in Morse code. I almost died laughing when the radio operator finished translating. Can you believe it? Just like one of the old rail barons' palaces on wheels. He said he needs something comfortable and regal to get him quickly around in all types of weather."

Ed started to chuckle. "Once word gets out that Gustavus has a private railbus, I'll bet that every nobleman will want one, too! Every politician, too, once campaigning starts. The old whistle-stop politicking will return! Arlen, I'll bet even Wettin gets with you after you get back from your honeymoon."

Arlen reached for a chair and dropped into it. "We may have to scrounge walnut for the bodies and old trucks for the frames, but we'll do it!" The rest of the conversation was lost as Mimi tossed her bouquet. Ed Piazza and Hugh offered a toast, "To Arlen and Mimi Goss, a long, happy and fruitful marriage." Ed Piazza gave Arlen a mischievous wink, and took a drink.

With visions of the future, Arlen kissed the bride and whispered, "And to the Goose, the founder of our future!"

Feng Shui for the Soul

Kerryn Offord

Grantville, 1633

Kurt Stoltz ignored the rumbling of his stomach and continued his careful scanning of the pages of the newspaper. He well knew that *they* censored everything. So one had to read everything to detect the tiny inconsistencies that hinted at what *they* had removed. He knew there were censors about, especially in Grantville. There was no way that they would allow easy access to all the information from the future, no matter what they claimed.

He turned the page and started reading the advertisements.

The ad in the "situations vacant" column practically leapt off the page. Kurt stared at it in disbelief. The Gribbleflotz Spirits of Hartshorn facility in Grantville was looking for multilingual people with fluent English (preferably up-timer English), Latin, and German to work in the research department. He could do that. He was fluent in Latin and German, and had spent several years in England. As for up-timer English, he was a regular user of the various libraries around Grantville. Not that he was well known of course. Anybody growing up in the Stiefel-Meth sect learned the value of keeping his head down and being inconspicuous.

He placed a hand inside his satchel where his notebooks resided. His personal notebooks, with all his notes about the research being undertaken by the great Herr Dr. Gribbleflotz. The doctor was publishing information that Kurt couldn't find in Grantville's libraries. Did he have a source of information the censors hadn't gotten to? This advertisement suggested a way to find out.

A position as a researcher with his company, even if it was in Grantville rather than in Jena, was an opportunity not to be missed. Kurt copied the address for applications, then for the first time since he arrived in Grantville to see the truth of the Corona Conflagrens miracle nearly two years ago, he left a library early. He needed an early night if he was to get to the Gribbleflotz Spirits of Hartshorn facility before any other applicant tomorrow.

HDG Enterprizes
Jena, 1634

Dr. Phillip Theophrastus Gribbleflotz glared at his special aluminum pyramid with the strategically placed faceted gems. He picked up his pen and dipped it into the ink. The pyramid wasn't working, but the world's greatest alchemist couldn't just write "it isn't working" in his notebook. That kind of comment lacked any hint of scientific credibility.

Phillip paused in thought, idly chewing on the wooden shank of his pen. Then he remembered how the Americans would record the lack of results. He dipped his pen again and wrote "No invigorations of the *Quinta Essentia* of the Humors were observed." It was nice. It described the lack of observed results in suitable language, but then, why couldn't he see anything? Phillip started worrying his pen again.

The obvious answer was that there was nothing to see, but that couldn't be right. Maybe... Phillip sat up straight. Of course! The changes in the *Quinta Essentia* were invisible to the human eye. What he needed was some method of detecting the invisible forces.

He'd found it. Photography. More specifically, Kirlian photography. With Kirlian photography one could record the image of a person's aura. All one needed was some simple electrical equipment... and some photographic equipment. That last brought Phillip back to earth. What was the availability of up-timer photographic equipment?

He went to the door of his office and called out. "Hans. I need you."

The normally reliable Hans Saltzman didn't answer. Phillip went searching. The first person he found was Ursula Mittelhausen, the housekeeper for HDG Enterprizes.

"Frau Mittelhausen, have you seen Hans?"

"He is in Halle helping set up the Oil of Vitriol facility, Doctor."

Phillip stifled an unsuitable exclamation. Just when he needed his personal assistant, Hans had to make himself unavailable. Well, when everyone else failed you, there was only one person left to do the work. "I need to make a trip to Grantville. Please book a seat on the train."

"Of course, Doctor. The evening train? Do you wish for me to also book accommodation?"

Phillip considered the work he had backing up, and the expense of accommodation in Grantville. "At the Higgins. I don't know how long I'll be. I need to ask about 'photography.' "

Ursula perked up. "Michael's sister, Maria Anna, sent a photograph of herself that one of the up-timers took. Are you going to be working on photography now, Doctor?"

"I wish to investigate the application of photography to the detection of the invisible forces of the invigoration of the *Quinta Essentia* of the Human Humors."

"So you'll be taking photographs, Doctor?"

"Purely for science, Frau Mittelhausen."

"Oh!" Ursula was crestfallen. "I was hoping that I could have my photograph taken so I could send it to my sister in Leipzig."

Grantville

Phillip had the choice of talking to the dreaded Frau Kubiak, or to Maria Anna. It wasn't that difficult a decision to make, so he caught the bus to Grays Run. He easily found the property where Frau Mittelhausen said Maria Anna worked. There was a sign declaring the house to be the head office of Brennerei und Chemiefabrik Schwarza. He looked around. It was vaguely similar to the property of Frau Kubiak—a large house on a few acres of land with a number of outbuildings. Obviously it was only a small company.

The door was answered by a little old lady, an up-timer.

"I am Dr. Phillip Gribbleflotz. I believe Maria Anna Siebenhorn works here?"

The little old lady shook her head. "Oh dear, I'm sorry, but Maria Anna's not in at the moment. She's in charge of the new explosives division at the Schwarza Gewerbegebiet and won't be home until late... Gribbleflotz, did you say? The Aspirin King?"

Phillip grimaced. "The Aspirin King" was not something the world's greatest alchemist wished to be known as. They could at least get the name right. "Yes, I am the Gribbleflotz behind Gribbleflotz Sal Vin Betula."

"Do come in, Doctor. Your people were most helpful when Celeste and I wrote asking about photographic chemicals."

They were? Phillip hadn't seen a letter from this company. "You wrote asking about photographic chemicals?"

"Yes, and we got such a nice letter back from your Mr. Saltzman."

Phillip made a mental note to remind Hans just who was in charge in Jena. So, the next question was, had they done anything with the information? "Did you take Maria Anna's photograph?"

"Oh, yes." The woman fluttered a bit. "Would you like me to take yours?"

Well, it seemed he'd come to the right place. "Yes please, Frau..."

"Sebastian, but everyone calls me Lettie. Come on in."

Several days later, the Spirits of Hartshorn Facility, Grantville

Dr. Gribbleflotz was doing what he did best, pontificating on his latest hobbyhorse. Michael Siebenhorn glanced over at his sister. She smiled back and shrugged. When one worked for the doctor, one learned to put up with his little foibles. He didn't force them on anybody, and the open disbelief of most of his senior laborants only made him work harder to prove his theories.

Michael shuddered. One of the consequences of the doctor's continued failure to invigorate the *Quinta Essentia* of the Humors in test subjects was Kurt Stoltz being authorized to work on artificial cryolite so he could make pure aluminum. Dr. Gribbleflotz had theorized that the impurity of the materials might be why his experiments weren't producing the results he expected. Well, Kurt was welcome to the task. Even the stink of ammonia that hung around the Spirits of Hartshorn facility was preferable to being around hydrofluoric acid.

"I have been unable to observe anything happening when I use my pyramid to invigorate the *Quinta Essentia* of the Humors in test subjects. I believe the reason I can't see anything is because the actions taking place are not detectable by the human eye. However, a special photographic technique I have read about should allow me to observe the otherwise invisible forces at work and help me progress my research. The diagram you are looking at is taken from a reputable up-time source, and both Frau Sebastian and Frau Frost believe that such a device should produce the Kirlian images I desire."

Michael dragged his attention back to what Dr. Gribbleflotz was saying. At least this wasn't going to be anything as dangerous as hydrofluoric acid. The diagram was a simple electronic circuit, easily understood by anyone with knowledge of the up-timer science. Of course, actually making the device needed a level of expertise he knew the doctor lacked. For that matter, so did he. What was needed was a specialist, someone who knew how to make a transformer. Fortunately, such people were relatively easy to find in Grantville. "Where are you intending to use this..." Michael paused to think up a suitable name the doctor would enjoy. "Kirlian Imager, Doctor?"

"Kirlian Imager... I like that, Michael. Yes. I will of course use the 'Kirlian Imager' in my laboratory for my research, but also, I am running short of the aluminum for my Candles of the Essence of Light demonstrations, and I hope that I might be able to add the Kirlian Imager to my seminars."

Michael grimaced. He suddenly had an idea where this meeting was heading, and an explanation for his sister's presence. It wasn't going to be a simple request to make a Kirlian Imager. No, nothing that easy. "That will require a lot of the new photographic materials. Can Brennerei und Chemiefabrik Schwarza supply your needs?"

Maria Anna, Michael's little sister, answered. "Lettie Sebastian knows a lot about photography, but not a lot about chemistry, and while Celeste Frost knows a lot about chemistry, she doesn't know a lot about photography. Together they make a competent photographic chemist, but neither of them understands production on the scale Dr. Gribbleflotz requires."

Michael sighed. He'd guessed right. "So you want me to develop the information your friends have into procedures to produce photographic chemicals?"

"Yes." Phillip smiled. "I've already talked to Frau Kubiak, and she is happy to make the necessary funds available. I'm sure you'll have no trouble recruiting additional workers for a new production line."

Michael struggled not to swear. He shot his sister another look. She was smirking quietly in her corner. The little witch. He knew why she was smirking. She'd been trying to get him to produce the chemicals her friends needed for their photography project for weeks. Well, it looked like she'd succeeded this time. One didn't turn down Dr. Gribbleflotz. Not when he had taken you, starving and desperate, off the streets and then trained you in the new alchemy. It wasn't even as if the doctor was interested in the potential fortune Maria Anna insisted photography could bring in either. For someone who must be one of the richest men in Thuringia, the doctor displayed a sometimes distressing disinterest in making money.

Michael tried a last, desperate rearguard action. "Doctor, I am currently running not only the Spirits of Hartshorn facility, I'm also running the production for the new fuel tablets. Couldn't you find someone else?"

Phillip shook his head. "There is no one else, Michael. Hans and Kurt are both occupied getting the Halle facility up and running. With Hans in Halle I've been forced to not only waste my valuable time supervising operations in Jena, but I've also been forced to endure the illiterate fool who is Hans' temporary replacement."

Well, that hadn't worked. Michael could well imagine how his boss might be suffering in Hans Saltzman's absence. Hans had developed from a scared teenager into one of the four best alchemists at HDG in the three years he'd been the doctor's personal laborant. That was why he was helping Kurt Stoltz, the last of the four, set up the new Oil of Vitriol facility in Halle. Remembering Kurt stopped Michael's train of thought in its tracks. He grinned. "Doctor, I think I might know of someone suitable as a temporary replacement for Hans. He's a hard worker here at the

Spirits of Hartshorn facility. He has steady hands, and he lived in England for a few years and has been living and working in Grantville for nearly two years, so he has a good command of both written and spoken English."

Phillip looked interested. "English is good. Frau Mittelhausen has been unable to find anyone suitable who can comprehend the up-time material. But is your man literate?"

"Of course. I wouldn't suggest him if he wasn't fluent in Latin."

"So, who is this paragon?"

Michael grinned. "Kurt Stoltz."

"What? But Kurt is running the Halle operation. He can't be... oh! Another Kurt Stoltz?"

"Yes, Doctor."

Michael watched Dr. Gribbleflotz worry his goatee and then polish his spectacles. Both well known signs that he was deep in thought.

"Would he be willing to move to Jena?"

Michael nearly burst out laughing. His Kurt Stoltz had been bothering him for months about a transfer to head office. To actually work as the personal assistant to his hero, even just for a few months until Hans returned, would be more than he could ever have hoped for. "There should be no trouble persuading my Kurt to move to Jena as your temporary personal laborant, Doctor. He has read everything you've written about your exploration of the invigoration of the *Quinta Essentia* using your special pyramid."

"He is interested in the invigoration of the *Quinta Essentia*?"

Michael wasn't surprised by Dr. Gribbleflotz's reaction. The doctor was well aware that a number of his senior laborants were non-believers. Kurt Stoltz the Second though, he was as close to a true believer as Michael could believe existed. Apparently he had been a follower of Johann Valentin Andreae, and was into spiritual alchemy. "He is most interested in your work, Doctor."

Michael returned from seeing Dr. Gribbleflotz out of the office and glared at his sister. "Are you happy now?"

"It won't be too bad, Michael. Lettie and Celeste have done all the hard work. All you have to do is take their production methods and increase the volume. Your biggest problem will probably be making the Kirlian Imager."

Michael glanced down at the drawings. "It doesn't look too hard.

I'll get Kurt to help. If he knows something about the apparatus, he'll be more useful to the doctor."

"And with an expert right there in Jena, Dr. Gribbleflotz won't need to ask you to travel to Jena to help every time something goes wrong," Maria Anna suggested.

Michael grinned at his sister. She knew him so well. "The thought never crossed my mind."

A few weeks later

Michael looked down at the finished prototype Kirlian Imager. Things had not gone smoothly in its construction. First, he'd been unable to procure a suitable transformer, so he'd been forced to improvise. That had resulted in a decision to build a big Wimshurst generator, which of course produced its own problems. The main one being that they didn't have any of the special discs large enough for the task. Fortunately, one of the laborants at the fuel tablet division had been experimenting with some of the surplus waters of formalin. Georg Heinz had been able to reproduce an up-time material with useful properties by using a cheat sheet and chemicals from the gas works. He'd been making "bakelite" insulators for several weeks now. Learning how to make suitable bakelite discs had taken over two weeks of expensive experimentation. However, the imager was finally ready for testing.

"Kurt, switch over to the safe light, please."

With just the red safe light to see by, Michael took a sheet of photosensitive paper out of its lightproof envelope and placed it on the thin sheet of rubber that covered the small sheet of copper that was the main electrode. Then he attached an earth to the specimen to be examined and placed it on the photosensitive paper.

"All right, you can start the generator now."

While Kurt pumped away at the treadle of the Wimshurst generator Michael counted the sparks snapping across the air gap until he thought there had been enough discharge to make an image. "Stop! That's enough." If the theory was right and the Kirlian Imager was properly constructed, the photosensitive paper should now contain an image of the aura of the object on the paper. Michael removed the coin and took the paper next door where a simple photographic laboratory had been set up. He could feel Kurt breathing over his shoulder as they watched the images appear.

Michael didn't see the fascination the Kirlian image had for Kurt. It was just a simple photograph of a coin. The books had much better pictures. Maybe it was the fact that he'd helped make the image.

Kurt looked up. "Could we try making a Kirlian image of a human hand?"

Michael had a quick look at his pocket watch. There was time. "Sure. I assume you're willing to donate the use of your hand?"

Kurt smiled and rolled up his sleeves. "Which one would you like? Or, better, why not both?"

Michael looked at the images of Kurt's fingertips. They were, to put it mildly, disappointing.

Kurt sighed heavily. "It doesn't look as good as the images in the up-time books."

Michael nodded. They didn't look very good. That was probably due to a lot of things. "The paper probably isn't sensitive enough."

"The books say an earthed subject's image is stronger. Maybe if we were to earth me?"

"Kurt, the books also say that you shouldn't earth a live subject."

"But, Herr Siebenhorn, I am willing to take the risk. What harm can it do? You have said yourself that you have been stung by the lightning from the generator, with no ill effect."

Michael bit his lip. He didn't like going against safety warnings, but Kurt was right. Most of the laborants had been stung by sparks when playing with the doctor's Wimshurst generator, with no ill effect. However, the new machine was significantly larger. It generated more electricity with a higher voltage, and could make much longer sparks. Further it had a huge capacitor. It was entirely possible they could electrocute someone. Michael thought about the description of the up-timer Benjamin Franklin killing a turkey with a similar device. "Very well." He quietly adjusted the spark gap to make it smaller. The zaps, while more frequent, would be less dangerous.

☆ ☆ ☆

Zap!

"Ouch!" Kurt jerked his hand off the imager.

Michael stopped spinning the generator and removed the wasted photosensitive paper. "Kurt, are you sure you want to do this?"

Kurt nodded. "It was just the surprise, Herr Siebenhorn. I'll be ready for it next time."

Michael sighed. He wasn't sure this was a good idea. He made a minor adjustment to the spark gap and drew another sheet of photosensitive paper from the lightproof envelope. "Right, let's try again."

When Kurt put his hand on the paper Michael started the generator spinning. He could see Kurt twitching as the current hit him again and again. "For God's sake, Kurt! Hold still or we'll never get an auroral image. The coin didn't move. Neither should you."

Kurt was still rubbing his hand as he examined the damp photograph. "It looks much clearer."

"Yes, it does. Would you like to try the left hand now?"

Kurt nodded. "Yes, Herr Siebenhorn. Herr Siebenhorn, could I please keep the images of my hands?"

Michael suppressed a sigh. Kurt, for all his experience with English, didn't seem to understand the concept of the rhetorical question. "Of course, Kurt."

A few weeks later, HDG Laboratories, Jena

Kurt still couldn't quite believe he was actually working as his hero's personal laborant. Even if it was just until his regular laborant returned from an important job. When Herr Siebenhorn made the offer, Kurt had been overcome with emotion.

He gave the safety glass of the fume cupboard a final polish to remove the last speck of dust and stood back to admire his handiwork. The fume cupboard was sparkling clean. Now to collect the various items for Dr. Gribbleflotz's next experimental session. Kurt's eyes lit up as he read the requirements sheet. *Another experiment with the Kirlian Imager.*

☆ ☆ ☆

Phillip walked into the small laboratory and nodded in Kurt's general direction. "Are we all ready to proceed, Beta?"

With two Kurt Stoltzes being employed in important positions, there had been several instances of confusion. Phillip had solved the problem by telling Kurt that, as the latecomer, he was to no longer respond to the name Kurt Stoltz. Instead, he should only respond to Kurt Stoltz Beta or Kurt Beta. Or, as it turned out, just "Beta."

Kurt had no problem with this. If learning not to respond to the name Stoltz and answer to Beta was what it took to remain as Dr. Gribbleflotz's personal laborant, he was willing to adapt.

"Yes, Doctor. The envelope of the big sheets is in the top drawer on the table. The trays in the darkroom have been filled with chemicals and are at the correct temperature. All is ready for your experiments."

Several weeks later, the public seminar room, HDG Enterprizes, Jena

Phillip held the static-charged rod close to the stream of water. There was an "oh" of astonishment from the audience as the stream of water bent away from the rod. Phillip started recharging the rod on the handful of wool in his other hand and smiled at his audience. He really enjoyed it when he got that reaction of amazement. "That was a demonstration of the repelling force of an electrical field. It is interesting to note that the same charged rod can also attract." Phillip passed the recharged rod above some small pieces of paper on his demonstration table. The paper leapt up to the rod.

The audience applauded the demonstration. "You have seen me use inanimate materials to make my electric fields, but did you know your own body also generates electricity?" He looked around his audience sympathetically. "I see a number of heads shaking. Yes, it is true. And now, using the wonders of the up-timer science of Kirlian photography, I shall prove it."

Phillip nodded to Kurt that he was ready. While Kurt made preparations, Phillip returned to his audience. "A gifted up-time philosopher, Semyon Kirilian, continuing the work of the great

Nikola Tesla, discovered that he could photograph the life force, or aura, which surrounds all living beings, as I shall now demonstrate. Could I have a volunteer from the audience, please?"

Phillip stood back while Kurt hung the wet prints to dry. Each was carefully labeled with the volunteer's name so that they could take their own Kirlian image home with them, and they were crowding Kurt so they could see the images.

Once the images were hung up, Kurt opened the heavy blackout curtains and turned out the red safe light. Phillip waited for his audience to return to their seats.

"As you can see, the Kirlian Imager can detect forces invisible to the human eye. Proving the existence of a field around our bodies..."

"Yes, but what use does it have, or is it just another useless party trick?"

Phillip froze. Was someone suggesting his Candles of the Essence of Light demonstrations were nothing but a "party trick"? He stared at the speaker. Could he be an agent from the university sent to try and discredit him? There was a gentle cough from his assistant. Phillip looked over at Beta. It appeared he had something he wanted to say. Well, Beta had spent a lot of his own time experimenting with the Kirlian Imager. Maybe he could silence the critic. "Would you like to explain, Beta?"

Kurt nodded enthusiastically. "Yes, and I have a number of Kirlian images that I would like to show everyone."

Phillip turned to his audience. "My assistant has made a personal study of the uses of the Kirlian Imager. If you will wait patiently for a few moments while he gathers some materials from the laboratory, he will attempt to answer your question."

Kurt approached the rostrum with his folder of notes and Kirlian images. This was his opportunity to impress his hero with his level of scientific knowledge and comprehension. He coughed gently into his hand to clear his throat and looked around at the curious faces and took a last steadying breath before starting his very first public presentation.

He held up an image of a modern coin so everyone could see it before passing it around the audience. "In this image of a coin we can see how the Kirlian image of the corona is regular and symmetrical. The life force follows the curvature of the coin." He passed out a second image. "This is the image from the same coin a week later. Notice how the 'flames,' those fine short lines radiating out from the edge of the coin, are the same."

He held up a new image. "And this is a Kirlian image of an old, well-used and abused coin. Notice how the corona is not symmetrical, showing the damage inflicted on the coin. Again, although I don't have a second image available to show you, the corona from this coin doesn't change.

"However, when we examine a living being, things are different." Kurt passed around some images of his own hands. "Look at the coronas around each finger. Compare the same finger on different images. Notice the variation. That is evidence of the life force interacting with the world. We as human beings have the greatest variation in our Kirlian images, clearly demonstrating the greater complexity of the human spirit.

"It has been my privilege to investigate many Kirlian images. In the course of my investigations, I have determined that no two images, even of the same person, are ever the same. I have found that the variation is due to several things. First, just like the stream of water can be moved by the charged rod in Dr. Gribbleflotz's demonstration, other life forces can influence your aura. Second, what you eat, drink, or even wear, can influence your aura.

"My investigations suggest that the flames of the corona should be symmetrical around the surface being photographed. This would indicate a spirit in its ideal state. By carefully analyzing the placement and the ratios between various lengths of the flames of the aura, one can analyze what is required to transform an individual's aura to its ideal state. Not, of course, that it is possible to actually achieve a true ideal state, not as long as there are other life forces able to wield influence. But my investigations have shown that one can 'manipulate' the forces acting on one's aura to arrive as closely as possible to the ideal state, where one is truly in balance with the universe, even by such simple things as changing the color of the clothes one wears on a given day."

Kurt held up his left hand so the audience could see the chased copper bracelet he was wearing. "Of course, sometimes a little more effort is necessary to bring a person's aura into balance. But since I have been manipulating my aura towards the ideal state I have improved not only my health, but my prospects. Clearly, an unbalanced aura is an indicator of poor health and vitality."

Kurt could feel that he had his audience in the palm of his hand. *So this is why Dr. Gribbleflotz continues to give his seminars. The feeling of euphoria as everyone listens attentively to one's every word.* "Of course, just looking at the fingertips doesn't tell us a lot about how our life force interacts with the world. Fortunately, Herr Dr. Gribbleflotz has a special Kirlian Imager that can record much larger images." Kurt unrolled a large Kirlian image and stuck it to the seminar backboard using magnets. With Dr. Gribbleflotz's pointer in hand he stepped aside so everyone could see.

"This is a Kirlian image of my head." He ran the tip of the pointer around the corona surrounding his head. "We can clearly see the 'halo' which is present around all of us. Obviously the head is not round, so the flames are not symmetrical, however, by analyzing the ratios of the length and density of the flames we can draw some conclusions as to what the individual must do to move their aura to the ideal state."

Kurt wasn't sure where the words were coming from, but he let them continue to flow. Anything to maintain the interest of his audience and the feeling of euphoria.

Phillip wasn't sure what to think. Beta had made a most enthusiastically received presentation. Even that dissenting voice was currently begging Kurt to interpret his Kirlian image and explain what he had to do to return his life force toward its ideal state. He shrugged. It seemed Beta had things well in hand. Meanwhile, he had papers to read and write. So Phillip left Beta to deal with the people crowding around him.

Kurt knocked diffidently on the door. He had a request that he hoped the doctor would approve.

"Enter."

Kurt pushed the door open and stepped into Dr. Gribbleflotz's personal office. He passed an envious gaze over the shelves of books that lined one wall.

"Ah, Beta, a most impressive presentation."

Kurt flushed with pride. Dr. Gribbleflotz had been impressed. "Thank you, sir."

The doctor gestured toward an easy chair. "Take a seat. What is it I can do for you?"

Kurt gingerly lowered himself into the soft easy chair. Previously he'd only been invited to sit on one of the hard wooden seats. He must have really done well. Maybe Dr. Gribbleflotz would be receptive to his request. "After the seminar today, sir, several of the attendees asked if I could take Kirlian images of their halos, and then interpret them so they could move their auras towards the ideal state. I was wondering if you would permit me to use your large Kirlian Imager to take the required photographs, and also allow me the time to interpret the images."

"The photosensitive paper isn't exactly cheap, Beta."

Kurt nodded his head rapidly. "I realize that, Herr Doctor. I expect to charge people a small fee."

"For the image and the interpretation?"

"If it is permitted, Dr. Gribbleflotz."

"Well, the Kirlian Imager isn't giving me the results I hoped for, so I don't see a problem letting you use it. However, I still need a personal laborant until Hans returns, so I can't really spare you."

"I wasn't thinking of performing the imaging when I should be working for you, sir!"

"You weren't? Very well. Make arrangements with Frau Mittelhausen."

"Thank you, Herr Doctor."

Two months later, Grantville

It was Michael's first visit to the explosives factory and he was curious. He paused at the door of his sister's office to look around. It was crowded with filing cabinets and wall charts. There was a good up-time typewriter on the desk and—wonder of wonders—a computer. Maria Anna was currently engrossed with the computer screen. "How come you rate your own computer, Sis?"

"Michael! Long time no see. I get the computer because I handle the books. What can I do for you?"

Michael had been so busy over the last couple of months he hadn't been able to spend much time with his sister. "I've got an order from Jena for some more Kirlian Imagers and photographic chemicals, and I was wondering if Celeste's daughter and her friends can get me some more milkweed latex."

"You could have phoned."

"Sure. But then I couldn't have shown you this." Michael tossed a booklet and covering letter over to Maria Anna. He was interested in how she'd react. He'd nearly fallen over laughing, himself. "Kurt's calling himself Beta these days. Dr. Gribbleflotz was having too much trouble with two Kurt Stoltzes on the payroll."

Maria Anna gingerly picked up the booklet and looked at it. Her head shot up. "'How to Manage Your Aura for Personal Health and Gain.' By Kurt Beta. What the hell is happening in Jena?"

"Read the letter. It explains everything."

Maria Anna dropped the booklet and opened Kurt's letter. "He's been teaching others to interpret the life forces made visible by the wonders of Kirlian photography. Is he for real?"

Michael shrugged. "I think so. That's why he needs the additional imagers. He needs them for his students. Frau Mittelhausen has authorized the order."

Maria Anna grimaced. "Kurt's students? What's he trying to do?"

"Franchise auroral interpretation, of course."

"Franchise what? He's selling snake oil."

Michael shook his head. "No, snake oil is a total fraud. What Kurt Beta is doing is merely pseudoscience, like the doctor and his pyramid. Frau Mittelhausen says people in Jena are lapping it up."

"You know what I think of the doctor's pyramid."

"Sure, but it's harmless. Think of what Kurt's doing as being Feng Shui for the soul."

"What the hell is Fung Shway?"

Michael paused to consider an answer. Feng Shui wasn't one of those things that were easy to explain. "I think I need to lend you the book I read."

Several weeks later, office of Boots Bank, Jena

Marguerite Lobstein called over to her partner. "Johann Diefenthaler wants a loan to take the new photographer course in Grantville and to buy a camera obscura photographer equipage. What do you think?"

Catherine Mutschler looked at the photographs of her and Marguerite's family displayed around the room. "Where does Johann hope to operate?"

"He wants to operate in Bamberg. There hasn't been anybody else saying they want to work there. Most of them want to operate in Magdeburg."

Catherine chewed on a lock of hair while she read the detailed loan application. "He's got a reasonable business plan. I think we can make the loan to do the Certificate in Photography at Brennerei und Chemiefabrik Schwarza's school in Grantville easily enough. Tell him the rest is dependent on his passing the course."

"Right." Marguerite made a note on Johann's folder and tossed it into the yes basket. Then she pulled out another folder. "Oh, dear!"

Catherine took in the grimace of distaste on Marguerite's face. "What's the matter?"

"Another Kirlian Imager application."

"Just because you don't believe in the interpretation of the human spirit doesn't mean it isn't a sound business proposition."

"Are you suggesting that you believe in that mumbo-jumbo?"

Catherine shook her head. "No. Of course I don't believe it, but I know there are lots of people who do. If your applicant has completed Herr Beta's course and has a good business plan there is no more reason to deny the application than there was to deny Johann Diefenthaler's. Remember, the only criteria we use to determine whether or not to make a loan is whether or not they can pay it back."

Marguerite tossed the application across to Catherine. "Very well, you sign off on the loan. I don't want to touch the thing."

A couple of weeks later, HDG Enterprizes, Jena

Ursula Mittelhausen smiled at the photograph her sister had sent her. It wasn't as good as the one she had sent to Margarethe, but her portrait had been taken by Frau Sebastian using a proper up-time camera, not one of the new manual exposure camera obscura photographer machines that the traveling photographers were using.

Phillip shook Kurt Beta's hand. "Are you sure you have to leave, Beta? There's plenty a man with your talents can achieve here at HDG Enterprizes."

Kurt shook his head. "Thank you for the offer, Doctor. But my time as your personal laborant has opened my eyes to a world of new opportunities. I intend spreading the science of interpreting Kirlian images. I already have a number of lectures scheduled in Magdeburg, and I have to see my publisher about my new book."

"Your new book?" Phillip asked.

"Yes. *Feng Shui for the Soul.* Herr Siebenhorn gave me the idea for the title. I had previously missed the obvious connection between the ancient Chinese science of Feng Shui and the new art of interpreting Kirlian images, but as soon as Herr Siebenhorn made the comparison, the relationship was obvious."

Kurt paused to consider just why he'd missed such an obvious connection. The Censors had been hard at work indeed. They'd hidden the truth with careful use of misdirection, surrounding the truths of Feng Shui with claims only the gullible could believe. It had taken him considerable time and effort to sort through all the up-timer material to discover the truth, but now he knew, and it was going to make him rich.

Ghosts on the Glass

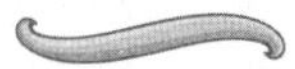

Tim Roesch

The first time Mary saw the ghosts she was transfixed.

In the beginning, they had frightened her, the ghosts. Now she found them before they found her. She knew where to look and how. With a clever smudge here or a bit of pigment there, she could enclose them or set them free or leave them completely alone.

She looked across the street in the early afternoon sun, and was again struck by the ghost on the glass. She looked at the ghost, watched it as the sun moved in the sky. Mary could tell this one needed help, needed her to touch it, embellish it, bring it to life. This ghost, of all the others, was special.

Mary sighed and felt in those wonderful things called pockets for the small piece of chalk she had borrowed from school and kept for moments like this. She would be late getting home again.

With a simple mark on the ground it began again.

Mary had learned not to fight beginnings. She would look at the glass and the ghost would tell her when she had done enough.

"Look at it! Just look at my windows. I've had enough, Julie."

Julie Drahuta tried really, really hard to see what it was that had made Audrey Yost this upset. A dirty window shouldn't cause Audrey to lose her cool like this. Sure, it looked someone had smeared her window with colored snot and dirt but a little Windex, or the 1633 equivalent, would clean it right up.

"What am I looking at, Audrey?" It was best, in situations like this, to maintain a professional demeanor, regardless of the circumstances. After all, it was probably a child; a child who liked to eat sherbet with their bare hands then wipe them on Audrey's window.

"Look!" Audrey pointed angrily at the large, smeared plate glass window.

In Julie's experience very little made Audrey this angry. She took two very considered steps forward, her eyes scanning the glass and trying not to look at the potted plants on display on the other side.

Audrey might not have access to flower networks but what she had and what she could do with what was available was truly a sight to see, smeared windows or not.

"See? Smudges! Smudges all over. Look!"

"Glass gets smudged, Audrey." Julie tried not to sound amused. "Hell, I press my nose against your windows from time to time. You have a green thumb and it shows."

"She does it on purpose! And not with her nose! Every day, I turn my back for one second. One! Next thing I know I have to chase her away and the glass is dirty. She stands there, right in front of my face, Julie, and messes up the window. She does it on purpose. She used her tongue once!"

"Her what?"

"Then she smeared it with her nose."

"With her nose?" Julie leaned in and scanned the glass more closely. Yes, indeed, it was . . . smudged. No, smudge wasn't a good enough word. There almost seemed to be a pattern . . .

"With her fingers too, Julie. Can't you see? Sometimes it's so thick you almost can't see through the glass. I think she sticks her hands in stuff just to dirty the glass. She has to and it isn't random. It's like she looks for clean places to mess up. Look at it . . . every day I have to clean the glass. Every day she smears a different part. If this keeps up, I'm going to wear the darn stuff out!"

"Just on the outside?"

"She'd never dare come inside and do that! I've never been this mad at a child, Julie. You know that . . . but, it's so . . . so . . . blatant. She's doing it on purpose!"

"Do you know who she is?"

"I'm guessing she's a German kid, a down-timer. She's blond

and blue-eyed and she has that look. She understands me when I yell at her though, so she at least knows some English. She glares at me then she's off like a shot. *Bam*. Sometimes she runs that way or that way... if I see her I'd recognize her but... I just want it to stop, okay? Can you talk to her parents or something?"

"About what time does she do this?"

"Lately? Usually about midday. She should be in school, right? I mean she looks like she's about ten or so. Sometimes it's after school or before. Some parents need to be reminded to have their kids in school. Schools are for kids... not my window. If she wants to finger paint, she should do it in school."

"About how tall?"

"She's a bit tall... maybe close to five feet. Look at the glass. That should tell you something. She leaves enough fingerprints."

"We don't have an FBI fingerprint database, Audrey."

"I know... just... make it stop, okay? It's really annoying and I'm... more annoyed that I'm annoyed. I like kids, Julie, you know I do. We adopted two, remember?"

"I'll see what I can do."

Audrey went inside her store. The tinkling bell drew Julie's attention back to the window.

There was something odd about the smudges. No, smudge just wasn't the word for it. Finger painting didn't describe it either.

Julie stepped back and struggled. The light didn't seem right.

Nothing on that glass seemed right.

It was almost like there was something... ghostly on the glass, an image that was almost there.

The light just wasn't right.

Julie looked over her left shoulder to see where the sun was.

Nope, not quite right.

Mary scowled at the glass from the beginning place she had marked across the street from the flower shop. The words painted on the glass were like rocks in a stream or trees in a breeze. The ghost simply used sunlight to make itself part of the letters.

The ghost flowed around the letters on the glass; changing as the sun changed. Mary had learned that the sun was never in the same place in the sky at the same time. It changed its position slightly each day.

It was hard to understand, like Grantville and the events that had stolen her family, left them scattered about the burned rubble of her home and memory.

Mary would understand though. She would work hard and understand. Like Grantville and this ghost on this glass, it would all work itself out.

All she needed to do was be patient. This ghost would wait for her and she knew another one would appear and it would not be happy if she failed to help this one.

Her new parents loved her and cared for her. There was food on the table again and it was warm and safe. She might even find another dog to replace the one she had taken for granted until she had found it, like her family, dead.

She would make this ghost she saw on this glass warm and safe like Grantville made her feel warm and safe. It was the least she could do.

This particular image reminded her of some place, some event, some person in her past life, the life before Grantville, the life she had tried so hard to forget. Maybe this ghost was all of those things. Ghosts could be whatever they wanted to be.

This ghost was trying to tell her something. All she had to do was follow the sun behind her and find the right pattern to clothe the ghost, surround it, enhance it.

Enhance was a word she would have never known before Grantville. Just as she knew she would never have seen this much glass before Grantville.

But if she hadn't, would there have been ghosts? Mary calmed herself.

Remembering was not enough; just as forgetting had been too much.

The ghosts reminded her to live. The dead didn't make memories. They were memories. She was alive and she made memories.

It was all complicated but it would all work out.

She would need to come earlier now. She wouldn't be late for chores but she would have to leave school early again.

The ghost didn't care. It would appear about noon now and she would have to be here to enhance and embellish it.

Julie made it a point to be somewhere nearby around midday. For three days there was no sign of a tallish, blond, German female between ten and twelve years old lurking about a flower shop at midday.

For three days Audrey said nothing about smudges though she did wave when Julie walked by. Walking by Audrey's flower shop was always a treat even if Julie "had" to because she was on duty. The chief was always interested in potential child abuse or neglect cases. Protecting kids and families was always good PR.

"Get her blond ass back in school," Chief Frost had said. "But do it nicely. It's probably just some kid who's never seen that much glass before and she likes to touch it or something. Make Audrey happy and me happy; get her back in school."

So, here she was, watching the flowers and plants through Audrey's clean windows. Clean so far.

It was day four into the investigation that yielded results. Patience and perspective are everything in police work.

This particular day Officer Drahuta was late. There were other issues in Grantville of more import than a glass window smudged by some truant girl. It was slightly past midday when Julie appeared. She noted her reflection on a glass window she passed and smiled.

Julie was just turning the corner when she heard the yell.

"*Get away*! Get away from the glass!"

Julie ran the twenty or so yards to the florist shop and was confronted by a fuming Audrey, a smudged window and the faintest glimpse of running feet turning a corner.

"She did it again!" Audrey pointed. "I went in the back to see how Mrs. Hardegg's miniature roses are doing and when I came out there she was . . . smudging my window! Where were you?"

Julie turned and looked at the window. There was still something . . . odd about the smudges. A barely discernible pattern of some kind.

"Can you leave the window just like it is, Audrey?" Julie asked, stepping back.

"Sure, why not? If kids can draw on the sidewalk, why not smudge my windows? I can have another installed! Plate glass is just all over the place, isn't it?"

"What?"

"Look!" Audrey pointed at the ground near Julie's feet.

There were a series of marks; lines drawn with a thin piece of chalk or maybe dry wall. There were words written next to them. She pulled out her clipboard and began writing.

"Does she do this to anyone else's store? No! Just mine!"

"Audrey, you're letting this work you into a frenzy. I'll catch her and we'll settle this. It's not like she's throwing rocks through your window."

"Yet," Audrey grumbled and stormed back into her store.

Julie looked up at the glass then back on the ground. The occasional pedestrian politely moved around her as she scanned the sidewalk. There were faded remnants of other marks.

She turned and looked around at the other buildings up and down the street. "Why this store?" Julie muttered to herself. There were plenty of other stores along the street, plenty of other windows. What was special about this store and this window?

She spent a pleasant few hours window shopping, asking other store owners if they had a problem with smudges or tall German girls with dirty fingers.

Some didn't know what she was talking about. A few had heard Audrey's complaints and smiled as they told her, more calmly, what Audrey had already told her.

Julie Drahuta, crack child protection officer, learned one more piece of evidence that Audrey either had forgotten to mention or hadn't noticed.

The girl would often appear just before sunset. She would stand on the edge of the sidewalk and stare at Audrey's window. Most assumed that, as a young girl, she was attracted to the pretty displays of flowers and plants in the window. Who wouldn't be?

Julie wasn't so sure. The smudges didn't appear related to anything behind the glass.

Sunset was a few hours off. Julie would be here then.

The florist shop had large windows.

Mary knew such places, with or without windows, simply did not exist in the time when her first family had been alive, when glass had been so much smaller and the ghosts had no place to be seen, to feel safe.

Now, if she could only find some way to stop the owner of the shop from washing this window.

Mary knew the ghost on the glass wasn't bothered by the washing. It simply moved with the sun, from one place on the glass to another. It waited patiently for her.

Mary would follow it.

Ghosts were slow, steady and patient. All she need do was be patient and even if the ghost disappeared completely, it would reappear later.

After all, where could a ghost go that she could not follow now that she was here, in Grantville, with all this glass?

The girl didn't reappear that afternoon but Julie hit pay dirt the next afternoon. She chose to stand at the line with the word "five" scrawled almost illegibly beside it before beginning her surveillance. Five what, she wondered.

Perspective and patience. The five didn't mean anything to her but it did to someone else.

"You need be standing here," a voice told her.

Julie turned to see a ten-year-old, maybe a year or two older, blond female glaring at her. Her arms were crossed across her chest. She was dressed in a handmade dress with what appeared to be food stains smudged across the front where she had obviously wiped her hands. There was a mother somewhere who wouldn't be happy to see that well-made dress smudged and stained.

Smudged and stained?

"There?" Julie smiled. Her smile often won over children when nothing else did.

The girl's expression did not change when she nodded.

Julie moved slightly. There was another line. This one had the word "six" beside it.

"Now look," the girl stated firmly.

Julie looked.

There were ghosts on the glass. There was no other way to describe them. The smudges transformed with the slanting, late afternoon light and the slight change in position, five to six, into what could only be seen as ghosts.

Reflections and smudges and light merged into something faint and beautiful, like forms in a mist that is slowly swirling in an unfelt breeze.

"Oh, my God." Julie moved her head slightly and the image was nothing more than smudges on glass. Then she moved her head back to its original position.

They were faint, startling images of faces and places and things. It was like laying down and looking up at the sky and how clouds changed from horses to sailing ships. She had done that with her father how long ago?

"That's her!" Audrey stormed out of her store. The words seemed to strike Julie straight across her face to wake her up.

"Stand here, Audrey." Julie grabbed Audrey as she stamped toward the girl with the blond hair, determined eyes and pale arms crossed across her chest.

"There she . . ."

"Look!" Julie aimed Audrey's face at the glass.

"It's those smudges! I tol . . . my God . . ."

"You need to see in the light," the girl said. "Can you wait for the day to end to wash them away? Can you wait for the sunset? I can pay. I can't wash window. I do not have the time to do so. I do not like to lie to Momma."

Neither Julie nor Audrey saw the youthful hand outstretched with a meager handful of random coins and slips of paper.

No, they weren't smudges at all, Julie thought.

"How . . ." Audrey took a step closer and the image was gone, the light wrong, the smudges had become smudges again. The ghosts had vanished to wherever ghosts go when pursued.

Julie remained standing right where she was. Audrey rejoined her.

The occasional pedestrian paused a moment to see what the two women were staring at and, if they were in just the right spot, stopped and started to stare.

"I have to go," the girl said.

"Don't. Move. Stay right there."

"Am I in trouble?"

"No . . . just . . . we need to talk. Stay there. Okay?"

"The sun will be setting soon. I will have to go home. Maybe tomorrow . . . and stop screaming at me. I can pay you for window."

"On the house." Audrey moved her head slightly from side to side. "Any time you want . . . smudge away . . ."

"The sun will change and I will see another window. Now is the best time for your window. Later . . . maybe down the street . . . It doesn't hurt the window. It washes off."

"Uh huh," Audrey muttered.

There was a long silence.

"I thought . . . what would people who used to live here . . . where Grantville is now . . . what would they make of this place? How would their spirits see what become of their home? They are ghosts of people who were here before Grantville. Some of the ghosts . . . are people I was knowing . . . before . . ."

"It's . . . beautiful . . ." Julie shook her head. "And they're just fingerprints."

"No." Audrey sighed. "They are ghosts watching us. They're reflections of us . . ."

"Can you keep them on the glass until sun sets?"

"Sure . . . sure. Of course, yes!"

"Good." The girl sighed. "They are beautiful, no?"

"You've turned my window into a work of art." Audrey nodded.

"Have you thought of canvas?" Julie asked.

"Canvas? You mean cloth? Cloth is for wearing. Glass is a window to soul. Cloth merely covers soul. I like glass."

"What's everyone looking at?" a voice demanded.

"Stand here!" a chorus of voices said. Hands pulled the speaker. Complaints ceased as the place was found.

The sun did set but not before at least ten people saw the ghostly images smudged carefully onto the plate glass of Audrey Yost's flower shop.

The ghost smiled at Mary.

As Julie walked her home, Mary looked up, knowing where the setting sun might expose another ghost.

There it was, high up in a window above her head, three stories up.

Story could mean a floor or a story you read, like a mother would read to a child. English was the perfect language for ghosts. Like ghosts on the glass could change as the sun changed, English could change too and be what it needed to be.

Mary liked English and she liked school and her new parents.

And the ghosts didn't frighten her anymore.

Three stories up there was a ghost of a dog lying on its side in the setting sun and Mary smiled. She had known that dog, seen it alive in the yard in front of her first home. Now it was here.

The ghosts were coming here, to their new home.

So was she.

Julie couldn't quite figure out how to write her report.

There is no art in a well-done police report. It states the facts, clearly and without bias or emotion. A police report reports a vandalized masterpiece with the same dispassionate words that it reports a gang symbol spray painted on an alley wall.

Signs of abuse or neglect? No.

Julie met the girl's adopted parents. There was no sign of abuse or neglect. Her papa made it clear that little Mary would have to clean the windows she had smudged. Mary wasn't to leave school without permission again.

Damage to property?

Julie closed her eyes and remembered the ghostly images on the plain, cold glass.

No, she wrote firmly.

Firm, bold strokes were the only emotion allowed on police reports.

Chief Frost accepted the report without comment.

To him, the case was closed, the "blond ass" was back in school and Audrey wasn't complaining anymore.

Grantville had lots of glass, a growing number of ghosts, and a young artist to smudge them.

To Julie, Grantville felt just a bit less cut off from the past and just a bit more attached to this new future.

Bunny B. Goode

Gorg Huff & Paula Goodlett

"These Americans," Don Alfredo de Aguilera said with a sigh. "They have no idea of the effects they have." He cast a sardonic look out the window, then sighed and turned back to his letter. The best he could do was the best he could do, but that didn't mean that his uncle Ramon was going to be any happier with him. But perhaps the letter to his cousin might help.

Mi querido Carlos,

As you know, your father has required that I stay here in Grantville, researching and looking for ways for the family to increase its wealth and influence. So I stay. In many ways, I do enjoy it. In some others, I simply do not.

There is bad news which I have shared with your father in brief but I share with you in greater detail. The woman will not sell all her sheep. The up-time Merino sheep will be bred in Germany. And she is selling some, but not all, of her Angora rabbits. Which, as rabbits do, are reproducing in great numbers. Rapidly. Very rapidly. So much so, that the insane woman is now furnishing breeding pairs of them to others. At no cost. With contracts to purchase the product of said rabbits.

While the quantities will be small for years to come, especially of the Merino wool, the quality of the fabric is better than anything we have. This is partly because of the

Angora rabbits, but I must tell you, Cousin, that the wool of the up-timer sheep is better than any in Spain. So Spain no longer has the best wool in the world. As well, these sheep produce more wool. They were bred to do so, after all.

Carlos, yesterday at the Exchange I saw a young woman, the daughter of a farmer, wearing an Angora-wool blend top. That girl was wearing finer woolens than Her Imperial Majesty, the queen of Spain possesses. A farmer's daughter! Can you imagine it, Cousin? "Here, Your Majesty, we have the best wool in Spain. Granted it's not quite so good as a farmer's daughter wears in barbaric Germany, but it's almost as good." What price will Spain's fine Merino wool bring when this becomes common knowledge throughout Europe? And it will. The farmer's daughter was quite proud of her "Angora sweater," marveling at its soft comfort, having her friends feel the softness while she spoke of its warmth. There is no keeping this secret, even if almost no one can get cloth made of the angora-wool blend. Simply the fact of its existence must bring down the price of our Spanish wool.

Yet there is good news, or at least a potential way to compensate for the lost profit that the family will face. Up-time they had machines to spin wool and other fabrics at tremendous speed and low cost. None of those machines made the transition. But, sooner or later, they will reinvent the machine. At that point, wool cloth made in Germany will cost not that much more than washed wool from Spain and the window of opportunity will close.

The opportunity I speak of is to become more than a supplier of washed wool. I believe that we should become a supplier of finished thread and cloth. I know my uncle will likely be opposed to this, but I believe it is essential. The cloth makers of England, France, Germany, and Italy will not pass on the savings from such a machine to the providers of the wool.

The National Library has very little available on the subject of the spinning jenny, spinning mule and other machines used in the "mass production" of cloth. I enclose what they have from the various encyclopedias and I will be continuing my research. Carlos, we have a window of opportunity here, but that window will not stay open forever. If the family's wealth is to be maintained, we must have those machines. We must be able to break into the cloth markets of Europe before they have the machines to compete with us or we will likely never gain the foothold we need. I know what Uncle Ramon thinks of the mercantile trades, and that his opinion of those who work with their hands is possibly worse. But for the sake of our family, Cousin, you must persuade him to invest in an experimental facility geared to the development of the machines used in the mass production of cloth.

Don Carlos de Aguilera sipped his wine as he read the letter from his cousin. After delivering the bad news, the letter shifted to asking after various family members, before switching back to matters of business. Business and trade weren't something his cousin seemed able to avoid. Don Alfredo suggested diversification into other crops. Which was a possibility. Cotton, peanuts, and corn.

In the next few weeks, as I acquire them, I will send you a pair of Angora rabbits and some seed corn. I have included what drawings I have managed to accumulate, as well as reprinted articles on many things of interest. I'm particularly interested in the peanut butter. Up-timers crave peanut butter, Carlos. Small children beg for it. We must discover what they're talking about and attempt to produce it. There's a market right here. As well, I'm told that it is "nutritious." It has "protein." And that everyone benefits from ingestion of such. Best of all, the plant itself nourishes the soil. Which should allow for the growing of cotton if you can acquire the seeds.

I strongly recommend that we attempt to breed sheep with better wool and size. Select the largest rams, the largest ewes and keep them isolated from the others. The shepherds have always attempted to breed the best to the best, of course, but they were as much concerned with the ability to traverse the meseta *as they were with size and wool quality.*

Do write me. I sometimes feel that I'm lost in time.

Alfredo

Don Carlos rang for a servant. He didn't look down on his older cousin to the extent that many in the family did. Granted, Don Alfredo wasn't very good with a sword and seemed unable to avoid involvement in trade. But that too had its uses. "I will be dining with Father this evening. Have my horse readied," Don Carlos spoke past the servant.

In spite of Don Carlos' best efforts, his cousin's report was laughed off. Until the matched pair of gleaming white Angora rabbits arrived. With them came a sample of the Merino-Angora blend, in the form of a scarf. Even Papa couldn't laugh that off. As punishment for being right when Papa was wrong, Don Carlos got placed in charge of putting together a research and development facility to develop the spinning machines. He naturally delegated the actual organization to his steward, Ricardo. Then he went back to his hunting.

Ricardo Suarez shook his head and considered whether or not he should just run screaming into the night and fall off a cliff. Then he sighed, and went back to writing letters, muttering all the while.

"Build a research and development facility, he says. And what do we do if we succeed, I wonder. That's the problem with the entire family. They don't think ahead. Not at all." Ricardo was actually quite fond of the de Aguilera family.

The patriarch of the de Aguilera family, Don Ramon, was a hearty man, nearly seventy years old. Upright, upstanding, bound by traditions . . . a bit hidebound, in Ricardo's opinion. Most of the de Aguilera scions were following in that tradition, except for young Don Alfredo in Grantville. Ricardo had hopes for Don Alfredo, although he knew that Don Ramon didn't have much use for him. The young man simply didn't meet his expectations. Don Alfredo liked making money and was, well, obvious about it. Don Carlos, his cousin, was much more the type to suit Don Ramon's expectations. Proud, courageous to a fault, honorable . . . but useless for practical things. Basically, a proud wastrel, at least in Ricardo's opinion.

Very well, Ricardo thought. I shall write young Alfredo and get more information. Carlos . . . well, Carlos won't pay much attention to what I do, so long as his pleasures aren't interrupted.

By the time Ricardo gave it up for the night, he'd made arrangements to hire an assortment of craft masters, journeymen and apprentices. As well, he'd arranged for them to travel to the most isolated village the family owned. It had been nearly depopulated by a virulent sickness two years ago, so there would be room for experiments and the surrounding hills and valleys could be used for the sheep-breeding program Don Alfredo advocated. Not to mention, the rabbits had to go somewhere else. The stable master was very insistent about that.

Agustin Cortez alighted from the wagon, happy to be out of it. It had no springs and was not, he thought, well put together. What he saw, however, was almost enough to make him want to get right back on it. Agustin was a journeyman cabinet maker, who was rather better with wood than he was with people. Which might have something to do with the reason that he was still a journeyman and not a master. He had a marked tendency to open mouth and insert foot. And always at the worst possible moment.

So when he was offered a job working on a special project, well, he needed the job. But he hadn't realized until he got here that the job was in the middle of nowhere. As he looked around, mostly what he saw were sheep. There was also what appeared to be a broken-down grain mill and the remnants of a village. All these things were located in a valley in the Cantabrian hills. What sort of a project could they possibly have in mind for this place?

Agustin's musing was interrupted when a young woman walked by, carrying a load of wool in a basket. She sniffed as she passed. Apparently, whatever it was that they were doing here, the young woman did not approve.

Well, he was here. Best to get on with it. "Senorita? Oh, Senorita?"

She turned and cocked an eyebrow at him.

"Who is in charge here?" Agustin asked.

"Montoya." She shifted the basket, then pointed to the best of the buildings. "There." Then she sniffed again, and turned away.

Not a friendly woman, Agustin decided. And plain as well.

He found Luis Montoya bent over a number of drawings of a strange-looking contraption. A contraption Agustin simply couldn't make head or tail of, although he could clearly see where his skills with wood were needed. The drawing showed wooden parts that were hopelessly unadorned. And Luis, it turned out, was not "in charge," but merely another journeyman.

"Gears I can produce," Luis said. "This I have the knowledge for. But I know nothing about producing thread. Women spin. Not me."

"Ah," Agustin said. "So that's the big secret project we're to work on."

"And secret it indeed is," Luis warned. "The de Aguilera, Don Carlos, was very clear on that. Not one word of what we do here is to be spoken of. Not to anyone."

Agustin looked at the drawings again. Then he looked for more, something to show how this was supposed to work. There weren't any. "How long have you been here?"

"Five days. Don Carlos, well, his steward, made me an offer I couldn't refuse."

Well, Agustin certainly understood that. Eating is better than starving, any day. "Are more coming? Surely you and I are not the only men to work on this."

"A master carpenter—he'll be in charge. Two or three other masters and journeymen, for wood and metal. Some apprentices, mostly, from the de Aguilera estates. The people here, only a few, are mostly herders and that ilk. Unlettered, of course. No knowledge of anything but sheep."

Agustin sighed, then they got down to trying to figure out how this machine was supposed to work.

As Agustin read through the sheets of paper, he kept running into words in brackets, with numbers. And at the bottom of each page were annotations. *"In 1828 Mr. Thorpe, also an American, invented the ring spinning frame, whose principal feature consisted in the substitution for the {flyer 25} of a flanged annular ring, and a light C-shaped {traveler 26}."* Unfortunately the annotations were not always helpful. {Flyer 25} was recorded as: 1) An advertisement (usually printed on a page or in a leaflet) intended for wide distribution. 2) Someone who travels by air. 3) Someone who operates an aircraft, followed by a note in another hand: *This can't be right. We are talking about a part of a spinning machine.*

It was very clear that several people had worked on this and not all of them had known what they were working on. Some parts of the notes were printed and others handwritten. The right definition was in the packet, but Agustin would not find it for over a week. By the time he and Luis knocked off for the evening he was exhausted from trying to make sense of the half-translated documents.

☆ ☆ ☆

The rather surly young woman delivered their evening meal. A thin soup, cheese, and bread. Luis did, at least, have a cask of reasonable wine. The de Aguileras weren't exactly generous with supplies, but they weren't entirely misers, Luis explained.

"So," Luis said, "the problems of getting the machine to work are . . ." He began a litany of complaints, possibilities, conjectures and outright fantasy. Even Agustin knew more about wool and how it was processed, having seen the *lavadero* Alfaro, near Segovia, in operation.

"Have you no sisters?" Agustin asked. "Have you not observed a shearing, even?"

Luis looked dumbfounded that he would even ask. "And what does that have to do with building the machine, I ask? We take the wool, we make the machine make the thread."

The woman, who had returned to pick up the remains of the meal, laughed out loud. Agustin, who had four younger sisters, joined her.

Luis looked hurt for a moment, then explained. "My family . . . my mother died, years ago, when I was small. So, no, I have no sisters. Only an aunt, who sent me to apprentice to a smith in El Ferrol, on the coast, after my father died. Which is how I became interested in clocks, because of navigation."

Luis' story was a long one, which involved quite a bit of travel, a number of misadventures, and untold heroism. At least, according to Luis. Through it all, the woman listened, leaning against the doorpost, spinning with a hand spindle. Agustin watched as the thread grew longer, then, when the spindle had nearly reached the floor, the girl drew it up and wound on the thread. Again and again, the thread lengthened.

Finally, Agustin could stand it no longer. "Why this way? My sisters use a wheel." He gestured at the spindle. "And what is your name, please?"

She cocked her eyebrow at him again. "Lucia. And you can't use a wheel when you're walking the hills, following sheep. So—" She gave the thread another twist. "—I carry this, always."

Agustin nodded. The production of fabric was time consuming in all ways. First the sheep grew the wool, then were sheared. The wool was washed, sorted, sold, then carded, spun and woven. Flax was worse, as the hard stalks had to be rotted in water before the fiber could even begin to be prepared for use. Silk wasn't something he'd ever seen produced, although that was done in

Lyons, he knew. His sisters, who made his clothing, were always moaning about wanting dresses made from Lyons silk. Not likely, even though Papa wasn't dreadfully poor.

The master of the project, one Pedro Munos, appeared three days later. And Agustin knew he was probably in trouble within moments. Munos was just the type of master he could barely tolerate. Worse, he was the type of master who could barely tolerate Agustin—and Agustin needed this job. It was clear that the man was more interested in sucking up to Don Carlos than he was in working the wood. More journeymen came over the next week, until there were eighteen men, along with the wives and children of the more senior of them.

Agustin thought that "wife" might have been an overstatement in some cases, but that was between them and God. Just when he began to think that he might as well leave now, before he got in trouble with Munos, Miguel Cortes showed up. And Miguel, thankfully, was senior to Agustin, so Agustin could probably avoid Munos' notice, with a bit of luck and care.

One of the exciting days that broke up the drudgery of making machine parts that no one understood was the day the rabbits arrived. They were, Agustin decided, very odd-looking rabbits. They were also, alas, not particularly friendly in spite of their incredibly long and soft white hair.

This was discovered when the man who was attempting to transfer the doe from the traveling cage to a larger cage screamed vituperations at her. Then dropped her on the ground, clutching his bitten, bleeding hand. Before anyone could reach her, she took off between the buildings.

"Catch that rabbit," Munos cried.

What followed was something of a circus, with men, women and children chasing a very frightened—and quite speedy—long-haired rabbit that didn't want to be caught. And wasn't.

Munos, huffing from his run, cursed everyone indiscriminately. The rabbit handler, with his wound bandaged, finally removed the half-grown kits to individual cages, along with the buck, these actions also accompanied by Munos' cursing.

"This will set Don Carlos' breeding project back by months," Munos whined.

"They're rabbits," Lucia pointed out. "It won't be that long before the young ones are ready to breed. Because they're rabbits, like any rabbit."

"Would you like to say that to Don Carlos?" Munos asked.

Lucia flinched.

"I thought not."

The rabbit handler carried a written explanation back to Don Carlos' steward. No one knew just how the temperamental de Aguilera scion would react, but they expected it to go badly for the handler.

Badly, it went indeed. A week later, Munos received a summons from Don Carlos.

"We are making good progress, Don Carlos, but it is a very complex device." Master Pedro Munos handed several sheets of paper to Don Carlos. They were the collected questions about the workings of the spinning machine so far. This was the first major status report since their discussions when Don Carlos had approved his hiring.

Don Carlos looked through the sheets of carefully numbered questions. "There are over a hundred questions here, Master Munos. Can't your craftsmen figure out anything for themselves?" He snorted. "See Ricardo with this list of questions. What have you accomplished so far?

"I have gotten most of the parts that were clearly shown in the diagrams made. There are a few diagrams that are less clear but they shouldn't prove much of a problem. Now all that is really needed is to assemble the machine, if the images are correct." Then, noting Don Carlos' look, Master Munos hastily added. "As I'm sure they are. There should be no great problems. I should have a working machine for you in a few months. As I said, it is a complex piece of machinery and these things take time."

Ricardo felt a good bit of sympathy for Munos when the sweating man entered his office. Don Carlos wasn't the easiest man to get along with, and was even less easy to explain things to.

Munos plopped into a chair and wiped his face. "That . . . that . . ." He stopped and shook his head. "It is most difficult to explain the mechanics, Señor. Most difficult."

"So explain it to me, please," Ricardo said. "Tell me what happened."

While Munos explained about the difficulties with the machines, and about the lost rabbit, Ricardo took notes and read over the list of questions. When Munos ran down, Ricardo settled back into his own chair and called for refreshments.

"I see. Well, I will arrange for a replacement rabbit, and, if possible, for more of them. And I will send your questions to Don Alfredo. I must say some of them don't make sense to me, so I well understand why they didn't make sense to Don Carlos. What could the color of the wool have to do with the machine and how it will work?" He tapped the list. "Wool is simply wool. It is all much the same, whether black or white. Do try to provide questions that at least make some kind of sense."

After three months, Agustin was nearly at the end of his rope. He, Miguel, and the other journeymen carpenters had built the parts they could see clearly on the drawings They'd also built parts they thought would work by extrapolating what they thought the machine should do. The smiths and Luis had done the same thing with the metal parts they thought the machine needed. But putting it together was not going well. Something was missing. Several somethings, probably.

In the midst of this, some of the shepherds came back, Lucia's father and older brother among them. They had been on the *meseta* for a year, herding sheep throughout the country. This year, though, would be different. Don Carlos had directed them to bring the best rams and ewes to the mountains after shearing, and keep them there. Now, according to Lucia, was when the real work started for her family. The men would shear their own small flocks, as well as care for the de Aguilera flock and supervise the breeding program.

It did mean that Lucia was in the village more, because she no longer looked after the flock with her younger brother and sister. It did not mean, however, that there was less work for her to do. In addition to the ever-present spinning, there was more food to cook, the garden to care for, sewing and darning of damaged clothing for her father and brother, as well as the wool to clean and card.

The villagers made something of a holiday of the shearing. And Agustin was surprised at how fast that went. Shearing, however, he learned, was not the biggest job. Even docking and culling the lambs was not as big a job as cleaning the wool turned out to be. There was, though, plenty of meat for several weeks after the shepherds decided which lambs to cull.

Washing the wool, at least in this village, took almost every hand that was available. And because he and Luis were somewhat extraneous to the machine project at the moment, they decided to help. Luis, it turned out, had his eye on Lucia's cousin, Beatriz, because of her cheerful, loving nature. Agustin had to admit that Beatriz was better looking than Lucia, but she was also a bit flighty for his taste.

So they both wound up putting the wool in cold water, which was then warmed until the grease and dirt loosened, then lifting out the heavy, wet, smelly stuff to drain and rinse. Throughout it all, the women chattered and made sure that no one poked and prodded the wool too much, as it would then stick together and become unusable. After rinsing, the wool was laid to dry in clean, grassy areas, where the breezes would dry it as quickly as possible.

Lucia explained that the wool would be turned several times a day, and that it would take about four days to dry completely. Surprisingly, they did not sell the finer grades of wool, not this year. This year, Don Alfonso had pre-purchased all of it, so that the machine team would have wool to experiment with. Rather a lot of wool to experiment with, Agustin thought. And too soon to be doing much experimentation, at that.

"If you want to make spinning faster," Lucia grumbled, "find a better way to loosen the wool and get all the hairs lined up in the same direction."

It seemed that if women weren't actively spinning wool, they were preparing it for spinning. Even after washing and removing most of the grease from a fleece, wool was just naturally clumpy. It grew in tangled locks, which had to be separated and made smooth before the wool could be spun into thread.

Carding and spinning were laborious, repetitive tasks, although not particularly difficult. Or so Agustin thought, until Lucia tried to teach him to use the carding combs she was wielding. In spite of Luis' laughter about it, Agustin felt that the machine would never work unless the men building it understood the process of making thread. Which, of course, none of them did.

So, Lucia not-so-patiently showed him how she loosened and

carded the fibers with a set of carding combs, then removed the straightened fibers and rolled them into what looked like a sausage. After that, the wool was ready to be spun, either on her hand spindle or a wheel.

"Why do you roll it that way? Why not just leave it flat?"

Lucia shrugged. "It is the way I was taught. I've never tried it any other way. Besides, it would take up too much room in my basket and might tangle again."

At Agustin's urging, Lucia sat at one of the treadle wheels he and the others had built from a drawing and began to spin the flat mass of fiber. After a false start or two, it only took a few minutes to spin. Of course, it only took her minutes to spin one of the sausage shapes, as she pointed out.

"But was this faster? At all?" he asked.

"Perhaps. But it would only make a real difference if the mass of wool was larger, I think. No. Not larger. Longer. And, maybe, thinner." Lucia used her hands to try and describe what she meant. "With these, I must stop the wheel, pick up another, attach it, then start the wheel again. With a longer, thinner, ah . . . I don't have the words. But if the wool was like a rope, long and thin, instead of a flat square . . ." She looked at him. "Do you understand what I'm saying?"

"I think so. And I think I read something about that, in all the papers. Let me think for a while."

It was often easier to understand Lucia's gestures than the stuff they received from Don Carlos. Rumor had it that the papers and notes they got from Don Carlos were sent to the de Aguilera family from Germany. Judging from the shape the papers were sometimes in, Agustin thought they might have been sent from even farther away. By now they were sending questions back along the route, wherever it lead. Agustin wasn't involved in that part. The questions went from him to Miguel to Master Munos. Agustin was increasingly concerned that the important questions weren't making it all the way to wherever the source of the information was.

The words were often unfamiliar, which frustrated everyone, as they would then have to ask for explanations. Still, every packet from Don Carlos gave them more information. The big breakthrough, though, finally came. The man in Germany—if that was where he was—had started tracking down the various names of the inventors, and come across more detailed information and drawings. Still not enough, but it helped.

The spinning machine was stalled. It should work. It was supposed to work. As they looked at each part of the operation, it even seemed to work. But the thread it produced was clumpy and came apart with even gentle tugs. Miguel, nearly howling with anger, had stomped away this morning, cursing all the way. Munos, who was being pressured by Don Carlos, wasn't in any better a mood, and had left for Zamora to explain the delays. With those two gone, Agustin and Luis had time to experiment with a better way to card the wool.

They started, much to Lucia's dismay, by tearing apart a set of carding combs to see how they were made. "Any idiot can see how they're made!" she said. But, better to check, anyway.

Agustin and Luis were a bit embarrassed to have to admit that she was right. The carding combs were just bent pins, stuck through leather, which was then nailed to a flat piece of wood. After a handle was added to the flat piece, the carding comb was complete. But it, combined with some of the drawings they'd recently received, did give them an idea.

It took some time to find enough leather to cover a large and a smaller wooden drum. It took longer than that to make the tiny pins to insert through the leather, bend them at the correct angle, and secure them to the drum. And more time to construct a frame to hold them.

It wasn't an exact duplicate of the "drum carder" in the drawing. For one thing, in order to take advantage of one type of motive power they had available, Agustin and Luis positioned the drums differently. The drums were laid on their sides, supported in the air by a pole that ran through the center of each drum. The drums were held up with a spacer, so that they could harness one of the bellwethers to a shaft that would turn the drum. The shaft was about five feet long and the large drum about three feet across with a radius of half that. A small boy was initially used to walk the bellwether around in a circle, but that same small boy eventually attached a turnip to a stick and hung it in front of the sheep. The sheep kept chasing the turnip but never caught it. As bellwethers were used to walking all day, leading the vast flocks throughout Spain, the sheep took no harm.

The smaller drum turned at a faster pace, of course, and quite a large amount of wool could be gradually placed on it. The teeth from the larger drum picked up and straightened the wool as it came off the smaller drum. Taking the wool off of the larger drum proved to be somewhat problematical in the beginning, but they eventually contrived a tool for that.

"Can you spin this, Lucia?" Agustin asked. He presented her with a blanket of wool that was about two inches thick, nearly ten feet long, and about two feet wide.

She looked at it carefully. "I think so. But it's too wide. We need a way to draw it out."

"Into sliver, yes?"

"Pardon?"

"Sliver. Or top. That's what the papers call it. Long, thin ropes of wool are called 'sliver' or 'top.' They call this a 'batt.'"

"Why? If it looks like a rope, why not call it a rope? If it looks like a blanket, why call it a batt?"

At her curious look, Agustin laughed. "I have no idea. But you can read them for yourself." He stopped abruptly. Probably Lucia didn't know how to read. Why would she, living out here in the middle of nowhere?

She didn't get angry as he feared. She just shrugged. "Or you can read them to me, if you think it will do any good. Which I doubt. Meanwhile, let's try this." She took the batt of wool and began to tear it into strips. With care, she could tear a two-inch wide strip of it from the batt without the strip of wool falling apart. These she coiled in a basket, pinching a new strip to each end as she tore it. That took a while. The "rope" they ended up with was over ninety feet long. Finally she sat at the wheel. And began to spin. And spin. And spin. The only time she had to stop the wheel was to move the thread from one hook on the flyer to another, so that it filled the bobbin evenly. Then to change the bobbin, after each of them got full.

"Aunt Lucia! Aunt Lucia!"

Lucia went toward the garden, where her niece was supposed to be gathering vegetables for soup. "What, Elena? What is the problem?"

"Look," Elena said. She pointed to a row of beans. "I was pulling beans and a rabbit ran out. It was that rabbit, the one that got away."

Lucia looked at the row of beans, then knelt down and fished around in the tangled plants. "Ah." She drew her hand out of the tangle. It was full of long, silky, white hairs. "Well, now we know where that dratted rabbit got off to. Perhaps we can trap it, now that we know where it is."

Elena tapped her on the shoulder and whispered, "Look."

Lucia did, then laughed out loud. The smaller rabbit, not quite as long-haired and not quite as white, ran away. "Well," Lucia gasped when she stopped laughing, "I see that Mrs. Bunny has been busy, hasn't she? We'll need several traps, I think."

In spite of the several traps that caught some of the half-wild, half-Angora bunnies, Mrs. Bunny managed to evade capture. That didn't, however, seem to lessen her fertility, as they continued catching an occasional half-breed rabbit well into the fall.

Which led to the question of who owned the half-breed rabbits. By long tradition, the wild rabbits of that portion of Spain belonged to the people that lived there. Mrs. Bunny would have been returned to the *patron* as a matter of course, but these weren't purebred Angora rabbits. These were the kits of Mrs. Bunny and the wild bucks of the valley, as could easily be shown by the fact that Mr. Bunny was still in his cage. And probably none too happy about Mrs. Bunny's errant ways. Those wild bucks had always been the people's rabbits.

If some of the villagers found occasion to slip a wild doe into Mr. Bunny's cage to give him a little consolation, what could be the harm in that? And later, how could anyone be sure that the newly-common long-haired rabbits weren't the offspring of Mrs. Bunny's wild shenanigans? Granted, Mrs. Bunny would put all other rabbits to shame in the productivity department if all the little kits that had been captured were hers. But in the case of any given rabbit, who was to say?

By the time anyone involved in the administration of the Angora project noticed anything odd, there was quite a little breeding program going on. Enough of the half-breed rabbits with longer hair had appeared that some Spanish Angora garments were appearing in the valley.

"Master Munos, what is the holdup?" Ricardo asked with a bite in his voice. "You promised us a spinning machine over a year ago. Where is it?"

Master Munos had been dreading that question. He considered claiming that the drawings and notes were incomplete but he suspected that it wouldn't work. It hadn't worked when the journeymen and other masters had tried it on him. "It's the journeymen. They talk back. They refuse to do as they are told." He honestly didn't remember that most of their talking back and refusing to do as they were told amounted to him telling them to make the thing work and them asking him how. They were, in Master Munos' memory, intentionally disobedient and disrespectful.

By this time, most of them *were* lacking in anything resembling respect for Master Munos. However, most of them were pretty good at faking it. Agustin Cortez was not so good at hiding his opinion. "That Cortez is the worst. He spends all his time with that village spinster. He claims that he is trying to come to know the process of spinning. Ha! That is not the sort of knowing that he is after with Lucia. And he encourages dissension among the other journeymen."

"Do you think he should be fired?" Ricardo asked.

Master Munos froze for just an instant. He knew that firing Agustin Cortez would be a disaster for the project and for him. Though he would never admit it, even to himself, Cortez had been the spark that had led to several of the minor breakthroughs that had gotten them as far as they were. Master Munoz desperately needed a reason for keeping Cortez that wouldn't sound like praise. "I wish we could," he said, "but he knows too much about the project. He could take what he knows to someone else and let them catch up to us in a few months."

Ricardo nodded.

"I wonder," Master Munos mused, "could that be what he's hoping for? To delay the project until he's fired. Then go to someone else."

Ricardo looked doubtful.

Master Munos shrugged it off as a passing fancy. "In spite of the difficulties with the journeymen, I have managed to get built a simple but ingenious device to speed up the carding part of the process." He snorted a laugh. "Part of what makes it ingenious is that it is simple enough that even the journeymen couldn't mess it up.

"It has turned the warehouses full of washed wool into warehouses full of carded wool."

"I will see about sending you some spinners until you get the spinning machine operational," Ricardo said calmly. "Do you have more questions for our source in Germany?"

"Only a few." Master Munos wondered if perhaps he hadn't been overzealous in weeding out the questions from the journeymen and the other masters. But he certainly didn't want a repeat of that first meeting with Don Carlos.

In the little village in the Cantabrian hills, they did in fact have a spinning machine that worked. Unfortunately it was a spinning machine for cotton. They, of course, were in a wool-producing area. If they had had some cotton to try on it, it would have spun decent, but not spectacular, thread. But they didn't have cotton or even realize that they needed it. They didn't realize that to spin wool they would need to adjust the machine. Agustin had considered the possibility and even asked about it indirectly, in one of many questions that he had included in the latest information request to go up the line. But he didn't really think it was important because, after all, who would send designs for a cotton-spinning machine to wool country?

"That works quite well," Lucia admitted a bit grudgingly. Then she sniffed. Again.

Agustin hid his grin. "I'm pleased you think so."

It was shearing time again. And if they couldn't get the machine to work, Augustin, Luis and some other journeymen had decided that perhaps they could do other things to help speed up the process. They developed a wooden cage to hold the unwashed wool. Then they were able to lower it into the cold water bath, with ropes and pulleys to make the lowering and lifting easier and keep the wool from being manhandled. Some of the metal smiths managed to tinker together flat pots that would need less water, and therefore less wood, for heating.

Cleaning the wool did take time, but perhaps a bit less than it usually did. As well, they had rigged up drying platforms, raised about eighteen inches off the ground, to allow for greater air flow around the wet wool. Drying was certainly sped up.

"More women will be arriving," Master Munos said when he got back from Zaragoza. "Beds will need to be arranged for them. De Aguilera is sending them to spin the wool that's in the warehouse, as well as the new crop."

Miguel nodded. "They'll need more wheels, as well. We haven't any extra."

Munos waved off the statement. "Just do what you have to. And get the machine working!"

Miguel left, steaming with anger. *Just do what you have to. And get the thing working.* There was a long list of questions that they had sent and most of them remained unanswered. How were he and his men to accomplish anything if they couldn't find the answers? If whoever it was who wanted this machine really wanted it, why didn't he try to find the answers they needed?

Miguel was afraid to experiment. It was an incredibly complicated device, the spinning machine. Able, the papers said, to spin fifty threads at once and have them all of consistent quality. No one had ever done anything like this before; it wasn't how innovations happened.

Honestly, Miguel wasn't sure how innovations did happen. It wasn't that he was either unskilled or that he lacked creativity. But his training had focused on quality and art, not whatever this was. Miguel could build a table that was a work of art. Show him a picture of something made out of wood and he could make it. He could inlay a family crest into the side of a chair using five different woods and make it look like God had grown it that way. He could also look at a piece of wood and know how strong it would be once it was cut and carved into shape. He could attach it to another piece of wood, never needing a nail. But never in his life had he been asked to do systematic experimentation. *Just do what you have to. And get the thing working.* Willingly. Except he had no idea what he had to do to *get the thing working.*

Agustin was frankly relieved that the women who arrived had done so unequipped with spinning wheels. It gave him something to do other than sit around staring at the uncooperative spinning machine. He and the other carpenters divided their time between the spinning wheels and housing for the new arrivals.

"Oh, yes. I heard him say that."

Lucia looked over at the scrawny young woman who spoke. How this one might have heard Don Carlos speak anything but an order was beyond her, unless she'd been eavesdropping. Unless, perhaps, Don Carlos was very indiscriminate about what he said in front of strangers. Well, he might just be. Nobles did tend to ignore servants. But had this girl even worked for the de Aguilera family? Lucia decided to find out. The rumors the new employees brought with them were somewhat distressing.

"We'll be provided with good beds and everyone will have their own room, when the factory is built," was one of them.

So was, "Ha! We'll never see another sunrise after we finish spinning all this wool."

One of the most reliable of the new women had indeed been a servant in Don Ramon's household. Lucia listened to her particularly well, as she might have greater insight into their employer.

What she heard was most distressing.

"I should say not!" Ricardo had decided to make a visit to the village and see if he could figure out what the holdup was. It was all well and good that the wool was being carded and spun, even if the spinning was still by hand. But this was outside of enough. "The mother of those rabbits belongs to the de Aguilera family. Therefore so do the offspring."

He was looking at rows of cages, each of which contained a half- or three-quarter bred Angora rabbit. The hair varied in length, and the colors tended to be much less spectacular than the colors of the purebreds. But for villagers to attempt this! Never would he allow it. Never! "These rabbits belong to the de Aguilera family," he repeated. "And they will be taken to the de Aguilera estate. Tomorrow!"

It was a bit cavalier of the steward, but not beyond the law. Agustin kept his mouth shut, although it was a struggle. It was obvious that the de Aguilera family intended to keep the Angora as their monopoly, at least in Spain.

"Foolish," Lucia muttered. "Pure foolishness." It was obvious to Lucia that the effort at monopoly would fail. Among the rumors the spinners brought was confirmation that the rabbits came from the up-timers in Germany, where they were sometimes even given away to poor women. If there were enough that up-timers would give them away, they must be very common and others would buy them.

Worse, many of the better of the half- and quarter-breed rabbits had belonged to her little brother, Juan. And Juan was very upset, since he loved those dratted bunnies.

The action with the rabbits did give credence to some of the other, less rational rumors. Like the one that said everyone in the valley would be held there for the rest of their lives to keep the secret safe. And the one that suggested those lives might not be all that long for most of them.

"Damn that woman!"

Agustin and Luis jumped. Lucia rarely cursed, and Beatriz never got angry. It was just the way these women were. Now Beatriz was cursing?

"What's wrong?" Luis asked. "Let me fix it."

Beatriz was apparently not in any kind of good mood. "You'll just mess it up, Luis. Stay where you are."

"But at least tell me the problem, *mi corazon*," Luis begged. Quite literally, Agustin noticed, trying to hide his grin. Lucia elbowed him in the ribs, but she was trying not to smile, he could tell.

"It's that dratted Isabel," Beatriz groused. "She never gets this right. Always, always, the strips she tears from the batts of wool are too fat. Always. She's in too much of a hurry."

"It's an easy fix, Beatriz," Lucia said. "Heaven knows, we've done it often enough."

Beatriz began stretching out the too-fat strip of wool. "I know that. The point is that I shouldn't have to. It was her job today, not mine."

Agustin found that his mouth was hanging open. He'd never seen Lucia do exactly what Beatriz was doing with the wool. The rope, when Beatriz was finished pulling, which she did very gently, was at least five feet longer than it had been, possibly more.

"I am an idiot!" Agustin shouted.

"Well, that's common knowledge." Luis grinned at his friend. "Lucia could have told you if you didn't know," he added winking at her.

"Ha! You're an idiot, too!" Agustin answered back.

Agustin's shout had distracted Beatriz, who had seen Luis wink and giggled at his surprised look. "That too is common knowledge. But what is the idiocy of the moment?"

"All this time we have been trying to figure out a machine to tear ropes from the batt. We could have been making a machine to stretch batts into ropes."

"That sounds like a lot more work," Lucia said. "Tearing them is easier. That's why we do it that way."

"Yes! Easier for a clever girl with clever fingers. A girl with the wit and skill to keep watch on how the wool batt is coming apart into ropes. But not easier for a machine that has no eyes, no fingers and no wit at all."

Luis was nodding. "Machines are stupid, even the most complex ones. They can't change what they are doing, can't adjust themselves."

Don Ramon de Aguilera was severely displeased. They had been pouring money into the spinning machine for two years now, and at the suggestion of his nephew. And now the boy had gone off to the Low Countries to save the guilder. What should a proper Spanish gentleman care about the Dutch guilder?

The idea had been that while there were restrictions on who could make cloth for sale, there were no such restrictions on who made thread. So if they could use the machines to make fine high-quality thread quickly and cheaply, they could have the savings of the improved production and slip through a loophole in the laws by exporting not washed wool, but thread. Carded wool was wool under the law. They could export no more of it than washed wool. They got a slightly better price for it, true.

He wasn't sure whether he was more displeased by Don Alfredo or the disloyalty displayed by his shepherds. Don Ramon felt he was a generous, if not extravagant lord. He didn't approve of extravagance, especially in regards to dealing with the lower classes. It only led to trouble.

In Don Ramon's world, there was a place for everyone and everyone belonged in their place. He was born a hidalgo and a Spanish noble, a defender of the church and of Spain. His shepherds had been born shepherds. He, like his father before him, generously allowed the shepherds to trap rabbits. But that was a matter of generosity, not of law.

Now, taking that generosity as license, his shepherds were stealing from him . . . stealing the expensive angora rabbits imported not just from Germany, but from the future. Apparently egged on by the over-educated craftsmen he'd had to import to build the spinning machine. Proving that education, especially of the lower classes, was a threat to the faith and to the social order. *Where was the loyalty?*

☆ ☆ ☆

Machines, it turned out, were even stupider than Agustin or Luis had thought. To stretch a batt into a rope, what the papers called a sliver, they were using a series of rollers, like those they had built for the spinning machine. Each roller turning a bit faster than the one before. "I don't understand it, Lucia." Agustin complained.

"Never mind about that!" Lucia said. "Don't you pay any attention to what is going on in the world?"

"What?"

"One of the other families in the Mesta has started selling limited quantities of Angora wool. From what I hear, the de Aguilera family is convinced that they got the rabbits from us." She looked down at the table. "It might even be true. A lot of people in the village were upset when they took our rabbits. And they didn't get all of them.

"They've placed guards at the mouth of the valley and no one is allowed to leave."

"It'll be all right," Agustin insisted. "Once we get the spinning machine working, everything will calm down." He tried to carry conviction in his voice, but it was hard going. The truth was that the improvements already made should have satisfied the de Aguilera family, at least for now. Cleaning and carding took at least as much of the time in going from wool to wool thread as spinning did. The project was already a success.

Not all the notes from the German source were directly on spinning. There had been some on more general mechanics and their impact and how that lead to the industrial revolution. Based on those books, they had done a couple of studies. The time saved by the cleaning cages, the drying racks, and the carding machines meant that more man hours, woman hours, could be spent on spinning. From the books, they had also made some improvements in the spinning wheels. They were producing a lot more thread for a lot less labor than before the project had started. Why didn't the de Aguilera family see that?

Things like this had happened before. The contractors would complain about a project, generally in preparation for extorting the costs back from the craftsmen or running the craftsmen out of town without the final payment. But that wouldn't work here because of the major concern with secrecy. It was starting to feel like a story from ancient times, about the workers buried with the Pharaoh to keep the secret traps secret.

To avoid thinking about the unreasonableness of the de Aguilera family, Agustin turned his mind back to the unreasonableness of the rope stretcher. It was at least something he had a hope of solving.

The rope stretcher consisted of five sets of rollers, each turning a bit faster than the last, and each a little closer to the next than to the last. Agustin had figured that the wider the rope, the more distance you needed to give it to stretch. Luis figured that it didn't matter, so he didn't argue the point, though—as a matter of aesthetics—he would have preferred that all the rollers be the same distance apart.

The first set of rollers was a foot from the second, the second was a half a foot from the third, which was a quarter foot from the fourth, which was only an inch and a half from the last set. But in spite of that, it took them a while to realize what was happening. Because you couldn't always tell that the batt of wool had lost cohesion between the first and second set of rollers, sometimes it looked like they were coming apart between the second and third sets. Or it looked like the third, fourth or fifth set was causing the problem by pulling too hard.

It was Luis that saw it. He was watching the stretcher shred rather than stretch another batt of carded wool and picked up a single strand of wool. He stretched it out as long as it would go and then pulled on it some more. Naturally, it broke. It really didn't have anything like the stretchiness of a piece of thread.

He looked back at the stretcher and began to visualize what was happening to the hairs as they went through the rollers. It wasn't that they were stretching; they were sliding against each other. At least he thought they were. He picked a fragment of the wool batt and pulled it apart. Slowly, carefully, watching the individual strands. Yes. It was the strands slipping past each other that allowed the wool to stretch. They were tangled together, but after being carded they weren't that tangled. Sort of half tangled.

He looked back at the rollers. Then he remembered something from the spinning machines. He was pretty sure that the rollers were all the same distance apart on the spinning machine. He picked up another bit of wool and slowly fed it into the stretcher. He wasn't really trying for a rope now, he was just carefully watching to see what would happen. He used very little wool because he wanted to be able to see what was happening to the threads. And see he did. Suddenly, he saw it all. A bit vaguely to be sure, but he saw it.

He started adjusting the distance between the sets of rollers. No easy job, because they weren't designed to be adjustable. That was what Agustin found him doing. He tried to explain what he was doing to the carpenter but the words came out jumbled. He wasn't used to being the one who wanted to try something different.

Even after the second run-through Agustin didn't get it, but he just shrugged and said, "Tell me what you want me to do."

BLAM! The sound of a shot woke Lucia. Then there was shouting. "Somebody catch that rabbit!"

Still only half awake, Lucia looked around and noticed that her little brother Juan was missing. Suddenly she had a bad feeling. She quickly put on a shawl over her shift and ran out of the cottage. And almost ran over a rabbit glowing white in the moonlight. The rabbit dashed around the corner and was gone.

Lucia could see lights waving in the distance, and went to investigate. The de Aguilera guards were milling around with torches, scattering in all directions. Except for one, who was bending over a slight form that lay in the dust. "Juan!" Lucia shouted, and ran toward the guard.

The guard sprang to his feet and pointed his gun at Lucia. "Get back!"

"He's bleeding. Let me bind his wounds."

"He's dead," the guard said harshly. "He tried to slip out of the valley carrying the white rabbit. Got shot for his trouble and now the damned rabbit has run off again." Then he shook his head and relented a bit. "Go ahead, girl. Talk to him while you can."

"It hurts, Lucia!" Juan cried. It looked like half his belly had been ripped away.

"Oh, Juan. What happened?"

"They stole my bunnies." Juan repeated a complaint that he had made ever since the rabbit crossbreeds had been collected. Then he added, "I caught Mrs. Bunny in one of my traps. I guess I shouldn't have tried to sneak her out but it seemed only fair. They took mine, I'd take theirs." He tried to grin.

"Oh, Juan," Lucia whispered. Then Juan died.

☆ ☆ ☆

"It's all that Agustin's fault," Papa said. Papa had been drinking ever since the burial. Juan was the youngest, and had always been Papa's favorite, as much for his independence of thought as for his resemblance to their mother.

"Agustin didn't tell Juan to steal the rabbit, Papa."

The look he gave her was ugly. Very ugly and scary. "Shut your mouth, girl. My son is dead, dead for a damned rabbit. I don't want to hear what you think."

It didn't quite work the way Luis and Agustin thought it would. Granted the wool did spin into better thread than it had been, but the thread was still weaker than it should be. It was all Agustin could do to keep from beating the machine into splinters, but he drew a deep breath and kept trying.

He went back to the papers. Finally, he had it. "Weights, Luiz. Weight on the first roller, to slow it down, so the wool will draw. A lighter weight on the second."

"Are you sure?" Luiz asked.

"When have we been sure of anything?" Agustin responded.

Lucia walked into the old mill upstream of the village with a breaking heart. She had just realized that she was truly and deeply in love with Agustin. Two things had told her so. She looked at her future without him and it was a bleak gray place that didn't seem worth the trouble. And she was coming up here to send him away because she cared more about him than she did about that horrible life. She had to tell Agustin that he had to leave but the words wouldn't come. She cleared her throat to prepare the way for the words she didn't want to say.

The two men looked up from the spinning machine. "We figured it out!" Luis said.

Agustin grinned at her. "I was waiting until we got this to work to ask your father, Lucia. But we're close enough now we know we can get it to work." Then he knelt right there on the dirty stone floor of the mill. "Lucia, will you marry me?"

"Yes!" came out of Lucia's mouth without her will. For a moment she forgot the news that had brought her here. Then they were kissing and the news was pushed back even further.

When they came partway back to earth, Luis was sitting on the frame of the spinning machine grinning like a loon. "So when is the wedding? From what I saw you'd better hurry." He laughed. "Besides, you still have to convince her father."

Suddenly, it all came back. "Father is on his way to the guards, to tell them that you're responsible, that you know where Juan hid his rabbit cages. You have to run, and you have to run now."

"Not without you, I'm not!" Agustin insisted. Then he shook his head in confusion. "What makes your father think I had anything to do with it?"

"Papa doesn't like you," was all Lucia could think of. "The way you talk about master Munos. And not getting the answers to your questions. Papa is very conservative. He can't blame Don Ramon, Juan or himself. It must be someone else, and he decided on you. He's been warning me about immoral townsmen for months."

"You both need to run." Luis was nodding. Lucia knew that he was more politically astute than Agustin. "Look, when this comes out Don Ramon is going to be very angry. He is going to want someone to blame and the people here know that. Munos is going to be looking for a scapegoat.

"I think they are misreading Don Ramon. He isn't stupid; he is just set in his ways. And Ricardo is a smart cookie. But they aren't here. What we have here are some guardsmen that figure they are going to be in trouble for letting Mrs. Bunny get away again, some scared masters and some upset villagers.

Besides that, there is no way Munos is going to want anyone hearing your version of events. I'm fairly safe because I don't answer to Munos. Master Guiterez will protect me from overzealous guards. But no one is going to protect Agustin and if he runs they will know you warned him." He gave Lucia a serious look. "All the guard will see in you is a village girl whose brother was caught stealing from the don. No one who can is going to even try to protect you."

"Are you sure that Master Guiterez will be able to protect you?"

Luis pointed at the cots that had been set up in the mill house. "I was asleep on one of those. I never saw a thing." He grinned.

More time was wasted while Agustin hugged Luis and Lucia kissed him on the cheek.

Agustin started putting stuff in a sack. "We'll have to head into the hills. Then on to the coast and somehow get out of Spain."

"Hills I know very well," Lucia said.

"Ah."

They looked toward Luis. "Ah. I know someone at the coast. He owes me a favor." He quickly wrote down a name and village. "Go to him. He'll get you out, if you can only get there."

It was the middle of the night when they left the village. They could see torches beginning to move toward the village from the mouth of the valley, but they had a head start, unlike poor Juan.

They ran toward the hills and didn't stop.

Lucia glanced back only once. Mrs. Bunny hopped out from under a bush, her white coat gleaming in the moonlight.

"Go," Lucia hissed. "Go, bunny. Go, go."

Mrs. December, 1636

Chet Gottfried

Justus Corneliszoon van Liede's smile was all teeth. Big teeth. Broad teeth. Dazzling teeth. Many men would have wanted to punch in his teeth at first sight. Many women would have been tempted to do the same. Flo Richards was different.

"Have another piece of cake, Herr van Liede." She daydreamed about the cavities that the rich white icing could cause in those brilliant teeth of his.

The Dutch cavalier accepted the cake with a flourish that went well with his flamboyant clothing, from satin doublet to orange breeches and tall red boots.

"Thank you, dear lady. My ride from Amsterdam was well worth the opportunity to enjoy your most wonderful cake."

Flo watched Justus' goatee move back and forth like a metronome as he chewed.

"How long did it take to travel from Amsterdam to Grantville?"

Justus smiled. "Not long at all. A few weeks, dear lady."

Flo didn't trust the smile. "Call me Flo."

"Of course, Flo, dear lady. And you may call me Justus Corneliszoon."

She sighed. Justus was the most difficult person she had ever met. He combined seventeenth-century courtier with twentieth-century used car salesman.

"I'm flattered by the letter you sent: your invitation. I'm impressed by your mastery of written English." Flo paused a moment. She wasn't at all sure whether she wanted to tackle traveling anywhere except maybe Jena. It wasn't like you could just hop in the car and travel a hundred miles in a couple of hours.

"Thank you."

"But a few weeks in each direction means that you expect me to be away from my farm for over a month. In autumn. That's harvest time, and I'm pretty busy."

Justus swung his arms wide and his smile grew wider. "But think of the honor, dear lady Flo. To have your portrait painted by Pieter Paul Rubens is a privilege you can tell your children and grandchildren."

"There's a war going on."

"What war? There isn't any war, not in that direction. That was settled last year."

"There are thieves and looters on all the roads."

"You shall have a dedicated escort. I have already arranged to have good men accompany you."

Flo was beginning to feel desperate. "I've never been away from J.D. for over a month."

"You mean your husband? Yes, I know about J.D., and we expect him as well. Dear lady Flo, you and J.D. will love seeing Amsterdam. It is particularly beautiful in the autumn." He smiled.

"Well, maybe." Flo tried to recall the last time that she and J.D. went traveling. They hadn't been anywhere since the Ring of Fire. Before that, all she could recall was their second honeymoon to New Orleans. And that was that. "I'll have to talk it over with J.D. first."

"Of course. I would expect nothing less." Then Justus cleared his throat. "Pieter Paul Rubens made a special request in regard to you."

Flo was on her guard. "Yes?"

"He has a certain technique in regard to his portraits of women."

"I am not—most definitely not—going to pose naked for him. I don't care how many portraits he's done or how many women he's painted. I am *not* appearing naked for him!"

"No, no, dear lady Flo. Whether you are dressed or undressed is your own decision. Rubens' request is different: He wants to include a few symbols of yourself in the painting, such as your love of coffee. You would bring a pot in which you brew your coffee, as well as a few cups."

Flo settled. "That's okay."

"And he would like you to bring your wonderful ram Brillo."

When J.D. came home later that day, Flo cornered him and took him into their bedroom.

J.D. began undressing. "A little early in the day for this, isn't it?"

"Keep your pants on, J.D. It's not what you think. Have you been drinking?"

J.D. hiccuped. "Gerhart opened a new pub in town. Calls it the Hole in the Wall. It's a small place but quiet. He's studied a variety of cookbooks from the library and is going to serve light meals. But you don't want to try his pizza. He uses Swiss cheese. Some of the other dishes aren't bad, I have to admit. Gerhart is trying hard enough, and right now he's in the middle of decorating. Today, we were sampling some of his brews."

"Smells like you've downed a keg."

He sat on the bed. "Real ale. You used to pay extra for it, but here, it's all they have. No fizz, but it packs quite a punch. I wonder what the alcohol content is?"

"Whatever it is, it's too high. Now listen, J.D. Are you ready?"

"I'm ready."

"I have a surprise for you. What are you doing?"

J.D. had stretched out on the bed. "I can take surprises better while lying down, dear."

"You'd only fall asleep. Okay. How would you like to take a trip together?"

"Like to Amsterdam?"

Flo became suspicious. "What made you say 'Amsterdam'?"

"It seems as good a place as any. Besides, wouldn't it be good to get away?"

"Who told you about Amsterdam?"

J.D. grinned. "Gerhart, me, and a bunch of us were talking about how good a painting would look over the bar. You know, a naked woman. Every pub should have one. Something by Rubens, since Varga hasn't been born yet. I hear tell that he's pretty good for that sort of thing. So we were talking about who in Grantville would look best naked and who would be most willing to go to Amsterdam. Opinions were hot! It could have become an out-and-out fight, but in the end we made paper ballots and had a vote. Guess who won?"

He patted the bed, and Flo, blushing lightly, sat next to him.

"J.D., you're not telling me that your buddies would prefer me to one of the young lovelies we have in town?"

Hugging Flo, J.D. gave her a kiss. "You'd be surprised the reputation you have. For starters, maybe you should remember to button your blouse more often."

Flo rolled her eyes. "And here I used to wonder what you geezers talked about." Then she looked at him suspiciously. "Just a minute. Would one of your drinking companions be a piece of fluff known as Justus Corneliszoon van Liede?"

J.D. smirked. "Do you mean Corny? He's a right good fella and a fine drinking companion."

"Corny? Not Justus Corneliszoon?"

"It might have been something like that for the first glass or two. Then he let his hair down. He could certainly talk up a streak. And he has to have the brightest teeth in the world. It's like staring at a laser. Funny though. Gerhart wanted to punch Corny's teeth in. For no reason whatsoever. Well, before Gerhart could do anything, out jumps Corny's sword, and four cuts later, Gerhart's shirt is in shreds. Then they were friends, slapping each other's back and laughing. I guess Gerhart was happy to be alive, and Corny is willing to be friends with anyone. Good thing too. A guy that good with a sword has to be someone to have on your side."

"And he told you all about our going to Amsterdam?"

J.D. gave her a hug. "Why not? We've been working around the clock, helping the town settle in, helping the Germans settle in, helping our kids settle in. So why don't we take a vacation?"

"What about Ed Piazza?" Flo asked. "We'll be gone six weeks or more. Can he spare you that long?"

"He'd better. I haven't had a day off since the Ring of Fire, so I'm due. Don't forget Mike Stearns is a long-standing union man. Try talking to the unions about no one having time off anymore, and then you'll see explosions that'll make the Thirty Years' War look like a kid's game."

"Now, J.D. It's a good job. I don't want you to get into any departmental fights and jeopardize everything for the sake of a picture."

"I was going to resign anyway, babe. I don't want to move away from the girls. So I talked to Ed and then talked to the tech school.

I'll be back teaching as soon as we return." J.D. grinned. "We're going, and we'll be having fun! And I'd like to get my hands on as many bulbs as I can. Tulips will help brighten our place, and we can sell them too. Not to mention it will be great to have a calendar."

Flo pointed to the calendar hanging on the wall. "What's that, J.D.? We already have calendars."

"But not a Rubens calendar. Didn't Corny tell you? Sure, part of it is to go to have your portrait painted. But Corny is putting together a calendar of Grantville notables—as painted by Rubens."

"Grantville notables, huh? I suppose that's why he wants Brillo along. Do you think it's going to be easy to get that ram to Amsterdam? He's almost as stubborn as you are."

"Why shouldn't Brillo come along? He can walk part of the way, and Corny said that he was hiring an up-time wagon, should Brillo be his rambunctious self and prefer to ride. Rubens included Anne Jefferson's pom-poms and baton in her painting, so why shouldn't you have Brillo in yours? Not every ram has inspired a rebellion. And a Rubens calendar would be a collector's item. Did you know that Rubens has a whole flock of artists and print-makers working for him? They've been into prints for years, but this will be their first calendar. I wonder whether it is going to be Gregorian or Julian. I hope Gregorian, but you never know. Down-timers never cease to amaze me."

J.D. was going a little too fast for Flo. "I'm going to be in a calendar?"

"Sure, Flo. How does it feel to be Mrs. December, 1636?"

"Get one fact straight, mister. I'm not posing in the nude for anyone. Look at me! I'm a grandma! Who's ever heard of fifty-somethings posing naked?"

J.D. agreed. "Absolutely not. It's totally out of the question."

Flo got off the bed and looked into the mirror. "Totally out of the question? Are you trying to tell me something, J.D.?" She turned right and left and critically inspected herself. "I still have a pretty good figure. Or do you think I'm too heavy?"

"Rubens likes well-rounded women, dear. And so do I. I'm sure you'd look great however you posed. One thing's for certain. The boys would really love to have you naked—over the bar." J.D. grinned.

For a moment Flo was lost in her thoughts. Then she snapped out of it. "Come on. Let's get Johan, Anna, and the rest for a decent dinner. Lord knows what we'll be eating on the road." Naked, she thought. And snorted to herself: That will be the day!

A week later, a procession headed into Flo's yard: a handsomely painted wagon drawn by two horses, with two saddled horses tied to the rear of the wagon. Justus rode a high-stepping black gelding in front.

Flo, J.D., their three daughters, and their partners in running the farm, Johan, Anna, Wilhelm, and Ilsa, soon surrounded the wagon. Justus casually dismounted while giving a nonstop description of all the wonders of his preparation for the vacation to Amsterdam, not least of all the wagon, rented from an up-timer. It had a seat in the front for two drivers, and the wagon had benches on either side that could be dropped down. "Very convenient for sleeping, should you stop between cities or inns." The wagon also had bales of hay for the horses and Brillo.

"And allow me to introduce you to your noble escort. I present my brothers Frederik van Liede and Johan van Liede. They are brave men, wonderful shots, excellent drivers, and will see you through every obstacle anyone could encounter."

The two brothers slouched on the front seat. For each aspect of Justus that said dandy, the two brothers screamed despair. Where Justus had finely groomed hair, wisps of yellow stuck out in random directions from their heads. From his brothers' lifeless clothing to their drooping expressions, they looked as if they had been dragged through every puddle from Amsterdam to Grantville.

Flo was shocked. "My God! Whatever happened to them?"

"Ah ha!" Justus declared. "You have noticed! All has not been well with my brothers. They were aboard the good ship *Brederode* in the battle along the English Channel, for which the English changed sides and attacked the Dutch fleet. The *Brederode* exploded, killing the entire crew except my brothers, who were thrown into the sea. They were fished up by the Spanish, and I, Justus Corneliszoon van Liede, had to pay ransom to release them. So, dear lady Flo, my brothers are in my debt. And until such day as they can repay it, they are in my service. It should only be another five years before they are free to return to the sea. And perhaps by then, the Netherlands will have another fleet, so that my brothers can be sailors again."

Flo asked, "What do sailors know about horses and roads?"

"My dear lady Flo, my brothers were farmers and often traveled these routes until several years ago. They would probably be farmers today if their joint farm hadn't burned to the ground. A pity we didn't know about lightning rods back then. Then they took to the sea. Or rather they were drunk and were taken to the sea. No matter, aboard the *Brederode,* they became crack shots, and between them killed twelve Spaniards before their ship went boom."

J.D. scratched his head. "Farmers? Sailors? They look more like flotsam and jetsam to me." The nicknames stuck, and thereafter everyone, including Justus, referred to the younger van Liede brothers as Flotsam and Jetsam.

Flo's one consolation was that however bedraggled Flotsam and Jetsam appeared, Justus knew his way around and was an expert swordsman. So her heart sank when she saw Justus mounting his horse.

"I've put together a farewell party with all types of meat, soup, and bread for us."

Justus took off his broad-brimmed hat and waved it with a flourish. "No, no, dear lady Flo. Business attends. I must ride on ahead, for there are other contracts to arrange. I leave you in the capable hands of my brothers. They won't let you down, for they know what will happen if they do. Farewell!" And he galloped away.

While watching Justus disappear, Flo had a brainstorm. She asked Flotsam and Jetsam, "Do either of you speak English?"

Flotsam looked at Jetsam, and Jetsam looked at Flotsam. After a minute of mute consultation, Flotsam shook his head.

"*Nee.*"

"But you do understand English?"

After another consultation, they both slowly nodded, as if any suggestion of speed would cause a head to roll off.

"*Ja.*"

Johan entered the conversation. "*Konnen Sie deutsch?*"

"*Nee.*"

It soon came down to the fact that the only language between the two Dutch brothers was Dutch, whereas they appeared to understand most other languages—to some extent. Flo turned to J.D. "I've lost my appetite."

J.D. patted her on the shoulder. "Remember, Rubens likes plump women. You don't want to be losing any weight."

She punched him on the arm and marched into the house.

☆ ☆ ☆

The following morning saw intense activity while everyone helped load the wagon—except Flotsam and Jetsam. They stood by and sadly watched the load increase and increase and increase. Food, clothing, blankets, dry wood, coal, coffee, soap, books, yarn, knitting needles, and sundry items were piled high into the wagon.

Each of Flo's three daughters managed to speak to Flo alone.

Kerry gave Flo a small package wrapped in brown paper. "You'll bless me for this."

Turning the parcel this way and that, Flo asked, "What is it?"

"A clean queen-sized sheet. You'll want to strip any bed in any inn and put this on. You won't believe the fleas."

Flo laughed. "I'm sure it won't be necessary."

Kerry asked, "Mom, are you going to pose in the nude?"

"Whatever gave you that idea?"

"If you did, what would I tell my children? What would happen if they saw their grandmother naked?"

Flo had to bite her tongue not to say that the children would hardly be scarred for life if that happened. Instead, she said, "I'm sure you can find something better to worry about. It's not going to happen."

Later, Missy trapped Flo in the kitchen and handed her a box. "Ma, here's something you'll really need."

The box was about the same size as the parcel. "Let me guess. It's a sheet."

Missy was surprised. "Did you pack any? Even if you did, I'm sure you could use an extra."

In the bedroom, Amy cornered and stared intently at Flo. "Mom, you're not going to pose naked, are you?"

Overall, Flo was starting to get a bit insulted by that question. She freely admitted that she wasn't as thin as Anne Jefferson, but it wasn't like she was fat. And she certainly wasn't old. She laughed uneasily. "Good heavens, no, Amy. Whatever gave you that idea?"

"It's what the whole town is talking about. Everywhere you go, people are saying that Rubens wants you naked." Amy gave her mother a heavy package in a small backpack. "You'll need this. It's a revolver and a handful of bullets."

"Are you telling me to shoot Rubens?"

"Don't be silly, Mom. It's for the road. You don't know who you'll meet. And if you want to protect your virtue when you're being painted, that's okay, too."

Outside, J.D. was also receiving gifts, from the men around the farm. His sons-in-law gave him a second shotgun in addition to J.D.'s own, muskets, and a variety of knives. Johan gave J.D. something particularly valuable: a large plastic tarp.

"Do you think we're going to have picnics?" J.D. asked.

"No. You will be in an open wagon and want some protection for when it rains."

"But the tarp's red," J.D. complained.

"So?"

"Do you have anything in green?"

Johan laughed and slapped J.D. on the back. "You need a vacation."

Meanwhile, both men and women found time to talk to Flotsam and Jetsam. Each person promised that should anything untoward happen to either Flo or J.D., the Dutch brothers would lose their hands, fingernails, private parts, eyes, or whatever piece of anatomy the speaker preferred. Tone and body language supplemented the brothers' limited German and English. With each additional speaker, the two brothers looked sadder, more forlorn, and more crumpled.

Early the next morning, Flotsam and Jetsam hitched the horses to the wagon and tied the saddle horses to the rear.

By nine o'clock, J.D. had a pleased look on his face. He had arranged all their belongings in the wagon. "I guess that's about it. We're ready to go, and I've used up every square inch of space. How's that for packing?"

Flo put her hands on her hips. "What about Brillo?"

J.D.'s face sunk almost as low as that of the Dutch brothers. "You get the ram. I'll begin rearranging."

Chuckling all the way to Brillo's pen, Flo never noticed the enormous grin on Johan's face as he followed her.

"Brillo's gone!" Flo gasped.

"Relax, Flo," Johan said. "I put him with the ewes for the night. I thought that might make him more manageable."

"Good idea."

The two of them found Brillo peacefully dozing among the ewes.

Johan laughed. "He's in heaven."

They pushed and prodded the sleepy ram all the way to the cart, in which J.D. had cleared a space for him.

"It's not much room," J.D. admitted, "but there's bound to be more space as time goes by."

Brillo blinked peacefully until J.D. and Johan swung him aboard. Then the ram was wide awake. His first baa was somewhat weak, but each succeeding baa gained in strength and terror.

Everyone pretended to ignore the cries while Flo and J.D. were kissed and hugged. She and J.D. got into the back with Brillo, and Flo stood up and gave her farewell speech.

"We'll go, we'll see, and we'll return."

Everyone applauded, Flotsam shook the reins and clucked at the horses, and the wagon rolled away to various cheers and ever-louder baas.

Flo closed her eyes. "However long this trip takes, it is going to be longer than I had imagined."

That was at the end of August.

Three weeks, four sweaters, five caps, and seven scarves later, they were still in Germany. Flo had calluses on her knitting fingers, J.D. was working on a beer belly, and Flotsam and Jetsam were more ragged than ever.

J.D. lifted a stein of beer. "It won't be long now."

Flo was working on another sweater for J.D. "You mean when we reach the border?"

"No, dear. When they serve dinner." He burped again.

They were sitting by a table in a small inn a few miles west of Osnabrück. It wasn't the most desirable inn, but the weather was stormy, and neither of them looked forward to another day of being stuck between inns and sleeping in the open at night while it was raining.

A fat man wearing torn clothes staggered over to them. He had a large knife stuck in his belt, a patch over an eye, greasy hair, and various scars. He was the innkeeper, and Flo didn't trust him.

A young woman followed the innkeeper. She was somewhat better dressed and was carrying a large tray with bowls.

The innkeeper spoke and understood English in terms of single words. "Dinner."

Flo groaned. "Stew?" She thought of chunks of indigestible meat sunk at the bottom of a bowl that had a scum of fat floating on the top.

The innkeeper smiled a terrible smile, exposing black teeth. "Mutton."

She gave a little shriek and thought: Brillo! Jumping up, Flo ran outside the inn and into its stable on the side. There she saw one of the van Liede brothers leaning against a stall. He had a musket lying across his thighs and was staring blankly in the distance. Next to him, Brillo was peacefully chewing his cud. A strange warmth descended over her, she was incredibly thankful, and she wanted to hug the two of them. Then she felt guilty that she didn't know whether it was Flotsam or Jetsam guarding her ram. The two might have been identical twins.

"Hello," she said somewhat shyly.

"*Goedenavond.*"

"Excuse me, but are you Flotsam or Jetsam?"

"Jetsam."

The indignity of calling these two men after the debris of the ocean occurred to her, and Flo tried to apologize.

The corners of his mouth turned upward. It might have been a smile. "*Nee, nee. Het Geeft niet.*" Then he thought about it some more. "Good name."

"Would you like to learn to speak English? It would help to pass the time on the road."

Jetsam nodded.

Where do I begin, she wondered. Flo pointed to her nose. "Nose." Jetsam repeated after her. After Flo ran through her face, she started on her body and worked down to her thighs.

Jetsam put his hand on her thigh and smiled in earnest. "Thigh!"

Flo recognized the look of the predatory male and hastily stood up. "I think we've had enough English for one night."

Going back inside the dark inn, she sat down by her table. "J.D., you won't believe what happened. J.D.?" As soon as her eyes acclimated to the numerous people milling around, she saw that the serving girl was sitting on J.D.'s lap. His right hand held a tankard and his left hand was inside her blouse.

Looking at her with bleary eyes, J.D. burped. "Strong ale."

Flo said pointedly, "I don't know about the ale, but maybe you should take it easy on the milk."

The girl removed J.D.'s hand, curtsied, and, laughing, left the table. J.D. said, "I think she'd like to come to Amsterdam with us."

"Really?" Her voice dripped sarcasm.

What began as a nod ended in a plummet, and J.D.'s head rested on the table. Flo finished her cold meal in silence.

☆ ☆ ☆

Three days later, in the bedroom at another nameless inn on the nameless road, J.D. complained, "I don't know why you aren't talking to me. It happens. I was drunk. I thought she was you."

Flo stripped the bed and put one of the travel sheets over it. "She was taller than me, had blond hair, a squint in one eye, and warts. So how in all hell did she look like me?"

J.D. began undressing. "She had your boobs."

After putting a top sheet over the spread one, Flo critically inspected the blankets for lice and fleas. "Maybe you shouldn't have mentioned her boobs. Maybe I was ready to forget."

"Honestly, Flo. You've a great body. I can see why Rubens would want to paint you naked. I mean, you'd be the naked one. Rubens would have his clothes on. Well, he better have his clothes on."

Flo warmed to him. "You think so?"

Nodding vigorously, J.D. got under the covers. "Let me show you."

She got into bed next to him. "I don't know, J.D. You're the only man who's ever seen me naked—if you don't count doctors. I don't know if I could do it even if I wanted to do it. What's that hand doing? Hmm." And the time for conversation rapidly slipped away.

By the end of September they had almost reached the border between the Netherlands and Germany. The problem involved a fork in the road and one of those rare occasions when there was no other traffic. J.D. and Jetsam had taken the saddle horses to explore the forks, as well as to buy some bread and other provisions. Flotsam was snoring in the wagon, and Flo was sitting on the driver's seat and stitching a ram needlepoint. She had drawn the design at home, and this was the first opportunity she'd had to finish it. Brillo was tethered nearby to a tree and was nibbling in the high meadow.

Half-dozing in the sunlight, Flo became aware of the large wagon drawn by a team of four horses when it drew near. She immediately recognized it as an up-time conveyance not only by the driver having a seat in the front but also by the "We Love Feet" logo and the "Eisenhauer Shoe Company" lettering on the side.

Flo waved to the driver. "Hello!"

The driver reined his horses to a stop. "*Guten Tag.*" He took in her appearance and wagon. "You are an American."

"Yes, and are you ever a sight for sore eyes."

"Do your eyes hurt?"

"No." Flo reminded herself to avoid being literal with down-timers. "I meant that I didn't know that Eisenhauer had expanded this far so soon."

"Ja, Herr Eisenhauer's shoes are very popular. We will be branching into the Netherlands next year. Why wear wood clogs when you can have leather boots at the same price?" He jumped off his wagon. "I'm Siegbert Zuckertort, but everyone calls me Ziggy."

She got down and offered her hand. "I'm Flo Richards, and I wouldn't mind another pair of shoes."

They shook hands.

"I'm sorry, but I've delivered all the shoes. You see, I'm taking hides back for more shoes." He smiled. "We don't want any wasted trips, and Herr Eisenhauer insists on a full load in both directions. But I have a catalog. Perhaps you would like to order something?"

"Another time maybe. When I'm back in Grantville."

"Flo Richards, Flo Richards," he murmured. "Yes, I know you. You're the one with Brillo the Ram. You're famous. He's famous! I have seen the video *Bad, Bad Brillo.*"

"Really? How did you like his performance?"

"Brillo is one hundred percent ram. So what are you doing here? Where are you going? And who is looking after Brillo while you are away?"

"We're going to Amsterdam, and Brillo is right over here..." Turning, she pointed to where she had Brillo tethered.

He wasn't there.

Looking in the distance, Flo saw three men leading Brillo away. "My God! They're stealing Brillo!"

Ziggy reached into his wagon. "You're lucky that they haven't killed you." He pulled out a heavy cudgel and charged the thieves. Flo took her wagon at a leap and began looking in all the green backpacks for the one that had the revolver. Finding the gun, she jumped down and started running. She prayed the gun was loaded.

One of the thieves threw a rock at Ziggy. It missed, and then he was on them and hit the first bandit on the neck. The bandit crumpled, but the other two used their clubs and soon had Ziggy on the ground.

By that time, Flo was close enough. Standing in her stocking feet, at only around five foot one, she wasn't particularly tall even by seventeenth-century standards. Flo was also a tad on the plump side and not accustomed to running. For this occasion, however, she had no trouble screaming curses while racing at full speed. It was enough to make the two bandits hesitate. When she began firing the revolver in the air, they decided that they had had enough for one day and ran away. The third managed to get up and didn't do too bad a job in keeping up with his fellow thieves.

Panting, Flo helped Ziggy to his feet. "Are you okay?"

He was bleeding from a head wound and seemed a little woozy. "I have had better days."

Facing Brillo, Flo asked, "What's the idea, you big goof? You baa your head off day in and day out, but when three strangers sneak over, untie you, and lead you away, you don't make a peep. What do you have to say for yourself?"

"*Baa*!"

Flo laughed. "I think he's gotten over his trauma of being ramnapped. I'm not sure about myself though. I could use a cup of coffee. Would you like to join me?"

"Ah, coffee! But of course!"

Half leading and half dragging Brillo, Flo walked alongside Ziggy back to their wagons.

"You saved Brillo."

Ziggy laughed. "You saved Brillo. I performed a delaying tactic." He shook his head. "I have had enough of soldiering and prefer a quiet life. Deliver shoes and buy hides. That's a good life. I have already earned enough for a roomy cottage outside Bamberg. It has been two months since I have been home, and I look forward to seeing my wife and children." He sighed. "I miss them."

By the wagon, Ziggy nodded toward Flotsam. "I wonder how he managed to sleep through it all."

Flo sniffed. Flotsam's state of unconsciousness was due to schnapps. "Yes, he's a great bodyguard." She bound Ziggy's wound.

"Thank you, Flo. You are kind."

"That's nothing. Let's see if this sweater fits you. That's the least I can do for a friend of Brillo."

When J.D. returned later that afternoon, looking rather beat, he scowled at the picnic that Flo had set up for Flotsam and Ziggy. "I wish I could spend all my time eating and chatting."

Flo laughed. "Stop grouching. If you brought back any cheese or fresh bread, I'll let you enjoy the last of our coffee supply."

☆ ☆ ☆

On a bright day in early October, Flotsam reined the wagon over to the side of the road. Approaching them was a sea of wool, a flock of sheep led by a young blond girl of about twelve. She smiled and waved her shepherd's crook, in thanks to the travelers standing aside.

Flo waved back to the girl. To J.D.: "Look how those ewes follow her. We should be so lucky back home."

J.D. nodded toward Brillo. "He's beginning to become restless."

Tied to the wagon, Brillo was pulling and straining at his tether.

"Relax, J.D. Brillo can't get away. I know how to tie a good knot."

"Was it a slipknot by any chance?"

Breaking free, Brillo charged into the middle of the sheep. Following him were Flo, J.D., and Jetsam. Flotsam was analyzing the situation throughout somewhat bloodshot eyes.

From the rear of the flock, a middle-aged farmer joined the pursuit. He seemed very upset and was talking nonstop.

While Flo and J.D. held Brillo, who was baaing for all he was worth, Jetsam explained in broken English and gesture that the farmer was taking his ewes to a different pasture. He was also a bit worried that the spring lambs would look like Brillo.

"Brillo didn't do anything!" Flo declared. She kept a tight grip around Brillo's neck.

J.D. had a less ambitious hold around Brillo's middle. "Not yet."

The farmer did a Moses act, parting the ewes and giving Brillo plenty of clearance. However, one particularly cute ewe was more than ready to respond to Brillo's advances. The ewe began running around them and avoiding the farmer's best attempts to have her move with the other sheep.

While the ewe ran her circles, Brillo dragged Flo and J.D. after him.

The farmer was shouting, Jetsam was laughing, and Flo and J.D. shared curses.

"J.D., why don't we just buy the ewe?"

Standing tall, J.D. spoke with the voice of authority. "If we give in once, what happens when Brillo meets another ewe he wants?"

"Let's handle one crisis at a time," Flo panted. "We can afford a ewe. Besides, look at her. She'd be a good addition for the breeding program."

Brillo baaed in agreement.

Flotsam, whether drunk or sober, understood the fine art of

negotiation and immediately got into the spirit of bargaining. The farmer haggled with equal enthusiasm.

The young girl walked over to see what was happening. After a few words from the farmer, she burst into tears.

"What's wrong now?" Flo asked.

Jetsam explained that the particular ewe happened to be the girl's favorite. She didn't want her father to sell it. She said that he should buy Brillo, but her father didn't want to.

Between the sheep baaing and the girl crying, Flo felt a headache stirring. But she persevered, and leaving Brillo in J.D.'s perhaps capable arms, Flo walked to the girl. "What's your name, sweetheart?"

Jetsam rapidly translated everything Flo said.

"Maria."

"Listen, Maria, you don't want money for your ewe, do you?"

She shook her head no.

"But what if you had something wonderful?"

Jetsam told her that Maria wanted to know what could be more wonderful than her ewe.

"Tell Maria to wait a few minutes." Flo got into the wagon and began selecting objects: a pair of scissors, strong thread, and the red tarp.

"You're not cutting our tarp!" J.D. said indignantly.

Flo cut a rectangle from the plastic tarp. "You never liked it." While the haggling continued, Flo worked wonders with needle and thread. "It isn't easy sewing plastic. You have to be careful or the plastic will crack and tear."

Fifteen minutes later, she was done, walked over to Maria, and held up a red plastic cape with a hood. "This is for you, sweetheart. It will keep you dry in the rain." She put the cape around the girl, who began to smile and talk rapidly.

"Maria is excited," Jetsam said.

Flo grinned. "I could have guessed that."

The farmer and Flotsam came to terms on the ewe's cost. Although Maria shed a few more tears over the loss of her ewe, she didn't make any more verbal objections. Maria and the farmer began moving their flock. The girl's step seemed lighter with her new cape.

"That wasn't so bad, J.D. And we've a good-looking ewe for our flock. What should we call her?"

"Pad?" J.D. suggested.

"Don't be foolish. That's a boy's name. I'll call her Pat. Or maybe Patty? Should we tether both of them to the wagon or let them ride?"

J.D. smirked. "I think they'll both want to ride afterward."

Flo saw what J.D. meant. "Honestly, Brillo, don't you have any self-restraint? Couldn't you have waited until we reached the privacy of a stable?"

Brillo baaed very contentedly.

The road to Utrecht was a traffic disaster. Carts, wagons, and what have you carrying fruit, wood, grain, and every type of dry good imaginable had ground to a standstill along the soft verge. Marching from the city, Spanish troops and cavalry dominated the road, and few people dared challenge the soldiers' right of way. Civilian opportunity arose between soldier formations, when everyone would go onto the firm grade and try to make some progress before the next group of soldiers appeared. Anyone too slow paid a high price: Earlier they had passed a smashed cart and its unhappy driver who didn't leave the road fast enough.

Perched on the driver's seat, J.D. idly held the reins. He snarled when a cart attempted to ride over the meadow next to them as a shortcut. But the cart didn't get far at all. It sank deep into mud hidden by the tall grass.

"And it serves you right!" he yelled. "Damned cheaters."

"What's that, J.D.?" Flo was busy giving Flotsam and Jetsam knitting lessons. It wasn't so much that they enjoyed knitting, but it was more comfortable sitting in the wagon than on the driver's seat. Whatever their interest in knitting, Flo was pleased with the progress that her students were making.

J.D. asked, "Do you think the Spanish are leaving the Netherlands?"

"Perhaps they intend to subjugate some other country?"

"They're subjugating us," he grumbled. "I hate sitting still."

"Do you want to try knitting? I'm sure Flotsam or Jetsam will let you have a turn."

"I hate knitting."

"Don't be gloomy. The traffic will clear. It always does. We should be in Utrecht by tomorrow. Then it's only a hop, skip, and jump to Amsterdam."

"Hop, skip, and jump?" J.D. grimaced. "And it's only mid-October. Some vacation."

"You shouldn't have taught them how to play poker. If you didn't owe them how many thousands of God knows what currency, you would be looking forward to a soft bed, a real bath, decent food, and warm water."

"Why are you so cheerful? Aren't you the same Flo who threatened Brillo yesterday with death and damnation? Something about sending him to a desert without a blade of grass for a thousand miles?"

"That was yesterday. Today I've made a decision."

"You mean like inventing an automobile for our next 'honeymoon'? Or putting in a train line?"

Flo stood up and put her arm around J.D.'s shoulders. "I mean a real decision, J.D. I'm going to do it!"

"Do what?"

"I'm taking my clothes off for Rubens. I've been debating that with myself every day since we set out from Grantville. Should I or shouldn't I? Don't interrupt! I want to say this straight. You tell me it's okay. Our daughters tell me they're aghast. So which way do I go? Well, what the hell. It's only skin, and it's not like I'm doing a bump and grind on the stage. It's art, and am I ready! As long as someone offers me a real bath, off they come!"

"All your clothes?"

"You got it, mister, every last scrap."

J.D. twisted around to give her a hug. As he twisted, he accidentally pulled on the reins and the horses reared, shifting the wagon into the road proper.

As fate would have it, an extravagant carriage passing in the opposite direction locked wheel to axle with them, tangling the two vehicles and jolting all the occupants. Flotsam and the coach driver began working to separate the two vehicles, and J.D. gladly gave the reins to Jetsam.

An official-looking head poked out the carriage window and began yelling alternately in Dutch and Spanish.

J.D. was in no mood to negotiate and cursed back at the official.

The personage managed to squeeze a fat arm out the window. The stranger shook his fist, and J.D. gave him the finger.

"I hope he understands that," J.D. muttered.

"No problem, J.D. Looks to me like you got your point across."

The door to the near side of the carriage was blocked by the wagon, and the carriage bobbed up and down while the person inside shifted his position. The far door was kicked open just as a cavalryman was passing, and the door swung out right in front of the horse. The horse performed various pyrotechnics and saved itself, but the rider was tossed head over heels.

After getting to his feet, the cavalryman threatened the fat personage, and the fat personage screamed at the cavalryman. The cavalryman pulled his saber halfway out of its scabbard, and the official puffed and postured while his face turned bright red.

"You see," J.D. said. "It's all sorting itself out."

As soon as the two vehicles were separated, Flo asked, "Maybe we should drive on?"

"Sounds good to me, but exactly how are we going to move?"

A crowd of curious onlookers had surrounded them.

"Rubberneckers," Flo moaned, "and in the seventeenth century."

"Makes you feel right at home, doesn't it?"

A Spanish officer rode up and dismounted. He silenced the angry official and cavalry trooper and then listened to each in turn.

"He'd make a pretty good traffic cop," J.D. said.

"I preferred it more when they were yelling at each other."

Flo's instincts proved correct. The fat official walked into plain sight and pointed at J.D. Then the cavalryman also came over and pointed.

"That's not fair," J.D. complained. "It wasn't my fault that the guy rode into the door. Fatty should have looked in both directions before opening it."

The Spanish captain approached them. Flo thought the captain's glare wasn't too cold. She didn't expect to be drawn and quartered for an hour at least.

In answer to the captain's questions, J.D. said, "Sorry, I don't speak Spanish. Or Dutch. I'm an American."

"Ah, American." The captain smiled, and Flo's heart fell to the subbasement. Somehow she knew that the captain was among the few soldiers who had survived the American attack on the castle Wartburg in 1632, during which the Spanish troops were not only killed by lead and fire but forced to listen to *Wozzeck*. To the present day, debate raged among the survivors about which was worse: to be honorably killed in battle or to suffer the torments of Berg's opera.

The captain continued to smile. "You will follow me." He pointed south. Away from Utrecht. Away from Amsterdam.

"I'm an American citizen," J.D. said.

"And you Americans are great believers in law. So. You have committed serious crimes against His Excellency. You have caused much damage. All this must be sorted out. Fines must be assessed, damages awarded." The captain nodded his head thoughtfully. "Yes, all this must be thoroughly looked into. You will be made quite comfortable, for you will be with us a considerable time."

Flotsam and Jetsam, never too cheerful in the first place, became less than splinters on the seas of life. J.D. was speechless. Flo broke.

"Two months! We've been on the road for two months to go to Rubens! We were almost there. Almost. Just a few days more and now this. I don't believe it. I honest to God don't believe it. Why in all the world did I ever listen to Justus Corneliszoon van Liede? I must have been freakin' out of my mind. There are dozens of painters. Hundreds of printers. Why Rubens? Why Justus Corneliszoon?"

It was the captain's turn to become pale. "You are acquainted with Justus Corneliszoon van Liede?"

If Flo's traits were to be assessed, among those highest ranked would be paperwork and organization. It only took her fifteen seconds to find Justus' letter and put it in the captain's hands.

After reading it, the captain handed the letter back to Flo and bowed. He said very quietly, "Excuse me one moment." He stalked over to the cavalryman, who had been grinning with delight.

"You!" the captain yelled to him. "Why are you standing here? Where is your regiment? Get on your horse, and if you fall off it again and do not break your neck, I will personally break it for you." The captain whirled on the fat dignitary. "Pig! Why were you driving on the road? Don't you see the soldiers? What gives you the right to be among them? Do you have a uniform? A rank? There's nothing soldier about you."

The official protested and waved his arms and pointed at J.D.

The captain drew his sword. "I envy you, for you have a simple choice. Move or die. Which do you prefer?"

Fat does not imply slow. Personage and carriage were away before the captain could return to Flo and J.D., whose mouths had collectively dropped open.

The captain bowed again to them. "I sincerely apologize for any mistakes."

"You know Justus?" Flo asked.

The captain grinned and suddenly looked years younger. "Of course I know him! He asked me to watch for you. That was maybe three weeks ago. It was odd meeting him. At first I wanted to punch his teeth in, because he was that type of fop. But before I could even draw my sword, he cut my doublet to shreds. Imagine that! Well, there's only one thing to do with such a swordsman. We promised each other eternal friendship, and I agreed to help you the best I can. Now, how may I assist you?"

Flo looked at J.D., and J.D. looked at Flo. They were somewhat embarrassed to ask, since they weren't accustomed to favors that put them ahead of everyone else, but the captain understood those glances.

"Attend! You will bring your wagon on the road and proceed after me. I will arrange an escort to guide you to Utrecht." He glared at the onlookers, who immediately dispersed. He was that type of captain.

And they were on their way, and Flo sang, "Amsterdam, here we come."

Flo slammed the door, and J.D. jumped a couple of feet skyward.

"Lord, woman! Don't I have enough gray hairs?" He waved the binoculars he was holding in front of her. "I nearly put an eye out. That would be a fine addition to this 'vacation.' You know, standing on a roof is perhaps the best way to see Amsterdam. Through binoculars. The tours are okay, but the canals stink. They're more like open sewers than waterways. I keep hoping to spot the Gretchen statue. Wasn't there talk of putting one up where she was on top of a building somewhere and waving a flag? We should be able to see it from here."

They were staying in Paulus Pontius' house, which was next to Rubens' studio. Between the two buildings was a large courtyard and stable.

J.D. noticed the expression on Flo's face. It was a cross between the Mother of Demons and Lucrezia Borgia, only not as pleasant. He asked innocently, "Didn't the first sitting for Rubens go okay? Did you have a place to change? Was the studio warm enough? Did Brillo do anything unmentionable?"

Flo grabbed J.D. by his shirt and shouted, "When can we leave?"

"Well..." J.D. was taken aback. He had never seen Flo so angry. "We'd have to send messages to Flotsam and Jetsam. They weren't expecting to be ready for another week. We need fresh provisions. What happened? What did Rubens say?"

"It's not my portrait!"

"Excuse me?"

"It's not my portrait. It's Brillo's. I'm not Mrs. December. It's Mr. December. I was only invited because they didn't think anyone else could manage Brillo. He has a reputation, you know. He's a one-ram revolutionary. What am I? Huh? I'm a frumpy housewife. That's all." She sniffed.

J.D. hugged her. "Those miserable bastards. I'm going to have a few words with this Rubens. I don't care who he is. No one can treat my wife like that. And after two months on the road to get here? They have their nerve."

Flo returned the hug with interest. "No, not a word to anyone. It's too humiliating. I just want to go home."

"We'll get started immediately."

She shook her head no. "I have to see this through. Brillo will be painted and get a month on the calendar. That's something. Then we'll have nothing to do with these people again."

"At least we'll have a fine portrait of your unfavorite ram."

"Not even that!" Flo wailed. "Someone already bought it."

"What? Has Richelieu been up to his old tricks? Sneaking and conniving among everyone?"

"No, it's some collector in Italy. I've never heard of him."

"Well, I'll be damned. I wonder how whoever heard of Brillo?"

Flo smiled glumly. "We have the most famous ram in the world."

Listening by the half-opened door was Paulus Pontius, Rubens' favorite printmaker. Deciding not to join his guests, he quietly shut the door and left.

A week later, Flo and J.D. were busily packing for their return journey when someone knocked on the open door.

Flo straightened up and smiled. "What a pleasure to see you!"

"A pleasure to see you, dear lady Flo." Justus Corneliszoon bowed deeply. "Flotsam and Jetsam have loaded most of the wagon, and I have a present for you." He offered her a small cloth bag.

"Can I believe that aroma? Can I?" Flo opened it. "It is! It really is! Coffee! It's been weeks since I've had any. Let me heat a pot of water, and we'll have some."

"Not to bother, dear lady Flo. I left some beans with the kitchen wench, and she's grinding them to make a fresh pot for us even as we speak. Shall I meet you in the dining room downstairs in half an hour? We can have a farewell chat."

Flo hugged Justus. "That's a date!"

He laughed. "Then I shall see you shortly." Justus left the room.

"Thanks for noticing me," J.D. said. "I don't understand you at all, Flo. You didn't get your portrait painted, we didn't get Brillo's portrait, and you're all smiles. That is, you're all smiles after Corny reappeared. Do you have anything to confess?"

She was all innocence. "Who? Me? No, I'm only happy that the calendars came out so well. Who'd think that Paulus could turn out plates for printing so fast?"

"You sure were happy to see Corny."

"Well, at first I thought that he ran out on us. But, who'd think he'd spend so much time on the road marking a route for us, making friends, and eliminating brigands. It's like having Ivanhoe on our side."

"Can't you think of a Dutch hero?"

Walking over to a tall and narrow wooden box, Flo tapped it significantly. "Rolled up inside is a wonderful drawing by Rubens of Brillo. It's almost as good as a painting, and maybe even better. I think I prefer his drawings to his paintings."

What Flo didn't mention to J.D. was that rolled within the Brillo drawing was a second one, in red chalk and white washes, of Flo reclining on a sofa. In the nude. Flo thought it was very flattering, but Rubens had a flattering manner in general. Perhaps she would give it to J.D. for his birthday. Perhaps. But it wouldn't leave their bedroom back home. Some things were too private.

"I'm really looking forward to being home. You know what I think, J.D.? I think we're going to have a fine trip back to Grantville."

J.D. looked out the window. "Maybe."

It had started to snow.

Nothing's Ever Simple

Virginia DeMarce

Grantville, December 1633

"That's probably about the best we can do." Roberta Sutter looked at the stacks of paper on the table in front of her with considerable dissatisfaction.

"We've interviewed everyone in town," Sandra Prickett said. "We've made them look for family Bibles and scrapbooks and newspaper clippings and birth certificates and applications for delayed birth certificates and applications for Social Security cards and... Anyway, quite a few people got annoyed and said things, like, 'Don't you realize there's a war on?'"

"We've gotten a lot that we didn't have before," Mary Jo Blackwell added her bit to the Genealogy Club council meeting. Mary Jo was always spoiling someone else's desire to have a good fight. She was a nuisance that way, sometimes.

Marian Butcher nodded. "Some surprises, too, like how Rose Howell's descendants knew that some of Cyrene's great-grandkids lived here in town and that they were related, but Cyrene's had forgotten all about it."

Miriam Miller looked at Jenny Maddox. "I guess the point is—does the Bureau of Vital Statistics want us to stop the blitz? Have we done enough for the records you need?"

"More than enough, probably. We're going to put copies of

everything in the public library. Marietta's fine with that. People can come look up their family trees if they're interested. Down-timers as well as up-timers."

Roberta frowned again. "The down-time stuff is still mainly oral history. It's not properly documented. When the wars stop, maybe we can write to the parishes where people told us they were born and married and get copies of their baptisms and weddings for our files."

"With your approach to genealogy, there will never be an end to it."

Roberta looked at Jenny, honestly surprised. "Of course not. Everyone who's ever been born has two parents, and lots of them have aunts and uncles, brothers and sisters, nieces and nephews. And cousins. Even Jesus had cousins. The historian Josephus wrote that Roman officials interviewed them, about thirty years after the crucifixion. Oral history *is* an important part of the process, even though it isn't sufficient in itself." Her voice was starting to perk up again.

Sandra Prickett sighed.

February 1634

"I hate to say it, Melvin, but I think they're losing their enthusiasm."

Melvin Sutter chewed his sausage. Personally, he had sort of hoped, after they adopted a couple of children after the Ring of Fire and Roberta got a full-time job, that she would lose some of hers. Not that he had anything against family trees. But their house didn't have just plain family trees. It even had family trees that Roberta had cross-stitched, framed, and put up on the walls. There was one hanging right over his head, here in the breakfast nook.

"I started to explain how we could supplement the oral history we collected for the new immigrants. I need documentation for our own children. I've already written to Gotha for Albrecht and Margaretha and to Kitzingen for Martin. Now if I could just find someone who remembers exactly where Verena was baptized, since she doesn't seem to be related to any other of the Elsisheimers who have immigrated to Grantville—not that I'm sure they're telling me the truth. They're a bit evasive, especially Magdalena Albert. She's Kunz Polheimer's wife—her first husband was an Elsisheimer, though she didn't have any children by him. If it's because Verena was born out of wedlock and her mother Maria was actually a relative somehow, then . . ."

Melvin, a veteran of such speculations, tuned it all out and continued chewing.

Until he heard the dire words, ". . . and I'm not going to put it off any longer. I'm not going to wait until it's too late."

"Uh. Put what off?"

"Melvin, you haven't been listening."

He didn't even try to defend himself.

"I know we don't have any natural children, but Marilyn has Matt and it's likely he'll marry and have children one of these days. So I really need to finish the Hooper side of the family. Before the Ring of Fire, I took it as far as the church records from Schwarzach that had been microfilmed by the Mormons would let me, but they only started in 1612. If I go to Schwarzach now, before it's too late, I can interview living ancestors. I'm sure with what they remember, I can add a couple more generations to the family tree. Huber, it was, in Germany, before the Germanna immigrants Americanized the spelling. I hope that my ancestor Georg Huber is still the mayor of Schwarzach."

"I hate to say this, but we've got four adopted children now. Their mother can't just go haring off someplace to do genealogy."

"They're not babies. Albrecht's sixteen; Martin's fifteen. Margaretha's eleven. Even Verena's five, not a baby anymore. Marilyn will help you. I'm sure she will, especially now that Matt's off in Magdeburg. It's her family tree, too, after all. You can manage on your own this coming summer."

"Marilyn just got married again last fall. Baxter Harris may not want for her to be babysitting a batch of kids all next summer."

"Since she married Baxter, she's Trissie's stepmother, and Trissie's the perfect age to babysit Verena and Margaretha, plus she's in the same class at school with Albrecht." Roberta patted Melvin's cheek. "Don't worry. It will all work out fine."

Melvin shook his head. "It won't be that simple. Things never are."

July 1634

Roberta sat quietly.

Roberta quiet was Roberta dangerous.

"Just where is this Schwarzach place, anyway? Why don't you write them?"

"After the Benedictine imperial abbey there was secularized in 1803, it became part of the Grand Duchy of Baden. That was the German state of Baden-Wuerttemberg in our day. I did write to the mayor, last year. And to the Catholic church, but I haven't gotten an answer. So I need to go."

"By my count, there's close to a hundred seventy-five years of politics between now and 1803. Where is it now?"

"Um. In Swabia."

"Horn has a Swedish army in Swabia."

Roberta tilted her head. "Not in the part of Swabia where Schwarzach is."

"Just what part of Swabia is Schwarzach in?"

"It's on the Rhine. And now I have a contact there, so..."

"You have a contact there? I thought you said that they hadn't written back."

"Well, Mayor Huber hasn't written back."

"And..."

"Uh, you remember that Duke Bernhard of Saxe-Weimar offered Kamala Horton a job? And she took it and shook the dust of Grantville off her feet, so to speak? She and the kids left right after school was out in May."

"Yeah..."

"Well, Duke Bernhard has his military headquarters at Schwarzach. That's where Kamala and her kids are. She's going to Besançon this fall, but there's stuff they want her to do in Schwarzach first. They've been given quarters right in the abbey buildings because she's working on military sanitation first. I can stay with her while I'm doing the research, which will save a lot of money in hotel costs..."

"Roberta!" This time Melvin practically shrieked. "You'll be walking right into a war zone."

"But not through a war zone. I can go straight over to Frankfurt and then take a boat down the Main and up the Rhine."

"Roberta! It's fucking dangerous!"

She looked at him, honestly bewildered. "Well, that's sort of the point." She patted his cheek again. "If the war is moving that way, I need to get in and copy the records for our family tree now, before things like tax records get destroyed or someone who remembers important information gets killed or dies. Think how many courthouses got burned during the Civil War up-time. It was horrible—just horrible."

"It's not common to have such a long family tree that's all made up of perfectly ordinary people," Roberta said. "There's not a famous person on it. Just farmers and innkeepers and stonemasons and carpenters. People like that. And their wives. I have all the maiden names back to the Georg Huber who is alive now, in this year 1634. Matt's the thirteenth generation. If I can just talk to this Georg Huber—a lot of the records spell his given name as 'Jerg'—then I'm sure I can add his mother's maiden name and he almost certainly knows the names of his grandparents. All four of them. His father was named 'Jerg' too. I've only been able to determine from the microfilmed church records that the older Jerg died some time between 1629 and 1641. If I'm really lucky and that ancestor is still alive, then he should remember the names of *his* grandparents, too. That would give us fifteen generations to my nephew Matt. At worst, I'll be able to find out Jerg, Sr.'s date of death and enter it on the charts."

Ed Piazza wished that he dared reach up and massage his temples. Roberta Sutter's family tree—to be more precise, Mrs. Sutter's extended disquisition on the topic of her family tree—was giving him a headache. Not only the abstract "problems for the consular service" headache that would result from her intention to go kiting off into Bernhard of Saxe-Weimar's little personal sandbox, but a very real one, here and now, in the front of his brain. This was worse than Count Ludwig Guenther's librarian in full spate on the topic of relationships among the ruling families of the various states and substates of the USE.

"Of course, it's not entirely a male-line pedigree. It was male-line up to my sister Marilyn, but then she married Harry Tisdel, so Matt's a Tisdel. Of course, she'd divorced that bum even before the Ring of Fire and Matt didn't see much of his father. Maybe he'd be willing to change his name to Hooper and carry on the family name." Roberta smiled brightly. "I'll write him in Magdeburg and ask. He's up there training to be a Marine since he graduated from high school this spring. There shouldn't be any legal problems."

Ed pulled his shoulder blades together as inconspicuously as possible, trying to relieve the tension in his neck. Roberta Sutter had been in his office for an hour. Unfortunately, he hadn't primed his secretary to interrupt with an urgent appointment. Maybe the kid liked being a Tisdel. Who knew?

A knock on the door. A wonderful, blessed, knock on the door. It opened. Jamie Lee Swisher's head poked through. "Mr. Piazza, guess what? Mr. Ferrara is here. I just knew that you'd want to see him."

"Yes. Thank you, Jamie. Get him a cup of coffee, will you? I'll finish up here." He prepared for some difficulty in disposing of his current visitor, but Roberta Sutter was already picking up her purse.

Unfortunately, as she went out the door, her parting words were, "I just knew that you would understand how important the project is. I'm meeting Melvin and Henry Dreeson for lunch at Cora's. I'll tell them that you don't have any objections at all."

He did. He could think of a dozen perfectly reasonable objections. He just hadn't been able to get in a word edgewise, which was—unusual for him.

If she had stayed a little longer, he would have told her no. Now, unless he actually chased her down the corridor, she would be out in public announcing that he had given permission to go to Schwarzach before he could do anything about it. That kind of announcement was hard to retract without ending up with egg on your face.

He looked at Mrs. Sutter's departing rear and reminded himself to be careful, because sometimes you get what you wish for. In this case, an interruption. One more premature than timely.

Anyway, why did Mrs. Sutter think that Matt Tisdel needed to carry on the Hooper surname line if the ancestor was alive right now? Presumably carrying the line on himself. Why couldn't anything ever be simple?

At least, Greg was carrying *two* cups of coffee.

Ed smiled. "Greg," he asked, "do you happen to be interested in genealogy?"

Another hour later, well into the permutations of the Ferrara family tree, which involved the Trapanese family and the second marriage of Greg's mother to one of the Zeppi boys, Ed made a note to himself in regard to an addition to his personal list of "Questions a Sensible Person Never Asks."

August 1634
Schwarzach on the Rhine

Abbot Georgius of the Abbey of Saints Peter and Paul at Schwarzach on the Rhine looked at the papers on his pedestal desk. Then he reached out and felt them again. Maybe for the tenth time since the up-time woman arrived. Perhaps for the twentieth time. Possibly for the hundredth time. So slick, so smooth. He had received descriptions of up-time paper from the librarians of the great *Stift* at Fulda, but this was the first time he had seen it for himself. Much less touched it.

Schwarzach was a Benedictine abbey, an imperial abbey, but not an important one like Fulda. One small town and a few villages, occupying seven square miles. Seven square miles—not seven miles square. Smaller now than it had been in the middle ages—the tribulations of the past couple of centuries had forced the abbey to sell some of its holdings to the margraves of Baden. A few thousand subjects. A ferry across the Rhine at Greffern—the tolls from that, far more than the modest taxes and dues paid in by the village farmers, kept the abbey going in a moderate sort of way. A very moderate sort of way, as evidenced by the fact that there was not a single nobleman among the monks and had not been for generations. Schwarzach did not have sinecures that would support the younger son of an influential family in the style to which he wished to remain accustomed. The monks of Schwarzach did not have to make any significant effort to fulfill their vows of poverty. They doubled as the parish priests for the villages. Sometimes, in difficult circumstances when no fellow villager would serve, they also doubled as godfathers for the children of the abbey's parishioners.

Or for children who did not belong to the abbey. His mind wandered back, briefly, to the *annus terribilis* of 1622, when the imperial troops had been quartered on the abbey. Sometimes he wondered what had happened to those soldiers and the women to whom the abbey's monks had married them that winter. What was the fate of the children who had been born in a dozen different camps and finally baptized here, on the banks of the Rhine, sometimes three or four years later?

He picked up a piece of the wondrous, slick, smooth paper.

"Photocopies" the up-time woman called them. "Photocopies" that she had made by a machine from something called "microfilm."

He turned to the other pedestal desk, the one he had borrowed from Father Gallus' cell. On it lay the church registers for Schwarzach and its villages, meticulously maintained—or as meticulously as possible, given the exigencies of the war—in accord with the prescriptions of the Council of Trent. He picked up one of the pieces of paper, turned a few pages of the register, and compared.

It was true. Exactly and precisely true, just as Father Gallus had said. This woman had brought, from the far future, copies of pages from their own church registers. Black, a bright white, and gray, rather than the gentle cream color of the paper in the church books. On the copy from the future, one could see little tears at the edge of some of the pages, broken corners, an occasional stain that didn't yet exist on the originals. But the abbey's own registers, without a doubt.

Father Gallus' own handwriting, plain and straightforward, just like Father Gallus himself. Gallus was a solid man. Plain spoken. Abbot Georgius' right hand in these difficult times.

Here was a page with Father Bonifacius' delicate script. It always surprised correspondents when they first met Bonifacius in person. He was a big man—bigger even than Gallus—who looked like he would destroy anything in his path, but somehow he walked without making a sound. Of all the monks, he was most successful at keeping the Great Silence. Abbot Georgius always chose him if there was detail work to be done.

The woman, Mrs. Sutter, had expected Father Christophorus to be much older. The style of his handwriting, she said, belonged to the middle of the previous century. But Christophorus, barely thirty, was the youngest of them all. Excited by new things, his writing was where he stepped back, at least in form. Not to mention, of course, that his village schoolmaster had been nearly eighty years old. Perhaps Christophorus simply shaped his letters the way he had learned them as a child.

Father Paulus wrote this page. His script, as usual, was clear, but a little cramped. Paulus was a fussy little man, insistent on getting the details right, sometimes at the expense of the big picture. But he was also the man who, wondering about the Latin baptismal record that listed a child's mother as "Regina" when no one in the village called her that, had gone back, year by year, realized that the priest from Lorraine who thought that he was hearing "Königin" and translated it into the Latin "Regina" was misunderstanding "Kunigunde," and had given the young mother her proper name back in the registers. Abbot Georgius smiled briefly at the thought of a village woman named "Queenie."

Father Augustinus, large and florid, but without flourishes. An excitable fellow. Sometimes loud and with just the touch of a fanatic about him. Very sure of his beliefs, but kind for all of that. He had spearheaded that 1622 campaign to regularize the military marriages and legitimate the children, completely ignoring demands that he first seek permission from the regimental commanders.

Father Anselmus. His handwriting was difficult, but consistent. The up-time woman had remarked that she had found it hard to decipher originally, but once she had become used to it, had no further problems. Anselmus was also difficult, in a way. *He struggles with his faith*, the abbot thought. Anselmus *wants* to believe as a little child, but he can't help questioning.

Father Beda's small, angular, uncomplicated script—as close to a printed page as handwriting would ever come. *A cold man*, Abbot Georgius thought, *though he tries to be a good one.*

Father Geroldus. He always had Father Beda enter clean copies of his scribbled notes, kept on random scraps as he went from village to village, into the permanent register. Geroldus was a natural persuader and organizer. The scrawl of his signature indicated that everyone else should be grateful that he had persuaded Father Beda to write out his documents.

Father Gabriel. Abbot George smiled again at the up-time woman's description. What had she said? "Presuming that he believes in purgatory, I hope he spends a couple of centuries there, writing on the blackboard, getting his cursive improved under a stern taskmaster who will also break him of that obnoxious habit of throwing in non-standard abbreviations at random." It was true. Father Gabriel was creative and sometimes half out of control.

His thoughts came too fast for him to keep track of. The other up-time woman, Duke Bernhard of Saxe-Weimar's "nurse," called Gabriel "an absent-minded professor type."

Father Antonius, whose writing was even worse than Gabriel's. The up-time woman had said, "I couldn't even decipher his surname. If anyone ever wants to keep a secret, just have this guy write it down; flocks of cryptographers will perish in despair." Georgius had thought briefly that he might be able to get some money from Duke Bernhard by loaning him a short little red-headed monk with a pot belly and a goatee. Then Frau Sutter had destroyed this hope by adding, "Of course, the recipient won't be able to make heads or tails of it, either. If possible, I would like to be permitted to work with him, and have him read his entries to me out loud."

And Father Gregorius, the paper consumer. One would think his entries had been written by a lady-in-waiting at the court of Ferdinand II, with the wide margins, the wide spacing between the lines, and all the flourishes on the capital letters. Still, the page was legible, and that was what mattered. Gregorius willingly assumed the tedious responsibilities associated with vestment repair, the mending of liturgical books, the cleaning of stained glass, the thousand minute and unending tasks associated with keeping a centuries-old church building intended for a far larger congregation usable and in a condition that honored God. In return, Abbot Georgius did not begrudge him twice as much paper as anyone else used.

And that was the venerable Benedictine abbey of Schwarzach *anno domini* 1634. An abbot and eleven monks.

Until Bernhard of Saxe-Weimar's *Kloster* arrived and took up quarters in their cloister.

Whatever else might be said about Bernhard of Saxe-Weimar and his advisors, they were scarcely monks. Georgius was grateful that they spent much of their time out campaigning or at the duke's new capital in the Franche Comté. Although, to give them credit, they appeared to be reasonably chaste. They had not defiled the abbey's walls with loose women.

The duke also insisted that his soldiers attend church services, albeit heretical Lutheran ones. His Protestant chaplains made an effort to keep a rein on the blasphemies falling from the soldiers' mouths, although they did little about other obscenities and profanities. Still, Bernhard's men refrained from taking the name of the Lord in vain. At least when the officers and chaplains were present.

Abbot Georgius picked up the sheet of paper again, sliding his thumb over its slick surface.

He was an old man. He had been in office since 1597. Every year became a little more difficult. He, too, like Father Anselmus, longed for the simple faith of a child. But it seemed as if nothing was ever simple. Duke Bernhard had recently gone south to join the troops he had called into the Breisgau. He would have to notify the duke of the woman's arrival. The duke would undoubtedly want to know that the up-time "nurse" had another up-time woman staying with her. One of Jerg Huber's sons-in-law could take a message down to Lörrach. They were reliable men, and close-mouthed. Simon Jerger, Sibilla Huberin's husband—he would do. Simon could take Susanna Huberin's son, young Regenold, with him. The boy was fourteen, and didn't get along very well with his stepfather. He was restless. Eva Reinlin had been complaining about his behavior, just the other day. The errand would do him good.

Lawrence Crawford hated this job. He was twenty-three years old and had been a soldier since he was fifteen. From the age of fifteen, he had fought in the armies of Christian IV of Denmark and Gustavus Adolphus of Sweden. He had fought in the name of young Karl Ludwig, the Elector Palatine, after the death of the Winter King, who was at least properly Calvinist. He had joined Duke Bernhard to fight, even though he, like the Dane and the Swede, was only a Lutheran, which was a poor substitute for the truth of God, if you asked him. Charles I and Laud were very close to being papists, and the Lutherans weren't much better.

Was he fighting? No. Instead, he had been assigned to a *monastery* to act as translator for the up-time "nurse." The woman's German was very poor. She said in excuse that she had spent the four years since the Ring of Fire mainly either at work in a nursing home, which seemed to be some kind of *Spital*, or attending her children's school events. In any case, it was still very poor and almost entirely limited to phrases such as, "When did her symptoms start getting worse?" and "Is his temperature coming down?"

The woman's English wasn't much better. At least not from the perspective of a man who had been born in Jordanhill in Glasgow. In Scotland. He and Mistress Horton were divided by a common tongue. Not to mention by the fact that she belonged to some kind of sectarian church. Crawford did not hold with toleration of Independents and other religious radicals. Disciples of Christ—that was what she called her body of dissenters.

And now she had brought another up-time woman to Schwarzach. Whom he was to escort to meet the mayor.

Mistress Sutter's German was better, at least.

Jerg Huber was nearly sixty-five years old. An old man. Almost as old as Abbot Georgius. He had been mayor of Schwarzach since 1615, and on the town council long before that. The two of them had worked together for half their lives.

It was one thing for a man to have children. He had seven children who had survived. Five had already married and established families of their own. He had nearly two dozen grandchildren already—a blessing from God in these days of war and disease, these latter times of tribulation.

Though he could wish that Hans and young Jerg would get married. Except for Michael's two, all of his grandchildren came through the girls. He had only one grandson named Huber, so far—Michael's four-year-old Jerg.

They were good, steady sons, though: hard-working and civic-minded, all a reasonable man could ask for. Barring famine and plague, one of them would probably, some day, become mayor of Schwarzach in his stead. Presuming Hans and Jerg got married, that is.

But.

He could not see that it was a divine blessing to have someone suddenly appear in the world who claimed to be his descendant thirteen times removed.

Not all miracles were necessarily blessings. Undoubtedly the fig tree cursed by Our Lord Jesus Christ had come to that conclusion somewhere in the process of being the object of a miraculous action. So he had ignored the letter from this woman, Frau Sutter, when it arrived the previous winter.

Now she was in Schwarzach.

It was hard to avoid a miracle when God wanted you to

undergo it. Consider the fate of Jonah. Jerg Huber paused during his morning's work and considered the efforts of Jonah to avoid destiny. The maneuvers of Joseph. The evasions of Elijah.

He had to answer the message from Herr Crawford. He sent his granddaughter up to the abbey to say that he agreed to meet with the up-time woman.

If a miracle wanted you, it would get you.

Although why God thought she really needed to learn his grandfather's name was well beyond his comprehension.

Anyway, it had been Huber. Of course. What had she expected?

Father Anselmus came with Frau Sutter, most times. Abbot Georgius thought that his faith could benefit from close contact with a modern miracle.

Officially, Abbot Georgius had assigned him to make copies of all the information that Jerg was remembering about earlier times in Schwarzach and the people who had lived there. He said that he would place it in the monastery's archives, next to the church registers. Perhaps, some day, if he had time, he could turn it into a chronicle.

Jerg Huber took exception to Frau Sutter's assertion that his family tree consisted of "perfectly ordinary people." He was, after all, a citizen of Schwarzach. The mayor of Schwarzach. Not some insignificant day laborer or vagrant.

"Well, I meant . . ." She sputtered a little. "Not nobles or anything."

Their conversations continued. One day, the topic was Jerg's maternal great-grandfather's sister's stepdaughter. Whom he had never met. That was the day that Father Anselmus mentioned that the abbey had tax and lease records much older than the church books. Mrs. Sutter gave him a blinding smile.

Jerg Huber gave him a blinding smile, too. Even if Father Anselmus didn't, quite, believe in miracles, he had performed one, at least in Jerg's opinion. Since then, the up-timer hadn't pestered him anymore, but rather had buried herself in the muniment room at the monastery, assisted by Father Paulus. From first daylight to the last dim remnants of dusk, according to Herr Crawford, the day he left Schwarzach to escort Mistress Horton to Besançon, she made copies of financial documents and put them in her files.

As Jerg Huber lighted a votive candle in the great church at the Abbey of Saints Peter and Paul, he gave thanks that the world still contained small miracles as well as large ones. Miracles such as the diversion of Frau Sutter to the abbey's archives.

Moreover, he had received, through this woman, the knowledge that his fatherly patience would be rewarded. Eventually, Hans and Jerg would marry—marry well, both of them—and father families. There would be only daughters for Hans, but four sons for Jerg.

If things remained the same in this world as they had unfolded in the one from which Grantville came, of course. A man could only hope.

September 1634

"Send her home," Bernhard of Saxe-Weimar said. Firmly. "By the time we wind things up here and *das Kloster* returns to Schwarzach to start planning next spring's actions, let her be gone. Absent. Removed. No longer present. While I admit that the likelihood that she is an intelligence agent seems to be..." His voice trailed off.

"Diminishingly small, on the basis of everything Crawford told us," Friedrich von Kanoffski contributed.

"Minute," Duke Bernhard admitted. "Minuscule. Nevertheless, we have Mistress Horton on her way to our civil headquarters, where she can do the most good now that she has provided directions for our new medical corps and well away from the location where we will be considering our... upcoming enterprises. Let the other one depart as well."

"You are assigning Colonel Raudegen to guard Frau Dreeson and Signorina Allegretti," Kanoffski suggested. "I will have the boat stop at Schwarzach. He is surely capable of removing Frau Sutter from the abbey and ensuring that she returns to Grantville."

"If anyone is. He can certainly try," Duke Bernhard rubbed his stomach. "But I remember all too well what it was like when I was a boy and my tutors started talking about the genealogy of the Wettins."

October 1634
Grantville

"Do you realize, Melvin?" Roberta asked. "The colonel would not even tell me his actual name. The one with which he was born. He claimed that he had used his military alias since he was old enough to run away from home and it was good enough for him."

"Ummmn," Melvin said.

"But I kept talking to him, and I got a lot of clues. I'm pretty sure I know what village he was born in, now, but I need a good map of Lower Austria. And his mother was called Barbel. I'm pretty sure that with those clues to go on, I could work out his family tree, with enough time and effort."

"Sounds like more trouble than it's worth, to me. Especially since Raudegen doesn't *want* you to research his family tree. Why don't you just keep working on our kids, now? There's a whole batch of stuff that came in while you were gone, from Kitzingen and places like that. I piled it all in your inbox. It doesn't sound to me that doing research on Raudegen's family would be easy."

"But it would be a challenge, Melvin. A *challenge*." Roberta waved both her hands. "Nothing worthwhile is ever simple. Nothing."

CONNECTIONS

Stories with a Common Ground

Editor's note: We play a lot in the *Gazette.* Periodically, someone comes up with an idea and other writers start riffing on it. What results is the literary equivalent of a jam session.

The Brillo stories which feature prominently in *1634: The Ram Rebellion* came about that way, and so did these stories. In this instance, the writers used software designed by the Kayuda Corporation to show and develop interconnections as the basis for developing story plots that intersected each other as much as possible.

Kayuda went out of business a while back—not our fault, I swear!—but the stories live on.

Supply and Demand

Rick Boatright

Tink tink tink . . . The little yellow screwdriver rang against the side of the Cora's mug as Father Nicholas Smithson sat silently in the rectory kitchen.

"Why so glum, Nick?"

Father Nicholas Smithson looked up from staring into his coffee mug to see his good friend walking in. "I was hearing confession, Gus."

"Well, it was your turn."

"I know, and I'm happy to provide the service. I still miss my parishioners in London, and this is a small way to be a part of the life of this community. But I'm afraid I may have to stop."

"Why?"

"Because it happened again today. Someone didn't want the sacrament; they had a job offer for Nicholas Smithson, expert on up-timers."

"Again? I am so sorry, Nick. It's so *sad* that people want to throw money at you. It's not like you were a Benedictine or something."

"They were demeaning the sacrament and the sanctuary of the church. Did not Christ himself overturn the money changers?"

"He did." Gus nodded, grinning.

"And when I do attempt to do research, I am pummeled with requests beyond what any man can do. It is not as though I am the only researcher in the library."

"Yes, Nick. But you are the only author of *How Not to Think Like a Redneck*. That may be the best-selling book in Europe."

"I know. But it's silly. Brother Johann is as good a researcher, and the others are just as good."

"Nick, they are good researchers, but you have found your place. You have a gift for putting the bits and pieces together into a whole that no one has yet quite matched. Then there is your reputation. I see only one way to control this. You must rely on the invisible hand."

"Gus, I've already doubled my prices over what everyone else charges!"

"Then double them again. Eventually, you will drive the crowds away. Then you can pick and choose the projects you want to work on."

"Double them again! I would be charging one hundred dollars an hour!"

"And if that's not enough, then you double them again. Eventually, the market will respond."

"Am I to be a prisoner of the Dark Science then?"

"Yes, Nick. A prisoner with an income which makes you able to do the things you want done. Oh, that more of us would have such a burden."

Nick stared into his coffee cup. "Let's go get a beer."

Gus smiled. "Your treat."

"Excuse me, Father Smithson?"

Nick looked up. The library table was covered with three-by-five cards, stacked in complex patterns like a tarot design, some with colorful ink staining the corners. There were pencils and strings linking the cards into an odd network. Nick set the card in his hand back onto his stack. "How can I help you?"

"My name is Johann Rademacher. I am with O'Keefe's Septic Tank Maintenance Company."

"Yes?" Father Nick looked at him questioningly. "How can I help you?" He gestured at the chair beside him.

Johann sat down. "We have been looking to open additional markets for porcelain. We have been working with potters and designing mostly sanitary pottery, sinks and toilets. Now we are wanting to move into 'higher tech.' Specifically, spark plugs. When we realized we needed help, we thought of you."

"Why me, Herr Rademacher? There are many researchers, and the library is open to all."

Johann pointed to the table. "This is why. Anyone can look things up in books, if they take the time. But few can do *that*." He made a sweeping gesture. "Your reputation is that you do not just research what the books say, you combine the bits and pieces into a whole which would not otherwise exist. We need your expertise. We have tried to make spark plugs. And we failed. We need you."

Nick sat for a moment. "You understand that I am busy? Your project is interesting, but I have work."

Johann smiled. "We can pay. We are prepared to pay. Further, we will pay extra for you to agree to keep the resulting research private for a period of time. A year perhaps?"

Nick thought about Gus' recommendation. "One hundred dollars an hour, and a six-month agreement of privacy."

"Done!"

Gus walked into the rectory kitchen. "I hear you turned in the spark plug report today."

Nick smiled and laid the check on the table. "I did."

"What was it, then?"

"It?"

Gus smiled. "It. There's always an it for you, the critical bit that everyone had overlooked. What is it?"

"It's the seals, of course. It is simple enough to make the bolt, to drill it out, to slide the porcelain into it and glue it in place. But with the pressure and heat of the engine, the gases leak out and burn the steel away."

Gus sat silently.

"Oh, very well. You need to use three different materials. One is braised onto the ceramic and is a substance that wets the ceramic, another is braised onto the bolt and wets the steel, and then a third braising welds them together in a flexible manner so that the differences in expansion don't crack the ceramic. Anyone trying to do it in one or two steps is doomed to fail."

Gus smiled hugely. "Well, then. Another success for the great Smithson, and hope for another new business."

Nick sputtered.

"So, let's go get a beer." Gus nudged the check. "And you're buying."

Plugging Along

Kerryn Offord

The Saale Industrial Zone, winter 1633–34

Larry Karickhoff turned the key of the pickup. The engine fired a few times, backfired, and stopped.

"What's the holdup, Larry? Day's over; everyone wants to get home," Johann Rademacher said.

Larry tried the engine again, with the same result. "I dunno, Johann." He flicked the fuel gauge. It remained steady. "Fuel's okay. I'll pop the hood and take a look."

Johann waited while Larry climbed out and opened the hood. There was a tapping on the glass behind him.

"Johann, what's the holdup?"

The workers in the back wanted to know what was happening. He climbed out of the cab to explain. "The engine won't start. Herr Karickoff is having a look."

"The same thing happened last week in this truck. Herr Straley said it was the spark plugs. He took them out and cleaned them and he was able to get the truck running again," Heinrich Bischoff offered.

"Thank you. I'll tell him. Hopefully the problem isn't serious and we can get home before dark."

Johann hated to disturb a man working on an engine, but it had to be done. He walked around to stand beside Larry. "Heinrich says there was trouble with the spark plugs last week."

Larry wiped his hands on his pants, then reached into the cab for the vehicle log book and flipped pages, checking the entries. "Shit! Typical bloody Norton. Has a problem and doesn't record it in the log." Larry made a note in the logbook, then put it back where it belonged before grabbing the tool box and returning to the engine.

"Damn it!" Larry waved the spark plug toward Johann and the others. "If any of you have to be anywhere soon, I suggest you start walking. This truck ain't going nowhere without a tow."

"What is the problem? If Norton could get the engine going by just cleaning the spark plugs, why can't you?" Johann asked.

"Because not only are they dirty, but this one's ground electrode is broken." Larry passed Johann the spark plug.

Johann held the spark plug up to see what the problem was. It was obviously very dirty, but... "What is a ground electrode?"

Larry handed him another spark plug. "See that little bit of metal hanging off the bottom? That's the ground electrode."

Johann could easily see the difference. "But why do you need to tow the vehicle? Can't it run on just seven cylinders?"

Larry shook his head. "It could run on just the seven cylinders. Not well, but well enough to get us home. But what's happened to that bit of metal? I hope it just fell off onto the ground. Because there's no telling what damage it could do floating around in a running engine."

"Ouch. Yes, I see. So you won't be running this truck until you find the missing piece of metal?"

"Or at least prove it isn't in the engine. Then we have to weld on a new ground electrode."

"Why don't you just get another spark plug?"

Larry stifled a laugh. "Where from? Nobody's making new plugs and nobody's selling their stock. We've still got a few left, but we're trying to put off using them as long as possible."

"They don't look as if they'd be too hard to make. Why hasn't anybody tried?"

"No idea, Johann. You're the guy with all the fancy letters after his name. Why don't you try it?"

December 1633

Johann Rademacher, B.A., M.A. (Leiden) slammed his fists down on the workbench and screamed to the heavens. "What am I doing wrong?"

Aurene O'Keefe, who had been attracted to the workroom by a continuous stream of swearing in no fewer than four languages, poked her head around the door. "Having a bit of trouble?"

Johann spun around at Aurene's voice. "My apologies for my intemperate language, Frau O'Keefe."

"Accepted. So what's all the fuss?"

"My latest attempt to make a spark plug failed. I'm at a loss what to do next."

"Um . . . How much do you know about spark plugs?"

"Not a lot personally, but Larry has been a considerable help."

Aurene snorted. "You can probably write what Larry knows about the things on a postage stamp. Have you thought about checking out the library?"

"No, Frau O'Keefe."

"Then maybe it's about time you did, don't you think?"

Embarrassed, Johann could only nod in silence.

O'Keefe's, two weeks later

Larry shook his head in disbelief. "You paid five grand for someone to go to the library and look in a few books. Hell, I'd have done it for free if you'd asked."

Johann pulled three sheets of paper off the top of the bundle of pages. "No. I paid five thousand dollars for these three pieces of paper."

"Three pieces of paper are worth five grand? Pull the other one; it's got bells on it."

Johann grinned. "I will happily pull your other leg. When those three pages represent the considered analysis of all the available information by none other than Father Nicholas Smithson, then they are definitely well worth the 'five grand,' as you call it. These three pages are a cheat sheet for making spark plugs."

"What? Let me see. Hey, I can't read this. What language is it?"

"Latin, of course. Now to see about making us some spark plugs."

O'Keefe's, a month later

Johann ripped open the package from Melba Sue Freeman's ceramics and porcelain company. Inside, in individual wrappings, were a dozen porcelain insulators. Carefully he unwrapped one. The shiny white insulator was beautiful. He reached over for one of the damaged up-time spark plugs and compared them. The insulators looked identical, except for the markings. Ever hopeful, Johann had already decided on the name he wanted.

Then he started to assemble Grantville-Zuendkerze-Kompanie's very first Series One spark plug.

With a dozen finished spark plugs in his basket, Johann went looking for Larry. He needed to prove they worked.

With Larry in tow, Johann headed for the workshop. First they tested them in the lawn mower. All of them worked.

"Well, Larry, what do you think?"

"I think you're going to be revoltingly rich. Let's try them in one of the trucks and see how well they work and how long they last."

A month later

Johann sighed. It didn't look like he was going to get revoltingly rich manufacturing spark plugs. At least not anytime soon. He'd invested heavily into producing a standard-size plug, as that should have been where most of the demand was. However, it looked like that might have been a mistake.

There were just too many of the standard-size plugs in Grantville, many of them still in vehicles that had been up on blocks since the Ring of Fire.

One problem was performance. Even reconditioned up-time spark plugs performed better than his. If they had been noticeably cheaper than reconditioning up-time spark plugs, he might have had better sales. But at the price he had to charge to make a profit, sales so far had been worse than disappointing.

He looked at the expensive equipment sitting idle on the workbench, and at the boxes of finished product stacked against the wall. Sure, there was some demand as up-time spark plugs failed beyond repair, but there was no driving need for lots of his new spark plugs. Not yet. What he needed was something to generate demand. Like someone making new engines. Because new engines would need new spark plugs.

Until then, it was back to designing plumbing installations.

Sunday Driver

Laura Runkle

Grantville
July 1634

Father Nicholas Smithson stood by the side door and shook hands after early mass at Saint Mary's Catholic Church. Father Athanasius Kircher was greeting parishioners coming out of the main door, but some always left by the quicker route.

He smiled as he saw three faces that had been missing for a month. "Lolly Aossey! Welcome back! How did the twins take to the field session?"

"It's good to see you, Father Nick." Lolly Aossey sent a tired look back at her older children. "Mimi and Larry are both teething." Cathy and Matt were each holding a plump baby. Behind them beamed Jim McNally, the proud paterfamilias, a hand on the shoulder of each teenager. If Nick knew anything about the older McNally children, it was to keep them from bolting.

Lolly brightened. "Since I'm back, come to dinner after the last mass? Jim's apprentices should be back from Countess Kate's by then. It'll just be the usual summer fare, but I'd love to tell you what all happened."

"I'm sorry, but there are a couple of out-of-town visitors I want to see. Otherwise, I'd very much like to." Nick's regret was real.

The conversation and the cooking at the McNally house were usually both lively.

Jim McNally smiled. "Bring them along. The more the merrier. That's what the Sunday usual is for."

Matt rolled his eyes. "The usual has got to be better than Cathy heating up one of Aunt Dina's casseroles."

"Ha! As if we'd want to eat your scrambled eggshells again!" Cathy's tone was sharp enough to cause the baby in her arms to stir.

"Let's go home, kids. I doubt Father Nick is interested in your unsupervised culinary attempts. If you want the usual, y'all have a bit of chopping to do." Jim pushed the kids out onto the sidewalk. "We'll see you and your visitors at two, Father."

Nick sighed as he waved farewell. Jim was right. After his visit last month, he'd had no further interest in the culinary attempts of either Matt or Cathy. Fortunately, today's dinner promised to be more interesting.

Nick regretfully decided that eating another bowl of the berries and cream would be gluttonous. There were still the remains of the wheaten salad and mutton pastries on the table. Across from him, Lion Gardiner and Henry Gage were enjoying the delights of fresh tomatoes with salt. Several conversations buzzed around.

"*Ja*, Mrs. Aossey. He says that when I've helped finish up this circular divider, and written the paper on it, I'll probably only have a year or so left until journeyman."

"Amsterdam? Really? If you could send on a letter for me, I'd be most grateful. Jake Koch has set up a correspondence back and forth from Augsburg, but I'd like to correspond with the Netherlands also. I've expanded from just optics to instruments, as well, but they have mighty fine opticians."

"No. Steel like this requires both nickel and chromium. Mom's graduates have found nickel in tailings from more than one mine, but no chromium yet. When? Any year, now."

"About half girls, again, Marie. And at the ceremony on Wednesday, Ron Koch told me that the instrument maker that Jake is visiting has started training his own daughter. You won't be alone when it comes time to do your journeying."

"No, sir. The ballet company has moved to Magdeburg, so there aren't any performances here this week. But I hope to go to school there this fall, if Dad thinks we have enough money."

Everyone focused on Jim. He said, "Honey, there's no question that we've got money. We've been putting aside your mother's fees for the field camp into a couple different funds, and they've done very well. The problem is that the twins' early arrival tapped us out for this year, as far as liquid cash goes."

"Daaaad! I've got enough money of my own from dancing to pay those fees!" Cathy wailed as only a fourteen-year-old girl could.

"But it's not liquid, and won't be for another couple of years," Jim said.

Young Cathy had a gift, and gifts were to be cultivated. Nick spoke up. "Don't spend so much time worrying about the future that you ignore what you have. Cathy should be studying with Mrs. Matowski."

Lolly sighed. "We're trying. But the only thing that would give us enough cash for the fees would be to sell the Subaru. No way are we selling the SUV. And you know that selling something as expensive as a car usually takes a month or so to get a buyer okayed by the bank."

"Subaru? That would be the car engine that makes a good airplane?" Lion Gardiner asked. "How much were you going to ask for it?"

"More than I'd feel comfortable talking about over a family dinner," said Jim. "Part of it depends on how much they cost now, compared to how much it would cost to make one. Marie, how long do you think it would take until your father can make an airplane engine at his foundry?"

Marie Schmidt, Jim's older apprentice, looked up. "Papa's foundry couldn't anytime soon. He's too committed to making the sewing machines. But someone could make one by hand, if they had the right materials. Right, Thomas?"

Thomas Swartz gave a wry smile. "That's why I'm here. I'm learning how to make all kinds of small instruments, and glasses and other things, so that my father and people like him can inspect small work. But the materials—?"

"Any year, now." The chorus came from around the table.

Henry Gage leaned forward, tomatoes forgotten. "Mr. McNally. We've come on behalf of a client who's not interested in waiting for 'any year now' to come. When would you be interested in discussing whether you think we could be approved by your banker? We have a letter of credit from the Wisselbank."

"You can worry about that tomorrow. Today, come look at the car." Jim stood up and beckoned to both visitors.

Nick winced. He'd learned what the visitors were doing in Grantville. Now he just needed to know who they were representing, before the banker cleared the letter. It was easier to worry about tomorrow than he would like.

As Henry Gage and Lion Gardiner left the McNally home, they were talking quickly, and waving their hands at each other. Nick was certain he caught a "vroom" coming out of Gage, but that could have been a trick of the breeze. They had certainly enjoyed their spin in the Subaru, "to make sure that the engine is in working condition."

Nick waited until the visitors were a block away. "Jim, aren't you wondering who the eventual buyer of this car is? For all you know, it could be someone who wants to destroy everything you stand for."

"And you're the one who says not to worry, Father." Jim sounded strangely smug. "I've just helped ensure tomorrow."

"What?"

"Think! What's the first thing that Father Larry—oops, Cardinal Mazzare—does when he has a spare moment?"

"He fixes cars."

"Yep. He fixes cars. And airplanes take a lot more maintenance than cars do," Jim said.

"So? Someone could still try to destroy Grantville."

"They can try."

"By all accounts, those Croats came too close."

"To make the airplane work well, they'll have to develop a whole support system. They'll need technicians, and measuring instruments, and eventually, they'll need materials."

"So you're just helping to develop someone else's economy," Nick replied.

"There's no 'just helping' about it. Lolly's driven home to me that the only way we'll get what we want for things like medical supplies is for everyone to be growing and changing. Everyone. Everywhere. Any year now."

Nick nodded. He knew just how close a call the twins had had. The night when he'd christened the early babies at Leahy Medical Center was still etched in his brain. "So by selling the car, you're removing worries from tomorrow?"

"There've been other interested buyers. They just didn't sound like they were able to follow through. Those two, though? Wherever they go, they'll help build the world my children need."

Jim turned around, and clapped Nick on the shoulder. "C'mon into the house, Father Nick. If I know Lolly, she's put together a basket of food for the rectory for tomorrow. Worry not."

Turn, Turn, Turn

Virginia DeMarce

July 1634

Father Nicholas Smithson, S.J., cleared his throat for the third time. Crossing his arms over his chest, he leaned back against the wall of St. Mary's rectory. After a pause, he cleared his throat for the fourth time.

With obvious reluctance, Father Athanasius Kircher, S.J., lifted his head from looking at the top sheet in a large pile of papers. "Yes, Nick?"

"I know you've been saving this evening for catching up on letters from your correspondence circle. I wouldn't interrupt if..."

"... it weren't important."

"Right." Nick moved over toward Kircher's desk. "Henry Gage is in town."

"This is important why?" Kircher, naturally, did not have the familiarity with England that a native son of the island did.

"He's from an old English Catholic family with strong ties in the Spanish Netherlands. His grandmother's family were merchants at Liege; his wife's mother is Flemish. Through his mother, he's a grandson of the late Sir Thomas Copley, the exile who was knighted in France and made a baron by Philip II of Spain, much to the displeasure of the late queen. He went back to England for a while in 1627, but returned in 1630. He's been commanding an English regiment in the Spanish service, under Don Fernando, now."

"Is it bad that he is in Grantville?"

"Normally, I'd be delighted to see him. His Aunt Helen, Copley's daughter, was the mother of the two Stanihursts. Given that we really need more English-speaking priests here at St. Mary's, I'd normally recommend that you approach him about trying to interest either Peter or William. They're both in their thirties, so they'll have the energy to keep up with the pace of things here. But they entered the order in their teens, so they're seasoned. It would make a nice balance."

"What is not normal?"

"Henry didn't drop by to catch up on old times. We had scarcely blown the foam off our beers when he asked to purchase a copy of that old report I did on spark plugs."

"You did say that he's an army officer." Kircher pursed his lips. "Is he working for Don Fernando? The cardinal-infante withheld his troops from active participation against the USE this spring, under various pretexts, some colorable and some . . ."

"Not so plausible. Yes. There's a truce, but not a treaty." Nick moved back and leaned against the wall again. "And then there's the man he's traveling with. An English engineer. He's describing himself as 'Master of Fortifications to the Prince of Orange.'"

"Is he?"

"He's definitely been working in the Netherlands for Frederik Hendrik. That much is true. He was born in London and the family is armigerous, I think. Or, at least, he's claiming connection to a gentry family. So there's no obvious reason for him to be working with Gage other than that, perhaps, someone has paid him a great deal of money."

"Or perhaps the rumors that Don Fernando and the stadtholder have come to some detente are true."

"Possibly more interesting is a book that Ms. Mailey loaned on deposit to the state library." Nick reached into the pocket of his soutane and read out, "*History of the Pequot War: The Contemporary Accounts of Mason, Underhill, Vincent and Gardener.* Reprinted from the Collections of the Massachusetts Historical Society. With additional notes and an Introduction by Charles Orr, Librarian of Case Library." He paused. "Nineteen eighty. Reprint of the eighteen ninety-seven edition, published by Helman-Taylor

Company, Cleveland. One of the relations in it, described as 'among the most reliable' by the editor, was written by Henry Gage's traveling companion. Gardiner seems to have trained under Thomas Fairfax—the old man."

"Puritan, then?"

"If it pays, probably. In the world in which he wrote his 'Narrative,' he worked for Lord Saye and Sele's company. He's married to a Dutch woman from Woerden. They went to New England next year, and eventually managed to get a manorial grant for an entire island off the coast of New Amsterdam. Which, by then, was New York, I believe. Or soon would be."

"Talk to them." Kircher turned back to his reading, unwilling to give up one of his rare chances to maintain his scientific interests.

Nick turned to leave the room.

Kircher's voice followed him. "Talk to them long enough that you find out who else they are talking to. And sell them a copy of the spark plug report. It's old news and the parish can use the money."

"Engines," Lion Gardiner said. "All the information about engines that you can provide. Especially airplane engines. Not that anyone involved with aviation wants to talk to us about engines."

Shelby Carpenter cocked her head. "Jesse the Mighty Colonel Wood damned well won't, nor any of his people. The Kitts won't either. And little as I like the Kellys, especially Madam Kay, who treats me like the dirt under her feet, they won't." She twirled her stein around in the puddle of water that had condensed under it on the table. "But I think I've met someone who will."

"What exactly did I do up-time? I was a mechanical engineer, that's what. With a bachelor's degree. Over twenty years of experience. I worked for GE in Baltimore, Maryland, that's what I did. And if I hadn't let my wife talk me into coming to her aunt and uncle's damned wedding anniversary party, that's where I still would be. Not here, slaving in a back room for Dave Marcantonio, because we were caught here with hardly a cent to our names and nothing but the clothes on our backs and I damned well wasn't going to take charity from her family. Marina didn't want to, either. None of the others who are doing aviation now could pay a living wage, at first, so we went with Marcantonio, who could—me as an engineer and Marina as a drafter. And that's where we're still stuck, working for wages while people around us are making fortunes, like those damned Sewing Circle kids."

He slammed a piece of paper on the table. "Look at the job description. That's the job I was applying for when the Ring of Fire happened."

Lion Gardiner craned his neck and saw magic words.

> . . . responsible for the design, development and test of aircraft engines or engine components. They are accountable to ensure that the product meets performance criteria, weight, and fit and function specifications . . .

"Why haven't you begun your own firm, as others have done?" he asked.

"For the same reason I likely wouldn't have gotten the promotion," Peter Barclay admitted a little ruefully. "People skills. It was that '*good interpersonal and leadership skills highly desirable*' line in the job descriptions that always shafted me. How the hell am I going to go out and schmooze the money guys to raise capital? But all the rest of it, I could have done. And done it well. Since when do you need to talk nice to components? Design them, test them, and be done with it. Now, what do you want to know about aircraft engines, and how much will you pay me for it?"

"Therefore," Henry Gage wrote, "I respectfully suggest that you modify your hopes to some degree. I believe that it would be possible to obtain not only an exemplar of one of the engines in question but also, if a sufficient financial inducement were to be offered, at least one trained engineer and several technicians. It is true that the great majority of the inhabitants of this Grantville are most zealous supporters of their Michael Stearns and through him of the Protestant Swede. However, they are human. Additionally, this Barclay is Catholic. Although, this will probably be of little matter to him, since Grantville is a far less hostile world for Catholics than is England. To the best of my knowledge, he has not even noticed that I am of the same faith as himself, whereas Gardiner is not."

Grantville, August 1634

Kircher looked at the pile of money on his table. Nick Smithson had dropped it into a small clearing produced by pushing a few stacks of paper closer together. "That's better than I was expecting we would do."

"Gage and Gardiner are definitely collecting technological information. I sold them several old reports and wrote three new ones, as well. Nor am I the only one. The Grantville Research Institute has done well by their visit." Nick resumed his favorite position against the wall. "But they are not collecting the material for Don Fernando."

"For whom, then?" Kircher raised his eyebrows.

"Their contact is Istvan Janoszi. He has been in Grantville, or at least back and forth between Grantville and Prague, for a year or so, now. I thought perhaps Wallenstein?"

"Very unlikely. Wallenstein has plenty of contacts here already. What is Janoszi like? I don't believe I've met him."

"A middle-aged man. Calvinist." Nick grinned. "That's probably why you haven't met him. He goes to the Reverend Wiley's church when he's in town. He serves as a man of business for Count Pal Nadasdy, who up until now has resisted all of the emperor's... incentives... for his return to the mother church."

"Austria, then?"

Kircher meditated a few minutes. "Nadasdy's children are still young, but he has a nephew, his sister's orphan—a Catholic, to boot, and therefore welcome at the imperial court—who is only a year or so younger than the emperor's son. The two have been companions, so he may be closer to the king of Hungary than he is to Ferdinand II. And the younger Ferdinand speaks for the peace party in Austria in this world, just as he did in the other."

"An arc across the Germanies, then? Fernando in the Netherlands providing access to resources for the voices of reason in Austria?" Nick nodded. "The emperor isn't well. Don Fernando and his advisers have to be thinking about what will happen when Ferdinand II dies. Or, if they aren't, they should be. But why technology? And would private citizens have the kind of money that Gage and Gardiner have been spending?"

"The younger Ferdinand will need some sort of a counterweight against his father's zealots. Technology would give it to him, in a way. A demonstration that he has the resources to defend Austria and Hungary, both in the Balkans and against Gustav . . . He has to be looking around, especially since he is spending the summer inspecting fortifications on the Turkish frontier. And, yes. Nadasdy is a magnate. He can afford to spend a lot of money. If he is drawing on his nephew's resources as well, he can afford to spend more than just 'a lot.' "

"And the man who brought that technology to him . . . a patriot, obviously, displaying zeal for the welfare of Austria . . . A Catholic friend . . . with a Protestant uncle who assisted . . . an argument for toleration . . ." Nick frowned. "I'm not sure where this is going."

Kircher stood up. "We cannot solve all the continent's problems in one evening, my friend. Yet, occasionally, we do solve one. Gage did write to his young cousins. One of them was interested. And Father Mazzare . . ." Kircher smiled. "*Cardinal* Mazzare, I should say, has written from Rome that the Father-General is looking favorably upon our request to have William Stanihurst assigned here. So, even aside from the money they paid for your research, St. Mary's, like the Grantville Research Institute, has done well from Gage's visit. Let us give thanks for God's providential ways."

The Spark of Inspiration

Gorg Huff & Paula Goodlett

Neil O'Connor looked over at Johan. "Say whatever you like, man, that girl is fine." He continued to turn the spark plug wrench as he talked.

"She may be pretty but she is too forward, I think," Albrecht Knopf said. "She is becoming too American in her attitudes."

Neil pulled the plug and glanced at it. Whatever he was planning to say about the girl was forgotten. "Damn! This thing is burned clear through. You guys have been running the mix too lean again, haven't you?"

Neil and Al were doing thousand-hour maintenance on the *Jupiter*, which was known far and wide as the *Monster*. Neil didn't know why Georg Markgraf didn't just give up and change the name, but he wasn't the designer, so what the heck.

Al poked his head around the cowling. "How's our stock?"

"All down-time made," Neil said. "Change them every hundred flight hours. Frankly, I'm a bit surprised that we can make them at all."

"Too complicated?" Al Knopf asked with a bit of a glint in his eye.

"No. Incompatible expansion rates." Neil held up his hand in surrender, or at least partial surrender. "More a chemistry problem than craftsmanship." He had lost a number of bets with Al over the last few months. They'd been bets having to do with what down-time craftsmen could do with just a file and a chunk of metal.

Neil looked back at the plug and then at Johan. "You know, I wonder how long it's going to be till we start building aircraft engines."

"Start?" Al asked. "We have already started! How much of that engine we're working on was made here? The plugs, the gaskets, three tappet valves . . ."

Neil held up his hands, interrupting the list before Al got good and started. Al could talk for hours about the parts of the engines that were now handmade. "That's not what I meant, Al. How long till we start from the design and make engines that are really for airplanes, not just auto engines pushed into service?"

"I don't know, Neil," Johan said. "But if we don't do it soon, we'll be buying our engines from someone who has." He shrugged and grinned. "Anyway, that's a management problem. I'm just a pilot. I just point the plane where they tell me to go." Johan made a great deal of money pointing the plane where he was told. Not to mention the stock options. Still, in spite of being unwilling to bet with Al on what down-time craftsmen could do, Neil didn't believe it. A whole engine was just too complicated for the down-time tech base to handle.

Magdalena van de Passe set down the phone with a sigh. If it wasn't the fuel, it was the engines. She had just had to turn down another job. Because they had just one airplane. Well, three, if you stretched it to include two two-seat small planes that ran with a pilot and a sack of mail. And they couldn't keep the *Monster* in the air all the time. She had had it all explained to her in great, boring detail. In normal use, an automobile engine might reasonably be expected to do thirty thousand miles a year. Perhaps fifty thousand, on rare occasion even one hundred thousand miles a year. But the stress on that engine during most of the time was not that great. The engine would spend time idling, and providing only enough push to maintain the automobile's speed. Not so in an aircraft. For all practical purposes, an airplane spent almost all of its time going uphill, even in level flight. The engines were forced to work as hard as a normal engine going up a grade.

TransEuropean Airlines was making money hand over fist. That was true enough. But they were turning down more jobs than they were taking because if one of their engines broke in a way they couldn't fix, they were out of business.

"Georg, we need more engines. We need more engines because we need more airplanes. And we need them soon."

"And I have the airplanes for you. Two more *Jupiter One* air frames sitting in the hanger, ready to go, if I could buy the engines for them. Find me eight one-hundred-plus horsepower engines and I'll have two new *Jupiters* for you in a month," Georg said.

He stopped talking when Neil burst through the door. Neil always burst through doors, generally without knocking first. Neil had apparently heard him, because he said, "Al and Johan figure you should build your own." He shook his head.

"I've been thinking the same thing."

"Maggy, you don't know how complex internal combustion engines are," Neil insisted.

Magdalena and Georg shared a look. It figured that it would be the up-timer in the room that brought that up. Sometimes the up-timer's constant harping on the great and amazing complexity of up-time technology got more than a little old. In point of fact, Magdalena did the in-flight repairs of the *Monster*'s engines. And she probably knew—well, almost—as much about them as Neil did. But Neil failed to grasp the degree of precision that fine craftsmen of the seventeenth century were capable of. Even Magdalena hid a grin after all the bets he had lost with Albrecht Knopf.

At first they were going to go with a V8 or perhaps a radial engine. Then a research project at the National Library suggested that the Wankel rotary engine made popular by Mazda was the way to go. This was because if it overheated you lost some power, but the engine didn't seize up, as well as the fact that it was lighter per horsepower. They also considered turboshaft and turboprop engines, but all three fell victim to the materials problem. Those would be better airplanes if they had the materials to make them . . . but they didn't. After much debate and several library research projects, they had been forced back to either a radial or a V-engine. Then to a radial design, because the radial design was simpler to manufacture and cooler than the inline cylinders.

Magdalena looked around the room like a nervous conspirator. Well, actually more like a twelve-year-old pretending to be a nervous conspirator. "Can any up-timers hear us?" she whispered, rather loudly.

Georg Markgraf rolled his eyes and Farrell Smith stuck his fingers in his ears. He was, after all, an up-timer.

Arnold Swartz snorted. Arnold, it had to be admitted, had something of a love/hate relationship with Grantville and its machines. He was a master blacksmith whose shop in Suhl now had several production machines running. His senior journeyman could run those, so Arnold felt a bit unnecessary there. It wasn't an especially comfortable feeling for him, either.

"It's not that bad," Georg insisted, looking apologetically at Farrell.

Farrell grinned. "You couldn't prove it by me." The issue was, of course, tolerances. Up-timers—some up-timers—were still insisting that down-time craftsmen weren't capable of the tight tolerances modern machinery needed. "Look, Dad is a good guy and a good engineer. But most of his work has been in the office and not that much on the factory floor. Mostly he's adapted well enough. I know he can be a bit of a by-the-book guy, but he is right about the fact that a lot of people died to write the words in FAA manuals."

"That is not what I object to," Arnold said. "I can deliver the tolerances and the material strength needed. But not if he insists on testing half the parts to destruction. The up-time engineers have told me that the usual percentage for critical components is ten percent. Granted, machines, at least well-made machines, produce more consistent results, but his attitude is both expensive and insulting."

Farrell just nodded. "How long will it take your shops per engine?"

"Less than you might think." Arnold smiled. "The cylinder casings can be cast to their basic shape, cooling fins and all, then finished by hand. We'll use crucible steel, not as light as aluminum but quite strong enough for what we need. By being extra careful with the molds, we will save finishing time on the parts themselves. I have craftsmen working for me, not what you call 'hacks.'

"But it will be expensive. Craftsmanship takes time and craftsmen need to eat. It's not the precision of your machines that we can't compete with—it's the speed."

"And that brings up another issue," Magdalena said. "To the extent possible, we want to use off-the-shelf parts, and adjust the design to fit them. That will save us money and save your craftsmen's time for where it's needed."

"How much can we get from the auto companies?" Arnold asked.

"Not that much. They still haven't fully finalized their designs," Georg complained.

"It's not that bad. They do have some of the parts in limited production," Farrell corrected him, gently. "Someone over there has been at least a bit clever and realized that some of the parts they would need for their automobiles would also be usable for other products. They prioritized those for production. They are building their heads to take the plugs Grantville-Zuendkerze-Kompanie makes. They've settled on a cylinder size, even if they aren't making them yet."

As a whole, the auto people were working in the red and probably would continue doing so till the assembly line got up and running a few years down the road. But by making parts that could be used in other devices as well as automobiles first, they were managing to keep the red ink from getting quite as deep as it would otherwise be. Standard-size nuts and bolts, ball bearings, brake pads, hydraulic brake systems—even, oddly enough, rotors. But they were still years away from a mass-produced automobile or a mass-produced engine. "On the upside, the parts of an engine that wear out fastest are coming into production pretty fast now. The biggest problem is going to be the engine-specific parts, especially parts specific to the radial engines. Things like the finned cylinders Arnold mentioned."

Arnold Swartz didn't seem at all put out by that. In fact, he grinned widely. With dollar signs flashing in his eyes, near as Magdalena could tell.

Six months later Swartz Aviation Engines delivered four seven-cylinder, 120-horsepower, air-cooled radial engines. They weighed 220 pounds each. By then Arnold wasn't smiling quite so widely. Word had recently arrived that another firm was also making aviation engines.

Georg Markgraf, on the other hand, was ecstatic. And Magdalena was pretty pleased herself.